ALEXANDRA NICHOLSON

Crown of Lies

First published by Kindle Direct Publishing 2022

This book has taken inspiration from Celtic legends and mythology but is not meant to represent it in its entirety. It is a work of fiction and the author encourages the reader to go through the right channels to learn more about Celtic society and mythology.

First edition

ISBN: 978-1-7779634-2-2

Editing by Isabella Betita
Cover art by Kelly Ritchie

This book was professionally typeset on Reedsy.
Find out more at reedsy.com

For Leo

Contents

Content Warning

This book contains content that may be unsettling to some readers including (but not limited to): Violence, death, genocide, mental illness, torture, gore, fantasy oppression, and sexuality.

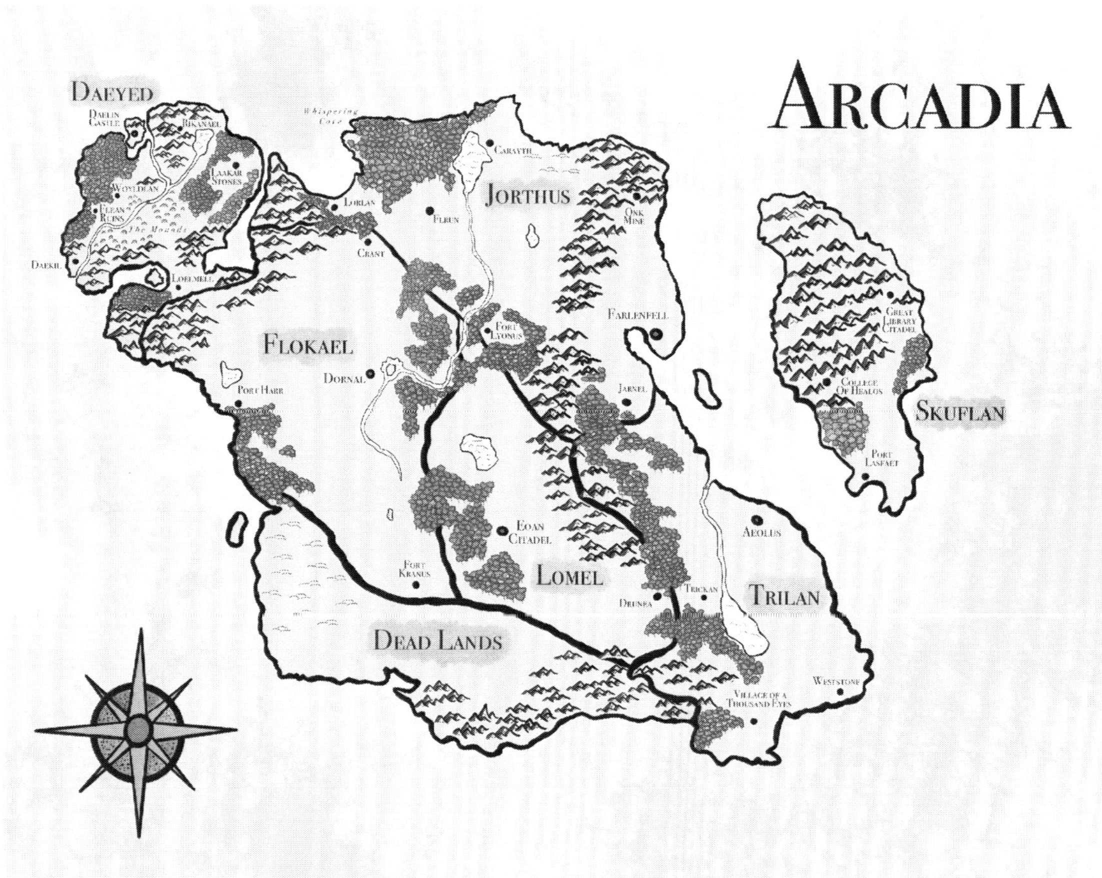
ARCADIA
DAEYED
DAELIN CASTLE
BIKANAEL
LAAKAR STONES
WOYLDEAN
ELEAN RUINS
The Mounds
DAEKIL
LOBLMELL
Whispering Cove
LORLAN
CRANT
FLRUN
CARAYTH
JORTHUS
ONK MINE
FARLENFELL
FORT LYONUS
FLOKAEL
DORNAL
PORT HARR
JARNEL
EOAN CITADEL
FORT KRANUS
LOMEL
DRUNEA
TRICKAN
TRILAN
AEOLUS
DEAD LANDS
VILLAGE OF A THOUSAND EYES
WESTSTONE
GREAT LIBRARY CITADEL
COLLEGE OF HEALOS
SKUFLAN
PORT LASFAET

Prologue

25 years ago
Whispering Cove, Kingdom of Jorthus

Tionne saw the creature on the first full moon of the year. Her slender frame perched atop a rock as she basked in the moonlight, while her ethereal viridescent hair flowed down her back as though she was underwater. A deep-sea faerie who dies at first light if left above water, among the last of her kingdom, an asrai.

She was said to have lived deep in the bay for hundreds of years. Tionne came here to hunt it for King Fyfe, as per his duty to the kingdom but upon this first sight, he fell in love with the creature.

"Hello," Tionne left his bow a few steps behind him. He knew not why he felt an immediate pull, yet it simply could not be ignored.

She whipped around, eyes wide and her strange webbed hands clutching the rock so tightly they bled. The bay began to swirl and crash into the shore as though it followed the will of her mind.

"I don't want to harm you," he spoke, taking a step forward raising his hands, showing her he didn't have any weapons. He looked very much like an ordinary human with high hopes of moving up in rank. As a boy, he had hoped to become a general but that would never come to pass.

The greenish waters began to calm as she sized him up. Her grip loosened on the rock as she stood up.

"*Ryste*! Your kind are not welcome here, leave before I *harm* you," she hissed his own word back at him.

He shook his head and sat down on the earthy floor a mere few steps from the water. She was beautiful, from her pale breasts to her misty eyes.

He had been warned against faeries his entire life, but upon seeing one in person, he became infatuated.

"Tell me about your world," Tionne said.

Her eyes widened, "And what do I get out of telling you about the fair folk? Death?"

"No. I will give you whatever you desire," he smiled at her.

"You are a fool to promise such a thing, your words are bound by magik." She slithered into the water. "I could ask for your tongue or firstborn..."

Once she sat on the edge of the Cove's shore, he dragged himself closer.

While remaining cautious, this faerie turned towards him and tilted her strange head and began telling him stories. At first to frighten him away, but then found comfort in conversing with him.

She didn't ask for anything for a very long while, even when they decided to meet each month during the full moon. It was on their tenth meeting that she led him to a sheltered cavern only accessible by swimming. She used an ancient deep-sea magik on him to keep him alive during the long underwater swim.

When he opened his eyes, he saw a cave glittering with gemstones and soft glowing orbs. The roof above looked as though the night sky had kissed the earth and became fused together in a loving embrace.

"What do you desire?" she asked leaning into the human as he sat down.

"To be with you." He looked at her, not realizing the words had slipped from his mouth.

"That will never be possible during your short lifetime," she whispered back.

"Then I want to make every moment we spend together matter," he spoke as he kissed the faerie's neck.

She did not resist him. It was the first time she had lain with someone so fragile. That night, something happened. She became pregnant, a child of asrai and mankind. After that, she did not return to the surface for months, until one clear night when the waves slowly crashed against the shore and the birds went silent in the trees.

It was the last time he would try to see her before going back to the capital, thinking she had abandoned him without reason or farewell.

His feet carried him up to the edge of her rock in the bleak hours after midnight until dawn. Just as the sun was coming up, she swam to the surface with a babe in her arms.

Tionne's eyes widened as she climbed the rock just barely holding the child. She told him that this child could not live like her, and that she hoped it could see the wonders of a sun-kissed land.

Tionne held the faerie baby in his arms looking into its murky grey eyes. It looked dead, like still water, with colourless skin, yet watched him carefully as though he were the strange one.

"Is it truly mine?"

"She is born through you and I." Then his beloved asrai kissed the baby before whispering, "Her name is Aurelia, and she must be protected from your king."

He agreed but watched as she began to melt in the sun.

"Go back in the water!" he cried.

She shook her head. "I want to spend my last moments with her in the sun. If I go back he will kill me."

"Who is he?" Tionne asked, grasping her wrist with his calloused palms.

"It matters not," she spoke kissing the baby's forehead. "She must live to unite the world of man and fae if we are to survive."

Her eyes shed pale tears as she held Tionne's hand. He pulled it back realizing that she used him for the babe. Within a few minutes, she was nothing more than a puddle on the rocks.

All that she was and ever will be is gone. And she took his seed to create a monster.

But this child was fine, the sun turned her pale grey skin gold, and her eyes a shiny copper. It was magik happening before his very eyes.

Glowing lights floated upward from the water to the sky, dissolving into the air. He had heard rumours that it was difficult for faeries to produce offspring, and when they did nature itself rejoiced.

But he did not.

I

Part One

Chapter 1: The Lonely Assassin

Present
Farlenfell, Kingdom of Jorthus

I hid in a small village for as long as I can remember. The villagers told me I was a creation of old gods and mankind, an abomination. Then the King found and fashioned me into a weapon.

There were many other paths I long for, but this would be the only life for me.

A black tunic and cowl shield me from the commoner's gaze. My hands are covered with pliable and worn ebony gloves, and my legs in tightly fitted trousers with knee-high hunting boots hooking upward with a silver tip. It was designed by my master so I could travel long distances and ensure no one looked upon me twice.

I am lucky, or so I'm told. I am the only one of my kind allowed to even be in Jorthus. The king loathed magik and ethereal beings such as the fae. Titus the Lion stole me away from my village when I was sixteen suns and trained me to fight in King Fyfe's army.

When I was older I was relocated to the capital where the king met me for the first time. He decided that I would be a useful apprentice to Cicero the Liar, his personal master of shadows. He was only several suns my elder but held the knowledge of a thousand spymasters.

Now at twenty-five, I have become the kingdom of Jorthus' most skilled assassin and second most skilled spymaster with the training of a warrior. Many humans train longer than I have and achieve little, but my one advantage over them is that I am not entirely human.

The king ordered that I always remain concealed and form no attachments. This meant I was the secret weapon of King Fyfe, who told me I could never have a family. That those he fought against would kill me given the chance because they were less forgiving of my existence than he was.

People walk around me in a hurry, jolting my mind to the present.

Today was the day we travel to the village of Lorlan in the northwestern corner of Jorthus. The king and his family would meet with the princes of the faerie country, Daeyed, there, as it was a mutually agreed-upon area without strongholds.

Cicero was busy planning and learning more about what the princes were like. It was a difficult task because they only met with a king of Jorthus over a hundred years ago. My duty was to linger in the shadows of their lodgings to steal information. There would be warding to prevent humans from entering, which meant I could be useful.

I step from the edge of the foyer into the sunlight. Dozens of people pause with their mouths dropping. They knew who I was but not what I was and they shiver with wide eyes.

If I lower my cowl, if I took off my gloves, they would see a grotesque person before them. A woman with gold skin and thick dark green hair, large eyes, and pointy ears. They would see that my teeth are not flat but sharp.

Everyone would be afraid and run in panic.

That is what Fyfe's family told the world of the fae. That they are the personification of humankind's worst nightmares. And I agree with him. Faeries are dangerous and wild creatures, longing to trick and kill weary travellers. When I was a babe, I was found in the very village we are travelling to, and the woman who found me, Lucia, the village huntress, told me that my faerie mother murdered and cooked my human father.

She raised me and called me her woodland sister, for many of the people of Lorlan believe the fair folk to balance the goodness. They saw me as a blessing while the world saw me as a curse. When Titus the Lion came, he stole me away by order of King Fyfe.

"Aurelia." Titus strolls over, his once hearty beard shaved and his hair flecked with grey. "Why are you waiting here? You should be with Cicero."

"I am waiting because Cicero told me to," I say simply.

"There is much to prepare for, you could make better use of your time," he counters.

I smile under the shadows of my hood. "I am afraid I only obey Cicero the Liar, and if you think I am not making use of my time you are mistaken."

"Do you think Cicero outranks me?" He crosses his arms.

"And do you outrank him? I do not follow a tired General's order."

"You are a half-breed who would be dead if I didn't vouch for you when King Fyfe called for your death," he responds. "I deserve more respect from you."

"You were only doing your duty, besides those like me are not welcome to live as you do," I say as Prince Lorkus walks towards us.

We bow immediately, our right arms crossing our chests.

When I saw him last, he had long, fair hair and now it is rather short. His face is clean-shaven and his eyes even more piercing. He will succeed King Fyfe in the near future if the king continues to be gluttonous.

"Shadow Master and General, how strange to see you two together," he smiles, "considering the last time you both were in quite the argument."

"Our factions in your father's service do not often get along," I say with a hint of a smile.

Prince Lorkus was charged with overseeing the shadow masters working closely with Cicero the Liar, and by default me. I was told never to speak unless spoken to while Cicero handled the prince.

"Aurelia," Lorkus says carefully, "I believe that is the first time you've spoken directly to me."

I take a breath, realizing my mistake. "I apologize, your highness."

"Have I even seen you underneath all those clothes?" he asks. "I don't even know what your face looks like."

"Few people have." I feel a pit in my stomach.

Lorkus touches the edge of my cowl, "I have never seen a faerie before, yet I spent many years in Skuflan at the great library learning as much as I could about them."

"I am human as well," I respond.

"Not enough to make a difference," Titus cuts in.

"General, perhaps you should join my father. I will be riding with the shadow masters," Prince Lorkus says before walking away.

I lift my head enough so Titus could see my shiny eyes mocking him before I walk away, cloak fluttering behind me.

I wish I knew who birthed me, what kind of creature would kill my human sire to keep me secret. Faeries speak truthfully but still manage to twist their words as smooth as rippling water. Humans hate them because they fear them. That is something I can respect, but I would still rather be a human pauper than an immortal queen of the fae.

* * *

The only time I lower my hood was whenever Cicero and I were alone, my thick hair spills around my face and down my back. He is the only one allowed to see me for who I was; even the king prefers I keep my cowl and scarf on.

"Aurelia, when we go there, I want you to know that the princes may question why you are covered—if they notice you." Cicero pulls down his own hooded cloak, revealing clean pale hair and a narrow, sharp ivory face.

"So I don't give them a reason to notice me. I stay in the middle of whatever crowd will gather and keep my gaze low. Cicero, I know what I'm doing."

He walks over without making a sound, our riding boots are designed to quiet footsteps. I can see the caution in his crystalline eyes.

"I know you loathe them, but I don't want the intended purpose of this meeting to become corrupt," he says. "King Fyfe still sees you as a threat, prove him wrong."

I nod as his fingers remove my gloves to examine the cuts on my hands; they were from an iron blade Titus used on me during training. While I was unable to become poisoned like the fae, they were never able to heal properly and reopen little by little. Since Jorthus was a land that resents magik, I went without faerie potions, salves, and remedies. Cicero has a special cream that helps the healing but never has any lasting impact.

"It's getting worse," he says, taking a cloth to them. "Perhaps I should assign you on a mission in Flokael, where you could trade something for a cure."

"You and I both know the king will never allow me to leave the country," I say.

Cicero smiles. "What he doesn't know won't hurt him."

"My, my, Cicero. You never go against what the king commands,"

"Well, I don't want you to bleed out now. You're the best I have."

I smile after he applies the cold, bluish jelly to my hands. I've always wanted to travel to other countries where magik isn't banned. Only Jorthus and Lomel outlawed it completely, both exclusively populated by humans. Flokael is where faerie outcasts live and are ruled by two arch kings, human and faerie.

King Fyfe refused to speak directly to the faerie-born arch king. Instead, he would send his own wife to deal with him. This went on for years until one day, he caught the former queen warming the arch king's bed. She had been banished from Jorthus and now resides in Flokael with her faerie lover as his consort. His hatred for the fae only grew larger. As one final act of power over her, Fyfe married her younger sister, who birthed Lorkus one year later.

Cicero told me all of this in confidence—that I wasn't alone in the world even if I thought I was an abomination. He told me that some faeries are stronger than others and all the faeries in Flokael are stripped of their illusionary glamour before being exiled.

"What if they find me?" I ask, referring to the princes.

"They won't," he says. "But if they do, they will either kill you or take you to Daeyed..."

"Then I won't get caught. I have a great master."

"A master can only teach you so much, then you must grow into your own skin." His voice was distant. "Some things are out of our control."

I look at him through his snowy hair. He was a spy sent from the moon, owning the night and hiding in the shadows.

"We should be going soon," he says and turns around to gather his riding gear.

I braid my loose earthy hair, clearing my face from any obstructions. I felt the air dance on the nape of my neck as though a spirit caresses my skin.

I open my silver tin to reveal talc-based powder to lighten my skin and remove the golden shimmer to it.

"Are you ready?" a voice at my ear asks.

I only nod once, sliding iron-tipped daggers up my sleeves.

Chapter 2: A Long Road Into The Past

Kingdom of Jorthus

I spend most of the journey staring out a stained glass window. Cicero sat beside me wearing a fine violet embroidered tunic conversing with Prince Lorkus. He loathes colours but wears them when visiting nobility. Usually, he and his subordinates wear black when the king wasn't around.

There were rankings in each faction of Fyfe's governance. Cicero is the head of shadow work, the lowest of which are Spylings. The skilled move on to become Spymasters, who only steal and deal information. If they wish to advance further they could become lethal Shadowlings with approval from Cicero and myself. It is at this stage, they learn to assassinate targets. If they excel as a Shadowling they can become a Shadow Master. For many, they remain as spylings due to the more demanding nature of the higher ranks. My nature allowed me to climb rank in a mere few years rather than decades.

Prince Lorkus yawns leaning forward, closer to me and away from Spymaster Rowyna next to him. Her role is to seduce the Daeyed princes for information; she dressed like the king's mistress as part of her cover. Rowyna is the Governor of the Spymasters, reporting only to Cicero, just as I am the Governor of the Shadow Masters. She and I used to get along quite well when we both were initiated in shadow work, but then I advanced rapidly.

"Governors Aurelia and Rowyna," Lorkus tilts his head, "Cicero told me you both were orphans. Do either of you have any tales of woe?"

Rowyna's head snaps to me as though expecting me to speak first. When I don't, she chuckles and tells a story of a horse she admired while hiding in a barn, a mare with a thick coat and eyes as brown as wood. She wanted desperately to ride it into the forest and never return but the owner had her whipped when she was discovered. The horse was sold for meat the next week.

Lorkus turns his eyes to mine when Rowyna finishes.

"Which story would you like me to tell? The story where I was a knight's daughter? A fisherman's wife? Second cousin of Lord Goern? Or perhaps all three at once? The truth is what I make it to be, what I want people to believe." I lace my fingers together.

Cicero smiles. This is the identity of a Shadow Master. We can be anyone in a matter of moments.

"Bravo," Lorkus tilts his head. "Tell me an early memory of something that may be remotely normal."

I look out the window for a moment with a smile tugging at my lips. "I would wake early to watch the sunrise over the water. The light would sparkle in oranges that cannot be seen at any other time. It felt so warm and comforting. I could be myself."

"The day's end colours are breathtaking as well," Lorkus continues. "Sitting on the edge of the city wall, I would watch as the ships dropped anchors in the harbour."

"I do not like endings." I turn my attention back to the prince. "Beginnings can be endless."

"You make many beginnings." Lorkus' voice is no longer soft.

"It is better than only one," I respond.

"You make a living to pretend, but deep down you have an identity and beliefs, ones that are so very finite." Lorkus glances from Cicero to me.

Rowyna smiles sweetly, steering the course of discussion. "What are the faerie princes like, your highness?"

"We don't know much more than their names, Vikorus the Wicked, Kynus the Proud, and Septimius the Wyvern."

"I never understood why people are given strange titles." Rowyna looks at Cicero.

"Titles are names man has given them, you see we are given a title once we accomplish something or have a defining trait," Cicero says. "I deal in information and lies, which is how I earned mine. I can only imagine what the faeries have done to earn theirs."

Those names were earned through fear, confidence, and control. They were ancient beings that once nearly conquered the entire continent. I don't know why they retreated to that small area that now makes up their country, but they were up to something. They hate humans more than humans hate them. Nothing good would come of this.

"What colour do faeries bleed?" Rowyna asks.

"When I was studying in Skulflan, I read a lore book that said they bled thick shimmering cobalt blood. That magik itself ran through their very veins," Lorkus explains.

He flaunts his education and vast knowledge in front of everyone. So few people could actually go to the great library of Skulflan to be educated in disciplines of illegal and invaluable information.

"If things work to King Fyfe's favour, magikal blood will be spilling across our country," I end the conversation.

"You mean my family's country and land you reside in," Lorkus sharply smiles.

I narrow my eyes at the prince.

"I apologize on behalf of Aurelia, she spoke out of turn and I assure you she will be dealt with after the faerie princes leave," Cicero cuts in before I can say anything else.

The prince cracks his knuckles. "You are a threat to both my family and my kingdom. This isn't your home, simply a temporary lodging."

Ever since I have known him, Lorkus looked at me as though he wanted to slice me open to see if I had a heart. As if I were some form of experiment.

Rowyna blinks. "How is she a threat? She is nothing but Cicero's servant!"

I say nothing.

Lorkus lets out a long exaggerated sigh. "Rowyna, little one, please just stop talking for once in your life. Perhaps you should sit with the coach driver."

I hold my tongue and bite back a laugh when Rowyna is escorted outside. I can only imagine her displeasure of climbing to the front in a dress like that.

Lorkus pulls out a book titled *A Fox named Arawn* and begins to read silently. I clench my hands carefully as I let my anger simmer down.

"Cicero, if I ordered you to stab Aurelia would you?" he asks, not looking up from his book.

"I would have to ask the king first, your highness," Cicero replies after a moment.

"What if I was the king and I asked you?"

"Then I would do as I was ordered," Cicero replies.

"Would you enjoy it?"

"If it pleases you, then yes."

"No, would you enjoy it without taking my views into consideration?"

"No, I would not."

The prince looks at me. "I have said things that you probably did not like, and you continue to say nothing. Tell me, faerie-born, if my father ordered you to stab me, would you?"

"Without question," I say. "I obey the king."

"Would you kill Cicero if I ordered you to? If I were king?"

Cicero turns to me. He knows I would never kill him; he was the closest thing to kin I had. However, when the prince demands answers, you answer the question to his liking.

"That depends," I say.

"On?"

"If I am already dead or not. You see, if you are king I don't see myself lasting very long. But if you did see worth in me, I would kill Cicero for you."

Lorkus forces a frown. "This got rather morbid. Trust me, Aurelia, I plan on keeping you around for a very long time."

A part of me wonders what he meant, but another part of me no longer cares for the conversation. Holding my tongue and honouring my master were the only things that matter at this moment.

* * *

We arrive in Lorlan several days later without stopping. While the king rested in his coach, the drivers were forced to overwork themselves. The king rarely strayed from the capital, which meant a journey like this was travelled as close to the date as possible.

I step out of my coach onto familiar green stones. These roads were formed from grionalite, a type of sea glass found only in the bay. They say this area once was the capital of the merfolk, faeries that once lived in the water.

I look at the shimmering blue waters of Laëran. The water always calls me. When I was a child, I would be allowed to stand on the shallow beaches letting it cool my feet, but never to swim.

My mind fills with thoughts of midnight swims, naked and unafraid to show who I was. To fall in love and have someone look into my disgusting eyes, unafraid and welcoming. These were dreams I would never achieve. I often hid these fantasies in dark parts of my mind, but sometimes in little moments they came pounding like a messenger at the door.

"Aurelia!" a voice alerts behind me.

I turn to see Cicero standing beside Lucia the huntress. She has grown older but still looks just as beautiful as when I left. Though now she has a thick black line inked across half her face.

"Hello, Lucia," I say as I walk closer to the only sister-like figure I have.

"It has been a long time," she says with her woodland accent. She was only fourteen when she took me in, but her maturity was that of a grown woman twice her age.

"I was never able to come back."

"Aurelia, I need to tell you something. I know this isn't the welcome you desire but it is the one you need. Please do not be angry with me. Your father will be at the opening ceremony when the faerie princes arrive." Lucia looks down. The woodland people were tribal and for centuries they worshipped the fae as old gods.

Cicero shoots her a look as if this was knowledge she should have kept to herself.

"My father is dead," I say through my teeth.

"I lied to keep both of you safe."

"Then he abandoned me and I no longer care." I let out a breath. "He chose to leave me."

She looks up at me and sighs. "He is a good man, trust me."

"Why mention him then?" I lick my lips. "If he were a good man, he should have killed me, instead he left me to grow in a world I didn't belong to."

"This may be the last time I see you," she pauses, "for a long while. Trust me, you need to know before they come for you. Even telling you this is dangerous but I may never get the chance to again."

"Come, Aurelia," Cicero motions for us to leave, "we have work to do."

"Who comes for me?" I ask her.

"If you want to truly live, you must find the Font of Lystál," she whispers in my ear before I leave.

I have no idea of what she's talking about or why she even dare mention that man. Her voice shook with fear, and that was not like her. I need to know who was coming for me and what they have to do with my father.

"Do not listen to her about Lystál or your father," Cicero sighs.

"He is alive and never bothered with me, he may as well be dead," I say, clenching a smile on my teeth. "What exactly is Lystál?"

He shakes his head. "A myth, nothing more."

"I would like to know, Cicero."

He pulls me aside, eyes scanning the area, "It's said to be a cavern in Daeyed that has mystical properties, including the font, which is said to turn the fae mortal and the mortal immortal."

Could it take the fae part of me away? Could I finally see the light without covering myself?

"It is not real, do not get any ideas." Cicero grabs my forearm.

"It's fine, I prefer myself the way I am," I speak plainly.

"Liar," he whispers, "I know you better than you think."

I continue to walk, shrugging off his hand and dropping the conversation. Cicero knows me best, and that is frightening because he is in deep with the royal family. If I were human I could be like him.

The King finally steps out of his carriage. He will be staying in Lord Yulin's estate just outside the village, but tonight the villagers and Lord Yulin are hosting a welcome feast on the shore of Laëran bay.

He is an average-size man who wears a giant fur cloak made from Rhinla wolves. His golden crown is almost as big as his thick beard. He is proud, clever, and once a scholar. He, like his son, spent many years in Skuflan.

Everyone bows immediately, peasants falling to their knees, while Lorkus simply nods.

His wife, Queen Selene comes next. Her golden hair is woven in flowery braids. She smiles at the crowd but says nothing.

"It is nice to see the western front of my beautiful country," Fyfe grins, "after all these years..."

"Sire," Yulin's rat-like voice squeaks beside his wife, Lady Hodna of the Woodland people. They were forced to marry as an alliance between the people.

"Ah, what has it been? Two, three suns?" Fyfe walks over to the scrawny lord.

"Four sire, come, let us head down to the gem of the west, Laëran bay." Yulin bows once more.

The king nods. "Did you know that legends say this bay once was the centre of a faerie empire, deep within its hidden underwater caverns?"

Yulin blinks, "We are aware that the bay is still named after the lost city."

"Not lost, destroyed by my great-grandfather when he purged this land for his new kingdom. I think it's time for a name change," Fyfe and the Lord walk to the shore.

Yulin called this faerie pilgrimage site beautiful. One strike. Proudly flaunting its name. Strike two. And finally ordering the king to come with him. Strike three. I suspect my next job will include the tragic death of one of Jorthus' least respected Lords.

I look at Cicero, who nods in agreement because he is observing exactly what I am seeing. I am always sent to kill important figures because I can do it without a trace and make it look very natural.

"Governor Aurelia, my dear, I would like to walk with you," the queen's voice is close.

I turn my attention to her and bow. "Of course your majesty."

I take one last look at Cicero before stepping beside the queen. I know he wants to give me the layout rundown once more by doing a walk through, but the queen's orders come first.

We walk along the shore of the water, my feet longing to step inside the sparkling water. I feel things most humans cannot, like the comforting energy that runs through the current.

"Aurelia, I understand you are from here," she speaks without looking at me.

I tense. "I was raised here, yes."

She shakes her head. "No, you were born here, in this bay." I am quiet. "You see, in a country like Jorthus, there are few places you could have been born to be a legal citizen. My sister once told me that there were only four faeries living in Jorthus around the time you would have been born."

"Your sister who fell in love with a faerie?" I whisper.

She frowns and looks around for eavesdroppers. "Yes, my sister Ambyr. I have learned a lot about you through my own network of informants. I am not an enemy of the fae, like my husband. I am an enemy of unfair situations, such as being placed in a position you had little or no control over."

"I am an enemy of the fae," I say all too quickly.

"You are still part of them," she reminds me. "I knew about Ambyr's courtship with the Arch King Whistryn. You see she never loved King Fyfe. She told me shortly after her exile that the faeries in Jorthus would be targeted and killed. My husband sent out two very skilled trackers, one of which came here to hunt an asrai—the last asrai."

Trackers or Legitars were mostly under the steward's control. They were called upon to hunt someone or something of importance to Fyfe, be it an animal or a faerie. Usually, they never gather together outside of capital meetings.

"The creature that gave birth to me," I nod.

"Yes, but you see, the hunter fell in love and lay with her." She stops and gazes at the water sadly. There is something hard in her eyes.

"How do you know all of this?" I take a breath.

"Because the hunter told me, because of my history regarding my sister," she says. "Fyfe does not know, all he cared about was whether or not the creature was slain."

"Was she?"

"No, she spent her last moments holding you under the sun before she died," the queen says. "Her name was Lythe and she was the last of her kind."

I stop in my tracks. This was enough, she has no right to bring up unwanted stories from my past. Stories that I could not even verify.

"I don't want to know why my fath—that man told you these stories, but I don't want to hear any more." I try to remain calm.

"You need to know, in case anything should happen in the next few days," her words are distant. "Do not blame your father, he was under a very unique kind of magik. He feared you would be killed if he kept you."

I wonder what, if anything, she means by that. My gut tells me that her intentions and heart are not the same as her husband's, that she is playing in radical ideas that will get her killed should the wrong people find out.

"I am loyal to my king and country," I say, ignoring what she said about my father, "I will not corrupt this summit, if that is what you refer to."

She looks at me with her bright eyes and sickly sweet smile. "Perhaps we should head back now, Master Cicero is expecting you, and I must speak to our host."

I couldn't tell the king about her, he does not need to know anything more about me. The queen knows this, which is why she also knows I would never speak against her, even if she were a traitor to Jorthus.

"I trust you will keep our conversation to yourself," Selene says.

"I will," I speak through my teeth, "I do not want to speak of my family again in return."

She nods even though she knows full well that she does not have to make any promises in return.

We walk onward, keeping an eye on our surroundings. Near the village, the seven royal Legitars emerge from the tavern. Selene looks at them curiously. I could have sworn one of the men smiled at her before noticing me and looking away.

"Have a safe ride." I bow to the queen.

Once she is safely in her carriage bound for the estate, I walk down into the basement of an abandoned home. This is where we would conduct our operations.

Familiar and new faces greet me. Cicero stands with his hood down, Titus leaning against the wall, Rowyna, Prince Lorkus, and two Legitars. So many important people in such an unimportant village.

"Did my mother bore you with talk of roses and gowns?" Lorkus yawns.

"I am afraid I would have very little to speak of in that regard."

"Everyone, this is Governor Aurelia, my second," Cicero announces. "Aurelia, these fine Legitars, Haerton and Tionne, are here to track and hunt any lingering fae."

I look at the Legitars, both worn from the frontier yet in regal garments from the capital. One is blond and the other has rather dark brown hair. I often wonder how they operate and why they were held in high regard. The one with dark hair is the same one that smiled at the queen earlier. This time, he seems uncomfortable looking at me.

"Pleasure to finally meet our Legitars." I nod at them both.

"Why are you covered?" the blond one says while the other remains silent.

"I have a disease," I say too quickly.

"I don't trust people who remain covered," he responds.

"And I do not trust anyone," I say, "especially those with fair hair, they are ever so tricksy."

"Hair colour has nothing to do with suspicion," he says.

"And neither does my choice of apparel, especially since the king tells me what I can wear."

"In my line of work, one may think you are hiding," he retorts.

"I must dress like this to hide because I murder people who pose a threat to the king." I shrug.

"I've heard stories about you, they say you aren't even human but a monster," the blond continues on.

"Enough," Lorkus commands the room, "let us begin our meeting."

Everyone quiets for a moment and then begins to discuss the plan. A guard will escort Rowyna as a gift to the princes. Depending on how that went, I will sneak into their camp and find out all I could. At the gathering the next day, I will stand directly behind the royal family during the meeting near Whispering Cove on the North Eastern edge of the bay.

"Aurelia will be wearing a hood but she will be painted to look human," Lorkus says simply.

"What do you mean to look human?" Rowyna and the blond Legitar ask at the same time.

"Everyone please calm down." Prince Lorkus smiles. "My father does not wish for anyone to know what she is, however in this trusted circle, everyone should understand our advantage. If anyone speaks of it, they will naturally face a death sentence."

"Prince Lorkus, if his majesty finds out, she will—" Cicero takes a step closer to the prince.

Lorkus cuts him off. "He and I already discussed that keeping her covered like this will not work long term."

Cicero only stares at him.

I'm unsure of what Lorkus is planning but these people are the least of my concern, it was who they would tell and who would rebel.

"Aurelia, I want you to show your face to these people." Lorkus turns to me.

"No," I say almost too quickly.

"Are you saying no to me?" he asks.

"Sire, with all due respect, you can simply just tell us what she is so she does not have to redress her face and garments," the dark Legitar interrupts.

"Legitar Tionne—" Lorkus begins, but Cicero cuts him off saying, "Aurelia is both human and fae, she was born in Jorthus but I assure you, she is more like you than them."

Rowyna takes a step back. "How long has the king known?"

Lorkus frowns. "Years, Aurelia is our weapon."

They all immediately bow without another word.

"Now is the time to finish our business before the hour grows late, I have dinner to attend."

Chapter 3: Whispers of a Time Once Forgotten

Lorlan, Kingdom of Jorthus

Part of my duties prior to the meeting is to take a personal look at Whispering Cove to note possible threats, escapes, or other strange things that may have been missed during the initial scouting.

I enjoy getting away from everyone during assignments like these. My mind could escape the politics of the crown and missions like these were very important to the foundation of much larger plans. New recruits miss many things that could lead to failure, which is why they often go on these with senior members before being trusted to be alone.

This meeting was organized by the steward and an ambassador of the faerie princes. It was the fae who contacted Jorthus first, to renegotiate the terms of the treaty as well as potentially integrate friendlier relations through trade and knowledge. Fyfe was interested only because he felt he could gain an upper hand against them depending on what they revealed.

The steward suggested three possible locations within Jorthus and the fae were to choose their desired place of meeting. The place of their choosing was no accident on their part. It happened to be a place that Fyfe banned his people from, and often there were soldiers scouting the area for trespassers. This cove was once a frequented path for the water fae. When the people claimed sightings in the area, Fyfe sent his Legitars, which led to the death of my mother and her remaining kin.

Once I reach the cove, my eyes immediately go to a rocky island near the middle of the water. It is large enough for several people to sleep upon but sharp enough to cut through flesh.

I climb down to the shoreline and watch as the moonlight turns the ocean spray into sparkling foam. The wind goes from howling to a whisper. Things like this always happen when I travel to any body of water.

A smile tugs at my lips as the water calms to a trickle as I stand on the division between land and sea. My toes curl and relax as the water laps the shore. They long to soak in salt and float amongst the darkest of depths.

I begin to turn, willing myself to ignore the pull of the water to examine other areas when something small and shiny reflects off the island. I can't help but wonder if I should stray off course and examine it.

I would not possibly get in trouble for doing my job, and if swimming happens to be the price I to pay, then so be it.

"It should not take very long," I tell myself before stripping my clothes.

I had very few encounters with true swimming, I was told I was not allowed to do it. Yet something about the act felt natural, like my body could finally break free of the dry air and my skin could regain its plumpness.

When I'm in nothing but my own skin, I dive in.

The water feels like a storm—thunderous against my body. I usually felt very anxious and wrong whenever I took my garments off, but here it is different, very different from even bathing in my chambers.

This feels like home, even though I will eventually drown and rot among the waves. I can only imagine what the water faeries did to lure men to the rocks at the bottom of the ocean.

With every stroke, I pull a cool silky quilt around my body. The warm autumn air feels quite gentle against the pools of water, like swimming in cream upon a spoon. The water is warmer and more inviting than in harsh winter months.

When I reach the island, I pull myself up with ease. The stone is mostly smooth yet some areas are jagged and sharp. A small sense of familiarity sweeps through my body but I ignore it.

My eyes fall down at the sparkle I saw earlier and find a very small ring stuck inside a small crevasse. It shines in the moonlight but does not look like any metal I know. The only way I can describe it was a ring made of starlight and ocean pearl.

I reach down only to find out it has been held in place by hard barnacles. My hands scrape against the rock and no doubt a little blood escapes my skin. My thick fingernails end up cutting around it after several attempts at pulling. Having hands like mine is an advantage in my line of work, but not something I can show or gloat about. My strength allows me to do what most humans cannot. I can break a man's neck while sipping tea at the same time. If I forget a weapon, I can use my hands to rip out a heart.

The ring breaks free just in time for me to catch it before it slips deeper into the crack.

In my palm, I can feel the vibrations of energy and life running through the band. It's as though the ring has a soul of its own.

I place it on my right middle finger, where it fits almost perfectly, which is concerning because my fingers are wider and longer than a human's. A woman's hand would look like a child's hand next to mine.

I decide to swim back quickly but when I take my first step, I do not sink into the water. It feels as hard as a stone but also spongy as I lift my foot.

"What wicked glamour is this?" I whisper, taking another step only to find myself unable to sink.

On my third step, I fall into the water. The feeling of uncertainty clothes and mocks me. I gasp for air when I surface. The world around me is chaotic and fuzzy as I try to float upon the water to regain my balance.

A sharp clapping echos the air around me as I turn towards the shoreline.

My eyes widened. An unfamiliar man was leaning against a tree.

"I think," his shadowy voice hisses slightly, "that I know why Fyfe neglected to mention you in our letters."

Once I make it to shore, I quickly dress.

"We aren't expecting the faeries until tomorrow," I carefully say as I watch him lower his hood.

His skin is a pale grey with what looks like scales clawing up his neck. His beady, pupilless red eyes send shivers down my spine. He is far enough away, and while his voice is quiet it's as though he is speaking at my side.

"You should turn back before someone hunts you," I say, not wanting to get any closer. Closer means he can attack or trick me into something unpleasant.

He raises an inky eyebrow. "Oh? Hunt us?"

I don't say anything. Instead, I pull a dagger from my pocket and throw it at him. High faerie or not, I have my orders. Kill any outside of the village unless they are being escorted by a guard.

He catches it in mid-air just before it could plunge into his heart. My heart pounds. He simply looks at it, and I can see his hands turning black as he drops the weapon.

"You dare poison me with iron?" His voice is dangerous as he steps closer to me, "Mortal."

"Enough, Septimius," another faerie says. "I'm sure she did not realize whom she tried to kill."

I am standing in the presence of Septimius the Wyvern, a powerful and old faerie prince.

The other high faerie runs a hand through his thick poppy hair. He looks mostly uninterested. The black line that runs along his cheekbone to each side of his face must have been some form of warrior's mark. I don't need to look at the leafy diadem atop his head to know he is of royal blood.

"Now, what is your name?" the red-haired one asks.

I shake my head, wanting to get as far away as possible from them. "I am just a servant to Fyfe. I apologize, your highnesses, for my behaviour."

"The creature knows our customs, names have power," he laughs in response. "A half-faerie in service to King Fyfe, now that is a fascinating revelation." Then he turns to Septimius. "We should interrupt their little revel."

It's as if I no longer exist as they walk away. All my training to protect myself and my country dissolved once I stood in their presence.

* * *

My legs wobble as I walk back into the village. The lights are burning but there's not a soul in sight. I can see many smashed plates of food on the ground as though everyone rushed away in a hurry.

They were terrified of the faeries that arrived early.

I look towards the shoreline where Lorkus, Cicero, and the red-haired faerie are speaking. In the dim torchlight, they all look so surreal, even the human men.

Then a voice directly behind me grumbles, "Where were you?"

I turn and see Fyfe before me. I bow quickly and lower my gaze; it is not polite to look a king in the eye.

"Your majesty, I was examining whispering cove for the meeting tomorrow," I say, "I was looking for traps, as per my orders."

"You shouldn't have left." He looks down at me. "Get inside before they see you, just having you here is breaching the iron treaty."

I nod and walk to my lodgings.

I sense their energy no matter how far apart we are.

Faeries have magik.

Faeries have Glamour.

High faeries can kill with just a single look.

"And half-breed, the time will come when all this work will either build up to something or end, along with your life," the king speaks quietly, but with my heightened hearing, it is enough.

I stop for a moment, catching my breath. It feels as though I never trained in my entire life and that I haven't slept in weeks. My legs wobble and swell.

When I look down at them, I tip over and fall on the hard gravel.

My arms pull me across the road to the building I'm staying in, but my stomach twists into a knot just as I reach the threshold. My teeth clench as I lose all mobility in my legs before the pain began.

I bite a scream back as my eyes turn inky and blur.

"Aurelia?" a familiar voice comes from the door frame.

I look up to see Titus' large frame. My cowl falls showing him my ugliness. "What is happening?" He bends down and lifts me up in his arms. I cry out silently from the pressure.

He pulls me inside and sets me on the table, his hands on my face, examining it. His warmth on my skin was like fire.

The pain lessens once the door slams shut.

"I-I don't know what-t..." I find myself able to speak. "Where is C-Cicero?"

Titus stiffens.

"I am here." Cicero's face appears next to the general's. "You were iron poisoned."

I feel my muscles twitch. "Iron does not affect me like this!"

Cicero's pale hands touch my face slightly, examining it. "It does when a high faerie uses glamour on a half-faerie. You are experiencing iron poisoning at an accelerated rate. The faerie, Prince Kynus, mentioned he met a half-faerie to Lorkus and I."

I crack my neck as I sit up, still wobbling from recovery and see my reflection in the window. Every vein in my body turns black.

I puke.

Cicero's palm goes to my back in support. When he looks down at the ring on my hand, his posture changes until he's staring into my eyes. I could see pools of knowledge swimming behind them, knowledge, wonder, and a dangerous drive.

"The plan is corrupted," I say, "because of me..."

Cicero shakes his head. "I suggested you go out, I take full responsibility."

"King Fyfe needs to know." Titus crosses his arms.

Cicero turns to Titus. "Not now, the faerie princes likely think she is dead from this magik. I need her for tomorrow, after that, you may tell the king."

"Are you planning something?" Titus asks.

"We all know the mission, but my apprentices and masters have their own smaller assignments that the military need not worry about."

"I am giving you until after the meeting, then I am going to the king," Titus warns Cicero.

"Aurelia, please come with me, I have something for you," Cicero says as he helps me down. For someone with a slender frame, he is stronger than many people I know.

"She should rest," Titus speaks quickly, as though he doesn't want me alone in the same room as Cicero. Very out of character.

My master looks at the general as though he said a silly thing. Yet there is something terrifying about the way he smiles, a killer even without lifting a finger. Cicero may be hard to reach at times, but he was always truthful and honest with his followers. His ironic title was gifted upon him by the king suggesting that he lied his way out of poverty to prove himself. Truth be told, I never knew much of Cicero's past. He told me he lost many loved ones and sought life without companionship.

Once we're alone, Cicero opens a pouch filled with white sand that sparkles in the lantern light. He grabs my palm and pours it on them. It burns a little but also tickles each nerve.

"What is this?" I ask.

"Crystallized starlight," he says. "I bought it off a faerie who came with the princes. It is rare but is the only known cure for lasting iron damage."

I smile as I watch the starlight twinkle, then frown once I realize something. "How much did this cost you?"

He looks at me. "It's coming out of your wage...While this is the only known cure, your hands will be scarred still."

I sigh in relief. I never accept charity from anyone, not even those close to me. Yet Cicero had done me a great service just getting this. I owe him for this and hope that one day, I could perhaps repay him.

The dust dissolves into my hands after a few more minutes. Then the fingernail on my thumb turns blue.

I look up at Cicero and ask, "A side-effect?"

He doesn't say anything for a moment. "I am no expert on this, but it would appear so."

Once again faerie magik has strings attached. It is almost ironic that I am once more marked to look less human than before.

"Why was Titus behaving so oddly?" I ask.

Cicero's face, like always, reveals nothing. Not one vein of anger, tear of sadness, or smile of joy. Whenever he did reveal something, it was forced and fabricated. I have never seen an emotion I could genuinely name or verify.

"He and I had a slight altercation after the meeting today. He no longer trusts me and I believe that once this is over, he will petition against me to King Fyfe." He cracks his neck.

I let out a short laugh. "You are very valuable to Jorthus, if anyone loses their position it will be him. He is replaceable."

Cicero smiles his false smile. "We shall see," he pauses and looks out the window, "You should get some sleep for tomorrow."

I nod as my master turns and leaves without another word. My mind lingers on his words about Titus. To go from respecting someone to no longer trusting them is never a good course of action. Either Titus is correct or Cicero is, and I really hope it's the latter. Fighting against Titus is natural for me, easy. Fighting Cicero is unimaginable.

I sit on the bed carefully, looking out the misty window. The nights here are cold, and the days warm. I almost forgot what it was like to work hard just to keep warm. The capital is loved by the stars. The heat radiates off the polished buildings and into the homes of the poor. I took it for granted even though I never liked the heat in the high season. I was grateful to live and work in the Ebony Hall, an underground mansion beneath the castle. It was cool and had many training rooms.

These lands raised me, yet right at this very moment, they feel so foreign. I'm surrounded by everyone I've ever let enter my life, and everyone who forced their way in, and yet I feel so alone and unsure of my purpose

So I begin to write two letters. One for my human father and one for my faerie mother. I need to let these feelings out once and for all. My mother did not murder my father like I was led to believe, which meant she was humane enough to spend time with him, and still give birth to me. I wonder what motivated her to carry out the pregnancy and bring in a half-blood child.

The Queen told me her name. A simple yet haunting word. Lythe. And that is how I start the letter, with her name scarred into the page like a memorable battle wound. I write down all of my feelings, past and present towards her. I tell her of my training as a warrior, spy, and assassin. The only thing I can't properly do is hunt animals.

The letter to my father is less fair in balancing the good with the bad. I let him know exactly who I am and what I am capable of if I ever meet him. How I would end his life and how long it would take, one week for each year he never came back to save me from this village, one week of pain in different parts of his body. An eternity of pain. He will regret throwing me away like a rock in a pond.

I look down at my hand, the tip of my quill pressed so hard into the parchment that ink has exploded and half the letter is in ruins and my hand is stained black.

I stand up and hold the letters in my hands. Feeling the weight of them linger on my skin, the raw emotions bleed onto my skin, the souls of them crumble and rebuild in seconds. Then I drop them in the fireplace.

They burn and I feel nothing.

Chapter 4: A Meeting of Snakes

Whispering Cove, Kingdom of Jorthus

There were six thrones set up on the hill just above Whispering Cove. The most intricate and decorated throne was for Fyfe. Painted with real gold, his seat was adorned with emeralds and diamonds while the others were wooden.

Cicero asked me to stand behind Lorkus' throne, which is covered in fine silk. If anything goes wrong, I am to protect the prince and get him out.

Seven faeries appear behind the thrones closest to the bay, just as Cicero and Titus set up the human side of the council. One of them seemingly crawled out of the earth, pulling loose soil and roots along with it.

The human mediator is sweating and constantly looking up at the sky. It's clear that he hasn't mediated something bigger than a farmers' council debate.

Trumpets sound and everyone immediately goes to their knees.

"We welcome their royal majesties of Jorthus, King Fyfe and Queen Selene, and his royal highness, Prince Lorkus," the mediator announces with all his courage. His nervousness would normally amuse me if it were an ordinary meeting, yet we are all on our toes. Despite the script and prompt, he manages to completely make a mess of their calling.

One of the faeries steps out from behind the throne, looking as though it were made of twigs and flesh with eyes as black as night. I wonder what it was exactly. I know there are many different kinds of faeries just like there are different kinds of humans, but I never thought I would see something so strange.

Everyone takes a breath.

"For the first time in many long years, the rulers of Daeyed step onto the once prosperous lands of the Unseelie Court," its voice sounds more like wind: wispy and deep, "Once there were four princes of Daeyed, each representing a former court, now there are three. They step back onto these ancestral lands hoping to see a sliver of what it once was, and they find a land nearly drained of life, magik, and beauty. My princes are in need of no introduction, but out of formalities for these..." He pauses, giving the king a once over. "Humans...they will be introduced."

Fyfe glares at his mediator, then at the faerie standing in front of him.

If Fyfe was in his prime, I have no doubt he would jump out of his seat and stab the faerie in the neck with an iron blade. He often commanded his armies during the Jorthus-Trilan three-year war. He is a king ruled by anger and often has his advisors do these meetings on his behalf.

"I take pleasure in honouring the ancient princes of Arcadia, the ones who have seen the beginning of the human empires, their royal highnesses, royal warriors, royal protectors, and royal immortals, Prince Septimius the Wyvern," the prince was already sitting on the chair, appearing quickly like the others, "Prince Kynus the Proud," Prince Kynus smirks, sitting on the edge of the throne's arm, "and acting high prince, Vikorus the Wicked."

The last one stands right beside the faerie. His long silver hair is braided down his back and his pale grey skin smooth, like death merely kissed it and nothing more. His eyes are a woodland green but rimmed with a deep crimson. This is the one we were all warned about. The one who hates humans above all.

"I thought we agreed on no magik for this meeting?" Surprisingly, it was queen Selene who spoke first.

Kynus tilts his head and smiles. "We keep our word, human queen. Our glamour is not magik—magik requires energy from nature, our glamour does not."

"Kynus, it is useless explaining, perhaps we should speak simply so they understand." Vikorus walks to the centre throne without looking at Fyfe or

Selene.

"You dare insult me in my home?" Fyfe stands.

Septimius yawns as if bored. "Is it an insult if it is true? Tell me, Fyfe, are you scared of Magik? You see this once was the land of the Unseelie Court, it was where Vikorus' blood held dominion, so would it be his home as well? Or mine since the Dark Court was annexed to the Unseelie?"

"You were born after your courts fell. You are not welcome here despite what claim you think you have on the lands," Lorkus chimes in. I feel his energy through the chair, his excitement.

I was hoping he would not speak, that he would not draw their attention towards him or me. I was unable to read the documents this morning because of what happened the night prior, and Rowyna was refused outright by the princes. The plan was already moving in a different direction.

"It appears not all humans are incompetent," Kynus says, "but you are wrong, child. We do not want to claim dead land. And I was born before they fell, I fought in the war."

Fyfe looks around at the green trees, water, and plush grass beneath his feet. He gestures to the sky with his hands and smiles. But the thing he did not realize was that faeries cannot lie. They only tell the truth, though they often twist it.

"Oh child, your land is barely alive, if only you saw Daeyed then perhaps you would understand." Kynus looks over at Fyfe. "To be alive means you can breathe in life, energy, and feel how the earth speaks..."

"I am no child, and neither is my son." Fyfe licks his lips. "You will not address us as such again."

"Do you know how old the youngest of us is?" Septimius' face darkens with delight.

"Septimius, perhaps move on from these circles." Vikorus paces in front of the other princes, observing each face watching them. "What I really want to know is why did you break our treaty?"

"You dare accuse me of such a thing?"

Vikorus sighs walking directly in front of Fyfe, so close that the king flinches. It is slight, but I see the faerie smile, eyes glowing greener than before.

"You have forced one of my kind into your service. Your ancestor made it clear when the Iron Treaty was signed that no human would force a faerie into servitude, that the human kingdom would never house a faerie unless approved by both the rulers of Daeyed and human country." Vikorus' teeth flash black like coal.

Fyfe says nothing for a moment... not a single word while everyone waits for a response.

Then the human king shut his eyes, "She was born on my soil, she is half-human, she is mine."

Septimius raises a finger. "Be that the case is irrelevant. If her faerie parent gave birth to her here, that means you were housing a faerie without our knowledge. These are grounds for war, you understand, King Fyfe?"

I take a step back when something grabs me. I look up to see the wood faerie. Its body creaks and wheezes as the wind snakes through some of its branches. The other humans around me scatter, too afraid to touch the creature or help me.

I try to pull it back but the creature only drags me into the open. Its strong, lanky oaken arms lift me off the ground, only to throw me through the air in front of Septimius and Kynus. Rocks press into the white leather of my gloves but not enough to cut through to the flesh.

I roll over so I can see everything. All eyes are on me. I'm a spectacle.

Seeing the cliff's edge, I roll upright and sprint towards the ocean. My only way out.

The twig faerie charges at me and pulls me down mid-leap into the water. Its pointy hands grab my tunic, and I am spun on my heels as it lifts me into the air once again.

I try to swing away but it grabs my silk cowl—my last defence between who I am and the world; then it is torn away.

My body hits the ground at the princes' feet and I roll onto my back. My green hair flies in tangles down my body and my copper eyes shine in the sunlight.

"It is without a sense of acceptance," Twig man says.

"She is not without fire in her soul." Kynus tilts his head.

"What do you want?" Fyfe demands, knowing that the other human countries would not be happy with the breach of the treaty. "I will kill her if you request."

I twist my body towards Fyfe. He is no better than I, a monster willing to kill me even though I was his ally, his weapon in the fight against the fae.

"Well, we don't particularly desire a war…at this moment. But payment is required. I want two of your people, including her, as prisoners," Vikorus chuckles.

"Father, she is important for us—" Lorkus' head shoots towards the king, completely losing his composure.

"Enough to start a war?" It is Selene who cuts her son off. "Why two?"

"You will give what is owed to us, and a human as payment for the faerie life that sired her, the one who is now dead." Kynus tilts his head at the queen.

"I will go." I look to find Legitar Tionne staring directly at the faerie prince Kynus.

"As if his life is worthy enough for our price."

"The crown does not have time for this. Who do you want?" Fyfe cracks his fingers.

Vikorus turns his head to where Prince Lorkus sits.

"Anyone but the crown's successor," Fyfe growls in response.

"As if we would want a human prince, no, we want the one called Cicero the Liar. You see, he knows far too much about us, more so than any other in your country." Vikorus looks at my master, who is close to Lorkus, then back to Fyfe. "Furthermore, should you decline, I promise I will kill your son and curse the *crown* of Jorthus to never have offspring. Have you heard about faerie curses, human king?" Fyfe nods, hands gripping the throne so tight it begins to crack. "Then you know that they are everlasting on humans."

"Cicero is valuable, but he is replaceable. The prince is not," Fyfe grits through his teeth. "The crown agrees despite the harshness of its guests."

"Is he though?" Septimius can't help but smile. "Not replaceable? He is fortunate to be in the position he is in. Being born in the right place at the right time, but there are others in your distant bloodline who would love nothing more than to see the downfall of Fyfe."

"We do not fear you," Lorkus shoots at Septimius.

"Oh?" Septimius looks down at me for a moment. "Then why be afraid of one like her?"

"Aurelia is useless to you, she is half-human and powerless," Lorkus stands from his chair, "she is but a beast at our beck and call."

Not true.

"This is a kindness, you should be grateful," Kynus claps his hands together, "She would have come to realize the disgusting cage you've placed her in and break free in a gruesome way."

"Why would she? We have given her life! A purpose." Lorkus steps closer but another faerie got between us.

"Do not heed the words of a boy. He knows not how much the crown has wanted to see the half-breed swine go," Fyfe silences the crowd.

"Right after you called her yours?" Septimius laughs. "Which is she? A weapon or nothing more than troublesome livestock?"

I can't remain silent. Not anymore.

"How dare you!" I nearly growl at Fyfe, "After all I've done for you! You are sending me to a fate worse than death!"

"The crown should have never allowed you to live in the first place." Fyfe closes his eyes, not wanting to burden himself with the sight of me a moment longer.

"Lovely," Kynus claps his hands together, "now onto the business we actually came here for. Lock our prisoners up, Guionne."

"Don't touch me, you filthy creature!" I try to wriggle away.

The tree-person snags my leg with ease and drags me as though I am as light as a pen. Cicero, on the other hand, walks without protest and simply lets the tree hold onto his arm. He understood when the battle was over, I did not.

"I swear I will kill you," I promise the king, "when this is over I will find you!"

"Is it still talking?" I see Fyfe ask the queen.

She meets my eyes and nods.

Cicero looks down at me. "Do not promise anything, do not give them leverage."

I forgot all my training in one fleeting moment and rage took over. My jaw tightens. "Why are you so calm? They are taking us to that disgusting country!"

"Aurelia, the calmer we are, the better the journey will be," he responds without looking at me.

Once we are far enough away from them, my teeth start to chatter and my body shakes. "Cicero, I cannot go there. I cannot be surrounded by faeries. I would rather die now."

He nods sympathetically. "I know that, but perhaps you should take this as a way to understand the other half of you."

"What do you mean?" I ask. "My mother was a water faerie. I may not know much, but I do know there is a difference between land and water fae."

He says nothing. Why was he like this? Why did we have to leave Jorthus?

My lungs gasp for air as though I step off a cliff. I'm falling through the cracks of my mind.

I scream and my voice rings through my ears, the windows of the nearby carriages breaking. Cicero winces and the tree creature nearly lets go of me as blue liquid begins to pool out of his ears. The tree tightens its grip around me. "You will not do that again or I will silence you."

Be quiet, Aurelia, I do look forward to meeting you, hush for now.

My eyes become heavy as my muscles relax. I try to look for the body attached to that voice but soon realize that it was all in my head. "Cicero, why are you alright?"

Wicked, Fair, Nocturnal, Diurnal, and Marine will unite the lands. They will reclaim the realm and heal it. For if they do not, they will end everything and anything that lingers as revenge.

"I am not alright," he responds.

I look upwards, seeing a bright light shining. It was calm. Heat dances on every surface of my skin. "What are you doing?" I whisper.

Calming you.

"Who are you?" I ask. This time, Cicero expresses confusion.

"Who are you talking to?" he asks me.

But I don't answer him, I just close my eyes as the tree creature pulls me along.

My name is Azlyon, first son of Oberon and Titania, and among the oldest of the fair folk left.

Chapter 5: Moth to Flame

Kingdom of Flokael

I open my eyes and I am inside a wooden cage. I touch the bark and my thumb burns. Cicero is nowhere to be found. Around me are four faeries on pale horses—the three princes, and an additional faerie with his head held high.

"Where is Cicero?" My voice cracks.

"She asks about Cicero the Liar," Kynus' voice muses.

"Cicero is here," Septimius smiles, "if you try harder, look deeper into your *wyld* nature, perhaps you could see him..."

What is *willed* nature? Was it some sort of glamour? I steady my shoulders as we pass a small village.

"Please let me go," I beg them but they do not respond. "I am useless to you creatures!"

Vikorus lets out a harsh laugh, but it's the newest faerie who lowers his hood and looks over with silver eyes and a sharp smile. His own wild hair seems white at first glance, but upon closer inspection, it is a deep plum that fades into a very pale white. I have never seen someone with hair so strange. His eyelids are lined with an absorbing black, standing out starkly upon his pale skin. I thought my features were too faerie-like, but looking at him and his companions, I suddenly feel so human.

"Your traitorous mother was called Lythe. She was the last in line to represent the Cold Court, she is the last high water faerie, which makes you...important, for now." He smiles sharply.

I take in a breath. "Are we in Daeyed?"

"It thinks so little of the great faerie kingdom," the tree faerie-cage says. "We are in Flokael, we travelled through the border city of Crant, and the village you see now is on the edge of the Mountains..."

I look over at the mountains, realizing that they are so pale they reflect light in unique ways. Like glass and stone.

"Sire, she has taken réalta!" the wood faerie screams as it stops directly in the middle of the road.

I blink and the cage is gone. I fall on the gravel road. The rocks are sharp and cause my clothes to tear. This tunic was only meant for the ceremony and made with weaker materials.

"Vikorus, take care of Guionne," the silver-eye faerie commands. He is like them—only so much more. He is a prince of Daeyed. One the world has forgotten.

I look at the cruel prince to my left, the one who took control at the meeting, the grey prince Vikorus. His expression is deathly and vengeful, but still, he nods evenly to the sharp, commanding prince.

"Kynus, ride on ahead and prepare Loelmell for court," the silver-eye faerie orders the princes. "Septimius, you and Vikorus are going to maintain order with the Warfellows until I arrive."

Septimius nods. Kynus says nothing but begins to gallop ahead at an unusually fast pace; the speed of ten thousand horses.

I begin to drag myself off the road slowly as the commanding prince attends to the other seemingly invisible faeries.

"Aurelia, you are staying right there or your ride into Daeyed will not be as comfortable," he says without turning his back.

I stop before reaching the edge of the road hoping to sway the conversation, "What is réalta?"

"It is what cured your flesh of iron poisoning," he says, "The starlight Cicero the Liar gave you."

"Why would a faerie be afraid of something that cures it?" I ask.

"All things should be feared," he says.

That wasn't an answer.

He turns around and walks swiftly over, cape fluttering behind him. His eyes glitter and shine before me, yet his energy does not affect me the same as the others. I feel nothing from him, as though he were a dead man walking.

"Come along, we have quite the journey ahead of us." He holds out a hand to me.

"Azlyon, that's your name," I say, standing without his help.

"That is my given name," he snaps as though I stated the obvious.

"Why have we never heard of you?" I look him straight in the eye. I must master this fear.

"Humans forget." His voice is clear though his lips never seem to move.

"We have records, records from the great war until this present day."

"I was around long before the great war. Do you think it would be difficult for someone like me to erase an identity?" he responds, grabbing my arm, "Besides, the great war was long enough for people to begin to forget."

The great war was hundreds of suns ago when the humans defeated the wicked faerie army that was plotting to end them. Back in those days, the fae controlled this world, and few humans lived freely in the land of chaos and beauty. I wish I knew more about the war but only royalty were privy to that information in Jorthus.

If Azlyon is telling the truth, which is highly possible because he cannot lie, then that means he has an ocean of knowledge. I was just a blink in his existence.

"Is Cicero glamoured?" I cross my arms. "Answer that and I will go willingly."

He raises a brow. "You care for your master?"

"He may be the only friend I have in this world," I say, looking away for a moment.

"He was glamoured and is headed to Loelmell," Azlyon's voice cascades down my spine, "He is sleeping right now, and will be as long as I say. So, my dear, if you wish him to remain safe, I suggest you do as you're told from now on."

"Very well." I walk beside him and climb the only horse remaining. The others took my master and I need to get him back.

I reach for the reins only to realize there aren't any, only hair and gills on its long neck. I look over at the faerie prince but he is already behind me. "How are you going to ride it with two people and no reins?"

His arms reach over to touch the horse's temples. The beast's eyes roll back into its head, and when they came back, they're a ghostly white colour, the colour of Azlyon's strange hair.

"He and I are connected, he is my familiar," Azlyon whispers like ice into my ear, "He can take on any shape I require, and we can look through one another's eyes."

"Why are you telling me anything at all? I thought you lot are very secretive."

"You will learn when we are safely in our territory," is all Azlyon says.

Then we are off like horses at the King's Match. Fyfe held an annual competition amongst lords where they raced one another for a hefty sum of money. The losers behead their horses in submission, and then a grand dinner would be made of the animals' flesh. Sometimes, if I was lucky enough, I was able to set a horse into the wild before the beheading ceremony even though I had been fined several times for being caught "interfering with tradition and sport." The one thing I do understand is the difference between cruelty, death, and suffering. Each is unique and often confused with one another, but I live on those fine lines. I kill on those fine lines. I grow on those fine lines.

"You should know," I say, smiling, "just because I was raised with humans does not mean I am soft. I've killed dozens of men."

I feel him almost laugh through my tunic. "The little assassin who's killed a few handfuls of humans. Tell me, did you enjoy it? Seeing their blood blanket them, knowing they will never wake again? Innocent and guilty people who disagreed with your king? Or perhaps you enjoyed the rush it gave you, taking away the only silver of magik they will ever know because in death there is nothing. What about seeing your own family torn from you? Yes, I am talking about the huntress who raised you, Lucia. Titus should have killed her, but his heart was too weak. And your father, he is an upstanding servant of Fyfe, does that disappoint or please you? The man who was too scared to care for you, the one who let his primal instincts control him long enough to get a highborn asrai pregnant, only to allow her to die in front of him?"

My breath falters as I grip his wrist tightly in anger. He doesn't move a muscle in defence or raise an arm in the offence.

"Stop!" I growl at him, teeth bare and eyes sharp. "How dare you? You have no right to my life!"

There they are. Your faerie instincts are rising in you.

I freeze. He pushes into the part of me that I locked away for so many years. All it took was some enticing. How did he know all of this?

"Disgusting, the lot of you," I hiss.

Azlyon ignores my anger. "Would you like to meet her? She could talk for hours and you would never feel the need to leave."

"She is dead," I say simply, "Unless you are suggesting I die."

"Just because she is dead does not mean you cannot meet her," he says and touches my temple gently.

I blink. Suddenly I am no longer on the horse, but instead on the edge of a dark cliff or an underground cave. The lights glitter and sparkle along the walls like tiny glowing gemstones. Not a single ray of sun or drop of moonlight in sight. I wonder how I could see so clearly despite the darkness.

I turn around to see Prince Kynus sitting on the edge of the pool of water in the centre. His pale legs swayed in the water and his fiery hair darkened to a whisky green as his skin further submerged.

"Kynus, we must make haste," Azlyon's voice came through me. Was I in his memory? "The war rages on, Oberon is making his last stand against them."

Just then a figure peeked out of the water near the opposite end of the pool. A horned woman with misty grey eyes, pale skin, and hair greener and paler than my own. She was wearing only a rag to cover herself.

"Lythe," Azlyon spoke without emotion.

"Son of Oberon," she said, sliding beside Kynus, looking as though she were perfectly dry, "has my brother behaved himself?"

They were related to one another?

"The sea obeys your family. Why have they not sent for aid since the first wave?"

She stood firmly and smiled with needled teeth, pointing a webbed hand at me—him. "The humans deserve revenge after all we've done to them, and with the fall of the Seelie Court, we do not stand a chance against them. Iron is already sickening Arcadia, I will not let it sicken my people, my family."

"Lythe, please—" Kynus began.

"She is not like you, she is not of the sidhe," Azlyon cut Kynus off coldly, "she is wild like the currents of the sea. She is too much like her environment, compassionate to those close but willing to drown anyone who touches her kin."

Lythe just tilted her head, letting her hair fall to her ankles. Something reflected the light from the walls. Upon further inspection, I saw the same ring I found stuck in the crevice of the rocks on the tip of her right horn.

"And you, Prince Azlyon, plan genocides as though they were nothing more than a decision to attend a royal feast. Yet you are correct, my brotherkin is more like you than his asrai kin, but that does not mean that he does not still care for us, and we him. I will ask my mother to beg the King of the Cold Court to send seven of our highest oceanic knights to aid you. This is not out of kindness, it is so my brotherkin does not die so needlessly." Lythe was standing so close now I could see the swirling grey in her eyes.

Azlyon stepped towards her, eyes glowing in the dark, "In return, I will try to remove the curse Oberon placed on you several years ago," Her eyes went wide as she touched her belly.

His hand reached over to her chest as dust began to swirl around Lythe.

"I could not remove it entirely," Azlyon almost sounded sad, "you cannot have true faelings, but you may have a chance with a human."

She snarled as she shoved him, "Which is entirely forbidden and you know that."

"Lythe, I called you here because I am taking Fryaen's place as High Lord of the Bright Court. The only stipulation is that I must cut ties with the

Cold Court for betraying Arcadia," Kynus cut in.

Lythe turned so sharply I thought she would fall over. Did faeries even fall? I can't see her eyes but the muscles in her back tightened in fury.

"Cut ties with the only kin who will be at your side in a moment's notice," I heard her whisper in an attempt to remain calm. "Kynus, do not do this. You are joining a losing side and you will never be able to return to us."

Kynus stepped up and his hair turned red once more. "I have outgrown you, I have outgrown being the bastard marine son."

His descent into power, Lythe could see it, but it was not she who spoke.

"Time to come home, Kynus, there will be a place in the new world for you," Azlyon said.

Kynus looked at Lythe once before jumping in the water. It seemed to be the only entrance to this cave.

"Protect him, Azlyon," she whispered. "he is still trying to find his place in the world at such a young age."

"I will never promise this, but I will keep an eye on him as long as I can," Azlyon responded, "The sea folk have become so soft over the decades, you must remember that you are still fae."

"We stopped behaving like your kind because you are the ones who brought this iron sickness here with every human you trapped, stole, or baited. We focused on all faeries long before the land courts united. Remember that. I hope we do not meet again. Once I called you friend, but my brotherkin is where our paths diverge." She stepped on top of the water as though it were solid, stopping to look back once at Azlyon. "In a perfect reality, both sides would coexist among one another."

"We did until we were driven out of our homes." Azlyon retorted.

I open my eyes. Standing before us are nearly a hundred warriors dressed in gold and blue, the colours of Flokael. A man in decorative gold armour stands several paces ahead of us. He has olive skin, a Harr warriors' braid woven with feathers, and narrow amber eyes.

The Harr are the human Flokael natives said to have been created from clay by the fae as frontline soldiers. Titus said that they were some of the best fighters he has ever seen. He once hired Harr mercenaries to take care of a mutated creature that escaped a famed alchemist's laboratory. A Harr warrior named Jaraet taught me some of their techniques when he was hired by the crown. No matter how hard I tried, I could not be nearly as flawless as he was.

This man was high in rank, perhaps a regional or territorial general.

"By the Order of Rhion, halt!" he orders.

He does not know who I am. You see, I haven't been home in years, his voice trickles in my mind.

I know the Order of Rhion very well. They are a faerie-human equality organization. It is said they originated from Daeyed, which I never believed, and Fyfe loathed them with every ounce of his being. According to Cicero, the Order's leaders are faceless. They want true coexistence and peace in every country, and their tactics were punishable by death in Jorthus. Flokael is an obvious choice for their operations.

I never imagined I'd see a whole army of them before me.

"I am just passing through with my companion," Azlyon's voice is emotionless.

"I am General Yvret," the man says, "and we cannot allow you to enter Daeyed without the permission from our arch kings. Heading there in that wildland is a death sentence. Who are you, sir?"

Azlyon presses his finger to his temple as he steps down from his familiar. Once closer to Yvret, I see the general shiver in the presence of a high faerie.

"I am a prince of Daeyed, and this is Aurelia, daughter of Princess Lythe," he laces his hands behind his back.

The general blinks, then bows. My mother was a faerie princess and somehow, this matters to them.

I crack my knuckles, which catches the general's attention. "Pleasure to meet you all."

"One of our founders was her royal highness, Princess Lythe," Yvret speaks carefully, "but I know who you are. You are one of Jorthus' assassins. You may look like her but you will never be one of us."

I shrug, hopping down with a hand firmly on my hip. "How amusing it is to think I would want to be part of such an organization. You preach peace but all you do is conduct violent acts."

"You disgrace your mother's legacy. Why are you here with a pretender prince?" Yvret crosses his arms.

"That is my business. What I find even more interesting is that you so willingly offer your name," I say licking my lips as I step even closer to him. He steps back as though I bore some illness he could catch. "I have hunted and killed on less than that."

My eyes meet his. This Harr is not afraid of me, per se, but he is scared of something. Does he have a family? Does he think I will hurt them? So many possibilities, just as there are so many outcomes.

"She is a permanent guest of Daeyed," Azlyon says behind me.

"A prisoner, you mean," Yvret replies, relaxing a little.

"Only if she resists."

"I'm certain our leaders would like to meet her," Yvret sighs, "but I am also certain upon learning their identity, she would smuggle the information back to Farlanfell."

"Kynus the Proud is her next of kin," says Azlyon. "Would you go directly against a prince of Daeyed? How would that fare against your organization?"

Yvret pales.

"Aurelia, please get back on Raenlin," Azlyon says.

I turn and climb on the horse without difficulty. Then Azlyon whispers to the horse and begins walking ahead. Raenlin follows without hesitation and fear, as though walking into an army of soldiers was just another day.

"My name is Azlyon," he says to Yvret, dagger in hand, "and you've delayed me."

He reaches up and cuts through Yvret's braid in one swing.

The world stills as the Harr soldier falls to his knees as though struck in the chest. Jaraet once told me that cutting off a Harr's braid is one of the worst punishments a warrior can endure. He said that their hair is meant to warm a certain kind of faerie's heart when they die. While it does grow back, they must wear yellow feathers so all Harr know he or she is not worthy to gift their braid.

The other Harr warriors gasp but do not move from their place, fearing that the strange pale faerie in front of them would do the same. Or perhaps because they are unsure of whether or not to obey their general now that his worthiness has been ripped from him.

When we reach the line of soldiers, they part before us. Azlyon walks gracefully, like the highborn he was raised to be. I, on the other hand, look around suspiciously. Trusting people is not something that comes easy to me.

"Tell me about her," I say to Azlyon.

"I've only met her eight times in the duration of my life," he says, "and what you saw was the very last time she and I spoke. I knew she formed that organization and operated it with another faerie because humans live such short lives."

I lean forward. "Which faerie? Is it still alive?"

He touches the horse's soft mane and smiles. "Still so loyal to the king who would kill you to appease us."

"They are poison," I grit my teeth, "and need to be ended."

"Does it bother you that your mother started this organization?"

"No, it bothers me more that my uncle is a high prince," I say without thinking.

"So you are going to try to end Kynus?" Azlyon asks without looking back at me.

"I haven't decided yet," I say quietly.

You stand little to no chance against him. Besides, faeries are not sentimental. They come together in celebration, produce offspring, and acknowledge their superiors. Lythe and her grandfather's people are different from most.

"So faeries cannot love?"

"They are capable of love, but rarely act upon it. For it is better to mate with an ideal faerie than a goblin in the name of love." He chuckles darkly.

I tilt my head. "Love is a fantasy, something I both crave and detest. That is why I kill people, it allows me to feel without becoming attached."

"The idea of love is your greatest desire," he says. "It only makes sense—a girl who lost both her parents, stepping in two different worlds, does nothing but work, and believes herself to be an aberration of what is normal."

I stare at him. "Why do you care?"

Oh, I don't care now, but the knowledge could prove useful later. You should at least try blocking my magik.

"Wait, what did you do to me?" I say.

"Think like a faerie, not a human, and the answer may come." He pauses but I don't respond. "I asked your soul to reveal truths to me."

I glare daggers at him a moment before leaping off the horse, raising my arm to hit him. I am fast. I trained all my life to outsmart my targets and reveal little, but this time I allow him to know just how angry I am.

I am fast.

But he is faster.

In a moment, he pins me to the ground. The pale prince's elegant left hand forces my arms against my chest while his right holds my throat down. He is stronger than he looks.

"Little River, tell me you weren't intending on hitting me, because if you were that would be a lethal mistake," he says.

"You won't kill me," I say over the pressure of his hand, "you need me alive."

"She is not as ignorant as she looks." He smiles like a cat.

"Did you just lie?" My eyes widen.

He tilts his head. "I never said I would kill you, all I said is that it would be a lethal mistake. Perhaps your dear friend Cicero will pay that tithe.

I have no idea what he means by a tithe.

"I adore how much Arcadian humanity has forgotten about both their history and ours," he says after my blank expression. "Our tithes are more than just money, they require blood and madness. Cicero could very well die as payment for your misdeeds."

Until recently, I never heard anyone still refer to this world as Arcadia. It was considered too tribal and too primitive…Just like the faeries. Fyfe described faerie supporters as Arcadians, and in Jorthus, it was the worst thing you could call someone.

"How did the fae let humans nearly obliterate them? After all, you had the advantage," I ask.

His grip tightens on my hands but not my throat. I hit the perfect nerve. If I was going down this path, I would not lock myself inside my skin as I did in Jorthus.

"We did not *let* them, I would remind you to mind your tongue," he says. "I lost my kin, my reality, and my world. The humans will pay one day for what they did."

"They killed the magik living in every stone, every breath, and every blade of grass," I say, meeting his eyes. "Daeyed is the smallest country, yet it holds all the remaining magik. Tell me, your highness, how do you plan on restoring magik to the entire land?"

He leans closer, his hair tickles my cheekbones as it shifts down the air. "There is a way, but that is wonderfully private information. Now is the time we continue ahead, Little River."

Then in one sweep, he gets up and pulls me along with him in an effortless swing. I swear that for a moment, I saw a sliver of pain in his eyes for what he had lost.

Chapter 6: The Stone Eye

Loelmell, Court of Daeyed

For the rest of our journey, I was silent.

Our descent into Daeyed was strange. Azlyon said the land near the border would look the most poisoned. It looked normal to me but felt different. The energy as we went deeper into Daeyed was stronger like my nerves were on the verge of being shocked by thousands of tiny lightning storms.

It also turns out that Loelmell was more than just a castle, it was a fortress. King Fyfe knew so little about this country. Not only is the presence of the Order of Rhion strong at the border, but there is also an even stronger military movement in Daeyed.

The fortress itself is made of solid obsidian and what looks like dark marble. The peaks of each tower are so pointy they look like they can carve the sky into a delicate sculpture. Spirals and intricate carvings decorate the outside. I remember at the meeting that faerie mentioned different courts that once ruled the land, and now I wonder if this place was once a centre of power.

"You are staying in the prison until I consult the other princes," Azlyon whispers in my ear, clearly amused.

"Lovely." I clench my jaw as a shadowy faerie pulls me off the horse.

"Take her to the East Wing cellblock," Azlyon tells the faerie.

I feel stiff bony hands wrap around my wrist, smelling of rot.

"Aurelia, the jailer is a bean sidhe," Azlyon says. "Also known as the wailing woman to humans."

I vaguely remember Cicero telling me about one King Fyfe could not kill in Jorthus. That he hoped I would be able to do it one day. The bean sidhe is a faerie woman who heralds the death of loved ones or betokens your own death with its distorted scream.

The cloaked woman guides me through the halls, stopping in a common area lit vaguely by candles. When I turn to face her, her red eyes meet mine, and for a moment I feel as though she is searching my soul and understanding my every action, past and present.

She holds out a clean grey tunic without a word for me to put on. Her leathery face cascades in wrinkles and her long hair is stiff like hay. When her mouth opens slightly in an attempt to smile, I see nothing but blackness in her body. I take the garments quickly and step back, changing my clothes.

Then she points to a swirling mirror in front of me. I shake my head and laugh, but this does not impress her. Her eyes sharpen as she pushes me inside the mirror.

I gasp and shut my eyes, expecting shards of glass to stain my skin with blood. When I open them, I am on the floor in a large cell. The mirror I came from is now a solid stone wall.

I climb up to my knees and press my hands to the stone, feeling cold energy vibrate through my skin for a fleeting moment.

"Tian, it is a girl!" an accented voice chuckles.

"A faerie girl or human? This is the best day!" another voice leers.

I turn and look across the slim hall where two very human-seeming men sit close together in another cell. Some sort of light streams through the top stones, glowing gold, red, and yellow. I shake my head once again blaming magik.

"Who are you?" I ask, rubbing my eyes. "How long have you been here?"

One of them has tan skin and curly hair. The other has darker skin with oily hair falling down his sides. Both have beady eyes in this light.

"My name is Jupa," curly says, "and this less handsome friend of mine is Tian. You look like a faerie but you also don't..."

I clench my teeth and look around, ignoring his question. "Are there any other prisoners?"

"Look at the girl, a curious one." Jupa raises his brows.

"Tell me I look pretty and I might answer the girl." Tian licks his lips.

"Do I have to? I am clearly the prettiest. I broke nearly half the hearts in Aeolus before I was arrested!" Jupa tilts his head.

"So you are from Trilan? The capital?" It is said that their skin is thick as bark, which helps them swim and stay afloat even in the strongest sea current.

"Have you been? It is quite nice around midsummer!"

I say, "I never left my country."

"Liar, you said it is too warm then!" Tian snaps at Jupa, "Guess where I am from!"

Tian looks like he could belong anywhere. However, based on the way he speaks, he would not survive a day in Jorthus.

"This is so exhausting," Tian pretends to pull his hair, "I am not from a fancy country like the both of you, I am from a land where people run wild. Don't even get me started on how few people live beyond the age of fifteen."

Then he is from the desert lands, formally known as The Dead Lands. It is a land where resources are scarce and mutiny is abundant. Only the worst prisoners in Jorthus are sent there to live out their days—a fate worse than the guillotine.

"How old are you now, Tian?" I ask.

"I never kept track after I made it past fifteen, but I think I am nearly twice that by now," Tian smiles. "All I wanted to do was find a girl and run far until we couldn't anymore. Oh, and this cell block is only for humans, which is just us now."

I raise a brow, crossing my legs and lacing my hands in my lap.

"So who are you exactly," Jupa asks, smiling widely.

"Aurelia, of Jorthus" I sigh, that life is more than long gone. It is no longer even an option even if I defeat all the faeries in the world.

"Hah! Called it!" Tian shouts. "Someone distant and entitled ought to be from that maniacal nation!"

"Excuse me, Tian, you did not call it! I believe I did!" Jupa scoffs.

"I didn't hear you, you coastal rat!"

"Neither of you spoke a word about it," I reply not feeding their insanity.

"Jupa, we appear to have called it in our minds." Tian tucks his hair behind his ears.

"Tian, now that we are all acquainted we should share prison stories!" Jupa grins. "I have been here for eleven years, I killed my family and ran all across the world. Then I hid in the Crystal Mountains where a troll found me! I was going to be eaten alive so I killed it. Then I was kidnapped and ended up here, where I am told I would live out my days for spilling the blood of the fae. Vengeful bastards!"

Tian rolls his eyes. "Liar, you have only been here seven years and you were caught courting a nixie in the Crystal Mountains."

Jupa shrugs. "I still killed my family."

"And you know what I did?" he asks. "I made a deal with a leprechaun and broke my end, so now I am to spend the rest of my life here before he claims my soul when I die."

"What did you hope to gain?" I ask.

"A woman who worshipped me!" Tian huffs. "Is that really too much to ask for? I'm a pretty man after all, but regular women don't like the whole idea of worship these days."

I roll my eyes. "You could have just saved a whore from a brothel and she would feel indebted to you. What you are asking for is a mindless servant who is pretty. Just hire servants once you obtained a real profession."

"I never said I was that smart, what would you have done if you met the leprechaun?"

"Do they grant wishes?" I ask.

"How do you not know about them?" Tian asks with wide eyes, gesturing to my strange body.

All I knew was what Cicero allowed me to know. "There aren't faeries in Jorthus. How much do you know?"

"I know things, but I am no expert." Tian shrugs.

"That's because there are no faeries in The Dead Lands..." Jupa hits Tian on the back of the head.

"There are sorcerers!" Tian complained.

"They don't have magik anymore!"

"They are still bloodthirsty, prickly bastards!" Tian hits him back.

"Gentlemen," I say, "tell me about the princes of Daeyed."

Both men pale. All sense of annoyance, anger, sadness, and pride vanish until only fear remains, and this was a fear that made children stay up late. It fell below their mind and into their hearts, which beat weakly.

"They kill with a single glance," Jupa whispers, grabbing the bars, the same time Tian says, "I saw the dark one make a man dance until his bones collapsed under his weight."

"When did you see them?" I ask.

"We are allowed to surface once a year as a tribute for their tithe," Jupa shivers.

There is that word again.

"What is a tithe?"

"A human sacrifice to what they call Hell." Tian shivers. "This year one of us will be their tithe. Until now, there were other humans here."

I jump up. "Are you sure there isn't another human here? His name is Cicero the Liar."

They both look at each other and shake their heads.

"Is he your husband?" Tian wiggles his brows.

I shake my head. "He is my mast—friend."

"Not a good friend if he was titled 'the Liar,'" Jupa barks out a laugh.

I take a breath, they were locked up here for a while. Time spent with the faeries can seem like a few moments or an eternity. Cicero told me little but he did teach me never to trust a faerie should I encounter one. They don't lie but they twist their words.

"Can half-blood faeries lie?" Tian asks casually.

"Have you never met a half-blood? Perhaps in Flokael?" I ask but they just stare on.

"Faeries cannot," Tian says. "I've seen half-faeries during my brief travels through Flokael but I never spoke long enough to find out."

Jupa looks down at my hand, noticing my ring. "How come you gotta keep that?"

I look down at the glittering gem. I treasure it deeply though I only recently found it. Just seeing it on my mother means it must be important.

"Because I am not a prisoner," I say meeting their eyes. The princes took me for a reason and I intend to find out the truth.

Tian sniffs the air. "Smells like your shackles are that of the invisible kind. The worst kinds of prisoners are those who are useful—to an extent. And when that extent runs out, you wonder about all the ways they will hurt you."

I lean closer to the bars and stare Tian in the eyes. It is at this point I notice that one of his eyes is not real. It looks like an endless black pit. Scars surround the edges as though the eye was ripped out by very sharp fingernails, or even knives. In that darkness, I knew he was right.

"Redcaps," he says, "they took my eye before I was brought here. Faeries don't just keep prisoners, for we are a waste of food, shelter, and space. The Loelmell bean sidhe wailed in our dreams that our fates were determined."

I shake my head. "Fate is not predetermined, you make your own choices, you write your own destiny."

Jupa claps his hands, "Such a heroic thought."

I wonder if the Loelmell bean sidhe knew my fate even though her voice never carries it into the wind. What is my purpose? In the grand scheme of all that exists, do I matter?

No.

I am done being a weapon. The best spies are the ones who fully infiltrate the trust of their target. The best assassins strike flawlessly when the time is right.

"If you are present during the tithe," Jupa says, "be the one to kill us."

I never make promises I cannot keep, but this is different. "If I am present, have the means, and am in the right position to do so, I will. If it jeopardizes my life, I will not."

Jupa tilts his head. "Spoken almost like a faerie. Yet I thank you, Miss Aurelia. To help a murderer out shows a great deal about your character."

Tian shakes his head, almost chuckling. "Pride, Lust, and Greed all together in one prison."

I raise my brows. "What are you talking about?"

"My mother told me of the seven sins. She said they came to this world along with humans," Tian says, "She was a believer of a different and old religion, one even I don't even remember."

Humans came to this world? I was taught they were born a repressed race that rose to conquer their faerie masters. The Dead Lands is known to house those who have erratic beliefs.

"Perhaps the princes know more about this religion," I say, mostly to myself.

"Doubtful. The fae are proud creatures," Jupa sighs. "Only humans worship the great creator, faeries worship themselves."

I smile weakly. So I was the proud one Tian was referring to. I will be the first to admit I feel pride in my achievements, but I do not believe myself to be better than anyone. Without pride, people have no sense of purpose.

I spot a perfectly circular stone by my feet. It is a soft, pale thing. In my hands it has a good weight; not too heavy but not light either.

When I look up, I see Tian staring at the ceiling. I wonder if I could fashion an eyeball out of this stone. I am a faerie, I have magik running in my blood. If I deny it any longer, I will not survive in Daeyed.

I open my palm with the stone in the middle, my right hand hovering over it moments before my forefinger pushes against the rock. My eyes shut as I picture it turning into a glass eye, one that is decent and soft.

I open my eyes. The stone remains the same. I frown.

Do you believe in magik? Do you believe in yourself? Most importantly, do you believe in your master and all he has taught you? Azlyon's voice echoes in my mind.

Cicero told me concentration was like a chrysalis and the butterfly that emerges from it is the result. It must wait, focus, and develop. And once it is strong enough, it will break free into something beautiful. Do I believe in magik? Yes. Do I believe I can conduct magic? Perhaps the butterfly inside me is waiting patiently to find out, but its hard waspish exterior is making it impossible to even see.

I breathe out, "I am of the fae. I can use glamour like the fae. My mother was a woman of the sea. She believed in a world both humans and fae could exist alongside one another. I am a creation—no—child of that dream. My mother loved me with all her heart but she died. I could walk on water like her."

I clench the stone tighter in my palm, feeling the deep beats of my heart.

"If I can walk on water, then why can't I touch the stone's inner magik with my own?" I ask.

"I think she is a nutter, Tian," I hear Jupa whisper.

"No, she just doesn't want to be useless, but I reckon she is partly a nutter for trying to be both faerie and human," Tian muses.

If you impress me, I will let you meet Cicero, Azlyon's voice caresses my mind.

I feel the stone crack and crumble in my hand.

I gasp as I look down at my now open palm. I put so much pressure on it that my muscles now twitch. There is nothing left. No stone, no dust, and no more energy. My only chance to see Cicero is gone.

I take a breath as I sink further into myself.

"I failed," I say.

"What?" Tian laughs aloud.

My head shoots over. In the dark shadows, I see a glittering eye in the once empty socket. High-ranking Jorthus soldiers lost eyes and were given gem eyes from the king's forge. Women clung to them as though the fake eyes were symbols of good fortune ahead.

"It worked!" I stand, grinning.

He stands as well, and says, "It more than worked, I can see out of it!"

Impossible. That simply could not be true.

But with our magik, miracles, as the humans say, can be performed.

Tears build in the corners of my eyes. I gave a man half his vision back. I gave him what the faeries stole all those years ago. Maybe if I gave him his vision back, his fate could alter.

"Jupa! I can see! Bless this woman and her odd appearance!" Tian grins, then smirks at me. "What? Now that I can fully see you, I think you should let your hair down, lose the resting scowl, and maybe stop staring at people like you want to eat their souls… What? I am just being honest. You could be really pretty if you…"

"If you were my cellmate, I would hit you so hard right now that your skull would split." I smile ferociously.

He returns my smile. "Trust me, honey, if we were in the same cell you would be begging me, even though you are not my type."

"Oh, you have a type?" I actually laugh.

"Yes. The I-want-to-live-in-your-trousers-Tian type."

"More like the will-anybody-look-in-my-direction type," Jupa chuckles under his breath.

"Excuse me, just because I don't run after the first nixie that flaunts her breasts at me does not mean other women won't worship at my temple." Tian crosses his arms. "I ain't about that faerie loving life unless it's with either of your mothers."

"Dead," Jupa and I say at the same time.

"Also mine was human," Jupa adds.

It is nice being able to speak with common folk like I am their equal. These men were clearly mad, but all the best people I've met were very blunt and live each day as though it were their last.

Their eyes widen, so I smile even wider, showing my strange teeth.

A hand lands on my shoulder. My body stills.

"Is it the bean sidhe?" I ask and only Jupa shakes his head slightly.

"Bonding with human filth?" A cool voice speaks monotonously.

I turn, only to face someone I was hoping to avoid.

Chapter 7: Wolf Among Sheep

Loelmell, Court of Daeyed

Vikorus the Wicked yanks my body off the floor as though it were nothing more than a rag doll. I gasp attempting to break free of his grip, but his eyes burn with dark violence. His hands are so cold they nearly freeze my arm.

"I will go willingly, your royal highness," I say avoiding his eyes.

"Azlyon, Kynus, Septimius, and I are inviting you to dinner." Vikorus drops me and scans my body. "You will attend and listen to us."

Vikorus is quite lethal. He has a rage in him that was different from what I saw in the other princes. I knew there was a promise in his voice. He is not afraid to use force if I break their rules.

He offers me his hand. When I make no move to reach for it, he grabs my wrist and pulls through the portal.

* * *

I am no longer in prison and the bean sidhe is nowhere in sight. Instead, I am in a room with a bed much too large for a single person to sleep in. White floors, cream walls, and blue silk curtains.

Vikorus turns to face me, eyes darting at the wardrobe "There are four dresses inside, choose only one."

"I doubt I could wear four at once." I look away forgetting where I am for a moment. He is not amused.

He leans closer. "We are not companions nor are we warfellows, you will not be speaking to me like that."

I don't meet his eyes. "My kin has power in this country."

He laughs, "Your mother has no—"

I cut him off, "My uncle is a prince here, the brother to my mother to be exact."

His face darkens, "I do not know where you learned that but you should know he left that side of him a long time ago."

He leaves without another word.

I saw that memory clear as day. I wonder if Vikorus knew. Approaching the snake at its mouth is a way to do this, but I feel my uncle would bite. If anyone knows Kynus the best, it would be Azlyon.

I walk over to the wardrobe and see four dresses within, just as the faerie prince said. One looks like living fire with the waves of silk and ribbon, and another is black as night with silver trim on its loose-fitting bodice. The third is shorter and human crafted, deep grey with the middle exposed.

The last dress falls in mossy green pools on the floor, crystal and glass beadwork flowing from top to bottom in shining sunset colours. Its translucent golden lace sleeves sparkle in the light. Hidden in the green fabric are embroidered flowers and vines which climb up the body of the gown.

I touch the dress without thinking. Never have I been allowed to wear something so intricate and fine.

When I step out of the wardrobe, I see another creature and nearly drop the dress as she curtsies to me. Her hair is not like mine, with strands blossoming pink flowers and orange leaves. Her arms and legs are wooden, and moss frames her face, but her eyes are bright orange.

"Lady Aurelia," she says, "I am your handmaid."

A handmaid? The faeries are treating me better than I would have.

"I am used to taking care of myself," I say, despite sounding very defensive.

"I am aware of your former life, but you are of royalty here," she looks at the dress, "Besides, I doubt you know how to put on a dress like that."

She has a point. "What should I call you?"

"Whatever you wish,"

"What about your name?"

She blinks. "Sorry, I am confused, this has never happened. You may call me Belousa, I am a wood nymph once in the direct service of Prince Vikorus, may she bless him."

"Who is the 'she' you refer to?"

She says nothing.

I step closer to her, handing her the dress, feeling the cool fabric fall from my fingers. Her hands have black bands in marking, almost like charcoal burns.

"What is the given name your mother or father gave you?" I ask instead.

She looks down. "I do not remember, they sold me when I was a girl."

"Are you a slave?"

"No, Prince Azlyon purchased me in Flokael and set me free, but offered me this position," she says. "Not many would hire someone like me."

She is doing her job. This is the only thing in her life that gives her purpose and a chance to earn a future. My heart longs for a purpose.

This girl can walk freely through the halls where they watch and escort me. I have been so focused on surviving that I wonder if I even have any control over myself. I couldn't help but wonder if the princes gave me illusions of false power through choice. When the other option was most certainly death there really wasn't one.

I let her help me into the dress, which she tightens, alters, and laces me into. Shockingly, it fits me. I may have faerie features but my body is closer to a human's with some small differences. I am taller and my bones are thicker. My muscles are not defined through my thick skin, but they make me look larger than I am, and my chest often needs to be bandaged to avoid any hazards on missions. I was not as slender as the nobility this faerie was likely used to dressing.

"You look beautiful, my Lady," she says.

"How does this fit?"

"The material shapes to each."

I turn and see a stranger staring back at me. She looks like she could be dining with Queen Selene. Every detail on the fabric appears to be living on her, as though the dress is an extension of her flesh and bone. Her long is styled in loose curls down her back and at her neck, a square emerald lies at the hollow, reflecting the light. A beautiful stranger in a killer's body.

"The ring, do you wish to wear it?" she looks down at my hand.

I nod, not willing to part with it yet. Right now, this is as close as I have ever been to my mother. She started the Order of Rhion, had a half-human child, and saw both the good and the bad on both sides. While her ideas have merit on paper, in reality, equality will never happen. One will always be treated better than the other.

"I was told to tell you that Cicero will be at dinner." She bows once more at me.

"Belousa, you don't have to be formal with me," I say before walking out of the room.

The halls are very dark and the roof is made of living tree branches that creak and slither into each other. The floor itself looks like a forest floor, roots and all. I turn back to the room and see marble floors and the plush bed. It went from luxurious to dangerous in a single step.

"Belousa, was I supposed to wait for someone?" I ask but she is already gone.

When I turn back, I see a small glowing light at the end of the hall—a wispy blue floating lantern effortlessly glimmering above a damp floor, which looks like a small marsh and smells strongly musk and earth.

It feels like I leaped off a cliff and into a strange new world. The light must be where I need to go for dinner. Yet something feels off. Faeries are tricky and walking in a swamp will ruin a perfectly nice gown.

"Azlyon," I say, crossing my arms, "do I go towards the light or not?"

No response.

"Please, you and the other princes went to so much effort getting me into a gown," I say with annoyance.

It depends if you want to make haste or be late, each end of the hall leads to us. Remember that everything is a game.

I sigh. The light is probably the quickest way but I don't trust it completely.

I will have to find some sort of weapon in case something jumps out and attacks me.

I walk towards the glow in complete elegance, stopping only once. I didn't want to take my eyes off it.

My hands reach towards the wall and snap off a dry root. It is a small weapon that could work, although I wish I have my blades—or even iron dust.

A screech sounds from above but still, I continue. Lingering will only bring problems.

When I come within a few steps of the light, it turns the corner. I bare my teeth at it without thinking. The marsh looms in front of me like poison—deadly to touch in this world.

The worst part was that I couldn't see where I need to step to avoid it. It was too damn dark even though my eyes could vaguely see direction and shape.

My hands reach for the wall, feeling around for roots like the ones I saw earlier. Perhaps I could climb along the wall; it won't be ideal but it will be the better of the two options.

When I find one, it slithers upwards and out of my reach with a low, growling chuckle. The plant apparently has consciousness and a personality.

"Of course," I say.

I turn my head upwards to see a stump-like spot in the centre of the roof. It has eyes, like many trees, only these follow my movements. Not only that, some of the vines near it form a mouth and smile with sharp thorns for teeth.

"I took something dead! You should be happier if it is gone!" I say to it.

It snarls at me, looking at the root in my hand, then back at me.

"I need to protect myself! I am not like you or other faeries!" I try, but its mouth shifts down to the wall, a mere step from me. A yellow residue drips from the thorns.

"Give it back," the mouth hisses, "give it to us and perhaps we will get you across the bog."

I look at the root and sigh, handing it over to the wall, which appears to consume it whole, smiling. The thorns shift against the stone as thick vines snake out, weaving into a swing hanging from the roof.

Before I can say anything, it slides under me and pulls me over the bog, which stretches farther than I even comprehend.

I turn my head back and see a pair of glowing red eyes looking up at me through the glassy yet murky water. Long arms slither beneath the surface. If I'd decide to walk through that, I honestly don't know if I would walk out whole.

The blue light drifts further the closer I get. When the bog ends, the vines dump me on the hard stone floor. I don't even want to know how badly the gown is damaged, let alone my tailbone.

I watch the face above disappear into the tangles of vines. Our bargain was over and I need to move on.

"Well, at least my dress isn't ruined." I chuckle, actually enjoying the experience of dressing up and playing princess, even just for a little while.

"Silence, shadow, slay, steal: the four pillars of the Royal Intelligence Masters," I whisper to myself remembering that this is not who I am, "the bureau I would have inherited from Cicero one day. It looks like I have strayed too far from that path."

Too far indeed.

"Must you listen in?" I ask. "How can you do that?"

Silence.

"Looks like I will never truly be alone, but always ignored." I sigh and begin walking again.

The blue light looks brighter and brighter as I step closer.

I hear faint music, string instruments playing hauntingly throughout the corridor. With each note, I feel as though I am on the right path. The light beating of drums begins and the soft melody of a pan flute pulls me closer.

Formal evenings always have music in Jorthus. The nobility would gossip and discuss to the tune of the mighty brass or harp. Poise and sharp tongues were something to expect at any royal event.

A hand wraps around my wrist. I turn, only to see a prince, the one I tried to kill by the cove. His red eyes are wide as he looks me over. They appear to glow in the dim light, reminding me of flickering candles.

"Aurelia, the last of the marine royalty," he says, "you really should not follow will-o'-the-wisp, nothing but danger awaits you."

I look over to the light. "It was leading me to dinner? The music..."

He smiles. "The castle rusalka and a few redcaps, waiting to eat you whole."

"What exactly are you?" I ask, still feeling the sway of the music. "You are different from the others."

"You mean not a sidhe?" He tilts his head. "I am and I am not, I am so much more and so much less. I am someone willing to forgive the misdeeds that occurred in Jorthus."

I turn away, "The dagger..."

"Do not fret, young girl," he says, "all has been forgiven, at least once you were poisoned. Now I come to whisk you away from this dreary place."

"To the revel?"

He laughs. "You are not ready for such a thing. You followed the wisp, not even the weakest faerie would do that if sane of mind..."

I clench my jaw. "Perhaps it would help if I knew about some of the different kinds of faeries."

He raises his brow. "Fyfe did keep you in the dark, how fascinating. A child of the fae trapped in the blandest of places. Bards may write epics about your life if you amount to what we assign to you."

"Whose court was this?" I ask.

He looks around with a sharp fiery smile. "High Lord Paeve and High Lady Wyntris were the last rulers of the Dark Court territory. They had a son and daughter; one stood beside King Oberon during his final stand and the other died in faeriebirth. This grand estate is running at the edge of magik's border."

I remember Septimius mentioning that he was from the Dark Court. The only highborn left of the Dark Court's ruling dynasty. One living survivor from each court to rule Daeyed. From what I gather, there were originally tensions between the courts, however as Lorkus said at the meeting, they were born after the great war.

"Who raised you?" I ask.

He turns his head. "Who indeed?"

I shiver. Then he wraps his arms around me as leathery wings tear from his back. With one kick we are off, flying through the corridor at a startling speed. I freeze in his grasp, trying to pretend that he doesn't look like a human-lizard creature.

"Are you some sort of bat?" I ask.

"No, though I do have the ancient blood of a fire drake," his voice caresses my ear as though I knew what he was referring to, "It is wondrous, you did not choose my dress."

I stiffen. "One dress for each court?"

He chuckles darkly. "Oh yes, you see no one would step up to be your keeper, quite frankly we all have better things to do. We decided to let you choose."

I look down at the dress, then at his hand supporting my body. It felt as though he would drop me.

"Whose did I pick?" I demand. These dresses hold different futures for me depending on my choice.

"It is not my place to answer, though you will find out soon enough. For dinner we are having roast ebony-breasted gulia trout caught from a pond near the castle, a rarity only found in southern Daeyed. To drink we are having thistlebre wine, a secret of the Seelie sidhe. Oh, and frozen rike berries in thick cream for dessert," he whispers, "Oh my sweet, remember to try all of our lovely food."

"Is Cicero going to be there?" I ask simply.

"...but of course," he pauses.

We land in front of a broad silver wood door. Bright golden light pours from the cracks like fire. The designs carved into the wood remind me of the forbidden symbols Lucia drew in her bow. She told me they were symbols of power, efficiency, wrath, and forgiveness—a huntress must respect and care for the sacrifice an animal brings her and her people.

The doors open.

Standing before me were two princes, four servants, and Cicero at the head of the table. Why is he at the head of the table? Vikorus is not angry, instead,1 he relaxes.

Kynus watches as Septimius lowers me. He isn't gentle about it when I hit the ground.

"Cicero? Are you ok?" I say, getting up and quickly walking over to him. "I was worried about you!"

Cicero stood, meeting my eyes. "I have been fine."

I touch his face, feeling the warmth of his skin and whisper, "We will get out of here, we can do it."

He looks up at me and shakes his head. "It isn't that easy, Aurelia. I have rejoined my brethren in Daeyed finally."

I shake my head, "You can't be a faerie! You lie all the time, you lived in a city made of iron, rowan ash, and holy sculptures! All things that can kill the fae!"

He looks at me. I look at him.

"What did they do to you?" I ask, eyes widening, "Where is Azlyon?"

Where was Azlyon?

Cicero the Liar was sitting in the High Prince's seat.

What if his title of Liar has more merit than cheating his way out of poverty? My trainer, my master, my closest friend—he was there for me when I needed him. I knew he was secretive, but I never thought this of him.

"You are not Cicero..." I say.

I step backwards when Cicero's features melt away into Azlyon's—his pointy face, ghostly eyes, and proud composure replace a trusting face I once knew.

"I am or rather was," he says.

Cicero lied, Azlyon lied. How could a faerie lie like that? It is physically impossible for them to do it.

My head jerks toward Kynus, Vikorus, and the new seated Septimius, all of them smiling as though I am the entertainment. They all knew about this, the long forgotten prince has been inside Jorthus the entire time.

Azlyon knew everything Fyfe planned. He had the king's trust, pretended to be friends with Lorkus, and probably ensured the only half-blood with royal ties was pushed in his service.

I told Cicero my darkest secrets. He saw the real me, taught me how to lock away myself, how to be the perfect killer. He showed me the path to accepting who I was no matter how much I hated it. He was the one person I thought I could trust and the only one who would not betray me without just reason that goes above the law.

"You see, I've known you for a very long time," Azlyon takes another step closer.

"No, no, no," my voice rises in a crescendo.

My body begins to shake. He should have told me Cicero was dead, I could forgive that. This? I've had a faerie prince in my life for many years without knowing. The spymaster was the mole that we've been trying to "hunt" down. The target he himself assigned me.

"You lied to me, you played with my emotions, I told you about my life—we were friends. I was just a tool for you, like how Fyfe treated me!" I snap.

You were never just a tool. I needed to train you, especially for what is to come. We will discuss more later, please sit down for dinner. Oh, and don't drink the wine or eat the berries. Your human side will be seduced by our food.

"How can you tell me to just sit down?" I snap.

Relax.

A calm whispers over me, caressing my mind and soul, as though this were a lazy afternoon. I breathe and take my seat.

I curse my body for obeying him. I curse the existence of magik.

I am on my own now. Cicero will not help me. I am set free from my master's influence, as well as Titus the Lion's and King Fyfe's and Prince Lorkus' control. I need to be there for myself now, and I am terrified.

Chapter 8: Dangerous Liaisons

Loelmell, Court of Daeyed

I want to snarl at them. I want to cry. And I want to fall into the cracks of nothingness. But I can't do any of it. All because I am bound by magik.

They bite the trout, crunching through the bones, leaving nothing behind in their warpath. Chunks of fish land on the table as they tear through its charcoal scales. Only Azlyon uses a fork, probably from years of pretending to be human.

Eat, you will feel better.

"I doubt that," is all my body will let me say.

I pick up my fork.

They thrive on reactions.

I stab the fish.

They love their games.

I bring it to my lips.

So let's play. I won't give you the satisfaction of my anger.

My teeth snap through the bone.

The trout is good, but it is also a bit raw inside and too crisp on the outside. To be honest, I don't even remember the last time I ate something. The goblet is still full of wine; both Septimius and Vikorus watch it like hawks. As if they want me to drink every last drop.

"What do you need me for?" I ask between careful bites.

"Straight to the point then," Vikorus says with a smile. "We need you to assist us in bringing the magik back from the lifeless lands."

I raise my eyebrows. "And you think I am capable of doing this?"

I must control myself and not show the hurt that burns beneath my skin.

"Not by yourself, but through your blood, we can accomplish this," Kynus says.

"Are you going to sacrifice me?" I look over to the head of the table.

"You are in no danger from us," Septimius says. "Your mother was the one who bound the magik in Daeyed so the humans could not destroy it all. We need royal blood from all five courts from five separate fae for the unbinding spell...among other things."

"Couldn't Prince Kynus sit in for her place as well as the Bright Court?" I tilt my head.

Kynus' eyes widen, realizing I know he is my uncle. For a second, his proud composure collapses into a spray of emotion and memory.

I shoot him a proud smile. So, uncle, how do you like the game now?

"He is not of the marine royals, for his father was Lythe's and he was not of blood," Septimius says.

"He paid a tithe long ago, we all did," Vikorus nearly growls. "Besides, when she died, she passed on all her power to you and locked it away. The wretch never trusted us or anyone with that power."

I narrow my eyes, ignoring the last part. "Call her that again and I will not hesitate to stab you."

"We simply want magik to return to the lands, before Arcadia dies completely," Azlyon crosses his fingers, "You see, this realm was never meant for humans to live indefinitely. They have far too much iron inside them and during the great war, they began spreading this sickness."

"You have no right to talk to me," I snap, turning to Kynus."If they weren't meant for this realm, how did they get here?"

"They travelled through a portal from a realm called Gaia, the Ériu portal was in a place called the Kingdom of Meath," it is Azlyon who responds with clenched hands, "and they were led by a chieftain. That was before the human wars that divided the land."

I cross my arms, turning to Azlyon and Kynus. "I should know more about what happened and more about your people.'

Vikorus stands, glaring. "They are not the only ones with power. And I think you should obey or we will tear each tooth from your skull."

I am about to respond but it was Cicero—Azlyon who speaks. "Need I remind you that you are no longer the acting high prince?" Azlyon stays sitting. "Need I remind you who has seniority?"

"Do not worry, my friends," Kynus chimes in, "I believe this should be the decision of the sidhe in charge of her."

Vikorus sits down, teeth bare and shining like black pearls, while Septimius shrugs without sympathy.

My heart beats faster as I sit on the edge of my seat.

"Aurelia," Azlyon says evenly, "you chose my gown. I know that we are no longer on any path towards good terms, but I promise to answer your questions."

Of course, it is Azlyon's dress. This is almost ironic, from master to mentor. He is the only faerie that can lie, and I plan on learning why.

"Show me what happened," I demand, meeting Azlyon's eyes.

Azlyon looks at the other princes and nods once.

"Azlyon is going to use the ancient magik he was blessed with to guide a child?" Vikorus crosses his arms, looking away from the table. "I want to make it very clear that if Laeraan was still alive, she would have been chosen and she would not give this...thing what it wants."

Azlyon leans on the table with his elbows, his brows raise and his mouth forms a hard line. "I was waiting for you to lash out upon our reunion. Go on, speak your mind, child of Daeyed."

"Very well." Vikorus leans closer to Azlyon, eyes fuming in cold fire. "I think you don't have the best interests for the courts in mind, I think the time you spent with those mice have rotted your brain, and this little half-breed," he gestures at me with a crooked finger, "is not worthy of anything except as a tool for our purpose. The Morrígan should have picked me to accomplish the task in Jorthus, my mother was more than you will ever be, and her Unseelie son is stronger than she dare imagine. I had to work for my accomplishments, they were not just handed to me."

The tension in the room is so thick, not a single soul moves. When Vikorus spoke, he was no longer a proud faerie prince but a monster craving more power.

"Many years have passed since we last spoke, but I am happy that at least now you speak directly to me rather than gossip like a nymph." Azlyon licks his lips. "However, there is one little thing you forget—I am the high prince, I know it's been many years since I physically set foot in Daeyed, but The Morrígan chose me to be the one. I know my destiny, Vikorus, I know who I used to be and who I am now. Laeraan was brilliant and one of my dearest friends, but it was I who was chosen and not her bastard son. I am back indefinitely now, and as high prince, ultimately I have the final say on issues such as this."

Cicero was this powerful the whole time. He never flaunted it; in fact, he was quite humble and careful. Yet, seeing who Azlyon truly is scares me.

"As high prince, you may need help mentoring her. Each of us could focus on one thing or another," Septimius calmly suggests. "You will be busy, and she is as highborn as most of us..."

Azlyon considers it.

"Daeyed was founded without the involvement of the Cold Court," Vikorus says through his teeth. "She will not rule in place of the Cold Court."

Azlyon raises a brow. "I never said she would rule anything. But you do have a point Septimius. However, I will only allow princes who desire to mentor her."

"I could answer her questions of our people," Kynus announces before anyone. His eyes met mine for a moment.

"I don't want anything to do with her," Vikorus snaps.

"I could teach her to fight." Septimius smiles.

"I was in the Jorthus military and the governor of the shadow masters. I know how to fight and to kill." I look at the scaly sidhe.

"Like a human though, we use magik and glamour." He blinks before turning to Azlyon. "It is good you managed to relax her mind and allow her to think coherently."

I surround myself with those not turning out who they appear to be often. Septimius was wrong though, they send chills up my arms and through my mind. Every nerve in my body is telling me to run far and hide, but I know the only way to get out of this alive is to play their game.

"I don't need to learn from you," I say and Septimius nods.

"I will bring you to the high lord's study," Azlyon says. "I will tell you what happened before, during, and after the great war."

"We really should rename Paeve's study to something more modern," Septimius sighs.

Kynus leans on his elbows, "You don't want the Dark Court once we reclaim our lands? Paeve was your grandfather after all."

"I don't know," Septimius frowns, "I never lived during the age of courts, I wouldn't know how to conduct affairs."

Kynus reveals nothing as he responds, "The faeries still remember, they could guide you. I remember visiting the Dark Court as a faeling when my mother attended a feast for High Lady Wyntris. That was when I met your mother and uncle. I learned a lot from them, I could assist you when the time comes for the right price."

"Who would help Vikorus?" Septimius asks suddenly. "It is no secret that former court connections have divided Daeyed's rulers."

I wonder if they are always like this amongst one another. When they were in Jorthus they were unified, but now they behave as individuals who are more divided than Fyfe initially believed.

"I don't need help, my mother raised me, unlike you." Vikorus stands. His hulking posture reminds me of a rag doll being held at the neck, sulking yet oddly limp as it moves. "This dinner was tedious and I will be retiring for the night."

Chapter 9: The Liar's Tale

Loelmell, Court of Daeyed

Study is an understatement.

Books, dark vines, and crystal fixtures fill the walls. The desk itself is pure obsidian with burgundy runes. All around us floating are silver balls like bubbles of pure light.

"Fascinated by the morstone light or the crystal?" Azlyon says behind me.

I turn sharply. "Morstone?"

"They are the glowing spheres, you see," he smiles, "named after The Morrígan herself."

I look pointedly at him. "Let's start with her. Who is she?"

He smiles. "Our goddess of war, fate, and death. She is the only one who believes in our future."

"You've lost me…"

"The gods are real and thriving. I've met some in my long life," he says casually, "but that is for later."

His cool finger grazes my temple and my eyes roll back into my head. Memories and fabrications flash in my mind. Azlyon stands beside me, holding my arm gently as we both watch horrifying details of the past.

In the beginning, a nymph climbed out of a hole in a very bland world. The colours were dull in comparison to Jorthus. The sky was a calm grey and horses whinnied in the background.

A man dressed in furs with a bushy blond beard followed her back into the hole. The scene faded as colours and light blinded us until we were in a place where flowers sang, morstone decorated the landscape, and laughter filled the air.

"Chieftain Brennon Fraser, the first human to be both trapped in Arcadia and escape," Azlyon's voice echoes. "My kind would often trick people and use them until they died or brought back to Gaia."

The scene blurs all around us again following Azlyon's words.

"He wanted revenge for what we did to him," he pauses, "we only take very few humans in this world compared to the amount of fae who have died on Gaia by mortals. Brennon came with thousands of men, he spent time convincing other clans and empires about what he believed was the real threat to humans."

Armies crawled out of the silver-leafed forests, carrying long swords, oval-shaped shields and spears. Their eyes were both in awe and brutal anger, and their bodies painted in blue markings. Some wore tribal garments and some were completely naked, yet nearly all had braided hair and beards.

"To them, Arcadia was called the Otherworld, and to their spiritual men, we were an important part of their lives regarding their gods and dead," Azlyon said. "This was only their first wave of soldiers. There would be two more, and one for women and children to populate these lands. My father, Oberon, called a high summit of all courts. Until that point, each court warred with one another, save the Bright and Dark and their master courts. Everyone met, including the Cold Court, and we all decided to unify to end the human infestation, though it was too late."

A young man with antlers and dark hair stood on near borderland we crossed coming into Daeyed. He held the hands of two female faeries, who in turn each held the hands of two male faeries.

"My father King Oberon, mother Queen Titania, the Unseelie Queen Marea, my half-brother Aeshlyn, whose mother was the high lord of the Bright Court's sister, and Septimius' uncle Drion," he nods to each of them individually, "this moment is known as the final stand of Arcadia. They sacrificed themselves to protect magik from the iron destruction in one corner of Arcadia where the faeries were pushed into. They sacrificed themselves to protect Arcadia, our home. This corner was originally called the Daeyedus province of the Dark Court."

Each faerie glowed brightly before they dissolved into shadows that sunk deep into the earth, leaving only four crowns in their place, solid as stone and becoming one with the ground.

"Lythe exchanged blood between the sacrificed, each had Seelie, Unseelie, Dark, Bright, and Cold blood in their veins. Five of the highest births must be sacrificed from all courts, while another had another role. Lythe read the spell that would sacrifice them when the time was right, as a result, she was bound to the spell more than they for only she could reverse the spell and bring back the magik. But then she fell and passed the curse onto you. Only you can bring the magik back to Arcadia when the time is right."

I stiffen as the scene shifts to four people standing before a very old man with wrinkles now cascading down his face. His blue eyes were cloudy and his clothes were fine and expensive. Several nobles stood a pace behind him, while two polished soldiers stood beside him. Four individuals across from him were faeries still wearing the red blood of the humans on their clothes.

"My late grandfather, Brennon Fraser the first, would have rejoiced on this day," the old man smiled. "After a long war between tricksters and men, we have finally completed our task, the court rulers are dead and we may come to an agreement."

There were two faerie females, one with glittering golden hair, and the other with ebony hair, grey skin and a very sharp chin. The males were recognizable as younger Kynus and Azlyon. Both wore braided hair along their backs, hard lines on their mouths and golden paint on their cheekbones. Azlyon looked different, less magikal than he did now.

"Have you had the chance to review our terms for this treaty?" the golden woman asked.

"I did, and found them reasonable," the old man looked at her. "Princess Laeraan, I must inquire, who will rule and govern the brand new territory," he looks down at the treaty parchments, "of Daeyed?"

"Four rulers from the four courts, one of which will be the high ruler," Azlyon cut in, his voice like acid dripping on all humans.

"You are Oberon's only interesting living son. From what I recall you are the oldest of the four," the old man sneered slightly. "I think you murdered half my grandfather's first reinforcements Tell me, why didn't you do that again to win the war?"

"Why indeed," Kynus nearly growled.

The old man smiled again. "Have you reviewed our terms?"

The faeries spoke quietly to one another before the dark-haired female stepped forward. "We have and we accept. We also would like to bring forward one of our key terms: If a human sets foot on Daeyed without us knowing, it will be killed without repercussions."

"If a man is simple and naive enough to even attempt that, they are not worthy to be in my kingdom. Now the signing begins."

Instead of ink, they used blood from each party to sign their names on the treaty. Azlyon signed last and crumbled the quill in his hand so it was nothing more than dust. The old man only chuckled a little.

"Welcome to your new life, Princes Azlyon and Kynus, and Princesses Laeraan and Juvelio," the old man smiled. "Tell me, who is the high royal?"

It was Laeraan who answered. "High Prince Azlyon is the figurehead of our table."

There was no protest from the other faeries, but the old man did narrow his eyes. "What do your companions think of this decision?"

"Let me make this clear if it wasn't already," she leaned closer to him, "he has the most power for one reason: You are afraid of him, and if you want to deal with us ever, he has the final say."

Azlyon stepped forward, smiling. "Relations between the gods and Arcadia go through faeries first, they won't be on your side from this day forward."

"You have no right—" The old man grasped his sword.

"We do, in no way did you write that into your demands, but we did in ours." Azlyon picked up their copy of the treaty. "'Humans shall not have any dominion over magik and its origin.' You see, magik comes from the gods."

"You did not specify!"

"We didn't need to, we knew you would agree because humans have no real way to wield or control it. Beyond this, one of your terms is that magik is forbidden outside of Daeyed."

The scene crumbles on itself as Azlyon removes his hand from my temple. He helps me over to a chair where I nearly collapse. My head is pounding and goosebumps crawl over my skin.

"Your parents, you saw them die," I say, grasping the chair's arm.

He nods. "They were among the last of my family to die that I am aware of. I understand why they did what they did but there was another way, I was just too late."

"How many siblings did you have?" I ask.

"Oberon had seventeen children, and of those only five were Titania's." Azlyon looks away. "Most of them died early on, not that he cared about many of his bastards, but he did ensure I would be held back until his sacrifice was complete. Of all my remaining siblings, I survived the hard world of Arcadia the longest."

"So that is what happened?" I shake my head, wondering why Fyfe was so stern about keeping all that secret.

"One day, you will step into the great library halls of Skuflan, where all that information is written in blood," he says. "I paid many visits to the great library, most of them during a period the humans call the Shadow Age."

"I know a little about that. It was a time where communication between daeyed and the world ceased," I say, "I don't even think they knew who was leading Daeyed."

"Since the Iron Treaty up until the Shadow Age, we never held summits or meetings with any of the human nations. After the treaty was signed, they squabbled and warred against one another until smaller countries were built."

"And you hoped they would kill each other off," I say.

He smiles. "We can dream."

"And The Morrígan?" I ask him. "How does she play into all of this?"

"She was the only god willing to help, and blessed me with more power than any faerie has ever had," he says. "Since then I have spied in all the lands, most of my time in Jorthus. I had different lives gathering information for Daeyed. That is part of the reason why I am called the Liar. I am the only pure-blooded faerie capable of lying directly."

I look away.

He lived so many lives and met so many people. It is hardly believable that he values our friendship after that. There were probably many "Aurelias" with different faces and different names, each one hoping to find a family in duty. Some could have even gotten to know him better than I ever did.

"Aurelia, I want you to understand that you are the key, and when I found you I knew I could go home once again." He places his cool hands on each side of my face.

"I am sorry you lost your home, but I never had one, not as a girl in Lorlan, and certainly not as a spymaster in Farlanfell. I understand why you did what you did, even though things between us will never be the same. I just don't see a reason for me to help you. I don't belong with the humans, though I want to desperately, and I certainly don't belong here with the faeries."

Telling the truth comes too easy in Daeyed, as if my nerves long to spill my true thoughts.

"You haven't spent very much time here. Give it a chance, and I promise you that you will belong in the new Arcadia."

"Take the word of a lying faerie?" I almost laugh.

"Take the word of your friend," he says. "I may have worn a different name but I never altered my personality for you."

"We are not friends, friends don't conceal that kind of secret from one another," I look up at him, "I won't answer you now but I do want to learn more about faeries."

He taps a morstone, "The winter solstice—we will be celebrating it in Daeyed's capital, Daelin Castle. Give me your answer then."

The mysterious land of Daeyed. This is a chance to understand the fae in a way no human has since the great war. For that reason alone, I nod once.

"And when is this plan happening?" I say, "The one discussed earlier?"

"On the anniversary of the Final Stand of Arcadia, which is seven days later." He leans on the desk, looking upwards.

"I also want to know more about my mother," I say, "and I want to know more about you, and before you say no, I'll remind you that I trusted you with my past. I also want to meet with my uncle."

He looks at me raising his eyebrows. If I wasn't who I was, he probably wouldn't even be considering such a thing. I want to get the most out of this transaction before I give my answer at the solstice.

"I will tell you about Lythe, and during your meetings with Kynus, you may be able to hear his perspective of her. As for learning about me, I have lived so many years I wouldn't know where to begin but I promise to tell you the important things," he says evenly, "Kynus, however, will have to agree to speak to you on his own. Finally, you must not tell anyone about our deal. Remember, once you and I strike a bargain, there is no getting out of it."

I take a breath and nod. In a swift moment he cuts my palm—and his—then mixes the blood together. He licks a drop and tells me to do the same. The only time I willingly drank blood was in the Yelt forest outside of Jarnel, the poor creature was the only thing my starved belly desired. This blood reminds me of bittersweet pomegranate seeds.

"You are not poisoned by the iron in my blood?" I ask.

"I am a unique faerie, and a blood bargain is so much more powerful than a traditional one."

I should have known better. Faerie deals were strong, but I never knew there were different kinds.

"Walking among the humans but not belonging…" I say to him.

He shakes his head. "I never tried to be human outside of the characters I played. My immunity to iron was the advantage I had over them."

"Advantage over them," I say, "I knew someone who said the same thing about his own people. He wanted his people to take control over Lorlan through blood descendants. He wanted to use faerie blood to ruin the people of Lorlan, most of them kind to me. This man betrayed me and since then, I denounced my faerie side."

I should not have said anything. It is hard to hold my tongue here.

"The Woodlander people, they remember us, they remember how the war brought forth the worst in humanity," he says, "but they cannot wield magik, even if they had the blood of the oldest faerie."

I look away. "You say I desire love, well that's because I had it once and it betrayed me."

His expression softens, "You never told me this."

"There was a man, a chieftain's son, who convinced me that I could be loved. The chieftain secretly wanted our union so that our children would be born special and able to take over more than just Lorlan. Then I found him with his lover shortly after he proposed to me."

Azlyon is difficult to read, but he does seem taken aback by my story. Having an advantage over people is key in this game of war and death, but hurting those who care about you is not right.

"I never told you because I believed love to be a weak emotion, but I cried after Beau's betrayal. Lucia left her people over it, and when I saw her last, I was cruel to her. The only person who genuinely cared for me." I shut my eyes. "I left that place a girl with ideas of love, hope, and compassion, and came back distant."

"You hated your faerie self because of what this 'Beau' did to you, and because his people wanted to use you to breed warriors." Azlyon presses a finger to his temple.

"It was widely accepted in Jorthus to hate the fae—Titus showed me that when he trained me to fight," I say, "and working with you, and being surrounded by the aristocracy. Prince Lorkus told me horrible stories about them and their power. It was a combination of things that created who I am."

Since the summit, I have had a few run-ins with faeries who probably would have killed me if given the chance. At least in Jorthus, if I remained covered I could pass as human.

"Lorkus is the key to Jorthus, you know, he may have radical ideas but the way he looked and defended you proved that he was willing to trust a faerie—even if it meant stabbing their back later," Azlyon sighs.

I wonder why Lorkus even bothered defending me. I would let them take me without question if I were in his shoes.

"Cicer—Prince Azlyon," I say, shaking my head, "I think that is enough for one night, I've already had quite the shock today…since the moment I stepped inside this castle."

"I understand," he says, helping me up. "Would you like me to escort you to your chambers?"

I want to say that I could find it on my own, but I am not in the mood for outsmarting the living walls and bog creatures so I nod slightly, taking his arm.

The path is silent and the hall brightens as we walk. The marsh and forest floors are gone, leaving shiny marble with gold fixtures. The living wall is still there, but even as it snakes along the walls and roof, it does not bother us.

Old paintings hang on the walls of sharp-looking faeries with dark ebony hair—flowing loosely, in braids, and crowned. These faeries had either red or glowing pale blue eyes. I'm not sure which was more unnerving.

Septimius is from a dark lineage with features so angular they almost look like something a faerie would call a creature. None of them had scales though, only Septimius.

"They want to scare you into submission, I do not. However, if you leave your room, you will face worse things than what you encountered prior to dinner," Azlyon says as we pause in front of a familiar door. "Unless you are with one of us, this is the only safe place for you. You saw the halls change in response to my presence."

"Are you saying this place is a living thing?" I look around.

"Very much so, that is why I've never shared any secrets out loud in fear of hungering whispers at the ears of this court's rulers," he says as my feet carry me inside without thinking. "The study and the High Lord's chambers are protected from eavesdroppers."

"Septimius let it remain dark and wild," I whisper.

"He is not entirely like us," he says.

"I don't even know who you are."

"I am Cicero, but I am also Azlyon. Perhaps Cicero is my human idea, one

I enjoyed playing but one I also learned a lot from."

"Did you enjoy tricking me?" I ask simply.

"I did not. There were moments where I wanted to help you grow into your skin."

"I meant at dinner," I say, meeting his eyes.

"I was relieved to be home, but the whole reveal was more for the other princes. I wanted to kill Cicero off without you ever knowing the truth, but they wanted a show."

"I'd like to believe you are telling the truth but I can never know, can I?"

Azlyon cracks a slight smile before turning down the hall.

I want to say more but I bite my tongue. Instead, I watch him walk around the corner.

The walls and floor immediately change behind him to what I saw before. As soon as the black hall reaches my door, I slam it shut. I swear I hear a deep, hearty laugh.

Everything lives and barely obeys its rulers. A nation forcing wild faeries to live together to preserve their species.

My bed is so far away, yet so close. I tiptoe there quietly, still wearing uncomfortable fasteners and string underneath the gown. I don't want to change out of this gown, mostly because I refuse to set foot off the bed in case something grabs it. After all, something could be lurking in the darkest corners of this room as I struggle to sleep.

Chapter 10: Familiar Faces, Wicked Places

Loelmell, Court of Daeyed

In the morning, Belousa returns and scolds me for almost ruining the gown. She tells me that this is no ordinary gown and I should know better than to mistreat something that has been in the Seelie Court for generations.

"It doesn't look that old," Perhaps to them, a thousand years is a short amount of time but to me, it was an eternity.

"The late Seelie queen, fair Titania, wore this dress when she first met King Oberon, it was one of her most treasured items," Belousa says once I am in nothing but my shift.

"Oh." I look away.

The dress is important to Azlyon. He used it to catch my attention so he could mentor me. It must have been a kindness for the friendship we once had, perhaps one he thinks may grow again.

"I tried to imitate what you usually wear with some adjustments," she says, passing me a deep blue tunic meant to be tied with a thick but pliable belt at the waist. The belt itself matches the dark skin-tight trousers made of ebony scales and leather. "Prince Azlyon assisted me with the sizing, it is why your clothes were taken by the bean sidhe."

When I put them on I felt nearly naked. It is lighter than cotton despite the hefty materials, but more importantly, it is flexible—even with the scales.

Then she passes me riding blue boots embroidered with the hook of a wave and a four pointed star in gold thread. They are also soft and pliable.

"In that tunic, you will never be too cold or too warm," she says, looking me up and down, "those trousers work your legs evenly to prevent fatigue or weakness, and those boots won't make a sound when you walk but will allow you to climb the iciest mountain."

"Thank you. What are they made of?"

"An ancient sea dragon, his name is Leviathan," she says. "He gave some of his armour-like flesh to the last ruler of the Cold Court in the hope that one day it would be worn by his champion. Since that day, no one on land has seen him."

"Who decided that was me? I barely know much about that court." I set my boots on the bed.

"He did," she said, "when you swam in the waters of whispering cove, he felt your soul enter his domain and sent word through the few remaining freshwater faeries. It was nixie who told the princes just before they left Jorthus."

I wait for her to finish braiding my hair in five strands before I slip on the boots. They are comfortable, practical, and even elegant.

"If you weren't a warrior, I would have made you something finer," she said, "but rest assured that what you are wearing is one of the rarest creations in existence."

"I'm not a warrior, in the sense you mean..." The fae treat combat differently than humans.

We both know this isn't court attire for someone royal. So if I am not playing aristocrat today, what exactly are we doing?

If I were the princes, I would travel inward to the capital. We were practically on the border of Flokael and Daeyed, an exposing position despite the things that lurk on the roadside.

"If you die, I will rip it off your corpse," a snake-like voice filters through the room.

I turn to see Septimius leaning against the doorframe. He wears a scaly tunic different from the ones on mine. A ruby circlet frames his face elegantly as his dark hair slicks backwards.

"You look like a dragon, from the stories in Jorthus," I respond, remembering the village children trying to scare one another, "like Riogus the Great, whose skull hangs in Fyfe's study."

His smile broadens. "Riogus was lesser, at least in comparison to the monstrous sea wyrm Leviathan. Once dragons and wyverns called the Dead Lands home before it was a barren wasteland."

"Is that why they call you Septimius the wyvern? Because of your knowledge of the scaled beasts?" I ask.

He tilts his head. "Oh, Aurelia, you really are immune to the whispers all around you." He pauses. "We decided to cut short our visit here, I come to say goodbye until we see one another at Daelin castle."

"Oh, you're leaving?" I ask, trying to hide the eagerness in my voice.

"Just Vikorus and I, we are heading there to resume court before you come. I believe Azlyon and Kynus are going to show you our beautifully damned country," Septimius licks his lips with what looks like a forked tongue, "Oh, and we found another human attempting to cross our borders, she claims that she was in servitude to Fyfe. He ordered her to bring you back. Do you want to meet her? Dine on her ribs after I tear out her heart? Or perhaps you would like to try and rip it out?"

My stomach drops a little. I have seen and done terrible things but cannibalism was not among them.

"Just when I was feeling a little hungry, you managed to change my mind about eating," I force a smile, "but I am interested to see who King Fyfe sent after me."

Septimius crosses his arms, tilts his head, and shoots out his tongue like a lizard. "I will smile on the day when you see humans as we do, meaningless lucky mice."

I shake my head. "Humans are kind but easily swayed, they are so emotional, yet faeries lack that empathy which makes humans so beautiful. Prince Septimius, as someone who has lived with them my entire life, I would not underestimate them. I think that's how the courts fell to begin with."

His eyes narrow. “Careful, princess, I was just starting to tolerate you.”

Even though I held their rank, these princes will never treat me as equal. Septimius likes to play but so do I, and in this game, only one of us will walk away. It could happen tomorrow or in a thousand years but ultimately, this game will end.

The tensions between the Daeyed rulers are apparent, and even if their plan works, I doubt there will be a lasting peace amongst the fae. Right now, their hands are tied to Daeyed. But if they succeed, with each prince in charge of a court’s territory, war will ravage the land. With the four of them, there can only be one faerie ruler. Septimius would step down for Vikorus, and Kynus would stand aside for Azlyon. Arcadia will be split in a war between the Unseelie and Seelie courts.

Right now I need to gain as much intel as I could and then decide what needs to be done. All I know is that Fyfe will regret tossing me away when I hold the key to his survival.

“Prince Septimius, before you leave for Daelin Castle, I would love it if you would take me to this human. I want to know who Fyfe deems worthy to catch me. You may think little of me, but in Jorthus, I was elite in my trade.” I walk over to the dark prince, every fibre in my body recoiling as I touch his hand.

He looks down at our hands for a moment, his glowing red eyes widening a little. “It would give you a perfect opportunity to say goodbye to Vikorus before we leave.”

I nod, knowing he is right, it will beneficial to be on a better side of that malevolent faerie. Vikorus and I will never be on friendly terms, but if I continually try to be, Septimius could sway him. The scaly prince is the key to Vikorus’ inner circle. I will need to alter my emotions and personality to get there.

“You read my mind,” I sigh, looking down, “I have been meaning to apologize to him after last night, I was scared and lashed out at him.”

Septimius reaches out and brings my chin up. “He was cruel, but if you prove you are more faerie than human, he will see that you are becoming like us.”

I latch onto his arm, pulling him outside the room. He resists at first but eventually comes along.

When we step outside I expect the same darkness, but I see bright light and clean fixtures just like last night. It looks like my plan is already working. Befriending this prince will work in time.

"Skaelean sidhe," he says.

I look up. "What?"

"You asked me what I was, that is my answer," he says, not looking at me. "A fire drake and my mother fell in love, she became pregnant and birthed a monster that tore through her skin, forcing her dearest friend to take care of something hard to look at. A skaelean sidhe prince called Septimius. That is why I am called Septimius the Wyvern, I am a half-breed just like you."

I look down. I was not expecting this from Septimius. He barely spoke loud enough for me to hear. Our mothers carried us to term and shortly died.

"I only told you this because I know you feel alone in this world," he says, "but eventually you will grow stronger and accomplish great things."

We reach an unfinished empty room, leaving only candlelight and black walls. Vikorus stands above a woman in a tangle of strawberry blonde curls, wearing ripped blue trousers and a grey tunic.

Then she turns to face me, her pale green eyes sharp, a familiar half-frown on her plump lips. Sitting in front of us was Rowyna, the spymaster governor of Jorthus.

"Prince Vikorus," I bow, "I apologize for my behaviour last night. I want to bid you a safe trip to Daelin Castle before we part."

Vikorus tilts his head and says, "This creature claims she knows you."

I don't look at Rowyna, not daring to take my eyes away from Vikorus. His long silver hair is tightly braided with an ebony circlet dipping down his forehead. He wears plain thin armour meant for riding.

"I do know her. She is a spymaster, but not a very good one," I state, "What are you planning to do with her?"

Vikorus tilts his head. "Sacrifice her at the next tithe, or use her for solstice amusement. Which would you prefer I do?"

This question is tricky. He is testing for my reaction. If I ask for mercy, there is no way he will deem me trustworthy. But if I look like I am trying too hard for his approval, he will see through my ruse.

"Well, if we kill her too soon, Fyfe would just send someone else," I say. "I think we use her for amusement at the solstice then kill her the next day. That way this plan can run smoothly and the faeries will have so much enjoyment."

I feel Rowyna glare at me.

"I suppose, however, I am leaving you in charge of her," Vikorus smiles, "and she will be your problem until you arrive at the castle."

"Aurelia may kill the human to silence her," Septimius laughs.

Vikorus cracks his knuckles. "I have ensured the human will die if it leaves Aurelia's side, if that happens then Aurelia has failed me."

This is my chance to prove myself to Vikorus. He believes I will fail because I care about humans, by letting her die a clean death instead of something worse at his hands. He wants me to fail.

I nod and Vikorus smiles unkindly.

Just as they are about to leave the room, Septimius pauses at the door. "Do not disappoint us, Aurelia."

Rowyna hobbles from the floor to stand before me with bruises all over her, finally letting go of her composure now that she didn't have to put up a front for the princes.

"So this is the real you," Rowyna spits, looking me up and down, "I barely recognize you."

I sigh. "I am who I am."

"You signed my life over—as though I were a pig for slaughter and not someone who trained with you for years." She tightens her hands into fists.

"You are not going to die today," I say, unable to move. "though I cannot say the same thing tomorrow."

"I know you hate them," Rowyna says, "but I never understood why until I stepped foot here. What doesn't make sense is why would you side with them?"

"Rowyna," I say, changing the course of discussion, "I know you very well, there is no need to pretend. They caught you because you wanted to be caught, you are using this as an advantage to gain information."

"I told Prince Lorkus you could see through me," Her eyes widen. "Always so clever, Aurelia."

I step closer to her, "I may be the only one left who can. Fyfe shouldn't worry about sending people after me when he should be reshaping his military. Tell me, is Jorthus still unprotected along the north coast?"

I blink twice. She knows I am lying. It was a way of telling her someone was watching us through our training.

The truth was that the army was stronger than they've been in years. Fyfe is so paranoid he made sure to place soldiers anywhere he could spare them.

"I am no fool, and I will not betray secrets," She steps back.

I shrug, "He will regret his choices. I would wager you are only here to prove yourself worthy enough to succeed Cicero."

"Where *is* Cicero?"

Travelling with us dressing in lies. "He is dead. They killed him in front of me."

Her composure sinks a little. I always knew she had a small dream of courtship with him. Yet this was better than explaining the unbelievable to her. I want her to know Cicero as Cicero, let that person live and die with her. The truth is far too painful.

"Rowyna, I know we've had problems in the past but I want to make a deal with you," I say.

She looks hesitant. Lorkus must have gotten in her head after we departed from Jorthus. "I am listening."

"Help me without question, when everything is over, I will disappear from Jorthus," I whisper, "and you will advance, maybe marry a nobleman."

I hate playing with uncertainty, but she dreams of being as close to royalty as possible. Finding any form of love is right for her, I just want to disappear into a more accepting country.

"Aurelia, I never hated you but I do not trust you," She shook her head, "I was angry and frustrated at how everyone adored how good you were at everything," she says carefully.

I wait.

"But you have problems I wouldn't wish upon anyone, you are chained more than I." She looks me directly in the eye, "are you on their side?"

I shake my head slightly but say, "I am on my side."

She nods, "I will do what you say to stay alive, for now."

I shake her hand in such a humanly gesture, one I have missed since coming here.

"I need to tell you a few things," I say before condensing Azlyon's tale of the great war quietly. I even tell her that they are planning on using my blood to aid their cause. I skip over every third word and use different names. It is enough information without going into detail, without mentioning Cicero or my bargain.

"That's a lot," She rubs her eyes and takes in a deep breath. "I didn't know you were royal."

I raise my brows. "Of all that, me being royal stood out the most?"

She smirks. "The first rule we learned was to expect the extraordinary, that way we are never surprised."

It was the first rule the spies in Jorthus learned. That way, when we come across any information, we are not unhinged, a tactic to avoid being caught right away. Rowyna and I went on our first mission together as spylings. Everyone mocked me then because I kept my face, hair, and skin covered. Rowyna never treated me differently, and when I rose in rank, everyone feared and respected me. She understood me until the time came for me to leave her behind as I advanced in the ranks and became closer to Cicero than she ever would. I knew she liked him more than she should, and I think she thought I did too as I overtook her in training. The truth was that Cicero became my dearest friend, but I climbed the ranks for myself.

"It has been a long time since I've heard that," I tell her.

"You know, you are prettier than I thought. When I heard you were a faerie at that meeting, I thought you'd look like an animal, but you look very...interesting," she admits.

I raise my eyebrows. "I wish I looked like the beautiful seductress Rowyna.

You had all the men wrapped around your finger and took information effortlessly. I was only good for my skill."

"You had Cicero's direct guidance. I only saw him when I was debriefing and during meetings with Titus." She looks away. "You were the lucky one."

"You loved him, didn't you?"

We never discussed how she come to love him out loud. It was the one conversation I never thought would happen between us.

"I love him still, even if he is dead," she smiles with tears in the corner of her eyes, "but your faction was more important than mine."

"That is not true," I say through my teeth.

We hear someone clear their throat. I turn to see Azlyon leaning against a shadowy corner; he is very hard to even notice until he comes into the light. My heart drops, wondering how much of the conversation he heard. If he knows our plan, it will be over before it even happens.

"How long were you there?" I ask, raising brows and crossing my arms.

"I walked in when you were complimenting one another." Azlyon raises an eyebrow.

Rowyna blushes as if caught in some dirty secret. I am glad she doesn't know who Azlyon really is. It is better that way.

So Cicero is dead... Azlyon's voice lingers.

I nod. "She is a spy sent to retrieve me—although I'm sure the other princes told you."

He smiles, looking directly at me and ignoring her. "I spoke with Vikorus as he was leaving. You are foolish to play his game."

I also was under the impression you were on unfriendly terms with Rowyna. His voice is amusing.

"I've known her for a very long time, we don't often get along but she is here. This task will calm the waters between Vikorus and I," I tell him.

Azlyon steps closer to me. "Village of Woyldlan or Laakar Stones?"

It is his way of asking me to do something. When he was Cicero, he did this to change topics that he didn't want to talk about for differing reasons. I was always first to pick missions.

"Village of Woyldlan," I say, "I want to see faeries, not dusty stones."

"Very well, let the four of us travel with three guards to Woyldlan."

Although Laakar Stones is very militarized with generals of Daeyed and soldiers training all day. It is clearly not a place for a spymaster.

I smile knowing he is tempting me to change my mind. It is a place of so much information for stealing but that information will still be there when I gain all of their trust. I won't have to sneak around to get it.

"Woyldlan seems like a wonderful place to learn about your kind," I say with a smile.

Rowyna watches us carefully. She is no fool and Azlyon still has Cicero's tendencies, even when he can finally be his true self. She may end up falling in love with him and side with the faeries, and that just won't do.

"Who killed Cicero?" she asks in a quiet voice. I feel her fear, smell it even. For her to ask a direct question like this in the presence of a faerie takes courage, and she knows little of politics and faeries.

Azlyon simply smiles like the court jester in Farlanfell, full of teeth and wild eyes.

"First we took all the information he had, over long involuntary sessions," Azlyon takes a step closer, "and finally we brought in Aurelia, we let her watch as he crumpled inside himself from endless pain only a faerie could imagine. Then we all gave him eternal darkness."

She is silent.

"He was your master as well, wasn't he?" Azlyon leans over her, fingers lacing under his chin. "Rest assured that he is better off dead and gone than in the wild of Daeyed, where we will be soon enough. And because of Aurelia's little challenge with Prince Vikorus, she will have a difficult time keeping you alive. Do you know what this means? I have to make sure both of you are safe. One must avoid the North and Eastern half side of the road, for that is where the wicked Unseelie and dark faeries live. The next rule is never stray off the road, for if you set one foot off, it may be ripped off in moments by a hungry faerie."

I feel my stomach drop and see Rowyna pale. Never has she been somewhere so dangerous and neither have I.

"Who lives on the southern portion?" I ask.

"The fair Seelie and Bright folk," he says. "Don't sigh in relief, they love to trick mortals. Luckily, you will be with Kynus and I, and they are our kin."

I take a breath. *Is Woyldlan on your side?*

Yes, it is. Azlyon responds.

I gasp, unsure how I just communicated with him like that. I just used my mind to speak with this faerie prince. It shouldn't be possible.

He smiles in response.

"Perhaps having someone you can trust will help you understand that we are not monsters."

"Yet you killed Cicero," Rowyna whispers, staring at the floor.

"Just another face who served their purpose, just like you," he says. "Death is easy for those without family."

I clenched my fists. "He had one before we came to Daeyed, we were his family whether he admitted it or not, and our hearts are broken to know his fate."

Rowyna meets my eyes. "Every family both hates and loves one another, and we always remember those no longer with us."

I could smile at Rowyna.

Azlyon raises his eyebrows but says nothing. I see something pressing against his mind. A black flame itching to take over. It is a darkness, an evil he hides from the world. It was the same flame I see in my own reflection.

When I was a girl, I stood upon the steps of the village temple of Dian Cecht and The Dagda. They were the only gods we worship in Jorthus. The Dagda was the chieftain god and represents magik and strength, and Dian Cecht was our healing god. In other villages, they have separate temples but in Lorlan, there is only one due to lack of resources.

I remember looking into the eyes of the priest who forbade me to enter because he believed I was faerie-cursed. He watched my lips burn slightly on the iron goblet used to bless the leanúna, the followers of the gods. Lucia was furious of course, but the priest promised to keep my infection a secret as long as I stood outside the doors every morning and prayed the sickness away. Lucia told me that he once spent time living with her people to study forbidden knowledge. It is an action punishable by death for those who aren't woodlanders, and she held that over him to protect my secret. Every morning, we recited prayers and he would drip blessed oil on my forehead. "Aurelia, poor child," he would say, "you are cursed by the others, and if it weren't for sweet Lucia, I would have spared you this fate with an early end. Together we must have faith that Lord Dian Cecht will cure you of your sickness. Perhaps a man can look upon your face and not see rotting skin laced with their magik. I know that when you look into a mirror, you see a dark flame, that is they who watch you and kill you from within. They possess you with sickness." And then he would blow iron powder into my face.

The dark flame the priest saw in me reminds me of what I now see in Azlyon. My darkness is of the fae, but him? It must have been something stronger if he carries it when the others do not. He was granted all this power but at what price?

Chapter 11: Kyn

Court of Daeyed

We begin our travels with promises of reunion at Daelin Castle. Faeries stand outside the entrance with their heads low at our passing, each uttering a single word—*"slán"*—even the bean sidhe, in a breathy suffocating voice that causes my skin to shiver.

"My kin," Azlyon bows back, "next time we meet, Arcadia will be a different place. As each day passes, our existence changes helplessly. Blessed be The Morrígan, the goddess of our age, and blessed be the fair folk who follow her into our future."

Rowyna looks at them with disgust but I see the dangerous fanatics of a goddess, one unsafe for the continuance of humankind.

Eventually, as you grow to understand, you will be bowing like them, Azlyon's voice comes through.

You say you've met a god but I have not. For all I know, you could be lying. I put all my energy into my response, hoping it reaches his own mind. *I only know what I've seen.*

Then you are in for a disturbing awakening.

Kynus appears at my side, his thick hair partly braided away from his face, revealing shiny eyes reflecting every ray of light in prismatic rainbows. They are golden gemstones with a colourful hue. I never paid much attention to them before, or maybe his hair hid them well enough.

"Azlyon, we should start moving," Kynus says without looking at me.

"Yes," Azlyon replies. "The carriage will take us as far as the Daelin fork, from there we will travel on foot."

"Inside seats four. We cannot allow the human to accompany the driver," Kynus responds.

"She will remain inside. Kynus, you are going to drive, I need your eyes on the roads," says Azlyon.

"I will sit beside Prince Kynus," I chip in.

They both turn to me, Kynus looking as if my speaking annoys him while Azlyon narrows his eyes.

"I want to see the country. Besides, you'll have guards on horseback in case anything happens. I am certain Rowyna and I will be secure," I pause then speak quieter, "and the two of us are not like typical humans, you made sure of that, Prince Azlyon."

They look at one another before Kynus nods, grabbing my wrist and leading me to the blue carriage. It appears to be made of a stone with black flowers and silver vines. The carriage is drawn by mossy horses with wooden legs. They snort out tiny butterflies when we approach, each one a different green before they dissolve in the air. I can't help but smile at something so beautiful.

"They are common Seelie horses." Kynus draws my attention to him. "Let me help you up."

"I am quite capable—" He pulls me up by the arm.

This is the first time he dares make eye contact today. His own are different from before. They are cat-like as he searches for any resemblance to his sister. I bear few asrai traits, and after seeing my mother in that memory, I know I look mostly different.

Kynus climbs up in one fluid motion, reminding me of a dove dressing in the deepest blue.

Everyone climbs into the carriage one by one. Rowyna shoots me a look before vanishing inside. Then Azlyon steps in after whispering something to the second guard.

The gate opens and Kynus speaks gently to the horses before they begin to move. They keep pace with one another as their hoofs gently clap against the ground. Kynus' eyes are sharp ahead, scanning the roadsides once we are far enough away from Loelmell.

"Prince Kynus, why are you our driver?" I decide to ask.

He sighs. "This is why I hoped you wouldn't be up here with me... Too many questions."

I cross my arms. "Who better to show me the wonderful world of Daeyed than my uncle?"

His mouth hardens into a line, knuckles turning white on the reigns, and his eyes narrow. The world almost slows in his irritation.

"I will say this only once: Never refer to me like that. I spoke with Azlyon and he told me partially of your deal with him. I will assist the best I can, but I have long since rejected that family, they are all dead—save for you, and we are strangers to one another," his voice is crystallizing with ice.

I wasn't sure what I was expecting but I was hoping we could become friends at the very least. That memory proves that he cares about power more than kin, but still, I hope.

"I've never had family and I don't expect you to even try, but I just want to know more about them. You knew them, Lythe was your sister and I think she loved you very much," I say after a few moments.

He said nothing at first, then his lips twitch. "My mother raised me in the Bright Court. It started with my asrai father not wanting me around for the first few decades of my life. She found her anam around then, and it just happened to be the high lord, just as my father found his before I was even born."

"Anam?" I ask.

"The human equivalent would be...mate?" He struggles for the right word.

"Mate sounds so animalistic," I say, wondering if their courtship was purely to have children, like animals.

"Humans fall in love and they marry, or they are forced to marry. Faeries are different, mates are soul connections. Most live together and have faelings, but others do not enjoy one another or love with another. Those faeries still feel obligated to care for their mate regardless of how they feel." He tilts his head.

"It's like a soulmate then. So all faeries have a mate?" I ask.

"I loathe the term." He shakes his head. "Sometimes mates are born outside of the other's lifetime or not at all. Some choose to ignore the soulbond because accepting that means they are obligated to that person in one way or another. They could be a faerie's dearest friend who cares for the other's offspring from another courtship. My father and mother are not mates but Lythe's were." He looks at me raising his brows, "And I have just lost you."

I shake my head slightly. "Well, it is just a lot to take in. I know many humans believe in the gods, and I hope that they are real and that there is an afterlife, but this soul bonding? It is not something I can fully understand."

"Think of an anam as two halves of a whole," he looks onward, "it is something only felt at the individual level. Most can tell because once you see two soul-connected in the same room you will notice their composure is different. They pull together like moths to a flame, and become hyper-aware of the actions of the other."

We hit the main road and the guard immediately rides ahead of us. It is wide enough for a few carriages to drive side by side, but still, we remain in the middle. Extra precautions, I assume.

"Have you found a mate?" I ask him.

"No, just as Septimius and Azlyon have not revealed such a bond to the princes," he says, "and Vikorus' died in the Dead Lands, he was never quite the same."

"It is hard to imagine him caring for someone like that," I say.

"When he was a child, he was compassionate. His mother Laeraan asked Azlyon to help her train him." Kynus says.

I nod, wondering what things in his life made him who he was. Faeries were a lot like humans in some ways. The innocent among them were very corruptible.

"Lythe was different from other Asrai, she played a large role in the beginning in the foundation of Daeyed, then she met her anam and the two of them were inseparable."

"Azlyon said he hadn't spoken to her since the great war."

"That is because she refused to deal with him, and he was far too busy trying to unite the faeries with Laerann, while Juvelio and I worked with her in creating a mutually beneficial set of laws for all faerie-kind."

"And how did you feel working with her?"

"Remember, you are on a thin line with me." Kynus clenches his teeth. "I treated her like an ambassador and nothing else."

"Tell me about her parents, please?" I can't help but smile.

"Her mother cared me more than our father. She treated me as though I were her own, which made everything worse," he pauses, "Lythe and I were inseparable for a time, she was both friend and sister. She was fiercely protective of her people and her family—as all Cold Court faeries are. It was ultimately their downfall, and hers."

"Do you know who my father is?" I take a deep breath.

He licks his lips. "I do. She met with me shortly after you were born in Rhionus cave where she nurtured you for three weeks before she died. Your father's situation was rather complicated. I am only to tell you when the time is right, and that time is not now."

I ball my fist together. "He is just a human! Why protect him when you've made it abundantly clear you don't care for them."

"Because Lythe knew he would not keep you, but he would protect you from the cruel world of the fae and human monarchies." He looks at me for a moment. "She spent weeks choosing your father to be the vessel to create you. You see, he is not a typical human—he spent time with the preceptors at the College of Healos on Skuflan. He spent his entire life learning about Arcadia and its people, he learned about us."

I raise my brows. "That's impossible, no one is allowed to live there unless they are born there or are a preceptor."

"Did you ever learn how the preceptors came to be?" he asks.

"They steal infants of people chosen on the continent."

"And the successors to all countries are allowed to study there for a time, no matter the age," he says. "Preceptors are not allowed to have children, or marry for the matter."

I nod as things become clearer. "And what does this have to do with him?"

"You are aware of Lythe's connection to The Order of Rhion? She chose him because he has a strong lineage, born of preceptor and nobleman. The preceptor that birthed him died in childbirth, and the man never knew of the son he brought into the world. The council of masters decided to take him in as their own until they sent him to Jorthus under the new King Fyfe's reign."

"How could you possibly know this?" This kind of information would not have been easy to find if it was real. He is also a faerie and could not lie, still, it was best to rely on caution.

"Lythe told me a name," Kynus looks at me with insult, "Azlyon was in Skuflan at the time. He investigated on behalf of me."

I clench my teeth. If Azlyon could lie to Kynus and Kynus believed it to be true, there was no real way of trusting the validity of his story.

"I need a name," I calmly press.

"I cannot tell you who he is just yet, it was a vow I cannot break," he looks onward, "yet I am sure you can figure it out if you pursue."

I consider this. "And what would you think if I did?"

"I enjoy watching people make choices," he says with a smile. "I have seen headstrong heroes—and villains—who will stop at nothing to achieve their ends, madmen who care not of their impact, and those who are content living an ordinary life. I thrive in the chaos people create with their choices."

Then he is mad himself. He claims to reject his family, yet he visited his sister near her end. Faeries don't lie but their beliefs can be confusing, I think. Kynus is happy with his position over all the creatures he rules over, but there will always be something clawing at the back of his heart, begging him to feel.

"You say you thrive in chaos, what do the other princes thrive in?" I ask.

"You are learning quickly, but I am not going to give you what you seek," he says. "Intrude on a faerie and suffer misfortune, we are beings of manners and respect. You may deal in secrets and lies so easily, but we must find ways around our values of life, amusement, and truth to behave like you."

The trees on our left clear out as black mountains with silver peaks rise. Navy smoke filters out of caves deep in the rock. The mountains themselves were taller than any in Jorthus, but still resemble something familiar.

"Treol Mountains," Kynus says. "Faerie witches live there guarding the last of the matron sphinxes."

"Faerie witches?"

"Oracles who vowed to serve the old magik," he says simply.

I look over to the mountains, smiling. "That sounds like an adventure."

"Do you know what a sphinx is?"

I shake my head.

"A master riddler with power stronger than the gods combined, they were killed by The Morrígan out of fear of being overthrown. She bore a weapon that could kill any creature, which has long since been lost."

"But there is one left?"

He nods. "Kynthia is its name. People who seek the wisdom of Kynthia rarely return, sometimes their entire existence is erased from history. Travelling through those mountains requires keeping low to the ground and not stopping. Most would rather go around if they need to travel in that direction."

"Don't you worry about them coming down here and killing the faeries?"

He shrugs. "They never have, and I doubt they will. Kynthia's guardians were blessed and cursed to follow and guard the great sphinx."

"How do you know it is still alive?"

"We don't but there is a reason the goddess of death left one alive."

* * *

Kynus holds his tongue for several hours down the road. I watch as the colours and lights around me change from auras to beams. More mountains show up on our right but they look different from the Treol range. They have snow caps and are made of dark crystals. Prisms glitter in the iridescent light, as do the trees below them.

I yawn as I adjust myself on the seat.

"We are going to rest for the night soon." Kynus looks at the pastel sunset at the peaks.

"We can pull through, I've travelled many places at night," I say.

"And if a hoard of Redcaps catches human scent? Or perhaps we encounter a Fachan, which can kill people simply out of fear? What then? Perhaps a Spriggan will find something offensive and trick one of you into doing something lethal?"

I sigh. "I suppose you're right."

"Listen to those who know this world best." Kynus tugs on the reigns and the horses go off-road. I immediately shift closer to my uncle, watching the sides of the carriage carefully. I can feel eyes all around me as if every blade of grass is plotting against us.

"Maikyn," he whispers elegantly, as though he were tucking a child in.

The ground begins to crack and shake as several feet of earth rolls up over the foothill, revealing a dark hole—and we are heading directly into it.

"What is going on?" I demand.

The vines close up behind us as the earth tucks us in, locking eternal darkness in, and the world out.

The air thickens around me. My breathing turns shallow. I grasp Kynus' forearm only to find the armrest on his side of the carriage. He was there one moment and gone the next.

"Prince Kynus!" I gasp.

"Ayrlan Kyn," his voice sifts through the hill's cave.

I feel cool air open up my lungs as though I were still outside.

Several lights flicker on in morstone orbs. Roots, hard dirt, and rock form the roof and walls of this blanketing hill. Kynus stands in front of the horses, feeding them something that green and slimy.

"When you are ready to sleep, simply say *'Slyye Kyn'* to the roots and they will take care of you." Kynus looks over at me as Azlyon emerges from the carriage.

"What does that mean?" I ask him immediately.

"Kyn means family, *Slyye* means blanket me in slumber," Azlyon says. "It is the language of nature, older than faerie tongues."

I walk over to Azlyon as the other guards begin sealing the carriage in mud. It glows slightly before the door disappears, leaving no escape.

"Is Rowyna coming out?"

"No, it is safer for the human in there than out here with us," Azlyon replies to me while nodding at the guards. "This is a mound bore, quite different from the natural mounds further ahead on the road. I suggest you think about sleeping soon, Aurelia. We have quite the journey ahead of us."

I nod but ask. "What about eating?"

Kynus and Azlyon just look at me plainly as though I were asking a child's question.

"The roots give with all their power as long as we are not greedy or intentionally place them in harm. When you wake, you will have a full belly." Azlyon laces his fingers together.

I turn to face a wall of vines. Magikal or not, it felt strange to talk to a plant. "*Slyye Kyn.*"

A vine wraps around me.

"What is it doing?" I gasp, trying to break away with my arms.

"Don't worry or struggle, our kin is just making sure you will be comfortable." Azlyon smiles before turning to Kynus as though I don't matter.

Shortly after he speaks, the vines lay me down on a bed of thick moss, branches, and soft leaves blanketing me. The vines cocoon me until the light disappears. The moss at my head rises like a pillow and my body warms.

The earth holds me so deeply as it breathes all around me. "*Kyn,*" the branches speak in my ear so softly I almost can't hear.

My eyes shut despite being wide awake moments ago. The beating of my heart slows into relaxing drumming, and my mind begins to feel fuzzy.

Chapter 12: Of Sympathy And Tongues

Three years ago
Kingdom of Jorthus

There was a young laird near Flrun whose name was Kenneth Murchadha. He had a relatively large estate that was always decorated with pretty things. He was an important target and one where my heritage aided me. He had a taste for the forbidden. Of course, there were many forbidden things, but only one was worthy of execution without trial, that was taking one of the fae to bed.

Fyfe was not pleased. Cicero and I avoided being in the king's presence for an hour after he found out, and Lorkus was the only one who could calm him down. I was assigned to kill him afterwards. This mission was so important and memorable because I could do it exposed. No more hiding and pretending to be human. I was the perfect bait for him.

When I first stepped into his manor, I noticed the servant, probably a footman, flinch at my green curls and sparkling golden skin. I came unannounced, in rags, and up until this point, this laird has been keeping his activities a secret from his servants. Once we were alone, he studied me in detail, from my legs to my breasts.

He walked over to me, reaching to grab my chin between his thumb and forefinger. His eyes wandered up and down my body like it was a feast after days without food. He leaned down to whisper in my ear. "You are very beautiful, and worthy of my protection—for a single night." The guards searched me for any weapons, I had none. If I weren't of faerie blood, the laird would not have let me into his home this easily. For this mission, I needed to be seen. When this man died, the king would use it as another reason to show people that faeries were wicked and untrustworthy.

Once we entered his private quarters, I noticed that the windows were boarded and that the candles produced red flames. It was clear that he created a private den where he could have his way with weakened faerie slaves he illegally imported in.

I looked at the clothes laid out for me—silk and lace that would hug me closely. I was meant to wear this for him.

"May I wear my pendant?" I showed him the large ruby at the base of my throat. Inside the pendant was powdered hileana, one of the only poisons able to kill within moments of contact with the eyes; it had no effect on other areas of the body. There was a cure but it would have to be placed onto the affected eyes immediately after administration of the poison.

"It does glow wonderfully on your shining skin, my dear." He ripped my ragged dress so my back was exposed.

I slid from his grasp and dressed in his silks so quickly that he frowned. Though it was disappointing for him, I saw lust and pride grow in his eyes.

"Do you want my body?" I asked him tenderly, stepping forward.

He nodded, reaching out for a moment.

"Do you want my body right now?" I asked, walking even closer.

"I beg of you…"

"Do you? Or are you drunk on the unnatural? Drunk on magik?" I asked, harsher in my step. "Close your eyes."

He relaxed a bit, sitting down on a large chair and did as told. "Faeries are mysterious in many different ways. Please, shall we continue?"

I sat on his lap, a leg on either side of his body. I held up the pendant to my teeth and when he opened his eyes, I bit down, shattering the hollowed glass gem and releasing the poison into his eyes. Glittering dust sparkled as it settled in his redding eyes.

"What are you—"

His eyes bled and his mouth foamed, body shaking. I don't know how he died, from ruptured arteries or choking.

I smiled down at him, tucking a loose strand of hair back in place.

"Ever fall in love, my laird? I doubt it." I stepped over him, plucking a silver blade from his deep jacket pocket. I held it by my fingertips at each end. It looked quite intriguing, its handle two strands of metal twisting together into some sort of horn. It was long, sturdy, and light. Someone took something from our neighbours to the West. As much as I wanted nothing to do with them, this blade was pretty.

Later, I met Cicero at the stables after the servants hid in an empty room. It was Cicero's second time seeing me without the cloak, only this time, he saw more of me all bloodied in silky scraps. He pressed a cloak into my hands as well as a clay mask, and I wondered if he'd thought of me as a monster or an asset.

Present
Court of Daeyed

I wake from my slumber not feeling the slightest bit hungry. I am still nestling deep within a root cage, but I am not anxious.

"Plants, roots—*Kyn,* could you help me out of here?" I struggle for the word.

The ground below me rumbles a little as it lowers a little and a tunnel-like hole begins branching out in front of me. It doesn't seem like it is going to let me out the easy way.

There is glowing light coming from the vines to my right when I reach the end of the tunnel. A dead-end leading me nowhere. I peek through the crack made by the vines anyway.

Kynus and Azlyon sit next to one another looking at an orange orb. Their eyes are training directly on it as though nothing else in the world can sway their gaze.

"Azlyon you must fight... If it takes more control, I fear for the future," Kynus speaks after the orb dims to a flicker.

I suppose I should thank the nature spirits for the position I currently am in.

"It is the only way. If I fight then our decimation is certain, it's what she told us." Azlyon continues to stare ahead.

"We did not anticipate things changing during your time away." Kynus turns around.

"As long as it remains on my path without any interference, the goal will ultimately remain the same." Azlyon's mouth forms a hard line.

"If the other princes find out, and they will, they will confront the three of you and revelations will come to light," Kynus responds.

The three of you? Who exactly was Azlyon working with, and why would Septimius and Vikorus have an issue with Azlyon when their country was on the line.

"The Morrígan is our salvation, they know this. She knows about my situation and mocks me everyday. I am to play the instrument of demise and revival."

"Are we going to tell Aurelia any of this? She is a creature of question and curiosity," Kynus speaks lowly. "She angers me with her ill manners."

"If I tell her, I may give in and be forced to fight The Morrígan, and doom my people. As for information about our goddess, I've told her only important things."

"Where will she sit when The Morrígan reigns?" Kynus asks, pulling a hand through his hair. "She is my only living kin."

Azlyon smiles. "You don't talk about it but I know after seeing Aurelia, you miss Lythe dearly, despite trying to remove that part of your life."

"She asked about her father, not knowing he has strong ties to Lythe's mate," Kynus sighs.

"Lythe's mate is a mockery of everything we hold dear," Azlyon nearly growls. "He and I could never agree on anything."

"Whistryn was always so eccentric and headstrong in his idea of living in the future and not the traditions of the past," Kynus sighs.

My mother's mate was one of two arch kings in Flokael?

"Whistryn was so quick to take the throne of a new nation when he realized he could never conceive with his mate," Azlyon sighs as well. "He isn't even a highborn. It is rather disgusting."

"He loved his anam dearly, and he needed a successor. His plan worked," Kynus says.

"Aurelia, by our ancient law is his child, even if they share no blood, which means if she ended up in Flokael, he would keep her like a prisoner in the name of protection."

"Here she could reign beside us, bringing the Cold Court back from ruin," Kynus tilts his head, "or she could bring peace between the courts and the humans, just like Lythe and Whistryn wanted when they formed the Order of Rhion."

"She must—"

I sink. My knees cause a branch to crack slightly, but enough to cut Azlyon off and make him turn in my direction. Almost immediately, the vines groan and shift around me.

I nearly gasp, my hand reaching up to muffle it. I crawl back to the area I fell asleep, the world behind me closing in.

Once I slide onto the now dirt bed I was resting on, I see the branches slide under me as the wood cage opens like a shell for me to step out into the main cavern. They lift me into a standing position before sliding back into the walls.

Azlyon and Kynus step out of the smaller room the branches made for them. The looks on their faces are nothing short of suspicious and I have to play my role.

"What happened? How long was I sleeping?" I ask, falsifying fatigue. "I'm not even hungry."

"You were given precious nutrients and sedatives," Kynus says.

"That can't be possible," I say, trying to distract them, and also wondering why this place allowed me to spy so openly on its leaders.

"Hmm." Azlyon looks me in the eye. "How long were you awake for?"

"A moment before I was spat out of that cage," I lie evenly. "I would have preferred sleeping out here."

"You didn't find it warming sleeping with our Kyn?" Kynus steps forward.

"I don't enjoy being defenceless against nature." I tilt my head.

Azlyon walks over to me, staring me in the eye, "Saying something like that is rather interesting, for the fae are nature and nature is the fae."

"I can handle myself against you, Azlyon," I say. "All I need is a sharp dagger and a temper."

He smirks. "You know iron does not poison me."

I smile back, leaning close to him "I never said I would try to poison you. All I meant was if needed, I could carve, say, a pretty flower into your skin."

He reaches into his belt and hands me a dagger, one familiar and ethereal. The one I took from the laird. I feel the magic hunger in each part of the intricate instrument of death.

"Go ahead, cut me." His voice is clear and challenging.

I look at the knife in my hands. This is the moment where I could do anything I want to the man who betrayed me. To the Faerie who tricked me. To the teacher I once trusted with everything.

But I hear the unspoken words between us. We were companions then and now, regardless of what our faces looked like. I shed a mask like he did. I revealed myself to this world and I revealed myself to him in ways different from before. I wore a gown like a normal woman. I let my face show.

Yet I want to help him. There is something in him that pangs of hunger and I want to put it out. Something that could place the world on the edge of his blade. And a kindness in his heart that was willing to help me, even though I could have been his prisoner.

I am not allowed to be attached to people, according to Fyfe. Yet I was to Cicero—Azlyon, Lucia, Titus, Rowyna, and Lorkus. Even though I wasn't fond of some of them, we were connected in one way or another.

I raise the dagger and spin it so I held the blade and he the handle. Our eyes meet with both amusement and deep interest. Wicked lives have wicked endings, but they are almost always worth living.

"We need some sort of agreement between us, so things can proceed normally once again no matter whose face you wear." I let go and he sheathes the weapon.

"Aurelia, I have no quarrel with you."

"I will try to treat you as I once did. However, I need assurance that you will be honest with me when it is important." I step closer to him.

We are so close to one another that I feel his breath on my face. It smells of sweet mint and magik, almost as though he fell from a cloud in the sky, beautiful yet dangerous.

"I do not have to agree with anything you say," he pauses. "I will out of respect for both you and your role here."

The endless silver pools in his eyes reflect the gentle glow of the Morstone. He is an old creature with a young heart, one that never had the chance to feel since the death of his entire family. It is tragic perhaps, but also curious to see what truly drives him each day.

I step away and walk over to Kynus; he is silent and expressionless. I wonder what he is thinking. One thing I do know is that he would rather remain silent than speak truths that prove himself compassionate.

"Do you have a map of Daeyed?" I ask him, perching a hand on my hip. "I'd like to know where we are going."

"You know where we are going."

"I know its name but if I am to trust you both, I would like to see what your country looks like." I snatch the parchment he pulls out.

A large river cuts the country in half and there are few roads. The capital is on an island in what appears to be a bay, narrow at the entrance to the sea but wide enough to be a large lake. There are areas in red marking called 'mounds'.

"There are few settlements," I say. "Your kind appear to prefer wild lives."

What interests me the most about this map is the area to the North East, a wall of smoke and mist meant to keep the humans from Jorthus out. It ends where their mountains began.

Little River, don't pretend you haven't spent most of your days under my wing longing to see this map.

I was expecting something more grandeur, I press back.

My lips curl into a smile upon looking at the map. Immediately, I begin memorizing settlements—Daekil to the Southwest, Rikanael to the North, and Woyldlan to the Northwest. There are war camps on the eastern edge of the country, closest to Jorthus and Flokael.

I am all too aware of the overshadowing presence of the fiery faerie prince. I feel his energy twist into annoyance and frustration but when I sneak a glance his face reveals nothing. I could feel the unnerving heightening of my ability to read people here.

"Shall we continue on?" I press the parchment into Kynus' palms. "I believe that it would be quicker if we cut through the mounds, at least a few hours ahead of schedule."

Kynus goes rigid.

Azlyon grabs my arm. I don't realize how close he is to me until now.

"Those who travel through the mounds are never seen again by the living," he says curtly.

"Surely a prince such as you could—"

"Perhaps we could, but our minds may be shattered by what we encounter," he whispers.

I shiver, imagining how little control they have over the area. A warning that even the princes carefully obey. From what I saw on the map, there were three clusters of mounds, and the largest is the one we will be travelling by.

Whatever is in the mounds...does it stay there? I reach out to Azlyon.

"Those that dwell there never cross the threshold of areas without mounds," he says. "It is the bargain we struck during the Great Seal of Druug."

"Pardon?"

"Once, the mounds were where faeries lived, they would have a door to Arcadia and a door to Gaia." Kynus sighs. "The Great Seal severed all ties to Gaia and Arcadia for a time, until we found a way to allow them to come back to this world. They were either dead or turned into something of distortion."

"Since then, they somehow know everything about you the moment you step on their land. Their own mound is their source of power. If they leave it for too long they will vanish into nothingness. They feed off of fear and dreams," Azlyon continues. "We call them the Unsidhe, or nightmare-walkers."

These faeries were cut off from both worlds and trapped inside the earth for a very long time. When we found out what truly happened to them, it was too late. Thousands of terrified faeries were forced into this or died from being trapped.

"Who did it?" I press.

"We did, after our defeat." Azlyon turns away. "We couldn't afford more humans coming in or out. It was the only way to ensure Arcadia wasn't overrun."

"You sacrificed so many." I turn away, not letting them see me like this.

"It needed to be done," Kynus says. "We all lost someone. The spells and magik to undo part of the seal took long to learn."

"Have you spoken to them? Told them why you've done this?" I ask.

They don't move or respond, answering the question for me. They haven't done it, though they do appear to be remorseful in their own way. A leader holds the ability to make difficult decisions and there is no doubt that this is something that has hung over their heads for centuries.

Faeries could be cold, cruel, tricky, wicked, kind, and generous. But they did care even though their feelings were never as clear as I want them to be.

Azlyon, will you ever tell them why? I ask.

His silver eyes look into mine for a moment before turning to Kynus.

"It is time we leave," Kynus says out loud. "Aurelia, will you be sitting with me?"

I shake my head. I need to see Rowyna.

"Rhoulus will sit beside me then." Kynus yawns as a faerie appears and bows.

I step inside the carriage to see a yawing Rowyna looking dizzy. Immediately, I take her face in my hands and examine each eye. She has trouble focusing on me.

"Cicero, why did you leave me?" she mumbled.

"What did you do to her?" I demand.

"I've done nothing." Azlyon climbs in after me. "Humans can become mad when surrounded by the fae. It is a natural response to this much magik."

He reaches over and touches her temple. Her body goes limp.

I immediately push him aside to check her pulse and breath.

"It is better than being awake. It will only last until the fork," He says against my ear, sending chills down my neck.

I climb into the seat across from him, but he raises his brows. "You are a faerie of royal birth, you should sit next to me. It is a Seelie custom."

I smile. "I am not a Seelie and I like looking at the person I am speaking to."

"Oh?"

"I cannot speak to Rowyna," I say.

"And our guards scare you?"

I turn to the one sitting beside him, proving he didn't frighten me. "Have you ever been to Jorthus?"

The guard looks at me, shakes his head and turns back with a frown. "I have not but one close to me has, and you honoured her."

"What?" I ask. "I can assure you I have never honoured a faerie."

The faerie guard's golden horns shine in the light as he turns to me.

"My war-sister was kidnapped and brought into Jorthus for a nobleman," the guard says through his teeth.

It must have been Laird Murchadha.

"War-sister?"

"Warriors who have fighting kin, those whose spirits work better fighting together than apart," Azlyon says, "a warrior's chosen kin when blood has all but abandoned."

"After that human had his way with her, she was left bleeding, broken, and iron poisoned at our border," the guard shakes his head. "Death greeted her shortly after. Then you killed that beastly demon. For that, I owe you a debt greater than all of Arcadia."

My eyes widen.

It would appear that attempting to make a wiseacre point, you've discovered something you did not want to hear, Azlyon says evenly in my mind.

"You don't owe me anything. It was an assignment for King Fyfe," I say, hoping the words sink in.

He reaches over with lengthy three-finger hands.

I pull my hands back slightly, but when it—he touches my own, I don't feel sharpness or aggression. I feel care, kindness, and relaxation. A warrior who is capable of being gentle.

"Regardless of your intentions, you ended someone of filth, someone who would harm our young, our old, and our innocent." He tilts his head. "When you need me, I will be there by your side without condition."

Such a promise you will never likely hear again. I could imprison him for making this promise because if you ordered him to go against his crown, he would have to, Azlyon's voice caresses.

"What is your name?" I ask.

"Lilon is what I am called," he nods to me, "my lady."

I shake my head. "Please call me Aurelia."

"As you wish."

I turn to Azlyon. He is smiling as he looks out the window, letting in the morning light. His face is quite unique, yet it is what lingers on his neck—several faint scars climbing from ear to ear—that distracts me.

Someone tried hard to kill him, and he should have been dead.

"Lilon is a nice name," I say.

The guard smiles. "Thank you, Lady Aurelia."

I smile for a moment without even commanding this display. I should not show compassion for faeries. They are using me for a purpose and there is a high chance they will toss me aside, kill me, or torture me when this is done.

"Azlyon, do you remember when I was training near Onk Mine? When I first joined the assassins?" I say, turning to the prince.

He raises a brow. "I do. I took you there and told you to separate the guilty miners from the innocent. Typically, it takes a very long time for a recruit, but you finished by the next morning when I was about to depart."

I shake my head. "I finished slightly before then, but the look on your face was priceless when I did come."

He nods. "I didn't expect it so I stayed."

He stayed and gave me different challenges, and I completed them with ease and haste. Except for one night when I'd been stabbed by a miner walking to my lodging. I was used to beatings under Titus but this was different. When I dragged myself in, I had lost a lot of blood. Cicero saw me and immediately went to remove my tunic, but my hand was quicker. He knew I was half-faerie but he never saw me truly before.

"And then you saw me."

He nods. "I did. And I wondered why you hated looking at your own reflection. I saw desperation to belong in your eyes because if it didn't work out for you under my instruction, you would have been put to death."

Cicero stitched me up and told me not to put the cowl on for one evening. He wanted me to tell him more about myself.

"I always believed myself to be an ugly creature," I laugh, "and still you wanted to talk to me, to my face. You know, that meant more to me than ever gaining praise from Fyfe."

"It was that night I decided to let Daeyed know that I found our last hope." Azlyon smiles weakly. "But you still had so much to learn before we could ever dream to bring you here."

I look at him. "I saw a letter with some form of runic language in a drawer, the characters were more circular than sharp."

"Arcadian in the Seelie dialect," he says without hesitation. "Only two others in Jorthus could potentially read it with refined and proper training."

I raise my brows. "Who?"

He glances out the window for a moment. "A former librarian from Skuflan and you."

I laugh. "I can tell you with certainty that I cannot."

"A gift from the gods. Through magik, those of fae blood enter the world knowing Arcadian, but unable to write the complex patterns of language."

I shake my head.

"How do you think we are communicating right at this moment?" He tilts his head. "How do you think you were communicating with all the fae you've encountered thus far? With the assistance of the ancient magik, you are able to communicate without realization."

I feel my cheeks turn crimson with the realization that there is no way the guard understands the human tongue. After all, this isolating country rarely interacts with the outside world.

"How could I not read the runes?" I ask.

"You weren't taught to read or write in our language," Azlyon says without missing a beat. "It took me four decades before I was able to read and write in the Seelie dialect; for some, it can take over a century. Slow learning in exchange for the ability to communicate with other faeries."

I look at the guard, then back at the prince. "How do I switch languages? Can you tell when you do? What am I speaking in now? How does it stop?"

"Calm down, Aurelia." He smiles. "It's all in the rhythm of the language. The Arcadian languages require more energy, whereas the mortal tongues are effortless. Think simple and small for them, for their languages have very little or no magic in its construction. It takes years of mastering before you finally can truly see the differences, though your body takes charge before your mind. There is one language, however, that you can never understand. One language that is all but dead."

I raise my brows. "I didn't realize you have dead languages here."

"Dead but never lost."

"So it's written down?"

He shakes his head.

"Then that doesn't make sense. What is this language I will never understand?" I ask

"Draevosun, the language of dragons and wyverns," he says. "It is the purest magic, apart from the gods' incomprehensible tongue."

"Do you know it?"

He shakes his head. "I was never privy to their vast knowledge of existence. They were the first creatures, then came the green, then the fae, the animals, and finally humans."

"What about the language we spoke to those roots?" I ask.

"That is a language you must learn by spending a single sun in green isolation from all creatures. It is older than Arcadia. If the earth deems you ready, it will teach you."

I look at him, the years in his crystal eyes flashing and fading. Is he trapping himself in the past and future, but never really considering the present? When he speaks to me, I sense detachment as though his soul floats just behind him. He is a book of immense knowledge of the world.

"What is the other world like? Have you been there?" I ask, leaning closer.

As though I snap my fingers, he looks at me. "Gaia? I've been there, though not for a long time. Let me think for but a moment... The last time I was there, humans were turning away from worshipping us and our gods to worshiping a single god."

"It's like the legends I heard Lorkus drunkenly telling another lad." I raise my eyebrows. "Is this god real?"

Azlyon's mouth tightens. "That god may exist in that plane but not here. The gods we worship are present in Gaia as well as Arcadia, under many different names depending on the region of that world. My last visit was near a place called Roma, and the hunted faeries who lived there for years were fleeing to Arcadia. They called us demons of false gods in their tongues. There was no place for us in that region of the world. Some fae moved north to pillage and outsmart the barbaric humans who lived there."

"So the stories are real," I say widening my eyes.

There is a world out there where humans live simply and without fear of monsters—and Azlyon has been there before. He speaks about it with little to no interest but this is intriguing for me.

"It is an iron wasteland now," he says. "We've peeked into the barrier and the humans use iron in everything. They cannot live without it. They live their lives inside their cages. They tear up the land to pour their metal and stone citadels"

"So the fae couldn't live there?" I ask.

"Many of us would die within a decade of living there," Azlyon narrows his eyes.

"Az," I say with a broad smile leaning on my elbows.

Az? He smiles.

What if we send the humans back to Gaia? I tell him, *They don't need to die.*

He tilts his head. *Do you think Jorthus will agree to that? Lomel or Trilan? Even the humans of Flokael? What of them? And the half-bloods? If we allow them to stay but not their human family, what do you think they will do?*

I sink back a little, feeling like an arrow pierces through me.

Regardless, there will be war no matter how you look at it. And how will they feel in Gaia? They won't fit in, and their very society will crumble under the highly advanced societies currently ruling there. They will be as good as dead, Azlyon continues very carefully.

I swallow and feel a deep, unsettling chill crawl over me.

Is there a way to make them integrate into that society? I say carefully.

Perhaps, but we would need a human from the other side, which is forbidden.

"I know you mean well and want the best outcome but blood will always spill. There is no world where we can coexist in harmony." He sighs.

I look away from him. Not all humans are bad, some are quite elegant in their sympathies. Like Lucia.

I treated her terribly when I last saw her. She sacrificed so much to keep me safe from the world. A stranger's child; not only that, a stranger's faerie child in a world filled with fear and hate towards the fair folk.

Azlyon was still cautious in what he revealed. He was always distracting me with stories about this country. He was even hesitant with Lucia back in Jorthus.

"What are you keeping from me?" I say firmly.

"You need only ask what you want to know, I've told you this," he says, looking at me.

"You tell me I hold the power of asking you questions, but you know I won't ask the right questions and you won't have to reveal anything," I say, leaning forward, closer to him. "You twisted the terms."

"I did not twist anything."

"No, but you know how to dance with words," I respond.

"The question you ask is broad. 'What are you keeping from me?' could mean anything and everything I have not told you. How do you expect me to know what you want specifically if you haven't asked?" he responds, this time with a smile.

"Ok, let's start with two very easy questions. What is so important about my father? And why has he never revealed himself to me?" I ask, ignoring that smile.

"He is a bastard child of an important human that has very close connections with the Order of Rhion. Your father also had a secret child with another important human to spread the Order's influence. As to the latter question, you have met him in your adult life. You know his name, you know his face, and you know his voice," he said. "Is that all Little River?"

I met my father already. He knew this entire time and neglected to mention it?

"Far from it," I say. "Tell me his name."

Azlyon shakes his head, "That is for Kynus to tell you."

"Fine. Who did he have another child with?" I ask.

He smiles. "A high ranking official in the Order of Rhion, one parading as a queen but smuggling secrets straight to Flokael."

Of all the kings and their queens in this realm, I could only think of two.

"Is it Ambyr or Selene?" I ask.

"Queen Selene has been keeping lovely secrets from the man she beds." Azlyon looks out the window.

"She has another child? Does the king know?"

Azlyon shakes his head. "She only has one child, a child who is the next heir to the throne of Jorthus."

I gasp. "Why are you telling me this?"

Lorkus is not the king's son. The queen was unfaithful. She wanted the Order of Rhion to thrive. Selene ensured a son who could easily be melded into what the Order needed. Lorkus grew up fascinated with faeries, often sickeningly fascinated.

And the most shocking revelation—he is my brother. I know he looks like his mother from his eyes and hair, but often children never look like both their parents.

"Because you asked." Azlyon leans closer, our faces nearly touching but neither of us surrenders.

"H-How long have you known?"

"Two years. While in Flokael I overheard Ambyr and Selene in the palace garden late at night," he says, "but that was not enough proof so I used my glamour to alter my appearance to look like him. Our conversations took place over three days."

I sigh and close my eyes. "You slept with her for information, didn't you?"

Azlyon looks curious but does not respond.

"This must be quite amusing for you. I never had a family. Now I have an uncle connected to Daeyed, my father is alive, I have a half-brother, and my mother ended up being a princess. You knew all this time and still watched me suffer."

He touches my chin with his pale hand. "I am not amused, I am more on the side of confused. I may have known this but it only makes me hesitant and cautious. Your existence is more than just to help the fae, it is heavily connected to the Order of Rhion. They are sinking in their teeth in every country, including Daeyed."

"And I am to choose between you and them?" I say, leaning back.

"Perhaps, but if you do choose them, Arcadia will fall and collapse on itself within a few centuries from human rule," he says. "We can save it with your help."

"Well, let's hope my experience in Woyldlan is favourable," I say regaining control, "for your sake."

"For *our* sake," He corrects me.

"So it would seem."

"You must visit the Eldyrgrove Springs just outside the village. The waters are wondrous for restoring your health," he tries to hide his enthusiasm and fails.

"Are they close to the mounds?" I ask.

"Aurelia, you cannot go to the mounds," he says, no longer looking at me.

"I am not. But you are going to," I say.

"I do not need to go there," he says quickly.

"You are going to talk to the unsidhe," I said evenly, "and tell them the whole story. You are the High Prince, explanation through compassion isn't a weakness. You are better than Fyfe."

"You are in no position to be demanding." His voice is sharp.

I lean in closer once again. "Perhaps you are right."

The tension simmers down to a calm but Azlyon isn't entirely himself. His eyes are darker than before. I'm not sure if it is the lighting but the once pale silver glimmers a slimy liquid-black. His jaw clenches and his hands are rigid. Could he possibly be sick?

"Little river," he says with a cracking laugh.

"Azlyon?" My eyes go wide.

"Play your tedious part soon or perhaps things will not be as pleasant... Don't mind me, though you must let me soon. It is not time. I am aware, you are taking far too long."

"What do you even mean?" I ask.

I see his legs shake slightly. His nails cut so deeply into his palms that blue blood spills all down his arms. The veins around his neck turn a dark murky grey.

Lilon reaches over to the prince and starts whispering an incantation over and over in his ear. I reach for his face, forcing him to look at me. His skin is as cold as frozen earth.

"Is he sick, Lilon?" I snap at the guard.

Lilon stops whispering. "Time is running out for him, I suspect he won't last much longer after the solstice."

"What does that mean?"

I press my forehead against Azlyon's and look him deeply in the eyes. "You need to fight this, you still owe me so much! Remember our bargain! You cannot flee it Azlyon!"

His eyes roll back in his head. "Aurelia."

I slap his cheek.

Almost instantly, his skin goes back to normal and his eyes turn back to silver. Whatever that goddess did to him is catching up quickly.

"*Kyn*," Lilon whispers, leaning back, his eyes directly on me.

Azlyon leans on his knees, "How long Lilon?"

"Seven minutes, my prince," he says, "five longer than last time."

Last time? How often does this happen to him?

He shakes his head. "Did you recite the bind?"

Lilon nods. "Yes I did, however, it wasn't working as effectively. Your highness, I tried, but I think Aurelia helped you more."

Azlyon's eyes shut as if the thought of me helping him is painful. I wonder if this was going on in Jorthus when I wasn't around.

Azlyon what is wrong with you? I ask.

Coming home was harder on my body than I thought. Do not mistake this for weakness because if I hadn't returned, you would be in the presence of a monster.

"I never thought you were weak," I tell him.

Chapter 13: The Hunter's Lie

The Mounds, Court of Daeyed

The carriage stops after a few days of riding in silence. We must be at the Daelin Fork they mentioned earlier. Just as Azlyon promised, Rowyna wakes slowly, her eyes puffy and her hair layering more mates and dirt.

Azlyon steps out as though being in the carriage any longer will suffocate him.

Lilon pulls out a jagged grey crystal and cuts runes on Rowyna's wrists; they begin glowing an eerie deep blue before they fade into an ink-like pattern. No blood or pain.

"Her body will go wherever you go, she won't be able to leave a mountain's distance without being pulled back," he looks up at me, "and what you saw earlier must not be spoken or thought of again."

"With Azlyon?" I ask. "What is happening to him?"

"We do not speak of princes," is all he says.

Rowyna pulls herself up. "Aurelia, I had the strangest dream that Cicero was speaking to a crow on the outskirts of Farlanfell. I couldn't understand him."

I turn to her. "You were spell sick, don't trust your dreams while you are here."

A small part of my mind itches at the fact that she dreamt of Cicero and a crow. Was it a warning or was it perhaps placed there by a faerie to further the charade of Cicero the Liar?

"He was so real," she mumbles as we exit the carriage.

I don't respond, instead, I stretch and look onward.

To my left are round barn-size hills as far as my eye can see; to my right are more mountains, dusty, misty, and sharp. The road divides through the mountains and to the edge of those hills.

"Are those the mounds I saw on the map?" I ask.

"Yes." Kynus hops down then turns to the two guards. "Head back to Loelmell and await further instructions. Do not leave Daeyed unless you hear directly from me."

The guards bow, then Lilon passes me a lightweight green satchel with gold embroidery.

Azlyon whistles and his familiar appears. He whispers something in an alarming hush tone, like two people speaking at once in different languages. As he utters the last word, the steed rides off through the mountainside of the forked road.

"Hello," I call to him, but he doesn't turn.

Azlyon you are going to have to talk to me, I call out to him again.

Nothing.

"Aurelia," Kynus is at my side as we watch the carriage head back the way we came, "I hope you rested because we are walking through the night. This is not a place to linger too long."

"Why did we leave the carriage then?"

I am curious. I haven't seen a faerie around since we began. The land is almost barren of creatures.

"It is noisy and being so close to the mounds causes the unsidhe to crawl from the soil. At least with us visible most won't dare attack," he says meaning Azlyon and himself. "This side is where the Seelie and bright fae roam mostly. We have more pull here than Vikorus or Septimius."

"Do you know what happened in the carriage?" I ask.

He nods. "Ignore it, he is fine."

"If he was fine then he would be the one talking to me right now."

"You may think that but he is concentrating on a partial cloak for us all. To trick humans is one thing, but to trick faeries is another," Kynus says.

"Hasn't he mastered magik? He used it during the war, right? And he is chosen or something? This should be easy for him," I say.

"He also may not wish to speak right now." Kynus shrugs. "That is what he told me he was doing, but I suggest you tread lightly."

"I wasn't supposed to see that earlier, was I?"

Kynus smiles. "No, but nothing can be changed. We must move on, and as I said before, he is fine now."

Faeries are stubborn and silencing.

I step around Kynus and before he can do anything, I hurry over to Azlyon. I peek back at Kynus and see narrowing eyes, yet he makes no move to stop me.

Azlyon does not acknowledge my presence, looking at the mounds cautiously. They are perfectly round. The blades of vibrant green grass do not move in the calm breeze. It feels like there is a hidden wall separating that land from this.

"Azlyon," I say.

"Yes, Aurelia," he remarks.

"I want you to tell me the truth." I look into his eyes.

He looks down at the ground. "I am a prisoner in my own skin."

"Even back in Farlanfell," I say, "you removed my shackles through training. If we work towards a fair future, I will help you rid this sickness any way I can."

Fair for whom?

He turns and walks away.

Fair for them, you mean. You did have me nearly convinced though.

Kynus steps to his side. I feel Rowyna nudging me. His voice is cold and distant, and he leaves me feeling small.

"If Cicero were here, he could help us get out of this," she says.

I smile. "There is still so much in this world, I don't know if even he could master everything."

"I actually hoped to find him here. I had a message to deliver to him but they took it. It was from General Titus." She looks away.

I tilt my head. "Did you look at it? What did it say?"

"I didn't read it, I will not betray Jorthus. However, if I knew his fate…" She shakes her head. "Titus also had a message for you, this one was verbal."

"And you only now tell me." I cross my arms.

She shakes her head.

"Spit it out Rowyna," I say, widening my eyes.

She steps back and freezes. I can't explain it but I feel her breath slow in the air. Her eyes lock on my mouth. She stares at my bare teeth like I'm a wild animal.

"I don't have time for this Rowyna, there are larger things at stake than meaningless fear. You know me, I am the same as I was when I left Jorthus." That is a lie. I want to tell her everything was going to be fine, but I'm not sure if everything will work out as I plan. I want to protect her, but I have other roles to play.

"You are turning into them." She looks at the ground quickly but doesn't step out of place. "Titus said, 'One way or another, you will be coming back to Jorthus,' and that I had to choose alive and able or alive and disabled."

"Why would Titus go to such a length to bring me back?" I ask Rowyna, "I very much doubt King Fyfe would waste resources like this." I look her in the eye. "And if you somehow died, who would be replacing you?"

Titus had to be doing this for another reason and without the crown's knowledge.

"They would send the Legitars that were at the meeting in Lorlan. Haerton Blackfell and Tionne Nyetynslae," she whispers cautiously.

Haerton was cautious of me. He is a true man of Jorthus and will hunt me down with his entire being. Tionne is different though. He is logical. His surname is Flokalan. His cautiousness and clarity must have been because of his connections to the fae-accepting country.

"Proper faerie hunters that have never even stepped into Daeyed," I almost laugh. "They will be eaten alive as soon as they step foot across the border. That is if the fae armies don't find them first."

"You are bold," Rowyna finally steps closer, "but the hunters should already be here, and they are looking for us. When they find us, they will decide whether or not to let me finish what I started."

So there is a timeline. The princes have no idea of this. If the hunters survive far in this country, then perhaps they could actually find us. Would it be Tionne or Haerton who drives the blade deep into my chest? Or will the princes save me? Will they hear out Tionne or Haerton?

Only one question remains: Should I tell the princes?

"Let's move." Kynus beckons me over.

I tug on Rowyna to follow, and she does.

The light is warm on my skin.

"Fall into the light, my child, the air will bring you life." I find myself saying.

"And with that life, you will begin anew, for both I and the gods watch over you until the end of time," Kynus finishes with a smile.

"What does it mean? I dream of a voice whispering in darkness." I turn to Kynus.

"They are the words we tell our faelings. It is an intimate moment of connection, I've only witnessed it twice. Once between my mother and I, and Laeraan and her adopted kin, Septimius."

"She was Prince Vikorus' mother, yes?"

He nods. "She was that and so much more, a fierce, cunning, and fiery sidhe. For her to take in Septimius was a testament to her being. You see, Unseelie faeries are a little harsher on their faelings than the Seelie."

"Where is his father?" I say.

"The drake? He was chained and crushed under Mount Reaun in the Treol Mountain range. For a Skaelean to live, his drake father must die within a week of birth."

"And the drake gave his life for Septimius? Just like that?"

"Of course, he loved Septimius' mother dearly, he wanted his seed to grow in a world of magik and power. Since Juvelio gave her life for her son, he did the same." He says, "Creatures of magik love with their entire being. They love their world, and poisoning it is something they will fight against."

A love so strong sacrifices had to be made. Yet where were words of encouragement, of life, hope always part of you.

"Did my mother say those words to me?" I ask in wonder. "About life and being with you?"

"She did, otherwise you would not be able to recite such words so effortlessly," Kynus sighs.

I look away. "If she could see me now, she would hate who I've become."

Kynus sighs. "I doubt that, though I cannot talk to her anymore. Your life is your own, she only helped you come into the world. Our gods meant for you to come here. To be born, to save or end us with a simple decision."

I shake my head. "It's not so simple."

He smiles. "It can be if you allow it to be, but the trick is to look at it as a matter of beauty and repulsion. Life can be both, but it is up to the individual to choose which is more intricate for their path. I have met humans who care for the land like us, and I have met faeries that want to see the world burn in chaos. Those who choose the ugly are distorted in themselves. Those who chose to renew, and to right wrongs can be forgiven by Arcadia."

"I could lie and say I understand what you mean, but I really do not." I reach to pull my cowl up but forget it's not there.

He continues to walk a few paces. "I will never make complete sense, I am a mad creature after all."

"Will I have a family here? People I could call family if I decide to help?" I feel like a child talking to him.

"You could begin a free life here," he continues to look forward, "and help us rebuild the world around us, and then perhaps rebuild the Cold Court."

"Kynus, answer me..."

I will try to be there for you. His voice is in my mind like Azlyon.

I gasp. "How did you do that? I thought Azlyon was the only one who could!"

"It takes a great deal of effort, and if you choose to stay, I will tell you why."

"Can you tell me something? Anything? I have been searching in the dark for answers and all of you keep playing with words—and emotions!"

"Too much can drive a person to insanity. It could shatter a mind with ideas and concepts hard to grasp. I am treading lightly with you, Aurelia, because you grew up in a different world," Kynus says. "I will tell you a story, one you may know, but not know enough. It may not be time for you to hear it but I feel this story will satisfy your lust for answers."

I look back at Rowyna, knowing she is trying to listen in, but can't understand what we are saying. When our eyes meet, she immediately becomes distrustful of me again. I was speaking in Arcadian with a high faerie. It looks like I was always a spy or at the very least a traitor to Jorthus.

I turn my head back to Kynus. It is a problem for later. If I have to end Rowyna's life, if she can't come to terms with this, then I will.

"There was a man who fell in love with a faerie, she wanted a child desperately and he forgot about the queen he loved back home. He worked for the steward—hunting faeries, and that is what he came to do. When she bore his child, he was scared. You see, if he were to be caught, his position would be jeopardized and the child would be murdered. So he kissed the babe on the forehead and found someone who still worshiped the fae, a huntress. She was barely a grown woman, forced to fend for herself after an assassin murdered her family for conspiring against the crown," Kynus whispers.

"How do you know this?" I stop in my tracks. My father is a Legitar and I have met him before.

"I sent a watcher to observe you," he responds.

My teeth clench. "Haerton or Tionne? One of them is my father."

"Reflect, and the answer will come to you," he says simply.

Images of both Legitars flash before my eyes. I saw Haerton and anger flashed in his eyes when he found out what I was. Then there was Tionne, who wanted to come to Arcadia with me. He, who was calm and careful around me.

My answer comes in the form of brown eyes and dark hair.

"Legitar Tionne Nyetynslae," I pronounce each syllable through my teeth.

"Silence," Kynus hisses, "names have power here."

"Aurelia," Rowyna curtly interrupts, "did you tell him?"

She could only hear names mentioned and not the faerie tongue.

"Rowyna, silence your tongue before I rip it out," I fume.

I look at Kynus, my fists still clenching tightly.

This man's name is my own by blood-right. I never had a surname part from the one Lucia told me in secret once, Cytheon. I was invisible to the king and his pure untainted records. To him, I was just Aurelia.

Am I now Aurelia Cytheon Nyetynslae? I am Tionne Nyetynslae's lesser child. How can I compete with a false prince? Lorkus will lead a nation, and I will remain invisible.

"Lythe chose him because of who he was. His proximity to the government of Jorthus, his relationship with Selene, and where he was raised. His surname is of Flokael. He is a bastard of an aristocrat from that twisted capital. Was I created for the of the Order of Rhion?" I speak my thoughts out loud.

Kynus smiles. "If that is what you choose to be. You could be their pawn, or you could bring the Cold Court from ruin and rule as its queen. Lythe is an enigma, but she made certain that no matter what you chose, you would succeed in the world."

I stop in my path. I can't talk to the dead, but I could interrogate a living tracker. The worst part was that when I met him back in Jorthus, he knew exactly who I was.

"Kynus, please tell me that none of this is true, that Lythe just wanted to have a child and he was the only human who would help her." I will not let myself spill a single frustrating tear.

"You know I cannot tell an untruth, Aurelia." He shifts away. "I do know that she wanted a faeling. Perhaps it was—how do you say that human expression—ah yes, two birds and a stone, I believe."

"Rowyna said the Legitars are coming for me," I growl. "Let me find them first."

Azlyon turns around sharply and advances with determination toward us. Once our eyes lock, he is a different person. He is the faerie prince no longer pretending to be human.

"Marine," he growls, "you have learned nothing."

Kynus steps aside, not wanting to be in the high prince's path a moment longer than necessary.

"Your impulsiveness will kill you," Azlyon snaps.

"You let him be around me, you knew the entire time I was in his presence," I snarl back. "You are disgusting, Azlyon. I understand why other faeries hid this from me, but you? I confided my feelings in you. You knew I have a brother, that I was terrified of the way he looked at me."

I march towards him, letting rage grasp me in its tight claws. Rowyna stumbles on the road, trying to hide behind Kynus. I hear her shallow breath falling beneath her skin. I feel Kynus raising his lips into a crooked smile. The ground beneath my feet is solid and almost like an extension of my body.

"How dare you pass judgment on something you know so little of?" His exposes his teeth in the light, looking like gleaming marble against his face.

"How dare I? How dare you lie to me all these years? If you can live with the knowledge that you've ruined my life, then you really are worse than any wicked thing that crawls on this land calling itself faerie or human."

I shove him hard with exposing my nails. He does not retaliate but his eyes are warning, testing, daring me to do something else.

"You tell me I should side with you?" I step closer to him.

"You say I hold the world in my hands?" I almost laugh.

"Yet you fail to comprehend that this world has never once given me happiness." I am practically touching him. "My friend lied to me, he played his game and enjoyed seeing me in turmoil."

He says nothing.

"You say you like to play games, you like to twist words, well, let's play, Azlyon!" I swiftly move to the edge of the road.

There is a flash of silver as he tries to grab my wrist before I fall off the road but I hit a wall of stagnant energy.

Azlyon is at the edge of the road instantly, holding an arm out for me.

"Aurelia, we can discuss anything, please step on the road now." His silver eyes switch to genuine worry.

"You told me to see your world, so that's exactly what I am doing," I say carefully.

"Aurelia, you know that my warnings were not for nothing."

Kynus crosses his arms. "Now is not the time to argue."

I take another step closer to the mound.

"Nothing has harmed me yet," I whisper. "I don't—"

Something grabs my foot and pulls me back. I fall on my face and see a grey face with flat yellow eyes half in the soil.

I hear someone say my name like I am submerging in saltwater.

Several more creatures crawl out of the soil, their dirty matting hair hardens into spikes. Each distorted mouth is bloody as though someone began to carve crooked smiles into their faces.

I gasp, realizing I am already waist-deep in the ground.

"Let me go!" I try hitting them with my free hands.

"Sshe ssmellsss like ssalt and deception," they all speak in unison.

"Let her go." Azlyon attempts to pull me away from them.

"Betrayer," they say, "betrayer, betrayer, betrayer, betrayer..."

And the earth swallows me whole, granting me a single glance of silver eyes before darkness.

II

Part Two

Chapter 14: To Be Born Again

Courts of Arcadia

I wake to see a brownie hard at work cleaning my chambers. His earthy skin contrasts with his straw-sewn hat. His hands are worn to the bone but still, he cleans and cleans. I always wonder why they love it so.

"M'lady," a lady goblin enters the room. With her pale grey skin, thin torso, and wide legs, it is obvious that she is my morning care-maid.

"Why do you enter so early, Friona?" I ask.

"Princess Lythe wishes me ta send for you, for you ar' headed ta tha Bright Court for tha spring equinox," she breathes, helping me out of bed. Her scaly hands are freezing and her blood is even colder beneath them. For a lesser faerie, she knows better than anyone how to navigate the tricky world of the high fae.

"Oh yes, I heard my uncle was named crown lord." I smile. "I am honestly surprised High Lord Fyraen and my uncle's mother never conceived a faeling."

It is difficult to have offspring in this world. The fae have with many gifts but always struggle to have their own sons or daughters. My mother had me from human seed, making me a demifae. The human who sired me died, and my father by right is her loving Seelie mate Whistryn.

"Tell me, who of importance should I impress this evening?" I ask her.

She helps me out of my sleeping robes and carefully begins to comb my hair. "Of tha Seelie, Queen Titania, Princess Fhanna, an' Crowned Prince

Azlyon will be attending. Of tha Unseelie, Crowned Princess Laeraan and of tha dark—"

"Do I really need to impress the Dark Court? They are so quiet and small." I look over the face paints on my shelf. Should I choose gold or silver?

"Lord Septimius and his uncle Crowned Lord Drion," she says. "May I be frank, m'lady?"

I nod as she finishes braiding my hair into flowers atop my head.

"Princess Lythe is second in line for tha cold throne." She brings over a silvery-blue gown crafted under the winter's eve star—a rare gift my great-grandfather, the king of marine, gave me years ago. "Play nice with 'em, for they may prove ta be n' ally in life should tha Cold Court declare war."

I gasp as she adjusts my breasts and arms in the gown before grabbing the face paint.

"Dark blue and silver," I say. "I want to look terrifyingly alluring."

"Of course." She snatches a pixie hair paintbrush off the shelf and dips it into the paint.

I love life at the courts. The scheming and the truthful deception are remarkably fun to take part in. One time, I tricked King Oberon into sending three of his knights into the Guul pond believing a rogue faerie lived there, but the pond turned their skin brown and red and they smelled of grass and sulphur for days. Oberon was furious of course but he never found out who the informant was.

"'Ere is also something at play m'lady," she hints, dipping a new brush in silver. "Yer grandmother is hoping te forge an alliance through yeh."

Servants play and listen to everything that happens in courts. They are invisible ears, and I take care to be kind and confide in them so a bridge of genuine trust can forge.

"The crowned princess of the cold wishes me to court a sidhe to strengthen our connections." I almost laugh. What they truly need to worry about is if another faerie can stand being near me longer than a simple revel. "I always thought I was going to marry a Reefthorn Knight one day."

"Yer not mad?"

"No, I knew this was coming sooner or later." I feel her paint my lips in a longer-lasting blue ink. I would certainly rather wed one of the strongest warriors of the sea over one of the land.

When she finishes, I look at myself and see a true creature of the sea looking back at me, commanding power and control. I finish by placing a large sapphire pendant in the hollow of my neck as Friona places crystals on my skin.

"My girl, you are a vision only that the deepest faerie could dream of." I hear my father at my door.

I turn to see Whistryn wearing in his usual green court garments, his long white hair braided at the sides and falling down his back. He wears a small silver diadem that falls close to his grey eyes.

"Father," I smile, stepping away from Friona, "will you be coming to the Bright court?"

He shakes his head. "I fear that Kynus will attempt to murder me."

It's true that my uncle never approved of the union between Whistryn and my mother, but this cannot be ignored. We live on land at the edge of the sea because he cannot live underwater longer than a month at a time.

"It will just be mother and I?"

He nods. "When you return, I would like to take you hunting."

"Of course, I feel as though we haven't been in years."

"That's because the Cold Court has been preparing you to rule one day."

"When I rule, I will dedicate the grand hunt to you. After all, I know of no better hunter than my beloved father." I take his hand and he leads me out of the room.

* * *

I ride with my mother in a shell-like carriage. She dressed with as much ferocity as I. One thing I envy about her stunning appearance is her horns, capable of wearing asrai-forged rings. They are among the rarest creations only an asrai water smith can create.

"So, who am I to court?" I finally ask.

She looks at me raising a curious brow. "Ever so clever, my sweet. I told my mother you would find out."

"There are few secrets you can keep from me," I let out a chuckle. "Do not fret mother, I am prepared to do what's best for the Cold Court."

She sighs. "Which is why I want you to find someone who will make you happy. Marriages are just contracts, but to find a companion in one makes a tiresome rule more desirable."

"Father is worried when the time comes for you to rule," I say.

She nods. "It will be an uncomfortable period. I won't be able to see him for weeks at a time. Every moment with Whistryn is a blessing, but I will have you. You are my greatest treasure, Aurelia."

"Many faeries do not love their faelings as much as you love me."

"The sea folk are different," she says. "No matter what the land fae say, love is an important rarity. If you can though, please refrain from bonding with someone of substantial power."

"Let's just see if someone cares to get to know me first, mother." I smile and gaze out the window as we cross into the Bright Court.

When we step out of the carriage, we greet the high lord and lady. around us are several of the Sunstone Laoich. Kynus will not be attending us until the evening, as per tradition. His appearance will be an official declaration of his new title in this court. My uncle was always quite proud.

"Princess Lythe, it is a pity that your mate could not attend," Lord Fyraen bows. He cannot lie but he knows that there would have been tension if my father came.

"My daughter is here though," Lythe responds carefully eyeing the warriors around us. It is said just one warrior from the Sunstone Laoich could cut down ten opponents in a matter of minutes.

"Of course. It is a pleasure to see you again, Lady Aurelia." Fyraen looks carefully at me for a moment.

My mother looks around. "Are we the first to arrive?"

Fyraen shakes his dark hair. "The last actually, everyone is inside enjoying a luncheon before the revel begins."

"I forgot how early the spring equinox begins. We usually do not celebrate it in the marine," Lythe says.

Kynus' mother, the high lady of the Bright Court smiles bleakly. "Yes, Prince Daeleon mentioned that once."

Lythe does not hesitate in her stride. It's no secret that her father had an affair while with her mother and that Kynus loves my grandmother more than his own. I believe that the high lady resents my family for that.

We walk inside the home of stone and orange moss. Roots hold the walls together in dramatic shapes.

The revel will have faeries of all sorts crawling all over the estate, but right now, this meal is reserved for each representing the courts scattering over Arcadia.

I feel the energy of the high faeries seeping through the walls. Being half-human is very tedious because it means I can never be fully immune to their tricks and charms. I know they see me as a slight problem, but nothing more than an annoyance.

The large troll opens the grand wood door to reveal a sun-adorning room with a long table, the food already gone, but the high faeries sitting in debate amongst one another. I have only met a few of these fae at court; the rest were at revels I've attended but never approached.

"Announcing her royal highness, Princess Lythe, and her daughter, Lady Aurelia." A troll peeks its head out of the wall before vanishing.

"Typical of the Cold Court to be tardy," Queen Titania announces at the head of the table, tucking a strand of golden hair behind her ear. Her daughter Fhanna and her son Azlyon sit to her right. His smirk snares my attention, as though he is pulling at my hair without even approaching me.

Across from him is Laeraan of the Unseelie, a strong warrior with a thirst for blood. She is also one of the most beautiful faeries I have ever met. At her side are the Dark Court royalty, Lords Drion and Septimius.

The Seelie and Unseelie sit across from one another as rivals. Their hate sinks so deep that one wrong move could start another war. The last one only just ended when I was a babe in my mother's arms.

"We don't celebrate spring like the land folk," I say for my mother. "Queen Titania, I believe you know that."

Lythe tenses at my side.

Laeraan smiles, allowing her forked tongue to flick out. "Oh my dear, you have matured so much since we last met."

"I'm sure there will be more time to become acquainted at the revel." Lythe looks around the room, pausing at Azlyon and his sister. "How has the Seelie Court been faring since the twins fell?"

The twins, Anul and Enal, were two lethal weapons in the form of Oberon's children. It was said that the king's first faelings were born of faerie and sphinx. They led his armies and served as the king's silver generals, the highest military rank in the Seelie Court. Anul cared more about fighting rather than politics. Enal followed her brother into even the most dangerous battles. If someone saw one, the other was near.

Azlyon turns his chin towards Lythe. "We lost two beloved fae. However, the Seelie will only prosper and grow. It is in our nature."

"My sympathies, you lost ones so close," I say, sitting down. "At the end of each day, kin are the only thing you have."

"I wouldn't expect a half-breed to even comprehend how the Seelie Court conducts itself." Azlyon does not even look at me.

"Just as a Seelie does not understand the Cold Court. I believe that in my short time of living, I've learned more about your court than you have mine." I lick my sharp teeth.

Azlyon is a faerie that many do not cross. He is dangerous, wicked, and quite calculating. Lythe has warned me about him. She said he was so emotionally detached that she wondered if he even had a soul.

"Enough," Queen Titania commands. "Thank you for your sympathies, Lady Aurelia. It has been quite a long day, I will see you all tonight."

The queen nods and the Seelie faeries stand and leave the luncheon. Then the Unseelie and dark follow in another direction.

"Aurelia, he is not someone to pick a fight with, I thought I taught you better,"

"I won't stand by as he and his family continue to insult us. We are not a lesser court!" I breathe deeply.

My daughter, we are here as officials representing our court. We are not in times of war. We must conduct ourselves with poise and careful selection. Her voice lingers in my mind.

I nod.

"I have to meet with the Unseelie, please do not stir anything." She kisses my cheek and walks out of the room.

I hear slow clapping as Azlyon falls out of the shadows like silk falling on the floor, elegant and fluid. Quite appropriate for a hidden prince to make himself known. The Seelie adore their dramatics.

"Does the prince of Seelie wish to treat with the Cold Court?" I ask.

He says nothing as he approaches like a wolf amongst sheep. It is only when he is several paces away that he stops and examines me.

"You are quite bold to say those things in front of us," he says. "You see, if you weren't of some significance to your court, you would be quite dead."

"We are not enemies Prince Azlyon," I say simply, "but how can I allow you to disrespect me when, in several centuries, I very well could be next in line for my court's throne?"

"The Seelie Court is superior to other courts, including your deep cold. We were the first from which all others came. The ancient magik we hold dear to us would make your glamour look like play." He pauses. "So little one, how are we going to settle this?"

"Simple—I am going to my chambers to prepare for the night, and at the revel, I will have a splendid time while you spend time with your folk." I throw him a sharp smile.

"Oh?" He cocks his head. "So you choose the revel then..."

He whispers something I can't quite hear.

A root crawls through the cracks of the wall and slithers towards me. I try to step back but it crawls up my body and secures itself around my wrist like a wooden bracelet, one on so tight there is no chance of sliding it off.

"What is this?" I narrow my eyes.

"You will find out at the revel tonight," I hear him say before he walks away.

"You have no right!" I try clawing it off.

"I have the only right," he growls. "It won't come off until I tell it to."

I can't tell my mother. She will scold me on how I react to his taunts and that I rely on my emotions rather than cold logic. I have but one person to turn to, someone who could actually help me without mentioning a single word to Lythe. My uncle Kynus, but he is staying away until the evening.

I step out to the foyer, where small green sprites tend to the roots and moss. As tiny and insignificant as they appear, they hear everything and are loyal to their masters. I know where my uncle's chambers are; as a girl I would drag him out to take me horseback riding.

Let's see if I can fit between the walls like I used to.

"Miss Aurelia," a sprite flew in front of me, "pathways are restricted in preparation for tonight, where do you need to go?"

"Can you take me to my room? The one I had as a child when I visited?" I ask. "I am feeling ill and that room always brought me joy."

She looks up and nods. "Follow me miss."

She leads me upstairs through the corridors. I peek down my uncle's hall and two warty grey trolls with rotting teeth and stone clubs stand at his large oak door. They see me and storm at me, a thunderous sound booming through the corridor. I would flinch if I am actually in any danger

"Whaaaaa-" one snorts.

"I am taking her to her room, don't fret, she needs to prepare for her uncle's revel tonight," the sprite scolds him with her finger.

He shrugs back and trudges down the hall, dragging his club on the stone floor. Trolls are not intelligent by any means and even the servants in this home hold rank. The head of the house was almost always a snowland elf, a close cousin of the sidhe. From there it fell all the way down to the brownies.

My door opens for me and everything is just as I left it before. It appears that this one space never changes even though it is regularly cleaned. The curtains along my bed are tied, ready for me to pretend I live in a dungeon where only the heroes go to save the court.

I smile and thank the sprite for her time. She tells me that if I leave, I am to knock on the door thrice. High fae are extremely proud but Lythe taught me to respect everyone because we are all connected.

"*Kyn*, reveal yourself should you be here," I call out, magik lacing in my words.

It is as though the room becomes clearer, as though I can see past all glamour through new lenses. If there are any faeries here, I would see through their magik.

I sigh in relief—there are none but I.

Immediately, my feet take me to the massive wardrobe built of a living tree trunk. I press inside one of the hidden holes I discovered long ago revealing my little tunnel connecting many different rooms in this manor.

I slide through, tearing the hem of my dress slightly. It matters not though; no one at the revel will notice. It is a tight squeeze, and I crawl and slide through roots and over stone. There are tiny pin-size openings where light pours in from the halls, looking like sprinkles of sunlight decorating the musty shadows between the walls.

I turn a slight left and find myself at a familiar dead end.

"*Kyn,* open," I say as the dead-end opens to a large curtain covering the wall. I slide out and lift the thick fabric of leaves and silk away.

My uncle is wearing a loose-fitting shirt, tight only at the cuffs. His bright red hair is pinned up with autumn leaves and citrine gemstones. His trousers are a bloodsilk woven from fallen wyverns.

He stands facing the window overlooking the blossoming grove of yellow and purple riken trees. A small stream flows gracefully through the trees. I didn't have to look to know of the breathtaking scenery behind the estate.

"Quite the little snake my niece has become," he says without turning.

"How did you know it was me?" I protest.

"You are far too loud," he turns, "but you are breaking the rules of today, of my day."

I nod. "I wouldn't if it wasn't important."

His cat-like eyes lower to my wrist. " An ororoot. Tell me, how did you manage that happening?"

"The high prince of Seelie thinks I offended him. I need to get this thing off."

"Aurelia, Prince Azlyon is not a wise person to insult. He is unpredictable amongst the fair. Only very powerful creatures can summon an ororoot and have it latch onto their target, and only they can remove it."

"So there is no way?" I ask, "What will happen?"

"You will be his toy for the duration of the root, I must tell—"

"Don't tell Lythe! Please!"

"Do not meet his eye tonight, that will solidify the strength of the ororoot since it is the third most powerful day of the year." He walks closer touching the root on my hand carefully. "It looks like you were fortunate, there is a time in which it will leave you."

"When?"

"I cannot read ancient Seelie arcadian." Kynus drops my wrist and picks up a paintbrush dipping it in ink. He wants to look perfectly wild tonight.

"How ancient?"

"The language the first fae created. It lives along with Oberon, and when Oberon dies, so will the language as well as any memory of the words that form it."

"So that's it?"

"What do you expect of me?" he says. "You are fortunate I took time out of my day to even look at that infernal root."

My uncle is helpful, but always leaves more undone than complete.

* * *

That night, I step out of the manner looking at all of the bonfires and drinking. Faeries dance, sing, and worship the spring moon. Others rut against each other like animals, while royalty sit elegantly on their stone thrones in clean garments.

Titania's crown illuminates her yellow hair as though she is born of starlight, while her daughter is more of a shadow, carefully watching all of the amusements. As to where her son is, I do not know.

Lord Septimius walks over to me, a naked elf clinging to his left arm while a nymph grasps his right. "We have humans to enjoy, to hunt, and to play with when Lord Kynus arrives."

"Perhaps I will partake in a little hunting later."

"Do you want to join us? There is a nice little cave for privacy near the pond." He raises an eyebrow.

Revels are nice because one can be wild and without remorse for one's actions, but tonight I will not let my body control me.

"Sweet Septimius, perhaps next time we can, but I don't like to share my conquests." I touch his sharp jawline, looking at the two faeries.

"Next time you could be married," his voice is seductive. "Word travels quite fast, my sweet lady."

"Are you offering?" I ask raising a brow. While it would be acceptable, I rarely care for his court.

"While a life with you would be most pleasurable, I'm afraid I don't wish to spend my life trapped in court duty," he responds.

I smile, changing the course of discussion, "Where is Prince Azlyon?"

"You are bold, my lady," Septimius smirks. "The Seelie high prince would be the biggest conquest you could ever make, but is it achievable?" He looks at my wrist.

"I don't intend on marrying one who has insulted me," I say, hiding my hand behind my back. "I would rather marry a troll."

"That could be arranged," a cold voice lingers behind me. I freeze at each word.

"Please don't marry too fast, I have yet to taste your skin," Septimius whispers before walking away.

"What are you planning?" I ask carefully keeping my eyesight down.

He walks around to face me and whispers, "I have discovered a problem between myself and the Seelie throne. I had every intention of you serving my family and I during tonight's revel. Since there are few things acceptable to do to high faeries without causing war. But then through long discussion with my mother, I discovered something disgusting."

"Seelies never make any sense." I throw my hands up about to walk away when the root tightens.

"And your half-blood makes you wilder than your marine family," he says.

"I have not spoken to you before today, and yet you have me breaking ancient rules and placed in an ororoot trap!" I make the mistake of looking him in the eye.

Kynus steps into view as sprites carry his cape behind him. The high lord of the Bright Court is making his grand announcement when my uncle and I made eye contact. His eyes narrow for a brief second before returning the revellers' smiles. Each royal nods their head in acknowledgement as he takes his place next to the high lord of the Bright Court.

"Aurelia," Azlyon tugs my attention back to him, "I never spoke to you because I never had any reason to. But now I know the truth, you and I are two of one."

Time freezes.

Chapter 15: Down Below Where Yellow Eyes Rot

The Mounds, Court of Daeyed

"Itss wearing off," a group of voices speaking in unison fill my belly with mud and sickness.

My eyes are shut, simply opening them is a battle I am losing. Did someone take me away from the revel? I didn't even get to speak to my mother after speaking to Prince Azlyon. It is the first time in my life I felt so unsure.

"Where—" I breathe weakly as if the weight of the winter star sat atop my body, crushing it deeper into Arcadian soil, "—is Lythe?"

"Masster sshe its sstill under—" a deep voice says.

"Shush, fiend!" a hungering voice growls.

"The one who rememberss orderss uss foolss, heed him!" several voices cry out in distortion.

I feel claws stroke my face. Was I kidnapped? I will have the ocean and the Bright Court ready to serve justice to my hosts.

"P-Prince Azlyon? Is he here?" I struggle to say.

The unseen creatures hiss at me.

"Oberon's favourite son," I hear him spit. "Azlyon stood aside as his father killed mine love and mine life."

"You sound alive," I gasp when the claw digs slightly deeper.

"Mine body is alive and well, but the soul is shattered!" I feel the venom in his voice, resentment trailing his words.

My eyes open slowly as though every fibre in my body commands them to work. The room is dim, save for a single candle at my side. There is pain in my arms, legs, and neck. As my eyes adjust, I see thin roots piercing my body, my torso wrapping in large sticky leaves.

Glowing pale yellow eyes pepper the shadows, but I can only see one clearly standing in front of me. His is very fair, but his face is cracked like porcelain. His eyes are a poisonous green but it is his mouth that frightens me. He has no lips, instead, his knife-like teeth point crookedly at different angles. A truly disgusting creature. I wonder if Oberon knew what it had become if it once been normal.

"Did you take me from the revel?" I ask, feeling more myself. "Why me?"

He cackles for a moment. "Aye. Mine sweet marine princess happened to step too far off the path."

"You are an ugly thing," I say without thinking.

"I was once quite quaint, a high-ranked knight wanting for nothing. I was even engaged to a kind lady of Seelie, who happened to be mine dearest companion. The cost for loving the wrong person is tragic forsooth," he says.

"I need to go back, my mother will worry. If you let me go, I won't tell her where I really was."

"I am afraid I am waiting for thy saviour to cometh. For thee is means to an end."

I was afraid he would say something like that. Perhaps I could pry information from him, command him with his true name.

"Well, since we are waiting for my saviour, whomever that may be, I do wonder what crime King Oberon charged you with...You mentioned love, did you fall in love with an inferior?"

He looks at me with a tilting head. "The lady's name was Elizabeth. The lady was a mortal mistress from a small village and she bore four of mine."

"Why should Oberon care? You were just a knight," I say, knowing that some knights swore to celibacy, but not all.

He stares at the candle, now half-melting. "I wast courting mistress

Taerlyn. She would come hither and sing to me after mine imprisonment."

He was engaged to a lady named Taerlyn. I wish I paid more attention to my mother during her tales of Seelie history.

"She must not have been from a very well-known family, if I've never heard of her," I carefully bait him, wincing as another root stabs my back.

"Villian, she wast Lord Rikkael's only daughter!" he growls, leaning closer licking my jaw, tasting my flesh as though I were a midsummer treat.

My mother mentioned this faerie. She said he was of the finest in all of Seelie's history. He had three children, all of which betrayed the crown. Dalziel, the golden son, was put to death for sympathizing with humans. Rhidion, the eldest, grew mad and tried to kill one of Oberon's lovers and was banished into the between. The daughter entered a forbidden pool and blamed Queen Titania for it. Things are becoming ever so clear.

"Elizabeth loved you, and when she died, your children perished. Bastard Prince Gideön," I whisper figuring out who he was.

He growls.

"Do they know you are alive?" I ask.

He shakes his head. "My kin think me dead. My father knows the truth."

"And does Taerlyn know what has become of you?" I press him.

He flinches in pain. "The world of mortals has killed her. The iron sickness. Her son told me so, through the stone and dirt."

"You should know that the world believes you to be gone. Your brother is expected to rule after King Oberon."

"Which one will rule? Will it be Azlyon?" He turns around to face the shadows. "Tis quite a pity that he who once resented the crown now wishes to leadeth."

I sigh and feel the roots dig deeper in.

"What are these things doing to me, Knight Gideön?"

"Stealing thy half-blood soul." He relaxes. "After we feast on thy bones and flesh."

Lythe would always find me when I hide in the reefs near the palace of clawing coral. It seemed wherever I was, she would find me. Could she see where I am now? Under so much earth and stone? The sea is vast and quite dangerous, but we cannot rely on Lord Leviathan's wisdom here. She will have to rely on our land kin, who are far more noxious than we.

I can't shake this strange illusion that I dreamt of another life where I was born in a human country, a place where faeries were feared like wild animals. A world where my mother could not raise me, and I was stolen away to be used by humans. It felt real to me, just like the revel only hours ago.

I blink. "No, something is wrong... My mother is so distant from me, my uncle... He is distant in another way."

The branches tighten as their master lunges at me, full of teeth dressing in rot. "A saviour doest not needeth to be a relative, real or not. Tis' just another tasty meal for us."

He bites my arm and I scream.

Something clings to my skin like acid eating away bone and flesh. The burning sensation sends jolts of lightning throughout my body. I taste blood in my mouth where my teeth bite down on my tongue. Never had I felt so much misery as I did at this moment.

"Do thee enjoy pain?" The candle goes out.

I hear a choir of whispers cloud the space I could once see, the faerie melding into shadows. My heart races until I collapse.

* * *

I cannot open my eyes when I regain consciousness, but I know I'm somewhere dark and damp. Where was I?

"Itss beginning again," voices cackle.

"Where is my mother—Princess Lythe?" I say weakly.

"Masster sshe iss sstill under—" a shrilling voice pierces my ears.

"Silence fiend!" an animalistic voice growls.

This seems somewhat familiar, but I was never trapped like this before. Someone from the revel must have been preying on me.

"The one who sstill rememberss demandss uss, we musst heed him!" several voices cry out in pain.

Something touches my arm, my eyes slowly open to a monster with rotting teeth and hungry eyes.

"Thee happened to step too far off the path," he snickers. "Thee is quite the sight, pity thou will not recall until death."

Just as the creature begins to lean closer, bright light engulfs the room.

I shut my eyes and hear screeching as hundreds of monsters hiss and cry out in blinding pain. The toothy faerie is easier to make out in the chaos.

"Villian!" His voice is sharp as he laments in torment. "That is magik of the heathens, the pure and deformed! How dare thee enter mine mound kingdom?"

I crack my eyes open as the warmth of the light bounces off my skin.

"It's been some time since you have seen the sun, I thought I would bring it here while I retrieve a dear companion." A dark silhouette steps in front of the source of the glittering white blinding light, a tall lithe figure belonging to a man.

"You?" the voice sobs. "I want that lady, for she is payment for letting the king sendeth me hence."

"I barely recognize you, Gideön." The voice leans over the crumpling figure on the floor. "I suppose since Oberon's death, the magik keeping you alive and trapped has distorted."

"Mine king father died?" the figure asks, trying to get up.

If Oberon died, war must be breaking out on the surface. This is not good for the Cold Court. I have to get out of here as soon as possible.

I wiggle and pain erupts in my body. My head rolls forward and I look down to see blood and yellow slime drenching me. Gashes and bite marks cover me as though I am being eaten alive.

I immediately feel sick.

"The world moves on without considering the values of the creatures that dwell here," the stranger lets the light die just a little, "but know that if you touch her again, I will rip you apart finger by finger, arm by arm, and leg by leg. Do you understand, Gideön?"

"I do. I need to know, is it true? When I reached into her soul, I felt something," Gideön cries out.

"It is quite true," he pauses. "May I take her peacefully?"

"Make the burning cease and thee may," the faerie moans. "I can only direct those folk for a time, but they ultimately doth what they wish. This means you must move apace."

I feel hands at my wrists at first, then a sharp pain shoots through my body as the roots slide out. I gasp at the familiar face above me—Azlyon.

"I-I know we've had our differences, but I'm so sorry to hear about your father," I whisper as I go limp in his arms.

He looks at me and sighs. "We must get to safety, and then I'll look into what he did to you"

He helps me into clothes that compress my wounds. Azlyon took these garments from the floor near the bastard prince.

Be quiet, they are all around us, but this cavern is safe—temporarily at least, I hear Azlyon speak directly in my mind.

Those muddy grey creatures that spoke in hissing voices were something I have never seen before.

What happens when we escape? With your father dead, there should be war. Does my mother know where I am? I ask him. *Does Queen Titania reign or will you?*

I felt him go rigid at the sound of his mother's name for a moment. *How far gone are you? Do you know who Cicero is?*

A human name? I've never held a conversation long enough with one to find out. I am surprised you have though, I respond, wincing from the pain.

He looks upward. *We have one chance at escape, Aurelia. You need to use all your might to hold onto me, I cannot support you without assistance. It will be painful but we are so close to the surface.*

I feel weak. If I were a pure-blooded faerie, these gashes would've healed by now.

"Am I going to die?" I breathe, feeling the weight of my eyelids.

No, you are not.

Faeries can't lie. Prince Azlyon knows something I do not, and I must trust in his words and fight the sleepy death that lingers around me.

I hold onto him with all my body and soul. I will every ounce of magik to keep myself from falling over. Death would be such a simple fate.

His tunic is thick but easy enough to grasp. I feel our energies touch, perhaps because I am fading and he is strong. I embrace his energy with my entire being bringing me relief and peace.

He helps me wrap my legs around him, careful not to touch the throbbing wounds. When they bend, a stream of thick, warm blood soaks my tunic. If the bleeding continues, I surely will die.

My father will kill you if something goes wrong. I wince.

I look at his face raising in confusion for just a moment.

A human? He appears to be attempting to conceal his disbelief.

How dare you mention that filthy creature. My father, Whistryn, may not be high in any court but he is still of the sidhe. I try to remain calm, for anger only opens my wounds further.

Hissing and snarling noises grow nearer. They claw their way through stone, clay, and moss. The grinding and pulling of things itch in the back of my mind to the point of worry.

Azlyon does not respond to me or them. Instead, he focuses on the earth just above him. He looks carefully at it but still does not move. His hands call forth roots deep within the earth, which slither around us and carefully clasp me to him so I wouldn't have to rely on my fading strength.

The noises stop for a few moments before they intensify, closer to our direction.

"They know we're here, it's time, little river," he says.

I raise my brows together, wondering why he is calling me that.

Just then, I see an ashen face snarling its way through the wall. I gasp at the creature, preferring the shadows that hid them before.

Azlyon chimes, his voice in another older language, and then we fold into a blinding light. More grey monsters claw their way through the walls, and as they crash into us, they burn away as though they were made of paper rather than flesh.

They howl like dogs as their limbs melt away. Others who stay back hiss at us. I roll my head back to look at Azlyon before a burst of magik throws us upwards, burning the ground away before it hits us.

Tears form at the corners of my eyes as the wind hits my face, I drop my arms and legs. The vine tightens as my grasp weakens.

"Hold on!" the prince demands.

"I-I can't! It hurts!" I cry out.

"Aurelia, you must!"

I try to put my arms around him. I feel our joining energies fading. He can only do so much for me and my body is dying.

My hands clasp at his back, giving both of us a sliver of hope of making it to the surface. "I cannot hold much longer!"

We break through the surface and moonlight greets us. The earth is already stitching itself back together to maintain the prison for the bastard prince.

The root holding us together slithers back down into the earth. Azlyon stands and looks me over. "We have to get off the mounds, I will have to carry you."

He lifts me in his arms before I can even respond. I look down numbly and see that he is soaking in blood. My eyes fighting to shut and my breath slow.

"Aurelia, I am giving you one single order, stay awake until we get to Woyldlan," He begins to sprint and I look up at his eyes. His focus is worrying.

"Tell my family that they mean everything to me," I slur my words a bit.

His grip tightens.

"You are not dying today. Daeyed needs you… I need you." His voice is absolute and commanding, but even he cannot master the goddess of death when she comes to greet a dying faerie.

I smile and close my eyes.

Chapter 16: Gentle Pain

Woyldlan, Court of Daeyed

It is dark. If this is death then perhaps it truly is as dreary as the elders claim. Or perhaps it is just one of many paths, and those who have killed so many people end up in this tormenting darkness.

I haven't killed anyone before, have I? Questions swim around my mind until I hear clear voices floating about in the distance.

"She must be foolish to even step on the mounds. What did she think would happen? Half-breeds are quite volatile, I think and lack the discipline of the fae," an older voice says. "She must be taken to the springs at dawn, then we will see if she will regain full strength or evaporate into unworthy nothingness."

"Be careful with your words, Sithen Dochtúir," I could swear it is my uncle speaking. "She is the last marine royal despite her impurity."

I hear a chair or a table move. "My apologies your royal highness, but if she truly is meant to save us then perhaps keep her on a tighter leash."

"I doubt that would have stopped her, but if she overcomes this she will learn a valuable lesson." Kynus' voice is quite clear now. "Sithen Dochtúir, where is Prince Azlyon?"

"It was a pleasure to see that he was alive and well. Truly my king, Oberon, lives on through his legacy of the silver prince." The voice sounds hazy with awe. "My prince was here all night, but he left this morning to the mounds."

"Seelie, take care of my marine kin while I step out, if she wakes send word to both of us," Kynus' voice is final.

I look for these voices but I cannot see them. Am I perhaps only dreaming of death? It would favourable than facing the wrath of my grandfather who would surely tear the world apart and destroy that trapped Seelie prince.

"Aurelia, if you are the end of us then I hope the gods take you from this world at the springs." Someone is close—the voice Kynus was speaking to.

I try to respond, unsure if my voice can be heard. "The gods would have taken me in the earth when Gideön harvested me."

There is the crash of glass and hurrying steps. "How fascinating, you are far stronger than I initially thought. Gideön betrayed all of the fae. Like your mother did, but at least his half-breed offspring died long ago. One of them fell by my blade, forged from breath by the last frosyre dragon. It's called Liebreaker, it silences those who tell untruths such as his son, and perhaps one day, you."

Magikal weapons are not always named, for they have to prove themselves worthy of a name. In a sense, they are like living creatures that obey their masters, and once they have a name they only respond to the warrior who helped earn that name. The weapon and wielder are companions.

"As long as your Seelie prince wishes me to be alive, that will not happen," I whisper into the void.

"Oh, my dear creature, I know the truth about his soul and your past, and while I may not enjoy those revelations, he will do good by us. When you slip up, he will be forced to make a choice. Though I am willing to challenge you to prove me wrong. Let Liebreaker remain sheathed," the voice coos back.

I take a breath and the air around me crystallizes into whites, greys, and blues. It is beautiful to see something begin out of nothing. Magik at this very moment feels so close yet so distant from me.

I close my eyes for a long moment, feeling the air around shift like sea foam surrounds me. I taste salt crystals at the corners of my mouth. The sea was a marvellous place close to my heart, but nowhere close to where I am at this moment.

I finally wake to a fire-lit wooden home. I'm on a table, tree knots digging into my back. The roof above me is leafy green and glowing pixies peering down behind the broad leaves. It is cottage teeming with life. Yet all I could think about was how sore my body is.

"Finally, I thought I would be speaking to a half-unconscious creature for a few more hours," a bored voice says.

I look over to see a faerie no more than several inches tall standing at my face. It had long pointy ears—like most of the fae—but its ginormous blue slanting eyes peer deeply into mine. It has wings but they were oddly still on its back. It was slightly bigger than the pixies.

"Were you the thing tending to me?" I ask "Sithen Dochtúir?"

It looks at me and vanishes, only to materialize on my chest peering down, "You are not very nice, but yes creature."

"I should know what you are but..."

"I suppose I better be the one to break it to you, but your family, your life in Arcadia was but a lie fabricated into your memories by the forgotten unsidhe. Their apparent leader, well, he has a vast pool of intact memories of the world he tricked you with to keep you calm." The tiny faerie's rough voice scratches my ears. "You did gain significant knowledge about us through him, it will never be enough."

I shake my head. "My mother, Lythe—"

"Is quite dead, died long enough ago for you not to have been raised by her." It cracks a blood-crusting smile.

"You are wrong," I say but am unsure of myself.

"The creature thinks I lie when only it has the power to do so here." It rematerializes across the room, picking up what looks like a tiny bottle of milk to drink. "Let the springs cure the delusion."

"What are you?" I ask.

He starts to laugh uncontrollably. "The creature needs to understand how the world of the fair folk works or it will surely die or become entrapped. Creature, your question has so many tedious answers, one must be more specific for a straightforward answer."

I blink. How dare he speak to me, daughter of Lythe, like this!

"What is the name of your faerie breed?" I ask tiredly.

He materializes with his bottle beside me. "I suppose that is good enough for a little monster like you. The mortal word for what I am is geancanach. You may know my cousins, the brownies? You should be kissing my feet, I healed your ridiculous wounds. If it weren't for the princes I would not have bothered, but you retained my services debt-free."

"Did they treat with you?"

It laughs. "I suppose they did. I owed Prince Kynus a seven-hundred-year-old debt. An easy task like this is far less than what he did for me."

"It must be ironic for you, I think, to heal me when you would rather end my existence," I say.

The faerie finishes the milk and sneers at me. "Who says I will not in the future? There are many possibilities."

I smile weakly as the creature disappears out of sight.

* * *

Azlyon returns with Kynus. They are deep in conversation until they see that I awake sitting by the fire. My body is healing quicker with the potion Sithen Dochtúir gave me, though my mind is still foggy with so many memories of two lives, one as a faerie lady and another as a trained killer. I'm not sure which was true and which was fabricated, though Sithen Dochtúir knows.

Kynus is the first to walk closer to me. His eyes are afire with relief as he pulls me close. I feel at home in his arms, like I was with my mother. I feel hidden desperation in him, one that longs for his kin. I also feel something trying to fight it.

"Uncle, don't worry," I say. "I am fine."

He stiffens slightly and clears his throat as he steps back. I see his bright red hair shining brightly in the firelight. He is truly the embodiment of a bright ethereal lord.

"I told you not to call me that," he snaps stepping behind Azlyon.

Sithen Dochtúir appears on the table next to me. "The half-blood is still under the silly, yet tricky, delusion of the Unsidhe. One of you must take the creature to Eldyrgrove Springs."

Kynus is silent for a moment. "In case something goes wrong, I won't be able to save her mind or body."

"Then I will go," Azlyon said. He hasn't taken his eyes off of me since he stepped into the home, almost like he is watching me to see if I will break at any moment.

Sithen Dochtúir rolls his eyes beside me. I look at him curiously but he only raises a finger to his mouth, telling me to remain silent.

"All of you are crowding my home, take the faerie born," Sithen Dochtúir waves everyone off.

I look at the geancanach in the eye. "If you are so small, why is everything in this cottage our size?"

The faerie looks at me as though I am ridiculous. "Perhaps you are too big for things your own natural size? Perhaps you are making do with things my size? Don't ask foolish questions, creature."

I raise my brows and Kynus lets out a small chuckle under his breath. Azlyon, however, turns and walks outside.

I look at my uncle and he nods as if to follow.

A few pixies fly down, their green skin reflecting the pale firelight. All seven grasp my sleeves, their tiny hands the size of a fingernail, and pull me up with a gentle force.

Sithen Dochtúir appears in front of my shaky legs- standing atop a wood-knot cane he willed into existence. I hesitate before taking it.

"Bring it back to me or I'll sew your liar's mouth shut permanently, always hungry but unable to eat," Sithen Dochtúir glowers.

I blink. "And if this spring ruins my mind and I forget?"

"Oh, creature, for your sake you must hope our high prince returns it to me, I can haunt those who are broken and make their lives quite uncomfortable." The faerie smirks.

I press the cane down and step out the door, into the night air. It smells of mead, and burning mutton. The energy is thinner and easier to disappear into.

"He used to be taller and far more handsome," Azlyon says. "He would lure human women and bed them before the war. Time away from the humans has given him a bad temper and changed his shape."

"He has a temper?" I respond with a smile.

I look around and there is an assortment of faeries dancing in the night. There are leafy homes built into giant trees and smaller huts. There are wisps, spriggins, goblins, and nixies celebrating the night together. They are among other breeds of fae I did not recognize. Even faelings are out dancing and pouring wine.

"This was who we were before," Azlyon says. "We were guardians, protectors, and lived mostly in peace with one another."

"Why do you say were? My pasts are confusing me." I shake my head.

"The truth is, as we have attempted to tell you, though your fabricated reality seems easier and preferable to this chaotic dying world we live in now." Azlyon takes my free arm.

I look up at Azlyon. "Perhaps after the springs, we could dance under the stars? It's been quite a while since I've had fun, and being around Sithen Dochtúir is about as uplifting as being around a bean sidhe."

He looks at me oddly, as though something has taken over me. I simply smile in return and continue forward on the path we were initially heading on.

"Do you remember when the king's servants had their own ball in the guest palace? You practically dragged me there, and I caught you dancing quite terribly on one of the balconies? You haven't danced in front of anyone since," Azlyon recalls. "Lorkus was with me, I think he was sent by the king to make sure nothing broke—which, I may add, is absurd because a party is not a party until the breaking begins. I think you were dancing with a spyling you threatened to be there."

I raise my brows. "That doesn't sound like me, I'm just a lady of marine."

Azlyon doesn't miss a beat. "I couldn't see your face, but I knew you were smiling beneath it. Even though you were quite tragic to watch, I enjoyed seeing you attempt to have fun because you often avoided it."

I glance at him strangely. "Then why did you put an ororoot on me?"

He looks genuinely confused for a brief moment. "I'm not sure how much you know about one of our ancient roots, but I assure you that I never used one on you. They are so rare since the iron came that there are only several in this world, and all almost planted at Daelin Castle."

"I am not sure if you are all tricking me to believe one past over another." I look away.

"Down in the mounds, you were the target of corrupted power," Azlyon says. "When you challenged me on the road and were snatched—let's just say I haven't felt fear like that since my family sacrificed themselves."

"You revealed something to me, and I want—no, I need to know if it is true," I say to him. "In one past you told me we are two of one, but I can't help but wonder if that means that you are my—"

We stand before steaming pools of the Eldyrgrove. The trees around us dress in white leaves as the ground below transitions from grass to shimmering black stones. Above the water are bright balls of light floating everywhere, a broad mixture of will-ó-the-wisp and morstone. My fate leads us here tonight.

"I will answer all your questions when your mind is clear. If this is successful, the real past will remain while the other will feel as distant as a memorable dream." Azlyon takes my hand.

"If I don't make it out, please bring back Sithen Dochtúir's cane." I look into the prince's eyes.

He half-smiles. "Of everything, you are worried about the cane?"

I shrug and dip my toes in the spring, every hair on my body standing straight as a surge of energy cascades upwards. I am wearing nothing more than a simple white nightgown with bloodstains.

Azlyon takes my hand and steps in the water, fully clothed, guiding me in. This magik, I fear, will be too strong for my weaker body to endure.

"Little river," he says, "you have to trust me."

I feel strange in the warm water. Surrounding the edges of the forest, peering at us, are little gnomes. Their cheeks are rosy, and their triangle teeth show when they smile back.

Azlyon steps backwards, but when I follow, I trip over a larger stone. He is quick to catch me but I am already neck-deep in the thick water.

"Close your eyes," he murmurs against my ear.

I close my eyes against the starlit sky. The darkness rushes around me again, like salting a wound, only the wound is my mind.

Chapter 17: Of Gods And Agreements

Eldyrgrove Springs, Court of Daeyed

A man stands under the moonlight of my mind, as though I am moving into the depths of another realm through the healing of the spring. He supports himself against a staff made of twining wood. He wears a blood-red cloak with white fur around the shoulders. I cannot see his face but I see long, greying hair pouring out of the hood. I can't help but wonder who he is but even now I am not afraid of this man, I feel the calm of early morning when bread bakes and birds sing.

"Come over here, my child." His voice is deep, raspy, and aged longer than the lifespan of many.

I walk over the darkness to him. A faint blue aura surrounds him. His worn face is cracking with wrinkles and his eyes reflect the world. Different images with different people, animals, land, and water flash through eyes the colour of life itself.

I fall to my knees after seeing my own reflection in his sapphire circlet. It is dull in comparison to his. I feel so helpless, and need him despite my unworthiness.

"May I ask your name?"

"Aurelia, my heart bled for you many times yet you ignored me. I saw you since you were a girl. We watched you at our temple every day, allowing that priest to torment and desecrate you slowly. If only you stood at my altar and genuinely prayed for me, I could have aided you."

I look up into those earthy eyes realizing who he was, "My Lord Dian

Cecht." My voice cracks as I begin to sob at his feet. "I-I..."

"You did not truly believe in me, and yet your anam-connected has allowed the essence of evil inside." He places a hand on my cheek gently.

I look down and hear a smokey laugh. "You do not know what I say. Let your blessed companions answer that. Now, you come to me to cure your mind of the falsities that plague it."

He pulls my chin up and his eyes now reflect the starry sky. I look up and see Azlyon holding my body reflecting in Lord Dian Cecht's eyes. Then I see Lorkus and Fyfe arguing near the castle stone. The world is moving along outside my mind.

"I will need you to side with the fae in exchange, for only you can ensure Arcadia thrives without the corruption of the crow." He pulls me up, looking down at the cobblestone well beside us.

I look him in the eye with careful precision. "I will."

"I leave a gift of knowledge for you, to navigate and commune with the fae." He smiles as the cane disappears. "I will meet with you once more before you finally enter Mag Mell."

I tilt my head and, in a flash, he pushes me down the well. The small light surrounding him goes out and I am falling into the darkness. My breath goes tight in my chest before I hit the bottom.

* * *

I gasp and look into Azlyon's eyes. He is still holding me as the night disappears into morning. The gnomes slowly fade into the trees as though their source of entertainment was now over.

I take a breath and stand on my own, shaking my head. The water turns violet and begins to bubble in the light.

Azlyon doesn't show concern.

"I trained with Cicero, who is you," I gasp. "My mother is...dead."

He sighs. "This is a relief, you were a completely different person."

"Azlyon, I saw a god!" I said. "I-I know too much..."

He shrugs. "These waters were blessed by the gods."

"You don't understand, I saw a god, something responsible for creation and I-I don't know why I was chosen to see him!"

"Slow down, you must remember that the fae are the chosen, we commune with the deities more often than other creatures." Azlyon places his hands on my shoulders.

"I had to make a deal with him," I say, "Lord Dian Cecht."

"Then you best keep to it."

"You don't sound concerned?"

"He is one of the better gods, fewer strings attached," Azlyon softly speaks.

Azlyon won't look me in the eyes after that. Instead, he helps me out of the spring, and all the scratches bruises and imperfections on my body are gone, as though I never left the luxuries of a palace…and I hate it.

"He did tell me something," I say as we sit on the edge of the springs.

There is a sweet smell that lingers in the air. The music in the distance dies, telling me that the small revel in the village Is coming to an end. I smile, remembering the dream-like world with my mother. It felt real, like a life I truly lived. A part of me wants it to be the real one, but I would have never sympathized with anyone but the fae.

"First, I need to know is why the gods care about what happens in this world, and second, what in the name of the gods is inside you?" I ask him.

Azlyon's eyes go wide. He is silent for a moment, probably trying to form his words carefully to confuse me, or perhaps to find a coherent way of speaking.

"If you're not going to tell me—"

"They care because if we are gone, their power will be as well. Arcadia is the root and birthplace of magik," he hesitates, lacing his hands together. "If the gods are gone, all the magik, including life itself, will fade away—in more than just our realm, though we will meet a more destructive end."

"Faeries were driven out of that other world? Why weren't they here to begin with?"

"The first faeries were born and lived here alongside their creators. This was once the realm of the gods until they decided that living in the void, a place between the fabric of life, was a preferable alternative where they could retain autonomy over their own individual magik." His voice is distant. "Yet they are tied to this realm for many other reasons unknown to me. We knew they would aid us, yet we did not know which one would come first."

I widen my eyes and stand to pace around. "Is this the part where you tell me that nothing is inside you?"

He looks onward at the pools. I can feel the tension building up under his skin as he battles his own thoughts. I hope nothing is inside him, because that would mean another problem that needs to be dealt with. I don't know if I could even consider dealing with that.

"Nothing is inside me," he pauses, "at the moment at least."

"What is that supposed to mean?"

"It means that I have the power to end the world or save it, because of The Morrígan." I hear him speak but do not see his lips move. "She chose me as her sword, her vessel to save Arcadia, all she needs is submission and to release the magik back into the world for a successful conquest."

"But you need to free the magik to fight, and only I can do that." I close my eyes already knowing my fate is bound to my deal. "Realistically, what would happen if I helped you?"

He catches my eye. "There would be tyranny and strict order for a while, for only the goddess will rule through me. Then when the world is saved from the mortal humans, the gods will bless the land to help restore Arcadia."

I look away and feel the wind caress my skin gently. I only want to continue doing my job for the king even though I despise him; then I could be safe and live as an example for other half-faeries like me.

"I need you to promise me that Lucia will live and be allowed to stay," I say.

"The Morrígan will not be pleased but I promise that Lucia, the woman who raised you, will not be killed, harmed, and will be allowed to stay in Arcadia by the end of the coming war," he vows.

"I also want my father and Lorkus to stay alive long enough for me to speak to them," I say.

"Very well."

"And Azlyon, I need you to promise me one more thing," I say.

"Getting quite demanding, are we not?"

"When the task is accomplished, come back to us without her inside." I sit beside him and lean on his shoulder. "I cannot lose you in this."

He raises his eyebrows, a careful smile tugs at his lips. "You must lose me if her vision turns to corruption. You must make the right decision for Arcadia even if I must be sacrificed."

"Is she with you now?" I press my palms into the cool grass.

"She is not, but one must remain cautious regardless," he looks around, "for other gods and monsters could be watching."

I shake my head. "I need you to promise me that you will come back before we consider the alternative."

He tilts his head. "A good assassin would not wait a good assassin would strike when the opportunity opened."

"A good assassin does what their master bids. I have no master. Should I decide to wait, I will most certainly wait. I don't want you to die as a martyr for the fae, I want them and whatever humans are left to be united and live together. You are my friend, and as a friend, I am asking you to promise me."

He sighs as though he had already lost. "I don't know how you'll achieve unification, but I will promise to try. In return, I need you to promise me that if the time comes, you will plunge a dagger in my heart."

"It won't come to that, but if you are truly gone, then I will end your suffering." I shut my eyes for a moment.

I feel a hand on mine, pulling me upwards in one cool stride. Light and shadows flutter around me as the cool breeze carries off a floral scent.

"Let us not waste time on such woes. I think it is time you meet the folk," he says against my ear, sending shivers up my spine.

My lips curve upwards. "I was wondering where they all were."

"Vikorus ordered them to stay off the roads." Azlyon allows me to take his arm.

"I see."

"I know you are wondering why, and I often forget how much slower human minds are—I don't mean to place you lower than us, I just mean that we are born with minds so developed we often do not have any meaningful interactions," Azlyon speaks quicker towards the end. "What we gain for knowledge we are underdeveloped in emotions."

"It does sound very belittling though," I sigh, knowing he meant no ill, "but in this case, I would wager that it has to do with the fact that he doesn't want me to see the fae?"

"Yes, that I suppose. Past that, I think he is trying to sabotage my plans regarding you."

"What exactly happened between the two of you?"

Azlyon runs a hand through his hair, "Do you truly need to know?"

There is that strange tension again, so I shake my head. Though I do need to know eventually because I fear my life depends on it. Vikorus doesn't like me and he doesn't like Azlyon. He does not enjoy that his future is in our hands.

Sitting on the edge of the stream leading out of the spring is a woman with very long blond hair and a golden comb. She is thin and naked, and watching us carefully through her dark eyes.

"As your high prince, I command you not to sing within hearing distance," Azlyon tells her. She bares her teeth in response.

"My prince is not pure, and neither is his mistress," she spoke hazily. "You will not choke, you will not go mad today."

"Are you a water sprite?" I ask.

She looks at me oddly. "My kind sang with your kin, the royals of marine, and yet you call a protector of the pure a sprite?"

I step back slightly. "Pardon me, I am simply trying to understand how this world—"

"Do not show weakness. If you weren't with the prince, I would use it against you." Her body starts to darken. "I would take your child years before you conceive, I would sneak into your home and change you."

I didn't realize until now but I was using Azlyon as a shield against her.

"Mother of Xaninos, protector of the pure spring, we take our leave and for any inconvenience or offence we may have caused, I will have three grains of pure gold scattered in your stream."

She smiles and then goes back to combing her hair.

The faerie appears as though nothing happened. And all it took was three grains of gold as compensation for offending her.

"We fae-kind take offence very seriously, and there must always be an exchange done to right the wrong, or else prepare to pay in blood or bone," he informs. "We are not greedy without reason, we expect what is owed and understand the importance of fair trade."

I blink for a moment. "I need to get the cane!"

I run back for the walking stick Sithen Dochtúir lent me. The gods have dealt me a hand with too many players, and I can't think about worrying over the consequences of breaking a bargain.

Ah, I was waiting for you to remember that. His words echo in my head once I return to his side. *The faerie we met is a Xana, one of the changelings.*

I roll my eyes and continue onward.

Back in the village, the sun slides in between the brilliantly rich colours of the trees. The tree trunks themselves are as wide as small stone homes in Jorthus.

Sithen Dochtúir appears at my feet and takes the cane, which shrinks to his size. He looks so different in the sunlight, uglier and slightly grumpier. Yet so many years are visible in his beady eyes.

He is looking me up and down. "Does the creature know who I am?"

"Yes," Azlyon says.

"Does the creature show dementia, loss of eyesight, hearing? Or perhaps the creature is following like a dog stripped of mind?"

"I am right here." I cross my arms. "And I am perfectly sane."

The geancanach narrows his eyes. "And what bargain did Lord Dian Cecht make with you?"

I tilt my head. "I don't know what you are talking about, besides if I did bargain with him, wouldn't that be my business?"

"Lying creature, if it affects me, then it very much is my business." The faerie was now on my shoulder.

"How strange it must be to be so small yet so persistent with those bigger than you."

"This monstrous creature will end us all, prince." He turns to Azlyon.

"She will be fine," Azlyon decrees and walks inside the geancanach's home.

I look at Azlyon, wondering how he lives day to day knowing he is a slave to his people.

"I know that look. The creature must not get any foolish ideas about the prince," Sithen Dochtúir's voice is firm.

"I don't know what you mean," I say, my eyes on the door of Azlyon's disappearance.

"Of course. Mortals are so oblivious to each and everything that goes on around them. The prince forged peace with the Unsidhe and apologized because you asked him to despite what they did to you. His undead kin will serve under Azlyon, yet when the time comes, they will be allowed to attend the revels so long as they harm no one. At least until he finds a way to change them back, which I know does not exist."

I blink.

Perhaps this was his way of showing me he was on my side. To further earn my trust.

"Are you against that?"

"It asks yet another foolish question. Of course I am!" Sithen Dochtúir pulls at my hair. "They are created from a magik so ancient, I fear what mark it will leave on Arcadia."

"Why would he do that?" I ask. "Is it because we are friends?"

"We do not have friends. We have arrangements, loyalty, and passion. I have arrangements with the princes and I will forever be loyal to Seelie leaders, but we do not do things like this, we don't tamper with ancient energy unless there was a certain belief in necessity." His voice is sharp.

I shake my head. "So then why listen to me?"

We have an arrangement but not blind loyalty.

"He may be able to lie but his actions are louder than the truth. Though I am only speculating, the whole story he told me could have been a lie, though I believe it to be true," he grumbles and disappears.

Azlyon, why didn't you tell me? I say to myself, willing him to hear.

"Sitting atop a castle, a maiden waiting to be rescued? Though what if she were a monster deceiving us this entire time, what if it were best if she died?" A plain voice muses before strong hands pull me backwards.

The wind sparkles in a beautiful silver flash. Flakes of metal cover the village and I whip around to see a legitar smiling at me.

A few sidhe turn their heads and disappear after screaming out in pain. A shrill of the wild pierces my ears, yet Haerton appears unaffected.

I turn to run but he clamps a manacle on my hand. Our eyes meet, and he looks like he's already won.

"If you come nicely, we won't kill Lucia," he whispers.

Chapter 18: When Sins Meet

Woyldlan, Court of Daeyed

I follow without hesitation. He leads me to the edge of the village where I see Belousa standing beside Tionne. There are prisoners in hoods held by thick rope. I meet my father's eyes, but he reveals nothing in his.

Haerton pushes me forward. "You shared secrets with the enemy. You are a disgrace to Jorthus, just like his majesty King Fyfe and General Titus warned."

"What of the man Cicero saw having an affair with the queen? What of the bastard prince who is less pure than you?" I ask.

Tionne goes rigid for a slight moment, revealing enough. "You know not of what you accuse."

"Oh, don't I?" I say. "I now know the truth. I know who my mother was and that she was third in line for the Cold Court throne."

Haerton turns on Belousa. "Why did you not mention this?"

I cannot go out, I cannot let them see me until you control the situation, Azlyon's voice is calm. *Do not make rash decisions.*

Too late.

"Fyfe will die, his kingdom will fall," I say, feeling a familiar dagger pressing into my free hand. How it got there, I do not know.

"You are foolish," Belousa says, before ducking around the Legitar and vanishing from sight.

"There are so many secrets hidden in this world, and your allegiance with the queen is no longer among them," I say to Tionne. "I know who you are, and I know who Lorkus is."

Tionne can't meet my eyes.

Haerton's grip is strong as he pulls me closer, whispering in my ear, "The general would prefer you alive, but I believe you are more trouble that way."

"It is time for this creature to make a choice," I say. I grip the hilt harder.

In a sliver of a second, I angle myself and kick him in the groin. As he grunts, I pull my arms up and plunge the dagger into Haerton's eye. The blade crunches through his skull as I fall on him.

Blood carpets the ground and splatters all over me. I feel it escaping through the back of his head. A gasp leaves his lips but he is already dead by the time I pull the blade back.

Tionne's eyes go wide.

This is the moment our true colours show. A moment of raw truth, betrayal, and unbridled anger in my eyes. For a moment, I see every memory unravel and every lie come to light. There is just us.

"Do you know who I am?" I ask, picking up a key that fell out of Haerton's pocket and unlocking the manacle on my left hand. He really should have put both on before we left the village.

"You are former Shadow Master Aurelia," he says carefully, "and you are an enemy of Jorthus."

"Both are true of course, but who I really am is Aurelia Nyetynslae, the daughter you sired and tossed away like nothing," I say, stepping closer. "I am the daughter of Princess Lythe of the Asrai. Tell me the truth, Tionne, I want to hear it from your mouth."

He shuts his eyes for a moment. "A faerie used me to create you, tricked me into love, but when she died, my mind cleared. I am in love with the queen, we were going to marry until King Fyfe forced her to marry him as revenge on his former wife...Why am I saying this?"

"Don't you believe in magik? Truths come freely where it dwells." I step closer, gripping the dagger tighter. "Does Lorkus know who you are? Did your chosen son know why you left me?"

"Stop please!" he says in pain, shaking his head. "I was going end your life the morning of your birth—but then you looked me in the eyes and stopped crying out for your mother. I couldn't keep you, it would be a death sentence, but there was this maiden in the village that prayed to the old gods. I gave you to her. I wrapped you in my cloak and carried you to her home."

I breathe in, releasing my pull on him a little bit. "You could have taken me into Flokael, you could have raised me there."

He nods. "I could have, but what of my son in my love's body? How could I abandon them in such a treacherous place as the palace?"

"Does the queen know who I am to you?" I tilt my head.

"I told her as soon as I could," Tionne sighs in defeat. "Aurelia, ever since you came to the palace, I watched you when I met with Cicero. I know we never met face to face until the princes came from Daeyed, but I was around."

"Stop." I raise a finger at him.

"Are you going to kill me?" he asks, almost challenging.

"Humans have a certain aspect of empathetic love that the fae lack, and you turned a blind eye. At the castle, you could have approached me and told me, but you didn't." I walk to him, leaving few steps between us. "I want to kill you—I deserve to spill your blood, but first, you are going to tell Lorkus how you betrayed him, how he is not Fyfe's heir and how you were a coward for not claiming your family. Then, and only then, will I end your pitiful disgusting life."

I look at my father's arms. They are twitching. I know he wants to reach for a weapon and fight, but he is a hunter. Hunters track and kill, but how would he fight against one who has trained to kill brutally and silently?

"Aurelia, there is so much I need to tell you, about—"

"*Kyn*, please assist my father, he moves far too much," I snap, cutting him off as roots crawl out of the ground, wrapping around his ankles and wrists tightly. He falls to his chest.

"I don't want to hear your tales. Perhaps you are content with all of your choices in life, but eventually, they do catch up to you," I say, my eyes trailing off to the other two humans.

I walk over, pulling the sacks off their heads one by one.

Two familiar faces peer up at me. Their wild grins stretch ear to ear looking clean. The legitars took care of them in a way I did not expect.

"Ah, Jupa, our lady is here!" Tian looks at the man from Trilan next to him.

"Lust and greed," I say, cutting their binds. "Tell me what happened."

"Only if you admit who is the most handsome, Miss Pride." Jupa stands up.

"Do not flatter yourself, rat." Tian sheepishly dusts off his shoulders. "There is no real competition here."

"Excuse me, sir, just because you have a fancy new eye does not mean you can see how terrible you look. It's quite tragic really."

I say, "Two of the princes are just in the village. I suggest you tell me what happened because they won't find your banter appealing."

They both stop and turn to me, a sparkle of fear in each of their eyes.

"The faerie woman released us from prison. We saw those men from Jorthus a moment before we were chained and bagged," Tian whispers. "She told the wailing woman as we left that we were to be transported to the princes for an early celebration, that the other men were enchanted. I didn't know a servant could get away with this!"

A servant couldn't get away with this. They do as they're told, the entirety of them did. It was also not a lie, she did bring them to the princes, and early was so subjective. One of the princes either betrayed the rest or this whole encounter was a setup. Whichever the case, the humans don't know the truth—but the faeries do.

"Once we were away from that black fortress, we were unbagged and thrown into the river to clean ourselves." Jupa looks around him.

"We saw a mermaid with plump breasts, shining hair, and eyes like rainbows. I fell in love..." Tian is dizzy.

"Tian, please, that creature tricked you into seeing what you saw." Jupa rolls his eyes.

I press my bloody hands to my temples.

"Er, lovely work," Jupa says, noticing the blood, "though the trick is not to make a mess."

I crack a smile. "We are in Daeyed, anything goes."

"I could marry you, you are the perfect lady," Tian smiles hazily, "deadly, powerful, and, my dear, we could make beautiful monsters."

I shoot him a glare. "As tempting as that sounds, Tian, the other women in the land would weep for a hundred years."

His eyes light up. "Jupa! I mustn't let the ladies down, so many to bed and too few to wed!"

Jupa crosses his arms. "Tian, get your thick skull out of thoughts of naked women and tell the story before we end up like her friends over there!"

"Very well, though this discussion is a bore. We were pulled out of the river and someone hit us, which, by the way, was not gentle. I then woke up sitting where we are now and then an eternity later, you came." Tian shakes his head and looks at Jupa. "I think we are the unluckiest men in the world!"

I smile, realizing they very well might be.

"Human," my voice calls for Tionne, when he doesn't respond, I kick him over so he is facing the sky. "Why did you take the prisoners?"

"Because he thought their intel of this world would be valuable to King Fyfe." Kynus strolls over with Belousa beside him.

"She—" I start but my uncle smiles.

"She did as I told her," Kynus states, "though earlier than I anticipated." His eyes fall to the female beside him.

I look at the two faeries and shut my eyes. "And why would you do that? There are so many problems with this plan of yours."

"It is a gift to you. I thought at least after some travelling, you could have a little celebratory treat, though he looks virtually unharmed..."

"I don't enjoy killing, but it is a necessity," I sigh. "I have plans for him to suffer, but right now I cannot stand the sight of him."

"How interesting. We may have a manhunt tonight, if you're interested," Kynus then whispers something to Belousa who in turn begins to drag Tionne away.

I look behind me to the two humans cowering into themselves. They are shaking and do not look at anything but their own feet.

"Did Azlyon know about your plan, Price Kynus?" I lick my lips.

His face twists into mischief. "No, and trust me, it was difficult keeping him inside that home."

"I don't trust you, but I believe he didn't know," I say. "As for these prisoners, they are better alive than dead, at least for now. They would be better suited for a tithe at Daelin castle."

"Hmm," he turns around. *You have two more charges under your wing. Any more and you will fall to your death. The crow will fly on.*

His footsteps echo in my mind. Two more I have to watch, two more lives on the line when they could have been spared by a quick death in this village.

"You are delaying the inevitable." Jupa sighs after the prince leaves. "They get what they want, and what they want is their country being rid of humans."

It is more like this entire realm, but I can't tell them that. There are ugly flaws in every creature, every sliver, and every blade of grass. Some kill, some steal, but all have a soul to hold compassion.

"Nowhere is safe," I look him in the eye, "so I need you both to bargain with me."

"She thinks she is funny," Tian says too quickly. "I will not make another bargain."

"What is the oath, Lady Pride?" Jupa tilts his head.

"You need to follow all of my direct commands without hesitation," I say. "In return, I swear I will not abuse this power in any way that leads you to harm."

Tian's eyes widen.

"How long?" Jupa asks.

"I will say the words 'his sins converge over a stone eye' and the bargain will be over," I say.

Tian steps closer to me. "I want to know why, and I have another thing I want."

I cross my arms. "You're getting quite demanding, but if you insist, this is to keep you safe for as long as I can."

Jupa's eyebrows came together. "We only met once before."

We are all murderers, scoundrels and outcasts, but we deserve to live just as the virtuous. We are capable of redemption and we long for life, not just survival.

"I want to do good by at least two people," I say, because a god gave me a choice and I chose to be selfish, so Arcadia will suffer for it.

"I want a kiss," Tian says.

I sigh. "No, you don't."

"I'm pretty sure I do!"

"Fine. Arcadia bears as our witness as we conduct a sacred transaction by the old gods," I say, not knowing how this actually works. "Tian of the Dead Lands and Jupa of Trilan, do you swear on every fabric of your beings to follow all of my direct commands that don't lead you into further harm?"

"I do," they reply.

"When I say the words 'his sins converge over a stone eye,' this bargain will be fulfilled, and in exchange, I bestow a kiss each," I say. "Do you agree?"

"I do."

"From this moment on, the bargain is struck and will continue until death or my words release us." I close my eyes and feel the wind circle us for one long moment.

It is time to give them my kiss.

"Close your eyes," I say and they do.

I step closer to them, feeling their breaths as I lean in and pressed my lips to each of their cheeks. I feel magik leave my skin, fulfilling my end of our bargain.

"What was that?" Tian frowns as he opens his eyes.

"You asked for a kiss, I gave you one," I smirk. "I command you to follow me into the village."

Jupa smiles just then, "Have you kissed someone before?"

I blink and turn away. "A long time ago, but working for the king, I wasn't allowed to."

Jupa and Tian laugh. Jupa asks, "Did you want to?"

I blush and storm back to the village. I hear their laughter as they follow.

Chapter 19: Anam Begining

Woyldlan, Court of Daeyed

Jupa and Tian sit on the grass outside Sithen Dochtúir's home. The grumbly faerie would not allow them to contaminate his space with the likes of "humans." I think that they were relieved with the decision.

Azlyon and Kynus are in deep conversation by the fire. Sithen Dochtúir made sure to lock the door with multiple locks before appearing on the table in front of me; he looks angrier than I was hoping.

"The creature and her royal kin conspire, and what does poor Sithen get? A town filled with iron powder and not one, but *four,* living humans and another spilling its iron-infested blood outside my village!" He points at me.

"I didn't conspire with Prince Kynus," I say, sitting on a chair next to him.

"Not directly!" He stomps his foot.

I look at the small faerie, holding so much distrust and disdain for the world.

"Tonight, there will be another small revel. This is when you will have the chance to meet our people," Azlyon says. "Though I warn you, do not take, eat, or listen to their honeyed words and food."

"What of Rowyna, and the two prisoners and the legitar?" I ask.

"They will stay inside here tonight," Azlyon says.

"I must have heard you wrong," the geancanach gasps.

"You did not. Aurelia has seen fit to make them extensions of her, which means they are extensions of Kynus and I," Azlyon says. "There will be no more humans ever though."

That last part was shot at me. He can only allow so many before they start causing a problem.

"Creature!" Sithen Dochtúir grumbles, "I am told that you want to know more about my people? Excellent, you will be sleeping on the roads, in the woods, and by the streams with them tonight."

"Sithen—" Azlyon steps closer.

"He has his right over his home, we must not infringe any further on his hospitality," Kynus cuts Azlyon off. I gape slightly and Azlyon clenches his teeth.

"Seelie prince," Sithen Dochtúir smiles evenly. "I am willing to make a deal with you—let the humans brave the revel and your half-blood can stay here."

Azlyon considers this for a moment, but it is I who decides to speak. "They are tithes for the winter solstice, they must be intact as proper sacrifices. I will stay outside because there are more important things than a petty faerie willing to spoil what could be the greatest tithe yet. A tithe that represents the renewal of Arcadia."

The lies flow so easily right now.

"I wonder if this creature is being thoughtful or has ulterior motives." Sithen Dochtúir narrows his eyes.

"I don't care what you think," I say, "I am doing what I think is right for everyone."

"Except me. You better do what is best for the better of all fae," Sithen Dochtúir snaps and disappears.

"So, what are we doing with the legitar I just murdered?" I say, grabbing a stone bowl and leaning over the dripping water in the corner.

"Tell the fae you killed him for them," Azlyon says, not batting an eye.

I take a long sip. "What will they do with him?"

"Cook him, skin him and wear his flesh, both?" Kynus yawns.

I sigh. "Well, they can do whatever they want, I just won't take part in that."

Azlyon tilts his head. "I never much liked Haerton, though his daughter did, or does until she realizes that he will never come home. She must be three suns by now?"

I look him in the eye. *What are you trying to do, Azlyon?*

He smiles.

"Spoils of war? Though at least her father will be dead. Oh, and she will grow to hate the fae. A simple idea could flourish, she could rise in rank and make it her mission to end us all," Azlyon continues.

"Do I have to kill a child?" My stomach sinks. The youngest life I've ended was eleven suns.

"You will be far too busy for that, though the order should be given sooner rather than later."

I shake my head. "I killed him, if she must die, I won't have someone else do it. She deserves more respect than a cheap assassin."

Kynus smiles. "Oh, Azlyon, she is so much more than I thought. I wasn't aware how well you trained her."

"That wasn't my doing." Azlyon smiles at Kynus. "Haerton doesn't have a child."

I throw the stone bowl at them. It cracks in half on Kynus' hand, which he raises to cover his face. The water splashes all over both of them. Azlyon the Liar and Kynus the Proud.

"Though she will have to work on that temper." Kynus steps around me. "Now if you'll excuse me, I have a body to drag over."

"As if you will drag it." I roll my eyes.

"Oh, my kin wounds me. By me, I simply meant my servants, who are a kind of extension of myself. Delegating is so much work but someone must do it. I suppose that's why the gods created the high sidhe to rule all of the fae," Kynus mumbles as the door shut.

"But you're not entirely high sidhe, are you?" I counter but he is already gone.

Azlyon saunters over. "As for the temper, know when to use it and when not to."

"I'm not a sidhe either, I am half asrai," I say.

"I didn't know Kynus planned this," Azlyon said.

"I believe you, though it can be difficult to truly trust anyone right now," I say.

He looks away. "I am trying."

"And tricking me into believing that I must kill a child?"

"I am trying, as I said. Though you are asking me to overcome something all faeries are born craving: madness and trickery."

I shake my head. "But why would you do this to someone you love?"

He blinks as his hands fall to his sides, not expecting me to say what I said. I lick my lips carefully, they taste of blood and salt, just like the air between us.

"I'm not sure I follow," He says, turning his head slightly to the left.

"I know what you did for the unsidhe, and from what I hear, it isn't very much like you. The liberties you give me when you have no reason to," I say, not looking him in the eye. "We've known each other for years but I could never figure you out until recently, until you stopped using magik as a shield."

He shifts on his feet. "Aurelia, once it has been said out loud, it no longer remains a secret. Are you sure you want to travel down this path?"

I walk over to him. His silver eyes finally met mine. This in itself is a game, perhaps the most dangerous one. But I need confirmation, and I sincerely hope I am wrong about everything I accuse him of.

My voice is careful, quiet, and clear. "You fell in love with me."

He sighs and gestures for me to sit down as he does.

"I am enthralled by you," he says, "and have been since I met you. This has never happened to me before and I could have ruined everything."

Enthrallment and love are different. I was half right about him.

Even back in Jorthus, Cicero did favour me more than the others. At least now I know why. Azlyon is a creature—one who masqueraded as a human and set his sights on me. He helped me grow while his feelings were shielded from my eyes, from everyone's eyes.

"I was planning on using the information I learned here to buy my freedom back into the human kingdoms...Before I spoke to Dian Cecht." I tell him, looking away. "I conspired against you and I don't want Rowyna, Tian and

Jupa to be sacrificed."

He lets out a soft chuckle. "I know."

I blink and turn to him. "How?"

"I know you, Aurelia, we are two halves of the same coin."

I shiver, remembering the memory of a world I could have grown up in. It is distant but still vivid in my mind. The god I met said that my anam-connected had evil in him. I have a suspicion that they meant one and the same.

"My anam-connected, it's you isn't it?" I ask him, grasping my knees.

"Where did you hear that term?"

"Lord Dian Cecht and Kynus," I whisper.

"Anam, soul, and essence connected, are older words for mateship," he says, "though one's paired anam may not love the other in the same way, there will always be a strong connection."

"Kynus mentioned that earlier," I laugh. "I picked your dress, I couldn't stay mad at you for your betrayal, you were my friend, the only one I truly trusted with my identity and what I looked like under all those capes and hoods."

"It comes from a language similar to Arcadian, one the gods' gifted humanity, so we could understand one another," he says, still being careful surrounding the conversation, "a language born of Gaia and Arcadia."

I look down. "Does anyone else know about you and me?"

"Kynus knows, and she knows," he says quickly.

He didn't have to say her name. We both knew who he meant and it terrifies me. He has some control over what happens to me. In turn, I could find a way to free him of her once the task is complete.

"Azlyon, I won't be with you that way," I say. "I have so much I need to learn about myself before I can let anyone—"

He presses a finger to my lips. "As long as I am myself, I will never push you into anything like that. I didn't even want to tell you any of this for this exact reason."

"Az," I say, stepping in front of him, "I think friendship is what we need to work on."

He stands and tilts his head.

My heart races and my stomach fills with butterflies. I picture living in a cottage by the ocean, him at my side and morstone light surrounding us at night. We were friends in Jorthus, and we can be friends again.

I lean up, his breath warm against my lips. I lace my hands around his neck. Being this close to a faerie was never something I imagined. His eyelashes brush against my face as he blinks sliver.

"Aurelia, why do you lie?" He smiles, still almost touching me.

"I'm not lying, I just think that—"

He closes the distance between our lips, cutting me off. His mouth is soft against mine as if I would break at any moment. My hands tangle in his hair, his glide to the small of my back, pulling me closer.

My lips tingle against his, no doubt the magik around us manifesting. He tastes of berries on a warm afternoon. His embrace is comfortable but there is a hint of danger in each touch.

He pulls away but still holds me close. "I shouldn't have done that."

I smile. "I would have if you hadn't."

He chuckles, letting me roll back onto my feet.

"It can't happen again though," I say.

He tilts his head, hair tangling and a sheepish grin on his lips. "Back to our tiring normal again."

I laugh stepping back. As normal as it gets, I suppose.

The door opens and Kynus strolls, head held high and arms at his sides, long coat trailing behind him in a gust of self-made wind.

"Why did you tell her, Azlyon?" Kynus asks after settling on a plush chair in front of us. Fingers lacing on his legs.

"How do you know?" I ask, not feeling my lips utter a word.

"Oh, Aurelia, do not give me that look. The human outside was peaking in when I arrived and told me. Though I may add, I did break one of his fingers, just for amusement after. Spying on the sidhe is a terrible offence. If only he was not untouchable, the things I could do…"

I sigh.

"Aurelia guessed the truth." Azlyon yawns.

"I thought we agreed to avoid this," he replies.

The look Azlyon gives him causes my uncle to shiver despite his composure. I see, for a sliver of a moment, a familiar darkness behind Azlyon eyes. She is here and watching us, her hidden presence swallowing the air up.

"I am almost king of the fae, protector of the courts, and Arcadia's redemption," Azlyon grabs my wrist forcefully, "and as my anam blessed, Aurelia will be the queen at my side."

Kynus bows immediately; he knows better than to argue with Azlyon. I feel a shiver and a coldness against my wrist as he holds it.

"Despite her less than desirable parentage, some things are forbidden to be meddled with." Azlyon looks at me, I felt myself drawn to his gaze. I see him but don't recognize him.

"She may not be sidhe, but she comes from the highest of the asrai after all." Kynus licks his lips, rising from his bow. "She is a perfect queen, one who can help unite land and sea for you."

"And you think I cannot do this without the half-blood?"

"I have no doubt you can, but she can help in other ways… Leviathan chose her as his champion."

By the gods, so much has happened since I was chosen as an ancient wyrm's champion—whatever that meant.

Azlyon shuts his eyes a moment and smiles.

When he opens them, the darkness is gone once again.

"An asrai and a Seelie, anam connected." Kynus laughs. "Can you imagine what Lythe would say if she saw the two of you?"

Azlyon's face goes dark. "Oh, it would be rather amusing. Of all the fae, she would hate it to be me."

"You know, in another time I believe she would have preferred to unite her child with one of the Reefthorn Knights." Kynus looks at me.

"The Cold king trained them well, they matched the Silvyrguard," Azlyon sighs, "but none could match the Sunstone Laoich on foot. Sometimes I wonder how they were bested."

"It was just before the final stand." Kynus looks away. "Did you ever wonder why your half-brother stood in place of my mother or her husband?"

Azlyon looks away, "I never thought much of it, I know your mother died in the palace of vines while High Lord Fyraen was away..."

"Few knew but she had just given birth to a female faeling, my sister, Aerona. She had the brightest red hair. Her eyes were a soft sage—I remember exactly how peaceful she looked." Kynus shuts his eyes.

"You never told me this before." Azlyon places a hand on Kynus' shoulder. "You weren't there though. I know you weren't."

"You are right, I wasn't there when they were all murdered. All remaining Sunstone Laoich were ordered back to protect them, and one of the human war chiefs came and blinded them with rowan ash before his men cornered and slaughtered them all. He was called Lynch, and he was in Fraser's council. Once the last of the Sunstone Laoich died, my mother took Aerona and hid her in the chest behind the vines in my chambers and went to hers as a distraction. Several arrows pierced her as she tried to fight them off. The iron was poisoning her as she fought them. Lynch watched as the soldiers forced themselves on her until death. When my mother...when she was dead, they impaled her to the wall." Kynus swallows. "I never told you because it is my burden to bear for not being there."

I feel sick. "What happened to her, your sister?"

"They found her and skinned her alive, leaving only her head untouched. A weakened sprite managed to hide and wait until they were gone. She told me what happened." Kynus turns to me, his eyes squeezing shut. "My sister was tucked in my bed when I found her. I thought she was sleeping at first. She looked so peaceful, and I hoped that after finding my mother, she would be fine. I hoped they drew a line at our faelings. I tracked Lynch down and paid him the same kindness that he showed my family and the Laoich. And that's what happened to the Bright Court's elite warriors trained for battle but not how to wield defensive magik."

"And your mother's husband?" I ask, letting cold tears collect in my eyes. "Where was he?"

"He died in combat or so the stories say, but one of his servants saw him walk into a battlefield unarmed after hearing what happened. He killed himself. And I was left to pick up all the pieces."

"I'm so sorry," I said, unable to say anything else.

"Why do humans say this? At everything?" Kynus shakes his head. "It was a long time ago, we all lost fae we deeply cared for..."

Azlyon nods.

I shake my head and close my eyes.

They are old creatures, I only lived a fraction of the time they did.

Chapter 20: Revelling With Púca's Fruit

Woyldlan, Court of Daeyed

The sun is beginning to set, painting the land in shimmering gold, orange, and red. I remember how beautiful it looks in Jorthus, but here it is softer, gentler, and yet somehow more explosive.

From what I remember from the dream, revels were dangerous play for the fae. Humans were targeted in ways that can turn a stomach inside out.

I step out of the bedroom and see Azlyon and Kynus standing there. I immediately look away. Too much skin is showing and I can't help but blush.

"Aurelia, why must you stick to customs from another country." Kynus sighs.

"How did your hair grow long?" I ask.

Kynus' amusing voice sounds out from behind me. "It is just a little evening glamour."

I raise my brows. "Of course."

"Human revels are so formal, Kynus, so many rules," Azlyon says, cutting in. "Aurelia, place modesty aside, this is how the fae are."

I sigh and face them. My travelling attire is a wrong but safe choice.

They both wear green and golden vines in their hair. Azlyon's crawls up his head into an antler-shape crown while Kynus' long red hair is braided into ram horns. Their eyes are plastered with shimmering powder and their lips are black. They both wear thick ropes with rune stones. Their lower bodies are covered with pale furs slit at both sides, exposing their outer legs.

"My dear," Azlyon tilts his head, "do you want us to help you?"

"Mistress can keep the trousers because they are stunning, though you will be needing a new shirt and hair befitting a princess." Belousa walked over.

I shiver as she touches my hair.

"Fine."

Belousa turns my hair into a sea horned serpent in honour of Leviathan. Pale ocean pearls form the snake's eyes, and blue flower petals and gems are woven in. My hair wraps around my neck once and hangs down my left arm. She places me in a small shirt embroidered with fish scales that a nixie from the village made several moons ago. The back divides into two long strands that hook into my trousers. A runestone necklace snakes down my neck, only mine is a pale blue rather than white. She paints my eyes in ribbons trailing down to my jawline. I feel the humanity leaving my features with every stroke of the paintbrush.

Silver bands adorn my arms and my neck—a mark of the sea, they tell me. Everything is about who I am and what I could be.

"I'm not sure how I feel about my skin showing," I say, touching my belly and arms.

"Are you sure the creature is fae?" A familiar small faerie chimes beside my ear.

I turn my head to see Sithen Dochtúir yawning. He is entirely naked and standing on my shoulder.

"Get off me!" I go to flick him in the chest but he disappears and reappears on the windowsill. "Where are the humans?"

"In the cellar," Kynus responds, "all four of them."

I nod and walk over to the cellar door only to find it locked.

"Best you don't mingle with them until the morrow," Kynus cuts through my thoughts.

"Who is going to watch over them?"

"Belousa," Sithen Dochtúir growls and disappears.

I shake my head.

"I know you want to talk to her," Azlyon says, "and that time will come, but now please stand by our sides as we walk to the revel."

I nod and take each of their arms. I walk in the middle of two towering ancient faeries. One who wandered the land in search of Arcadia's cure, and one trying to maintain order in a faerie country while struggling against the ideas of two darker counterparts.

I hear voices singing and laughing as I take my first steps, my bare feet on the soil. It feels like an extension of myself, so soft and yet so lively. The air flickers in the morstone, the other floating lights I recognize as will-ó-the-wisp and fireflies.

In a short distance, there are faeries with antlers, goat heads, sharp teeth and no eyes, large red noses and small bodies; they are winged, hoofed, made of earth, made of water; some look like cats, some like wolves, and others look in-between many things. They all gather here and drink strange murky liquid and eat golden fruit, green meats, and other assortments of sweets and bark. There were smaller faelings, older fae, and those in-between.

The music shifts into a lullaby and all these creatures turn to watch us. Then they all roar in unison before silence overtakes the village.

"Is this not a revel?" Azlyon grins. "I feel as though I am standing amongst boring mortals."

With that, all the fae erupt in growling and dancing. Some claim others under the stars and in the open for everyone to see. Others bite and fight each other like raging animals. Others nakedly walk through flames and leap into trees.

Blood splatter my arm. When I go to wipe it off, Kynus shakes his head. "It's time to let your inner animal out, be one with the moon and the wild."

I go rigid at the thought.

Kynus chuckles darkly and raises his voice. "Princess Aurelia, heir to the marine folk has never revelled."

The faeries reach out to me and I let them pull me. Azlyon sits on a wooden throne made from driftwood and bark, while Kynus pulls an elf aside and whispers in her ear. I see the creature blush and pull him deeper into the woods at the village's edge.

"What does the highborn desire?" A male nymph licks the blood off my arm.

A dark-skinned elf runs her hands down my back and I shiver. "Does your highness crave flesh?"

A green gnome presses a knife into my hand. "Does she crave blood?"

A winged woman flies over. "Would you crave a golden apple from a sylph?"

"Would you like flesh, food, and blood?" The elf's hand goes to my stomach and I step backwards, bumping into a troll.

"I'm sorry!" I say not realizing.

It peers down at me before raising its fist and hitting me in the stomach, enough to make me step back a few paces before it returns to dancing.

My eyes narrow and the hand on my stomach is ready to give it the same courtesy, but another sylph flies over and lands on the ground in front of me. "Little lady, how about a hunt?"

"A hunt?"

"Oh yes, you see we are looking for the silver-eyed faerie with skin as dark as night, she stole from us little under a fortnight ago." Her blue wings fall behind her like a cape. "We know you can find her, little assassin lady. We want her, alive or dead it doesn't matter."

"Why haven't you found her yet?" I dodge a drunken faerie swinging too close to the fire.

"Our village only permits hunts at night, and she is like a dark elf but not." The sylph flies away.

I shake my head not knowing what that was supposed to mean.

A small grey-speckled black cat with the palest amethyst eyes sits on a stone several steps away, watching me. It is long-haired but despite the eyes, it looks relatively normal.

I don't like cats, they are tricky. All animals are unpredictable. While Fyfe kept several dogs, not even including the hunting beasts, they all saw people as food. Smart enough not to attack, but always gave away their desires through their eyes.

"You won't want to miss the hunt," a shadowy voice speaks at my side.

"Why is that?"

"Despite what these fae say, the creature you hunt is better an ally than foe, especially for a demifae such as yourself."

I turn and see the cat peering up at me.

"A talking cat? Of course." I sigh.

"Looking for a sliver of the mundane you cling to?" he yawns, licking a paw.

"What is your name?"

The cat laughs. "Names are gifts, names hold meaning—but you knew that, didn't you? I'm different from these fae, and I know more about the worlds that exist in different realms than any living creature. Even your princes wouldn't be able to understand some of the things I've seen."

I place a hand on my hip. "That's what they all say though, the fae. It's quite arrogant you know."

"But were all the fae once the familiar of a god?" The cat steps away. "Whichever you choose will have differing consequences."

I watch it leap into the shadows between two dancers.

I glance back at Azlyon but he just sits there looking bored as several faeries fight each other to sit beneath his feet. His eyes are sharp and his face is like a perfect stone sculpture. I suppose being near him is enough for some of these faeries.

"Who is hunting along with me?" I called.

A few drunken redcaps hobble over and three naked, lusty elves nod in response to my question. The sylph flies over but says it isn't going to hunt tonight, though she offers all the details before her friends pull her away.

It turns out that the creature we hunt has no known name, though it does have one of the most beautiful faces in existence. On her face is a tree inked in silver, the branches and leaves form on the forehead and around the eyes, a permanent magik that would stay on the faerie until they take their last breath. She supposedly has very metallic eyes without pupils. They say she is part dark elf, that her skin is a dark brown rather than inky black. While it is enough to go on, I doubt the creature would remain close to this village.

"Where was she last seen?" I ask.

"Near the ruins the last few times," a redcap points west, "but she won't hide there every time…"

Unless this creature wants to be found. Maybe I could pick up a trail there.

I smile and instruct the redcaps to go north and east. The elves will go south but avoid the mounds, and I head west.

Aurelia, what are you planning?

I ignore the voice in my head.

What of Rowyna? You cannot go very far. Perhaps limit yourself to Flean Ruins, for any further she may die.

I sigh, forgetting all about Rowyna. *You aren't going to stop me?*

Is there a reason I should? Enjoy your hunt.

"Then the Flean Ruins it is." A faerie pulls out a map and hands it to me after I ask where the stones are. They weren't very far, it turns out, maybe an hour by foot. Revels last until morning which means my disappearance wouldn't matter until then.

I step away from the crowd, feeling the wind, earth, and heat from the flames behind me. The woods cradle silver trees and white grass, lush and lively.

My body takes control through sense and quick footing. To hunt one must be both prey and predator, as a half-blood, I already am both.

I sniff the air and smell something different. It leads me to a loose strand of black hair stuck on a branch. There is something almost too earthy about it, which tells me that this individual has been living off the land, probably alone for hundreds of years or more.

I continue to follow the trail, which is quite linear and direct as if calling for me to follow. All my training tells me this is a potential trap and I should turn around and forget the hunt.

Then I catch the scent of Jupa—the human who should be locked up.

My brows rise and my heart slows. Why would Jupa be here? The trail is so fresh, it must only be an hour old. I must forget the faerie and focus on locating him after all the work I did to prevent him from getting killed.

Little pixies fly around in the night, conjuring morstone as they dance in the sky to the moon.

"Have you seen a human male?" I ask one that lands on a branch near me.

It looks around nervously but nods and points in a direction.

"Thank you," I say, giving it a jewel from my hair.

It smiles gleefully, then flies away with the stone too small for me and much too large for it.

"It's a setup," I say, stepping away from the group. There is no other possible explanation. It is an easy trail to follow, meaning whoever took Jupa wants to be found with the human. They want me to find him.

Whatever the truth, I must be careful.

I pick one of the few colourful plants I take notice of. The petals are a striking red, the leaves an inky blue. A simple but deadly thing I once found in Cicero's garden. It was one of the few things that caught my attention while looking for his book of poisons. What a shame it would be to ruin a wonderfully beautiful plant.

I tuck it in my waistband before continuing.

Ahead of me are enormous standing stones with rune engravings, crumbling stone houses, and one ruined edifice in the middle looming over all others. This place isn't small. The ruins span the size of several villages in each direction. It's been long since abandoned, yet a hum of energy vibrates through the soles of my feet through the bone.

I lick my upper lip and take a step forward, feeling lighter, almost as though I were swimming in water. I could easily leap my way over to the ruins, though I fear that this is what Azlyon meant when he told me this distance would be as far as I could go.

I feel the eyes of someone—or something—on me.

"I believe you have something of mine." I lean against a tree. "Whoever or whatever you are, I don't have time to play games. You see, I have a party to get back to. Please hand my pet over and I won't kill you."

I hear the silky chuckle of a woman with a deep voice. Something about it sets my nerves on high alert.

Jupa steps out of the shadows, looking petrified, yet he does not move closer to me. "Oh? Please come over here and take what's yours. Though you will be taking it back quite dead."

Jupa is speaking in his voice but it was her words

"I see, we must make a bargain then? Typical of the fae." I mustn't falter.

"No, I just want to have a little chat," he says. "I wanted to understand the creature in which the fate of my home lingers with.'

"How did you get him?"

"The human? Not very many people can sneak up on the good doctor and the servant, and steal from him, but I did." His voice is shaky. "Now my turn, why do you trust them?"

"Them?"

"Let's not play coy with one another, I have all the leverage my sweet." A dark hand lingers by Jupa's throat. "I can smell the poison on your fingertips, acena flower, very potent...and could kill someone like me, though you would have to reach me first."

"I have no other choice, and they've been decent thus far," I say, answering her question.

"What weak answers, my dear. Word of advice, do not trust any prince, they use honeyed words far too often."

"When one is my uncle and one is my—" I shut my mouth before I say anything too revealing, "—my friend. It's difficult to say no."

"Oh? Little seabird, kin are far from trustworthy."

"Who are you?" I ask.

"A faerie, a bastard, and one of the most skilled hunters in this world. I rode next to Herne the Hunter, I've travelled to different worlds, reaping and pillaging."

I shake. "I don't know who that is."

"Have you ever heard of The Wild Hunt? Fae who travelled between the worlds hunting humans, spirits, and animals?"

"For argument's sake, I will assume they are the best at their trade," I shake my head, "and hunting with them was an honour?"

"Yes, and no, hunting with them was a curse. Few can leave and those who do can be hunted themselves." It is her who speaks now, this time stepping out of the shadows. She is just as the other faerie described her. Her skin is covered in silver markings, clean of dirt and blood.

"Are you a sidhe?" I ask.

"I am pure faerie yet a mixed-breed fae," she says. "Herne hunts me to this day. When my time was up he expected me to stay, yet I did not. Where are my manners? Aurelia, I know your name, it's only fair you learn mine. I am called Scátha and we need to discuss the goddess who will rule."

"Who?"

Jupa drops down as she touches his cheek. "He is fine, only asleep, and I am not foolish like the other fae you've met. I'm sure by now you know I live alone, but my web of informants is quite large."

"Did you work for the princes?"

"I worked for King Oberon once, I was Lady of Elderflowers," she looks over, though I am still confused. "It is what you would know as the leader of spies."

I cross my arms and smile. "Scátha, what exactly do you want me to do about the goddess?"

"Do what she says, be her right hand, until she brings life back to Arcadia, then you must do what is necessary to end her presence here," she says.

"She will possess Prince Azlyon you know."

Scátha smirks when I mention the prince. "We would be much better without him."

I shake my head. "He knows the old world, he knows how to rebuild."

"Very well, if he catches on—if she catches on—you will find sanctuary where the red-tailed hawk screeches under the mountain and above the cold, an area of thy only son's domain. Take care, Aurelia, and remember to trust the green mice, for they will send word to me."

"How do you know I will go to you?" I raise a brow.

"Because I know the gods, and I know the princes, I know what those in every country say, and I know you will need me to face her in time." Scátha tilts her head and Jupa disappears.

She tells me he is back safe in the village and will wake with nothing more than a headache.

"It's best you don't tell Azlyon anything about me or our meeting," she pauses, "or anyone for the matter."

I nod and she blends in with the shadows again. "It was a pleasure meeting you."

* * *

I wander back to the revel, deep in thought as dozens of creatures, most of them naked and drunk, eat slippery food. My heart pounds as the haunting melodies of a pan flute whisper stories of death in time with the banging drums.

"Good thing I found the lost princess." Kynus appears beside me. "This apple is safe to eat."

I look at my uncle and take the apple from him; it is green and ordinary.

"Where is Azlyon?" I ask.

"The prince of princes is dancing on thorns, bleeding for his kin." Kynus smiles. "Take a bite, I find them quite scrumptious."

I look at the apple again. "What about not eating any food?"

"From them," he gestures to the crowds. "I made sure to find the right thing for you."

I smile and take a bite, tasting honey milk with slight citrus notes. While there is an initial crunch, the rest melts on my tongue and slides down my throat.

I look at Kynus and see the world in vibrant colours, rainbows and shadows move around everyone slowly. The air was heavy like a blanket on top of me.

Kynus grins again but he wasn't my uncle, but a dark-haired creature that looks like a mix between a rabbit and a tiny human with a long slender tail. Thick, long ear-like horns lay atop its head while its feline face mimics my own look of surprise. Small dragonfly wings fold backwards.

"You're not my un-un-uncle," I say, my speech slurring.

"Puck the Púca," it bows, its golden eyes glowing, 'keep the sharp things away and we can play."

It hops away, grinning like a goat.

"Your highness, we have a pretty crown for you!" A creature with a flicking snake tongue and glowing white eyes pulls me up.

"A crown." I smile hazily.

"Beautiful, for a lady of noble birth. Harsh, like one who has been burdened by the weight of so many, a princess of light and the darkest cold, bound to do great or perish and burn," Snake chimes.

"Which should I do? Perish and burn or do great?" I ask the man with a smile as I trip over a root.

"Little dove, little tree, little lake, little hill, for you will do both by the time your life is over," he tantalizes, "you will beg like a peasant, you will love like a queen, and you will hate like old Queen Mab on her throne of webs and bone. Rage will consume you until you crumble away, crumble and crumble and crumble to the day you are old and young with no one left but someone who betrays and hinders and lies."

I feel thorns press into my head. My scalp bleeds but I feel no pain.

"La La Lala La La Lala," I sing to the tune of the fire.

"Who do you desire?" another satyr hobbles over.

"Who do you want to dance with," a sprite chimes.

"Who will smile upon the princess of roses and thorns?"

"Did you hunt the faerie?"

"Did you kill it?"

Something pulls at my clothes and hair.

The world swishes and melts around me. Faeries come closer and closer, their faces reflecting the orange copper of flames. If one took the sharpest animal and bred it with people and other things, these creatures would appear, with smiles and teeth to cut you open.

"How about a game of riddles?" I say.

"Oh?" Several faeries lean in closer as others let go.

"Wagers then?" A faerie with a grey warty face asks, "I demand your firstborn should I win!"

I shrug, feeling so light and fuzzy "Sounds fair, I desire to be brought to my anam."

They blink and grin wider. "Tell us who that would be…"

"Well, that is only if I win!" I declare. "Trust me, ladies and gentlemen, I used to play games of riddles with... Oh, I cannot remember but..." I touch the warty nose. "I think I can win."

"Me first!" snaps warty, who demands the child. "What goes up but never comes down?"

I smile widely. "Oh, easy enough! It is age!"

The faerie crosses its arms.

"Ok...Ok, I have one...I make two people out of one. What am I?" I ask, crossing my legs.

"Is this a human trick?" another faerie grumbles.

Warty riddler only smiles at me though. I laugh out loud, feeling tears burn my cheeks.

"You are a mirror, though one must be careful with those here, just like our delicious food," the faerie responds by licking its lips. "When is it bad luck to see a black cat?"

"Are there more of those apples? They were quite good." I lazily look over to an elf at my side.

"My dear we don't want to get in too much trouble," it said with a wide grin.

"Did you hear me worm princess?" warty yanks my face back.

I blink.

"When. Is. It. Bad. Luck. To. See. A. Black. Cat?" It spoke slowly and with a growl.

"Black cats are good," a gnome cackles.

"Not if they are a Cait Sith!" another chimes.

"Only if you are human, but if they are fae, you must think truthfully," another cackles. "A real cat is a cat, not a faerie."

"We are losing the princess' attention." A horned man with bright blue skin leans over the flames we sat beside.

I smile, thinking about what they could mean.

Black cat. Bad luck. Black cats are omens, at least in Jorthus. I never believed it, though this is a riddle. I have to be clever.

"Does the girl have an answer?" Warty grins.

My eyes glance down, trying to look for more time when I see a small creature crawling between feet and hooves.

"When you are a mouse?" I ask slowly, raising my head.

There is a pause then a frown. "Oh, dear, perhaps we should call it a game. I hoped to have an upper hand but I don't foresee your faeling in my life soon enough."

"I don't even want to have children." I snort a laugh. "I don't even know if I can!"

They all burst out laughing as they drink more mead.

"I think that means I win!" I grin, trying to stand but end up falling on my arse. I blink for a moment, trying to remember who I was looking for to begin with, "Friends, I believe the name slipped my tongue… Silver eyes, hair—violet or white, I think, I can't remember if he is small or tall though?"

"My sweet, as you can see, there are fae here that match that description." A slimy green troll wiggles its eyebrows.

"You got me there!" I declare with a laugh. "I came here with him originally."

"Do you mean Prince Azlyon?" a pixie chirps on the shoulder of warty.

"What a silly name, but I think so." I laugh. "Take me to A-Azlyon then!"

What once was amusement on all their faces turns into deathly intrigue and looks of fear. I have confirmed something that they didn't expect.

"Oh, dear, if I had won I could rule the country," the warty riddler sighs, "one babe at a time."

"I would not face Prince Azlyon's wrath!"

"This is good though, information is always fascinating," an elf chuckles in passing as they walk by.

"Thanks for a good time." I laugh as warty pulls my arm along.

"Goodbye, princess!" they cheer in unison.

I hiccup as warty lets me go in front of several fancy faeries. I squint my eyes, trying to make out their faces to no avail.

"Which one of you is the fancy prince?" I chuckle. "Which one of you is the prince everyone keeps talking about?"

I look at them all before yawning.

"Aurelia," a voice at my side.

I turn and slowly look up to a familiar silver-eyed faerie.

"So you are bigger and not tiny!" I let out a cheer.

He sighs. "What did you eat?"

"None of your business, mister!" I point a finger at his chest.

"I ask only because it looked like it may have been tasty," he leans down and touches my cheek, "perhaps I could get more."

I giggle. "A lovely apple of honey milk! You should have one!"

He almost looks relieved, "Thankfully it wasn't the golden apples, otherwise your mind would be long gone. How was the revel? The fae?"

"I think I tried a hunt, but it failed. Then uncle Puck the Púca gave me a yummy apple. Oh, and I wagered my first born's life to warty! Don't worry, I won, you should have seen me, Azlyon!" I speak quickly and with intrigue.

Something flashes in his eyes, anger and disappointment.

"You know, you are by far the most handsome of all the faeries I have met." I fall against his chest. "Why haven't you married?"

"Aurelia, if you really want to know, you will ask me when the food runs its course through your body." Azlyon supports me with his arm.

"If… If I could marry someone, it may as well be you or one of those elves! Though your father wouldn't like that, since I'm not like you," I whisper in hiccups.

"Who said we would get married, you silly creature." He laughs for a moment.

"Well, you are stuck with me," I laugh, "want to play a game of riddles? I think I can wager my—"

He puts a finger against my lips. "I taught you all your best riddles, there is no way you would win. Perhaps it's time for you to retire for the night…"

"A revel isn't over until the sun comes up, " I complain.

"Not for you, not tonight, there will be others and I can tell you've had quite the time already," he says.

I smile lazily. "If you don't want to revel, we could always—"

"No," he commands quickly, "you are not in the right mind to make a coherent decision about that."

I smile into the stars as he takes me back to a home I vaguely remember.

I fall asleep on the floor, not wanting to walk another step to comfort.

Chapter 21: Morning Delights

Woyldlan, Court of Daeyed

I wake with a headache and a stiff back. The scent of fresh tea brewing drifts through the air. The fire is warm against my side.

I look over to see Azlyon and Sithen together at the table. They sip on warm liquid and eat a variety of fruits and root vegetables.

"Do you have peppermint oil?" I ask Sithen.

The small faerie chuckles. "The creature asks for something to soothe its blasted headache! To answer its question, yes, I have the oil, but no, the creature cannot have it! Suffer, you fool!"

I groan.

"Azlyon, can you do anything with your magik?" I ask the prince before remembering how I treated him last night. "Oh gods, never mind!"

Azlyon smiles. "Are you sure that's all you want from me? No marriage today?"

I pick up a pillow and throw it at him. "Not another word. I get it, I didn't listen to your warning, and clearly, I embarrassed myself. Let's just move on and forget."

"It was all in good fun, Aurelia, though there were some things I wish you didn't do." He takes another bite. "I had to spend a good while convincing the rest of the fae that there would be no marriage celebration."

"Any excuse to revel and the fae will take it," Sithen says. "I am still annoyed I couldn't revel last eve."

"Sithen, if I ever marry I will invite you." I smile sweetly.

The faerie cracks its back, stretching. "Why would I attend your wedding revel?"

"Who knows, maybe you will be my suitor?" I wink.

"Disgusting! As if I would marry a half-breed! Especially one as tall and annoying as you!" He spits. "She is just like all humans, not knowing when humour crosses a line!"

Azlyon smiles. "It's what makes her interesting."

"How was the rest of your night?" I turn my attention to him.

"After I dropped you off, I went back to the revel and enjoyed many fae... " He looks at my wide eyes "I'm lying. After I spoke to the fae at the revel, I stayed here for the remainder of the evening making sure you didn't get up and do something foolish while the fruit was in your body."

"I fear I am jealous," Sithen sips milk like an angry child, "the faerie who can lie so nicely."

"Need I remind you to keep that to yourself?" Azlyon turns his attention to our host.

The small faerie scratches its back before disappearing.

"Do you enjoy lying?" I ask.

"In the beginning it was interesting but I feel as though I rely on it more now than speaking deceptive truths. It is just far too easy. The human realm of influence is easier to see through but also easier to become part of." He stands up.

"I went to the ruins before I embarrassed you last night." I yawn suddenly, still exhausted. "They are magnificent, to say the least."

"And did you see your prey there?" He looks me dead in the eye as I focus on my wobbly legs.

"To be honest I saw a few sprites along the way but that was it."

"Those ruins were once the capital of faerie before it split into the Seelie and Unseelie Courts. It was where the first four of my siblings were born. It was where the first Unseelie prince was born, Eldran, son of Mab. When the faeries were forced to choose sides after decades of tension between Oberon and the darker-minded Marea, the citadel was all but destroyed. Marea's twin sister, Mab, did not like where the Unseelie were heading after the courts split and screeched atop the largest ruin and thus the Unseelie civil war began." He looks down with a sad smile.

"How did the war end?" I ask.

"With the decimation of Mab's family, though some say she cursed her son to live on as a silver wasp before the war ended. The sister queen was impaled several times by Marea and Ralean the summer elf."

"Summer elf?" I wonder.

"Marea's mate was of the Seelie, and Oberon struck quite the deal for her to keep him." Azlyon smiles as if remembering a fond memory. "It was the first council I ever sat in on."

"When were you born?"

He lifts my chin with his finger. "Didn't anyone ever tell you never to ask a sidhe how old he is?"

I smirk. "Must have slipped my mind."

"I was born just before the courts separated, though I cannot remember that time, I do remember the civil war very well. It was sort of an amusement for the Seelie sidhe. While Mab hated us more, Marea was the clever one. We knew how to deal with both should the need for war happen again."

"It happened again though?"

It was like reading an adventure book in Jorthus, of a made-up world with histories so deep yet fleeting. These lands changed and so humans chose to forget. Only the great library in Skuflan remembered, along with the remaining faeries that wander in Daeyed.

"We've been at war off and on up until the humans invaded. We've had so many truces and soaked the forest floor with blood that even I cannot remember who was in the right at which moment." His hand slides down my arm.

"Tell me one where the Seelie were in the wrong."

"I was supposed to marry Marea's daughter once. She was a close friend of mine though Oberon disapproved of it, at least until it may have been the only thing to bridge the hate between the courts."

"But you didn't?" I ask shyly.

"No, I did not. Nym and the Unseelie Princess Laeraan were caught in his chambers, in the Seelie capital of Tír na nÓg." Azlyon shakes his head. "That brother of mine enjoyed stirring the cauldron until there was a mess."

"Why did she do that to you though?" I ask, pulling Azlyon to sit by the fire.

"She didn't want to marry me, and that was an easy way out. Oberon started that war, accusing her of seducing Nym. He was a pitiful excuse for a sidhe."

"He was your brother though," I say. He had many kin and still chose to be solitary in his own family.

"He was apathetic and gluttonous," he says. "She knew how I felt about him and she still did what she did."

I look away, feeling a slight sink in my stomach.

"You loved her, didn't you?"

He cared for her so deeply. They were friends and I wonder why she wouldn't marry a friend, even if arranged. It certainly could have been much worse. Maybe she didn't want to put Azlyon through the pain of someone who would never love him back that way.

"I once thought she was everything I wanted. What I felt for her was not nearly—" He shakes his head. "It matters not to speak of the dead. They are gone and we are here."

"Maybe she wanted to be unbound from the crown when it came to the heart," I say. "Perhaps she wanted to love someone deeply and without constraint. Azlyon, just because she didn't want to marry does not mean she didn't love you differently."

"Have you truly met the Unseelie?" Azlyon asks. "They consist of malicious and more evilly-inclined fae. Vikorus, while being Unseelie born, did not grow with them. He does not know their ways. Laeraan had moments of kindness but she always crawled back to her dark roots no matter who got harmed along the way."

We are silent after that, at least for a while. His stories were his truths, but to me, they are something out of a book.

"I better check on them." I gesture to the door where the humans were.

Azlyon doesn't look at me, instead, his eyes soak in deeds of the past.

"They aren't there," a voice slips through the cracks of thought.

I glance up to see him free of his bindings and eating bread as he struts inside. My father. Tionne.

"Who let you out?" I demand, standing up.

Azlyon is quick to grab my wrist.

Then Tionne slips into the shapeshifter faerie I recognize from the previous night. Amused and pleased with its own actions, it saunters over to catch the heat of the flames.

"Aurelia," it says my name, "how very oceanic, I believe your name comes from the Asrai people, meaning golden river." It tilts its head. "You are quite the golden creature."

"Puck the Púca," I remember.

It smiles through its teeth. "Unlike most of my fae kin, I enjoy the lies of humans. It brings forth many curiosities and puzzles."

"I am not a human. How did you see my father if he is locked up?" I wonder.

"Your words make me itch. Your born father is tied up outside with three other humans. Did you think our good doctor would keep them in here?" Puck the Púca mocks in Tionne's face again. "Though I wish my prince wasn't here so I could play with you awhile longer."

"Are all the fae out to play?" Azlyon's voice is stern.

The púca shivers as it shifts into a rabbit with wasp wings. Why that exact thing? I suppose only it knows.

"Grehyl has chosen you, I only wanted to tell you." Puck stretches before leaving.

Azlyon turns so fast but the faerie is gone.

"Who is Grehyl?"

"A unique familiar who is a cousin to the Cait Siths," Azlyon's eyes are wild, "the only one who can switch attachments after death. He is said to have been once the familiar of Lord Manannán's wife, Fand. He also was the familiar to Mab before her death. Each time his bonded died, he shed his coat, revealing a new fairy with a different appearance. Did you speak to anyone unusual last eve?"

I almost laugh. "Apart from every faerie?"

Azlyon sighs.

I remember Scátha's cryptic warning and instructions, not to mention anything to Azlyon. It would be foolish to trust a faerie, let alone a goddess. Talking to Azlyon feels as easy as breathing, the meaning of anam really did this feeling justice, though it could be very easy for the goddess to manipulate him through me.

"A spotted cat," I say, "a troll or goblin, that shapeshifting púca, a few elves—I think they were elves, they are a little shorter than you but taller than me… I think their eyes were bigger."

His eyes open slightly. "Few fae have familiars, and those that do meet shortly after birth."

"Yes, but I never met any of them before," I say.

"A familiar is not an ordinary faerie, and Grehyl is something more entirely. He would have watched you as you grew." Azlyon ponders it for a moment. "It was the cat."

"He did say something about being a god's familiar."

A loud crash distracts us as Sithen swears in the distance.

I run outside and see Tian throwing clay cups at Sithen. The tiny faerie's lips are up to his eye in a furious snarl. Jupa keeps passing the cups and plates from the washbasin to Tian with a broad smile and a sunken concentration.

"I curse your firstborn human!" Sithen keeps disappearing and reappearing.

"Like I am going to have a child, you tiny ugly insect!" Tian calls back.

Jupa chuckles before he looks up and sees me. Both pale as the dish drops to Tian's toes.

"You fools, why aren't you bound?" I crack my knuckles.

Sithen appears and pulls Tian's right arm out of its socket with a popping sound.

Tian screeches and falls backwards onto the dirt. Not broken but dislocated.

"Sithen, was that necessary?" I ask.

The faerie snorts. "If the half-breed wasn't here, the smelly human would be sliced into twelve pieces and given to the crows."

Jupa looks at the ground.

"Bind them," Azlyon's voice was behind me, "Sithen, you may take a memory from each of the humans as payment for creating such a mess."

I turn to see Azlyon towering behind me. He has been there the entire time and they were scared of him, not me.

"A memory?" I ask.

"They are lucky it isn't their life," Azlyon says, "they must pay a price."

"What if it is something important? And Rowyna and Tionne?"

"That is not my concern, a payment must be completed however Sithen decides." Azlyon walks away from the home into a nearby apple grove.

"From the girl, I take away your memory of love." Sithen licks his lips.

She has been quiet until now. "No please, don't!"

I hold Rowyna's hand as Sithen extracts a memory with a hazy yellow glow at the tip of his finger. A memory of love for Rowyna, a memory of loss from Jupa, a memory of Tian's mother, and a surprise memory from Tionne. By telling them ahead of time, he relishes in their squirming. He wanted them to beg and plead as he took away something fundamental to their very soul.

And Azlyon told Sithen to do just that. He announces it in a cold, sure voice. It was the voice of a leader passing judgment. A voice of the fae I've been warned about in Jorthus. It was also something I couldn't ignore, but could not speak out against so openly.

"Do you know Cicero?" I ask.

"Of course I do, he was our leader," Rowyna says after Sithen's extraction.

"How do you feel about him," I ask.

"I think he favoured the assassins, but he was fair enough, kind of stiff, I think," she said. "Why?"

I sigh.

"The creature thought I'd take the memory entirely? Sithen is not a monster," the faerie smiles wider than comfortable.

I let go of her looking downwards.

He appears in front of Tian next, his eyes wide and smiling. He was waiting to punish the two men.

"Aurelia, remember my mama's name, it was Hazel." Tian shuts his eyes. "She had skin like sweet Lomel caramel. Her hair was dark—down to her calves, and her eyes, well, they were brown. I want you to know how she looked, maybe one day you could tell me about her. She called me her child of the earth."

Sithen touches his forehead.

Mothers were loyal to their babes. They can make the difference between a good or great man. Quite often children would only grow up with them, while their fathers were conscripted or working. I was robbed of a chance with mine and now his was taken away.

When I look back at him, the embers of remembrance fade into a dull voice behind his eyes. His once clenched hands fell to his sides like someone disturbed a corpse.

"Oh, my," Sithen says with a smile, "this one gave me quite interesting information. Quite a fitting name, child of the earth"

I glare at the faerie.

"I enjoy trading in secrets, one could call me a master of whispers when I am not healing generous fae-kind." Sithen licks his lips.

He turns to my father and I snarl, "Take everything from him, let him live in the pain of not knowing."

Sithen raises a brow. "As tempting as that is, it is not part of the exchange. We would be rather monstrous if we did that, now would we?"

I stand up, feeling my legs wobble. "You feel no ill about taking away two beautiful things from those other two humans, there is a line between punishment and torture, and I think you have crossed it. Why not go all the way with Tionne?"

Sithen only smiles and continues.

Chapter 22: Vesagona

Woyldlan, Court of Daeyed

I walk through the silent village alone but I feel eyes all around me.

There is a stick faerie with a goat's skull head sitting in the centre market space. It is a quiet creature, almost lost in its own thoughts. I sit beside it, knowing we're the only two in the area.

"Fall forward on your face or fall backwards and face the stars," it says to me in a low, fizzy voice.

"Sometimes it's easier to see nothing than everything," I reply.

"Easier but also cowardly," it says back.

I pull out a small pot of honey from my satchel and push it close to the creature. It was from Sithen's home but was given to me by Belousa.

"What is that?"

"A gift," I say with a tiring yawn, "for coming out to talk to me."

The other faeries would peer at me through the foliage and windows but not approach me. I wonder if it was because of the revel. Perhaps they were scared of how close I am to the crown.

"We do not accept gifts," it says. "I must give you something in return."

I raise a brow. "Why?"

"It is how it is done, I will answer three questions without trickery in exchange for this," the faerie says.

"Why is it always three?" I wonder.

"Three is a good number, and it is a number that originated in magik," it answers. "You have two questions left."

I laugh. Of course, it would take that as one of my questions.

"Why do they avoid me," I ask. "The fae here?"

The creature appears to stretch its wooden body. "I cannot speak for them, but I know the majority of them were told not to speak to you and the rest are scared of how close the princes keep you to them. You have one question left."

"Do you trust in The Morrígan?" I ask.

"The gods are our teachers, our protectors, and our life keepers." Then it looks me in the eye. "Even though she can save us, it is hard to trust one that is said to foretell doom and death with her appearance. I believe it is wise to always remain skeptical of the gods while giving them all the attention they need. Someone as curious as you should not trust The Morrígan, for her attention for the fae is different from one such as you. We are loyal to the gods, but humankind is not. You are not, and that is what could tip whatever opinion she has of you."

The creature then looks down at my hand. "They also fear being touched by you. The mark of réalta has changed your hand forever. It is a bad omen, though some enjoy the risk at night or during revels. In truth, it is no worse than a scar."

"Réalta?" I remember vaguely.

"I will explain it for a lock of your hair." Its voice is shadowy.

I could easily ask my uncle or Azlyon without worrying about the price. I have no idea what kind of wicked things it could do to me through my hair.

"It is fine, I have other places to get information." I shut my eyes for a moment, grounding myself.

"It is not fine, my knowledge is grand and you insult me by turning to lesser fae?" it asks.

My eyes open and I see it grinding its jaw as it grows into a mossy beast, no longer made of twigs and branches. I hobble back, holding my hands in front of me.

"I meant no offence, I just don't want to give you my hair," I say. "The princes are close to me, they can tell me."

It pulls more earth into its wooden bones, growing bigger. Stone wouldn't do any good since it came from the earth, and this thing ate the earth.

It roars angrily, "Whether you meant no offence makes no difference. Through trust, they will take you bone by bone until you are entirely theirs."

I dash circles around it. If I made it dizzy I could have a chance.

"How do I kill it?" I call as I side-step a claw now half the size of my body.

What destroys earth-bound faeries? Fire could burn wood, but not stone. I doubt anything would be useful against the stone.

I roll towards it, through the legs and grasping onto the thick roots that made up its back. I pull myself up as it begins to buck and snarl. I knew once it grabs me I would be as good as dead. I have one shot to end it.

I pull the horns atop its head. It jerks and shakes me but I am holding it so tightly the thorns began to cut my skin. The answer was fire.

Burn.

Burn.

Burn.

I saw a tiny spark light the wood as I was thrown off. The beast screeches as it begins to claw itself to put out the fire.

"I don't want to fight you." I jump back, gasping.

"Do you understand why I am doing this?" I hear it whisper as the fire nearly consumes it.

The Faerie only charges again, this time knocking my leg off balance, causing me to tumble. I could feel the heat from the flames as I fall to the ground.

My belly has been cut open, blood splattering over the ground and on my body. The faerie must have sliced me as I went down. The wound is deep enough to make me stagger but not kill me.

"*Skartha*!" I hear Azlyon before I see him.

He looks furious.

The faerie is snapping and ripping apart piece by piece as it makes its final charge at me, flames no longer in sight. Each twig and stone floats in the air like a dismembered skeleton in water. It yowls and cries, but does not stop until its head is the only thing before me.

Azlyon's hand circles the creature's beating heart. It is green and brown, but it glows brightly against the sunlight, smaller than an apple.

"Still so young for your kind," Azlyon said. "I don't want to do this, Vesa, for your kind were loyal to the blood of Oberon."

With one fluid motion, he takes the heart in hand and squeezes it causing each part of the faerie to explode and snap.

"Aurelia," Kynus is at my side, "are you alright?"

"It does not matter if she is alright." Azlyon walks past us. "She provoked a peaceful wise fae, and I had to destroy it. She nearly let it burn to death, let her suffer some more before Sithen sees her."

His voice is cold and angry.

Kynus sits next to me.

"Why is he like that?"

"The Vesagona are wise, they are caretakers, and one of the only kinds of fae who will approach anyone and treat them as their equal. Killing them without just cause is a sin, and even if one does, it is not without remorse," Kynus says.

I tell him what happened and he only shakes his head with a mortifying look.

"What's wrong?"

"While other fae use hair for deviant purposes, the Vesagona collect the hair of those who inspire them and then braid it around their hearts, to keep them warm during long winters to come. The Harr worship them, and keep their hair long should the Vesagona need warmth."

I feel sick.

* * *

The village disappears behind us as we walk down the road after meeting with Sithen once more. All of us are on foot, with Kynus walking beside me and Azlyon in front. The humans are bound behind us with a single woodland elf warfellow at the rear.

I never had the chance to speak to Jupa about what happened the night of the revel, but if he did remember, he wasn't about to say a word. Tian seemed the most empty of the two, he knew he had a mother but no memory of her. I told them all what they lost but they looked at me as though I were talking about strangers. Rowyna couldn't comprehend the possibility of her falling in love with Cicero. As for Tian, he didn't want to hear who his mother was until he was more comfortable with the idea of a memory being stolen.

Tionne hadn't uttered a word to me since the memory was taken, only passing words in the common tongue to Rowyna. He would speak to her and barely look at me. Sithen wouldn't tell me which one he took from my father.

Azlyon did not speak to me directly since he killed Vesa to save me. He was furious but silent. When I tried apologizing, he walked away, pretending to be preoccupied with "more pressing matters." Kynus warned me not to push him until he was ready to speak to me. He told me Azlyon could be unnecessarily cruel without thought.

"Cheers round," Kynus says. "You won't have to see the good doctor anymore."

What an odd expression. "I'm surprised he even healed me."

"I suspect for a moment, he pitied you or enjoyed the pain you suffered. It can be hard to tell with that faerie."

"Interesting things happened in that village," I say. "It can be hard to tell if the core of all were good or bad."

Kynus half-smiles. "I am less of a purist than Azlyon, I've had my share of mistakes, though I believe one can grow from them. Of course, it does depend on how I'm feeling that day, punishments could be light or they could be severe. When it comes to highborn fae, the rules are quite grey. Usually, each court decides the fate of the accused."

"If each court chose the fate of their own, wouldn't they make it light?" I ask.

Kynus chuckles darkly. "Oh no. While a highborn is usually never put to death, they usually undergo something we call the cataclysm. Mental and physical pain for months. It is not pleasant."

I shiver.

"He chose to undergo it once every few years," Kynus nods at Azlyon, "something inside him is broken. I say that as one of the last fae to know him, or at least know him enough to understand him."

"Were any Seelie highborns executed?" I ask.

"Yes, though I only know of one, Dalziel Skeasun, nephew of Titania," Kynus reminisces. "He was sentenced to a mortal death, and his twin sister and older brother were banished to Gaia during different times."

"Is it the same family Gideön mentioned?"

He smiles. "Back then, the worst crime was to love humankind. If you were alive then, you would've been smothered as a babe."

Humans now treat the fae like the fae used to treat them. It was a cycle of hate and forbidden temptation. I wonder exactly what went through Azlyon's mind when he realized I was not pure. Was he angry, annoyed, or perhaps afraid?

"What did Dalziel do?" I ask.

"Dalziel was caught with a human lover," Azlyon says shortly. "'We must remain firm in our laws, even if one of our own kin breaks them.' My brother was sealed away for committing the same crime, except with four of his demiblooded faelings roaming the world."

"Are you trying to figure out how to punish me?" I ask.

He does not respond.

I feel the fae before I could see them. Some were on the side of the road, basking in sunlight, others walk alone and with few belongings. Some flew above the road.

We appear to be backtracking to the Daelin Fork.

"My daughter," I hear Tionne speak and my body goes rigid.

"Aurelia," he says my name this time, "we can go back to Jorthus, I can petition to the king and we can move into a home on the edge of Farlenfell or we can move to Trilan. We can find a home that overlooks the sea. We can talk to your brother, tell him who he is and we can all move to a place where we can finally be a family. I can take you hunting, we can all be together."

Kynus only smirks at my side, finding Tionne's words humorous.

"Tionne, you are as good as dead after you tell Lorkus." I retort.

"They won't kill me, don't worry, my girl," he responds, now closer to me.

"I don't know what they took but I am the one who is going to kill you." I clench my hands into fists.

Rowyna scoffs. "So that is how you managed to go undetected. Papa was high enough to hide you."

"Rowyna," I say, "careful with your words. You must understand that what is revealed in this country must stay here."

I fall back so I'm next to her. I feel a small hesitation in her composure. She isn't sure if I am on her side or theirs, so she had to test the waters. My fate is already partially written through a contract with Dian Cecht.

Kynus coughs. "Aurelia, stop playing with the humans."

"You forget, I know this one—far more than the rest," I tell him. "She was always so terrible, playing is rather fun."

Kynus shakes his head in laughter before walking ahead with Azlyon.

"You deserve a life outside of the spymasters," I tell her quietly. "A husband who will come home at the end of the day, babies who will cause a stir in the capital, and a home near the market where you can smell freshly cut primroses. I have no doubt you dreamt of a life with Cicero once before your love was stolen from you."

"Aurelia—" she warns.

"Isn't Rowyna the most beautiful thing?" Tian begins with a smile. "She always tells me to 'shut it' or to 'stop talking,' but I know she is happy to have me for company."

I want to smile but she shoots the outlander a sharp glare.

"Darlin'," Tian licks his lips, "if only we met differently. I'd have you chuckling in a matter of moments."

"Oh, Tian," Jupa sighs, "as if you could woo a regular lady, let alone a pale-skin from Jorthus."

"Aurelia, kindly tell the prisoners—in small words—to remain silent," Kynus smiles tightly.

They don't need me to tell them.

"This will be over soo—"

My voice is cut off with a bang and my body was flung in the air.

Chapter 23: Falling Into The Cracks of Chaos

Court of Daeyed

When I open my eyes, I am laying in a ditch with the humans on the side of the road. I heard the snap of an arm, not knowing whose it was. My head is underwater, or at least it feels like it as the dust and dirt begin to clear around us.

Another bang sounds and I can't see anyone. I've never seen war or any form of battle. I only know basic training along with my shadow work skills.

I grasp the soil, sifting it between my fingers as I pull myself up through the loose earth and stone. I need to do something but I have no idea what. Every instinct tells me to run and never stop until my feet are worked to the bone.

The princes—what happened to them?

I cough, feeling a thick layer of smoke and dirt pepper my lungs.

Someone yanks my foot, pulling me back down into the ditch. I can't stabilize myself against the loose dirt so I tip backwards, my fall broke someone—or something.

Boom.

The place where I just was explodes into millions of pieces.

This is human warfare, laced with some form of magik. Humans cannot wield magik, at least not enough to cause this. Jorthus cannot be behind this, it looks like the work of a Flokael-born force or an inside rogue living in Dayed.

"Aurelia, you fool, you could've killed yourself!" I hear Rowyna before I see her.

"Wouldn't that be a treat" I let out a harsh, laugh which turns into a cough.

"You need to lead us to safety, none of us are safe up there or down here," she replies, looking me directly in the eye.

"Who is this, Rowyna?" I look up.

She shakes her head. "I have no idea, they aren't of Jorthus though."

I look around for any path of escape.

"Over here!" Jupa cries out.

I look at where Jupa was pointing and see a hole in the earth made of stone and moss. Too small to notice at first glance but large enough for us to try and fit down.

I pull at Tionne and we crawl over to take shelter.

Boom.

Our time is running thin.

Boom.

I push Rowyna in first before we start arguing.

Boom.

The earth next to us explodes as Jupa, Tian, and Tionne fall into the opening. I can only pray we wouldn't be buried alive or blown apart.

"Gods let us live," I catch myself saying.

There is no more denial, I saw one before my eyes. They are playing with all our lives, so the least they can do was help.

A mist hovers around me as I let myself fall into the hole, which turns out to lead to a cavern. I can't see anything but I do hear the breathing of what I hope to be the those that went ahead of me.

The earth grumbles and the hole closes. It was not pleased with all the stone and dirt that fell from the blasts.

I remember that Kynus said something once and morstone flickered on. What was it? I search my memory, watching it play in front of me.

"*Ayrlan Kyn*," I whisper, closing my eyes.

When I open them, I see morstone lighting the walls and floating between us. There is a tunnel several paces across from where we stood. The walls are made of a kind of marble with strange blue lichen climbing from the cracks.

"Is everyone ok?" I ask.

"My forearm is broken," Tian complains.

"But we are alive," Rowyna finishes in a stern voice.

I look around once more. "I don't know if Prince Azlyon or Kynus survived, but we are on our own for now," I pause, looking at Tionne, who silently watches me back, "and on our own, meaning we don't have protection against any faerie who hunts us in these tunnels."

"We have you, Aurelia," Tionne remarks.

I begin to scan the area, "I can only get you so far. You each have to rely on your own wits and sure footing. Do not leave the group, do not talk to anyone other than each other. The quieter we are, the more securely we can move. Ignore all taunts or illusions of good."

"We should all have a partner to look after," Jupa suggests.

I nod. "Pairing up is a good move, in case something does happen and we are separated."

Both Tian and Jupa eagerly say, "Aurelia will be my partner!"

I shake my head.

"You know we will be quite useless without you," Tian says. "Mostly me, look at my arm."

"Rowyna and Tionne are skilled in certain trades, they also happen to be stronger than the two of you," I say.

"Ouch," Jupa whines.

"I am meek around the fae, I'll admit it," Tian says.

"Tian and Rowyna, Tionne and Jupa, watch over each other without complaint until we are safely out." I cough out more dust.

Rowyna raises a brow. "Why are you the leader?"

"Because I—"

"The last time you were alone underground with the fae, didn't you lose your mind? Or when you came back from the party intoxicated also without a sound of mind?"

I look at her challengingly. I couldn't let anyone die and they would without me.

"You forget that when no one notices you, you tend to learn a lot more, and the fae weren't being discreet," Rowyna says. "I saw you each time you failed. They don't care because they think I am going to die when we reach that castle."

I know she meant the princes.

"You will die without me," I hate using this to my advantage, "Need I remind you?"

She raises her hands in defeat as the lights fade away. An uncomfortable stillness settles over us except for quick breathing. The morstone obeys me because I conjured it.

"I do not need you, Rowyna," I hear myself saying.

What I said is not true in the slightest; I still do not know what I was doing half the time. Yet she saw me remove the light that we need to see our way out.

"Ayrlan Kyn," I say and the morstone flickers on again. "Rowyna, I want you to live on in Jorthus."

She walks closer to me, her eyes cloudy and whispers, "I wish I could believe you, I do. But things have changed. You follow them around too much. Remember, I am the governor of spymasters, I think you forget this at times."

She is right about some things. The details of our arrangement have changed, and telling her would mean losing her and much of my old life.

"Aurelia," she says, louder this time and extending her arms at each side, "if you are so special, open the ground up with your magik, let us take a safer path!"

Everyone turns to me. They expect the world to flow from my fingertips and wouldn't accept anything less of extraordinary. This is more than just bringing everyone to safety, it is a test. Rowyna is challenging my ability and authority, and she's reading my weaknesses.

I only smile. "You act as though I've been practicing my entire life. If magik worked as simply as you think, well, I'd have a bottle of Wrenchworth wine sitting on sandy shores. If it was so simple, I would be like the princes of Daeyed and not who I am now. Tionne, perhaps you can tell her what it would be like if I were like them?"

My father sighs. "We would have already been dead."

"You are all alive because I made it so. I think it would be best to listen."

Tionne watches me curiously.

I began to walk.

A hearty chuckle echoes in the shadows. The morstone flickers into an eerie dim green as we go on. No one speaks or protests as we climb to the edge of an underground cliff with barely enough room for one person to step.

I turn my head and see that everyone is practically clutching the wall for their lives. I'm glad that it is dark in here, for one look down a lit cavern may cause panic.

"There is a landing over there," I say looking onward, barely making out a hole in the shadowy wall.

I cling to the rocky wall tighter as my body swings around the corner where the ledge ends. My nails dig into the stone to regain my balance.

"To kill or hide, a creature walks humbly through these halls," a deep morose voice echoes through the air. *"We wonder if you have seen the face of death, for we look similar."*

"Ignore it," I command, "be careful as you swing around, the edge is further than I thought."

The edge ends and several feet across is the landing. Between that is a drop so deep, I would most certainly die should I fall. I hear someone grunt as they swing their body around the stone.

I shut my eyes. "We are going to have to jump a good distance."

"Jump? Are you sane?" Jupa gasps as he makes the swing.

I clench my teeth, going back is a possibility, though we will have to dig for a very long time through the stone. That isn't an option for me. So I bend my knees and propel my body forward, feeling the air swirl all around me as my soles leave the ground. My heart races as my arms are flung backwards while I kept my head up.

Before I know it, I am on the other side, holding my breath as a few tiny rocks fall.

My eyes examine the now visible runes around the hole. They are dark, hollow, and tell a story I cannot possibly read. I wonder if even Azlyon or Kynus could.

I hear Rowyna gasp as she lands behind me. Her hand immediately goes to my shoulder as the next person makes the jump. I only wonder if Tian or Jupa hold enough nerve.

"Are we going through there?" she asks.

I turn and see Tian dusting himself off with a wide grin.

"We haven't seen any fae down here yet," I say. "You are right to feel afraid, and that voice taunting us isn't helping."

"What voice?" Jupa asks as he pulls himself up from his jump.

"A deep voice, I think a male voice." I look at them. "Rowyna?"

She shakes her head. "I'm sorry but I didn't hear it. If there is a voice it only wants you to hear."

"Or Aurelia is losing her mind like us!" Tian claps.

Rowyna slaps him across the face. "If you don't have something useful to contribute then perhaps you should stay quiet, Deadlander."

Tian only smiles at her sheepishly.

"Tionne," I say, walking back to the edge, "you need to jump."

"I don't know if I can make it," he responds, looking down at the chasm.

I look him in the eye. "Yes you can, you are a legitar!"

"I've fallen from less."

"If I can do it, so can you."

His leg begins to shake as he prepares to jump.

"I don't know, perhaps you should leave me here." He looks down again.

"You can do it!" I call back.

He nods and pushes off the cliff, jumping forward.

Time moves in slow motion as he pivots at an unfavourable angle. I reach out for him, his hand grabbing my arm, dangling off the edge and dragging me flat on my belly. Someone holds me by my legs so I don't fall.

I feel like my arm is ripping from the socket. I grimace as Tionne grips my forearm, thankful his wrist is broken on the other arm.

"Hold on!" My hair is in my face and my arm is going numb.

"Aurelia, I left a letter with Lucia, it is for both you and Lorkus." He looks down into the chasm then back up to my eyes. "You need to let me go."

I clench my teeth. "It is not time for you to die! You need to tell Lorkus yourself!"

"I should've taken care of you, I should've been there as you grew up." Tionne's eyes are wet. "I hope you will do good by Lythe, by your brother, and by this world."

"I won't let go!" My torso slides down the edge of the cliff.

"Aurelia, you need to let him go, we can't hold both of you!" Rowyna cries out.

I look behind me. They are holding my legs and anchoring each other.

"Tionne," I say, hearing the pop of my arm sliding out of place. I cry out.

"My daughter, the Order will keep you safe when they cannot," he says.

"What?" I gasp for breath.

He lets go and slides through my hand.

I watch his face fade as he fell into darkness.

My heart stops. For a moment, the world falls in silence, even as they pull me up. My mind is numb as someone pops my shoulder in place. I feel my breath against my upper lip but I can't force myself to move. It is one thing for your father to betray you, it is another for him to be gone from your life permanently.

Chapter 24: To Challenge A God

Tech Duinn, Court of Daeyed

"Aurelia," Rowyna touches my hand, "do you need a moment?"

"No." I need several moments but I can't let anyone else fall victim to this place.

I stand up. Jupa and Tionne are at each of my sides. I could feel their warmth and hear their soft comforting breaths.

"A father moves on, into the land of in-between where the fae fall though, he leaves a daughter more broken than a shattered glass crown," the voice calls again. *"Did the daughter care, did the protector take what was his without asking, or was it simply meant to be in this hall of cackling bones and whistling spirits?"*

I clench my fist.

"Who are you?" I scream into the cavern. My own words echo back at me sevenfold.

My feet pull me deeper into the tunnel and others follow without another word.

We appear to be in some sort of throne room. The stone is dimly lit from luminescent crystals. A dark throne of smoke and shadow sits in the centre and pews of bone craft seats for worship.

"We are the past," the air becomes cold, *"the present,"* then crystal throbs brighter, *"and the future."*

I turn and see that the humans appear to be petrified in fear behind me. I try to touch them but they don't move.

"That is not a good answer," I say, walking closer to the throne.

"It is the truth as your false gods refuse to claim." The voice became shallow and inhuman.

"The gods do as they please, I want to know who you are to me."

"Possibly the oldest and the youngest of them," the voice cackles. *"We are your future, you will pass through our gates, everyone does."*

"Are you a gatekeeper fae?" I decide to ask.

It laughs. *"We are so much more and so much less, we are the lord of the afterlife, my child, you are in Tech Duinn, our home and the doorway to the dead, the living, and each plane of existence."*

I bite my lip. "You are a god?"

"We were once, now we are the humble servant of hers." A shape materializes, a dark figure with skin so dark it reflects no light, and long hair matching the deep blackness of his body. The only features visible are yellow eyes without pupils. He appears to wear a cloak woven from bone and mist, though looking closer, I see the faces of the dead in the clouds.

I fall to my knees without thinking. The dead come alive here and the living die in his home. He is in control of everything and nothing all at once.

"How did we end up here?"

"You were in danger and the god of seas led you to us, thinking we would be kind and let you leave through the door back to your world." The figure floats like a spectre closer to me.

"And will you?" My face is on the floor.

"Perhaps, or perhaps we will allow you to find your way out." Skeletal hands pull my face to him. His skin is scarred and thick, and I can just barely make out his face in the darkness.

I meet his eyes and see my mother's reflection in them.

"Mother," I whisper.

The creature opens its mouth with a smile of red and yellow teeth. *"Your mother stood in this very hall before entering Mag Meli, they all do, just as you will. She begged us, you see, she wanted me to refuse you when you came, it is a fickle rule when one sacrifices themselves for someone. I suppose this happening is her last wish fulfilled, you see, no living soul can enter here and continue a life in the living world. You will be spared only this once, as for your companions, well we have already claimed one, the rest will follow."*

I pull back. "You can't take them, they've done nothing wrong!"

"Oh but they have, they stepped into Tech Duinn before their time, they cheated their fate on the side of that road. You are the exception because of your ties with the gods and mother's tithe. We simply cannot let them leave alive. She wouldn't let me and we wouldn't want to." The god pulls me up on my feet.

"You killed my father," I say.

"Our shadows did." Beneath his cloak, sickly black masses crawl out and slither all around the room like snakes. *"They pushed him slightly too soon as he made his final leap, and hung onto the mortal's boots as he clung to you. Our dear creature, they will do the same, to these tiny souls."*

I look down for a moment. "What can I do to change your mind?"

"You speak to us in such a tone, it is almost amusing, the desperation and determination," he says, touching my cheek.

I gulp. "L-Let me be clear, I am not going to leave without them. Wouldn't that ruin the nature of Lythe's tithe?"

"We are being quite clear, though we do love games and the folly of mortals. We are called Lord Donn," I hear him say, *"and we do not make these rules that you are so instant on breaking. If they all live to find the right door then only one of them will die and the others can leave with you."*

"That's not good enough!" I step backwards.

"You are bold," he grins. *"Little creature, you forget we do what we wish, and when it is no longer amusing, we could end everything simply by removing the air from the room. We don't care for your gods, your faeries, or your people. We will have another soul or all of them."*

"We will see," I tell him.

I hear a layered chuckle magnify throughout the corridor.

When I turn around, they are no longer petrified. They are all rubbing their eyes in unison as if waking from a long slumber. Rowyna smiles at me slightly when our eyes met.

"We need to find a way out," I say, starting towards the hall behind the throne.

"Aurelia who is going to die?" Tian asks.

I freeze. "No one."

"We heard your voice though we couldn't see," Rowyna says.

"No one will die today," I growl.

"We trust you," Tian says, "just get us out of here."

I nod but still feel my body shiver.

I look at each of them. "Do either of you know about Lord Donn of the underworld, someone who was once a god?"

Rowyna looks back into the room for a moment. "If he is a god, then he is not privy to those outside of Daeyed."

Tian looks at me curiously. "We have a goddess in the Dead Lands who presides over the dead, though I never followed her teachings."

I sigh. His goddess and The Morrígan were once and the same no doubt.

Rowyna stands beside me. "Despite all our differences and the trouble we face, I need to tell you that I am sorry that your father died."

I shrug her hand off me. "I never knew him. He betrayed me. His being gone changes nothing."

She breathes deeply. "I saw your face, Aurelia, just for a moment your world broke. You no longer have a chance for him to redeem himself, to both you and your brother, Prince Lorkus."

I look her in the eyes. "This information can never go to Fyfe. Lorkus is his son in every way that matters."

I want to tell Fyfe before I plunge a dagger in his heart. I want to tell him that his bastardly seed will no longer taint Arcadia. A new generation of royalty could emerge should the fae fail. But I could not forget that Lorkus is more manipulative and cunning than his father, who relies on brute force and threats.

"I have no way of proving that the Legitar is his father, and the king would not believe without substantial proof," Rowyna tells me.

"Cicero knew for years? He knew all the palace secrets yet never once whispered a word," I tell her, before covering my mouth, realizing I let this information slip. Rowyna is so easy to talk to that I forgot about my role and duty to both the fae and myself. Truths long to expose as though air pulls them from the tongue.

"That is news to me," She looks forward, revealing nothing. "As the Royal Master of Shadows, I should hope he kept the information to himself."

I breathe deeply. She knows far too much.

"What will you tell Fyfe?" I say, attempting to side with her.

Rowyna nods. "King Fyfe will need to know as much as I can tell him if there is to be a war."

"War?" I say carefully.

She looks back at the two men following us for a moment. "I'm not foolish, I can put things together. They are bitter and angry with us. Why would they take you away from Jorthus for the sake of your protection? They have motives behind every action. Nothing is genuine."

What do we do with people who know too much? We cut them loose and erase them from the world. If Fyfe even learned one morsel of information uttered in these stone halls, it would be too much.

"Your skin crawls," Donn's voice slithers into my head, *"your mind numb. We see those ravenous eyes as you kick down and climb over the hill of rotten carcasses you once called friends."*

I shut my eyes. Every action has a consequence, and by attempting to keep Rowyna alive I have only guaranteed her death. She knows too much.

"Let's worry about war when we get out of here," I say instead.

"Aurelia, will you fight in this war?" she asks.

I say nothing at first because the answer for me isn't clear. "I'm not fighting for Fyfe if that's what you mean. Perhaps I will slide into the shadows and move south."

She looks onwards.

"Lady Pride, do not trust the serpent's promises," Jupa walks up beside us, "I do not think this god is a good god and if he is pushed under ancient laws, then we must be wary of our actions."

I smile at him. "I do not fear him."

"Tian, did I ever tell you how thick the people of Jorthus are?" Jupa looks backwards.

"At least we are down one. My god, that tracker fellow was so dull! He had no sense of adventure. Have I ever told you when sandsick cannibals ambushed my clan as we neared the ruined Drakespin hills? It was a bloody massacre but I managed to get a few pretty scars from it."

"I've heard of Sandsickness, but you've never told me what exactly it is," Jupa inquires curiously.

"It's a disease only found in the western Dead Lands. There is something in the ground that enters the body through the lungs, bringing madness and a lust for treasure and insatiable hunger," Rowyna explains.

"Believe me, I know all about it, my second clan turned on each other. They all went mad 'cept me," Tian says. "Wager a guess and say I'm immune?"

"I thought you lot didn't know about magik?" Jupa said.

Rowyna laughs. "Disease and magik are not synonymous, and I thought you knew nothing of it."

Jupa shakes his head. "The Dead Lands may be lost of all spells and magik, but the drought of it left a mark in the form of illness no doubt."

Rowyna turns sharply to Tian, examining him.

"Open your mouth," she says.

He tilts his head with wiggling eyebrows. "What will I get in return?"

"I'm not a faerie, I am not enthralled by the idea of a deal. You are going to do as I say or I will sacrifice you to that nasty little god." Rowyna grabs his face, forcing his mouth open.

A slightly forked tongue and sharp back teeth.

"You said your ma did that to you when you were a boy, there is little vegetation so she sharpened your teeth into points and cut your tongue to look menacing," Jupa says as Tian plucks her hands from his face.

"I don't remember my ma," he says, looking frustrated.

"Then how did you survive the plague?" she asks.

She thought Tian held some form of magik in his blood. It is entirely doubtful and absurd. Even I knew that some people have a natural immunity to disease. While in this case, it may be rare, it is still possible.

"I wore a mask made from ocean kelp and bark," he explains.

Jupa speaks again. "Your ma was a healer and a wise woman, she knew the hidden truths of the way of life down there."

"My mistake then." Rowyna steps back at my side then whispers, "There is something he is hiding from everyone."

"We all hide things, and if I were from the Dead Lands, I would hide many things to start a new life."

We walk in the dark for a while, nothing but the cold pressure of a light wind against our skin and the soft fall of pebbles from above us now and then. On the walls are carvings of the past, great heroes, the gods themselves—or maybe they were the fae. It is becoming difficult to tell them apart from one another.

The ground is thick moss covers the ground, cushioning our feet, our breaths making the only noise. Jupa and Tian sink into the moss deeper than Rowyna and I, not because they are larger but because we know how to walk carefully and they do not.

Azlyon, if you are out there, we are alive. I push my words out as far as I can to no avail.

They could be dead, or at the very least far from here.

There is a small pool of pale, glowing water. It is warmer the closer we step into the chamber. The floor begins to vibrate and hum with every step we took. Faint hissing echoes above.

A tangled mess of snakes fall from the ceiling into the shape of a person as a hooded crow flew over to the edge of the pool watching us.

The mess turns into Lord Donn, though different from the one I saw before. Sharp teeth, broken dragonfly wings, six legs, and a half-melting face.

"Escape is one thing you will never have." Lord Donn smiles crookedly. *"You cling so elegantly yet so dangerously to the line between reality and nightmare. Escape from the loss you caused will hunger so close to your tainted heart."*

The bird caws and flies up to a ledge as if to get a better view.

"We are going to have to fight him," I say quietly to them.

Tian and Jupa gasp but stand at my side. Their madness will either help or hinder us.

"Aurelia, is there no other way out?" Rowyna asks squeezing my shoulder.

I shake my head. None that I could even remotely think of.

"Lord Donn, why let us come here?" I ask, walking closer to him and the pool. "Why not end us all back there?"

I look around the chamber for a way out. I remember stories of mirrors and holes being portals to different worlds. We climbed into the earth and walked right into one. There had to be something similar.

"We wanted information for her, we wanted you to feel a sense of fear, for no one loves to die," he says. *"Aurelia you may leave untouched, leave them for us."*

The crow looks down at the pool of water and back to me. I remember that I met Dian Cecht through spring water, and I couldn't help but wonder if perhaps the way out lay at the bottom of this small pond.

"Jupa and Tian," I decide, "I command you both to jump into the pool now."

They have no time to protest, for their legs are already carrying themselves to the pool. They have to listen to my direct commands and obey. I can hope the door back to Arcadia is through the pool.

Lord Donn growls and leaps for them a sliver of a moment too late. The water has already concealed and sent them far away.

"Reo!" Lord Donn cries as he clatters onto all of his limbs and runs at me. The waters begin to harden into a thick layer of ice or stone.

I get out of the way. He screeches and Rowyna is sent flying backwards into the wall.

I leap on the false god's back and try to strangle him—them.

"Aurelia, you can't kill a god! You'll die!" Rowyna spits blood as she gets up.

"Listen to the girl," Lord Donn chuckles darkly before his head turns back to face me like an owl.

I stab him in the eye with my claws. Their laughter only becomes louder.

I remove my hand and there is no blood, no mess, nothing.

"Our turn," he says, picking me up and flinging me so hard into the pool that my back cracks a little.

I open my eyes and see Rowyna between me and what would have been a killing blow. Lord Donn only grins wider as my shock melts into fear. His insect leg impales Rowyna. Her eyes are watery, glazing over.

I place my hands on her cheeks and shake my head.

"Go," she whispers, "my friend."

I shut my eyes a moment and then slam my fists on the ice.

The crow caws again and Lord Donn stops before he nearly crushes me with his body. Instead, he pulls Rowyna back onto the moss. His eyes are wild and a cursed smile graces his lips.

"Our mistress wishes you to leave. We have enjoyed this, thank you, faerie born." Lord Donn's mouth opens wider and tears off half of Rowyna's face.

I wince and stab the ice once more until it cracks.

My body falls through.

Chapter 25: The Font

Font of Lystál, Court of Daeyea

There is a light at the bottom of the pond, or perhaps it is the sky. My blood stains the water around me as I float down. My body is a shell, broken and leaking. Above me is heart-stopping blackness, one I long to cling to if my soul allows. My mind blocks out the pain and any sensation; it had to be the work of magik. I fell so hard against the frozen pond I felt the cracking, the creaking, and the shifting of everything within.

I would have died instantly if Rowyna hadn't acted. My friend and enemy chose my life over hers when there was so much at stake should she die. I was the last face she ever saw before she slid into the eternal darkness of life's end.

Then that god ate her.

My body is numb, but still, my eyes leak in this chaotic underwater nightmare.

Azlyon, if you are listening, let the tide take me, I am sure to die soon, my mind whispers everywhere.

My eyes shut.

If I die here, it would be as I deserve.

I've killed so many people, I led more to their death, and I sent so many to prison or exile in the Dead Lands. Before Rowyna died, I already planned on letting the princes end her life once we reached their capital. A friend wouldn't even consider such a thing.

The abomination should be silenced, it has become far more trouble than it's worth. Perhaps Fyfe truly understood what I was all those years ago.

* * *

"How do we heal her?"

I open my eyes and I am halfway on the shore of a small pond in a grassy cave. Moonlight shines in from the crack in the ceiling and the mouth of the cave. Luminescent orange dragonflies fly in circles as a single pale, root-like hand touches my forehead.

A tree-like figure towers over the humans at my side.

My eyes roll over to the left where I see a tree with bark white as snow and leaves as orange as the sun. A small hole where she must have crawled out of lays crookedly against the cool pond.

"W-who are you?"

I cough and examine her face, hollow eyes, branches for hair, and a small crack on her cheek. She is tall and magnificent.

"There are only two ways to enter this cavern, and coming from Tech Duinn has only been accomplished twice before your trinity escaped through." She presses a hand on my stomach and I cough out more blood. "You need to stop the magik if I am to heal you with the waters of Lystál."

"They can turn me into a mortal?" I ask, blinking.

The woman closes her eyes. "That path is no longer yours, lest you wish to die. For your wounds will kill you before they can be healed."

I shut my eyes. "What will the waters do?"

"It is up to them, child, they've healed your companions' memories as well as their insanity," the woman whispers. "Let your pain flow and then open your mouth."

I release the magik and the pain shudders through my body. I cry out and feel my lungs fill with splatters of blood.

"Lystál must be passed through the guardian hamadryad, for its waters keeps her living forever," she says, cutting her wrist and letting water flow into my mouth.

My throat seizes as my body begins to shake.

"What is it doing to her?" Jupa asks.

"Child of the East, it is doing one thing and only one to her, she will live," the hamadryad whispers. "When she is well enough to move, travel out of this cavern, to the light, and you will never find this place again."

The woman touches my cheek. "Thank you for your gift of conversation and greeting, Aurelia."

I look her in the eye. "I barely spoke."

She smiles. "You've told me so many things, your mind is truly wondrous."

Warmth wraps around my body as she kisses my cheek before walking back to her grand tree. She folds inwards as the tree moves to cover her body, exposing only her face as she returns to her deep slumber.

I follow soon after in sleep.

* * *

When I wake, the cavern is darker than before. The hamadryad looks even more statuesque than before. My body is no longer broken, it has a certain glow to it. Jupa and Tian are asleep when I crawl over to them, letting my muscles stretch. They feel one with the earth, and I hear every hum and breath of each blade like they are whispering and gossiping amongst one another.

"We need to leave," I say, looking at the water and wondering what exactly it did to me. I am not mortal, but I am not as I was before.

I shake each of their arms, and they wake looking at me.

"Aurelia?" Jupa asks, clapping my back. "It's about time!"

I look at Jupa, confused. "What do you mean?"

"It's been at least eight days." Tian rubs his eyes.

"What did you eat then?"

"The tree dropped fruit whenever we got hungry," Tian says.

What did I eat then?

"Let's get out of here," Jupa says, helping me up with him.

I look back at the hamadryad and whisper thank you before we walk out of the cavern. I use Jupa for support since my legs are still wobbly.

We step into morning light slightly shadowed by the mountain we emerge from. I feel a whip of air hit my face. The valley is green and full of life, and a small herd of centaurs trot along the forest edge. Lanky spriggans hulk outside of their stony mounds in search of mischief.

"It is nice to be out of the dark." Tian stretches.

"How are we going to avoid all fae until we hit the road?" Jupa asks. "And get out of this godsforsaken country?"

"The gods bless this province, you need a different word," I correct him.

"Province?" Tian asks.

I shake my head. "It used to be a province in the Dark Court. Sorry, my mind wandered as I spoke."

They look at each other.

"I have to find Azlyon, I need to fulfill my contract with Lord Dian Cecht," I say. "You both can leave when I see you safe on the road."

Tian shakes his head. "We are not leaving you with these monsters."

"They aren't monsters, at least not more than the average human, everyone has a dangerous side to them," I say.

"Relia," Jupa sighs, "let us at least make sure you can travel alone by the time we hit the road, if not then we will go with you as far as we can."

I smile. "Relia?"

"I give all my friends nicknames, for example, Tian is 'arsehole' sometimes." Jupa snickers as Tian punches him in the arm.

"Are you certain you wish to be my friend? I hear that I'm not the nicest person to be around," I say as we walk down the mountain slowly.

"Well, it's between you and the world that wants me dead," Jupa laughs. "Besides, we've been through a lot together."

I look back. The cave we exited is now just a wall of rock, as though it never existed in the first place. The woman in the cave is forever bound there, alone until someone finds the font.

"There you are." The spotted cat with amethyst eyes appears at our side.

"A talking cat?" Tian laughs as he inspects the creature with his own eyes.

"Mortals are quite delicious, it's been quite a while since I've devoured one," Grehyl speaks, silencing Tian.

I look at my familiar. He chose me for a purpose and I have yet to learn why.

"How long have you been at my side?" I ask him.

"I've been near you since you were born," Grehyl replies with a sneeze. "I met your mother when you were in her womb. I have not always been in sight, nor always in the same place as you, but I have been there when you've needed me."

I tilt my head. "And have you spoken to Azlyon?"

"So many questions..."

"Just this one more," I coax.

"Very well, I have spoken to Azlyon," the cat looks at me before rolling its eyes, "lifetimes ago when I was the familiar of one of his kin, and recently when he asked where you were."

I blink. He is alive. He survived the unknown attack after all.

"I am not loyal to the faerie prince, only you. I will not tell him anything unless you wish me to, but right now I am here because you surfaced and I can rest." Grehyl smiles.

"Relia, what are you saying?" Jupa asks.

I shake my head and turn to them. "Sorry, sometimes I—"

"Speak in faerie tongues? We know," Tian says. "The last bit of the common tongue was when the feline threatened us."

I look back to Grehyl but he disappears as though he was never there. He simply came to check in on me. It would have been nice if he led us to a road or even point us in the direction of one.

"Pretend to be my servants should any faerie take interest," I tell them. "I don't feel like fighting again."

Fighting and losing more people.

"Yes, ma'am." Jupa salutes.

"She is not our employer, she is our owner!" Tian punches Jupa's shoulder.

"You both will not speak unless I speak to you directly," I say touching each of their shoulders. "I won't take any more chances."

I walk apace in front of them. As far as anyone is concerned, they are simply toys to amuse me until I dispose of them or reach my intended destination.

A limping redcap with hair the colour of straw takes notice of us immediately. Where there is one, there is a chance more will follow. This one's large woven hat stands stiff at the nape of his neck from years of soaking it in fresh blood. No doubt the wound on his leg is probably from larger and trickier prey.

"An elf walks towards Fral Gwin looking lost, will Fral Gwin help?" The redcap licks his lips with a bloodied tongue.

"I am no elf," I say. "I am a princess of Daeyed."

"I hear the new princess is half asrai, you look nothing like an asrai." He hobbles closer.

"I am so much more," I say. "Have you seen an asrai?"

The redcap looks at my sharp fingers and my pointed teeth. Both are not common in elves, but it is easy to call anyone an elf, most fae had pointed ears and an aura of mystery around them.

"I have not seen an asrai in hundreds of years. Will the princess allow me to nibble on one of her slaves?" The redcap looks behind me.

"I would if I didn't need them for a grand tithe at the solstice. Prince Vikorus will be displeased if they aren't whole," I respond then tilt my head. "I would rather dine with you on human flesh if it were another time."

The redcap grins. "I am pleased to know there is someone on the throne who shares the same tastes as Fral Gwin."

I return the smile. "Unfortunately I separated from my guide, will you point me in the direction of the road to Daelin Castle?"

Fral Gwin looks at the sky for a moment and raises an arm to point with a long rotted finger towards the fruit-bearing side of the forest. I smile but also remember that nothing came for free in this world.

"In return, I offer these words to you: Fral Gwin, brave and vicious, you pave the way, though malicious, one day I hope to see that not all who cross your path are suspicious."

Fral Gwin snickers and begins to hobble away, looking for a bite in other areas. Sometimes the creation of words lined together musically creates memories of those they are about. Belief is another form of magic one must never pass up. Redcaps are Unseelie and Dark. That much is known. A way to appease them is to pretend to be like them. I just have to channel Vikorus and Septimius through my words.

"Handling redcaps with ease." A shape steps out from behind a tree.

The owner of that voice sends shivers down my spine. A human with the ferocity of a monster, a demon hidden underneath a proud face.

In front of me is Titus the Lion, general of Jorthus.

"You need to come with me," Titus says.

"I am not going back to Jorthus." I pull my brows together.

"I never said anything about Jorthus. We are going to Flokael."

Chapter 26: The Mighty Fall

Court of Daeyed

My eyes widen yet my lips maintain a hard line.

"Out of words, Aurelia?"

"No, I am just wondering when you decided to betray Fyfe." I cross my arms.

"I haven't, I've never been loyal to him." He steps closer, "One may say the Order has roots everywhere. Your father is where my allegiance lies."

I laugh curtly. "A human servant of the steward? One who is very dead?"

Titus' mouth gapes slightly but his stance is firm. "It is sad that Tionne is dead but I am talking about your real father, not the human vessel Lythe used to create you."

Whistryn, an Arch King of Flokael and Lythe's mate, is the leader and his claws were deep in Arcadian soil. Titus is the last person I expect to be part of that Order.

"Selene, Tionne, Lorkus maybe, and now you," I muse. "The Order has been quite busy. Tell me, Titus, is everyone I grew up with part of the Order?"

Titus smiles. "Of course not. Aurelia, you were created to unite the world. Come, we can take you home."

I could meet my mother's mate. I could finally fit in somewhere. Yet there was an itch that begins to peck at the back of my mind that I was not created out of love, but to be a beacon for change, a puppet, a doll. My whole life was fabricated and sewn together so perfectly, no doubt Titus was angry when Azlyon—Cicero—took me. He couldn't control me.

Azlyon was yet another person who wanted me to serve his own needs, but at least he made it my choice after my arrival. He showed me that I could be in control of myself and what I did here.

"It is convenient," I say, "that when I surface, you show up."

Titus looks around, uncomfortable to be in such a place. "We aren't very far from where you disappeared. I am relieved you were so close after the time that's passed, but now that I've found you, you must come back to my camp."

"Why would I go with you?" I ask.

Titus looks confused, "You are a prisoner with them, you can finally be free when you come with me."

I shake my head. "No one is ever free, but maybe a Queen could be..."

"Aurelia—"

"Remember when you used to hit me when I did a drill wrong?" My fists clench, "When you kicked my stomach until my ribs broke and I was coughing blood? Or maybe when you nearly let those soldiers rape me, but you came last minute and told them to stop just as they were taking off their trousers while others pinned me to the ground. I knew you waited because I saw you watching from the door, just before I could be stripped."

I do not like to think of the time when I was under Titus' direct influence. It is something I try to block out.

"You needed to be strong for the Order, Aurelia—"

"You are beneath me," I sneer. "You call me by my first name, yet you of all people should know the proper way to address a princess is your royal highness."

"Aurelia, I don't know what sort of unnatural magik they are using on you but you can finally have a family." Titus clears his throat.

I narrow my eyes. "I have family here, more so than I would with the Order."

"You don't know what you are doing!" Titus grabs my arm as I walk past him. "These creatures will only do what's in their best interest. You will only be half best, half worthy, and always lesser than them. In the Order, you will be seen as a true leader."

His words sound like the leaders of the Order are puppeteering him even at such a distance. It makes sense, he loves to follow orders.

"Titus, you don't care about the fae, you don't care about me, there is something in it for you." I grab his arm and slowly pluck his fingers off my wrist, each time nearly cracking bone.

Titus' mouth falls into a hard line as he winces slightly. Soldiers were taught to hide their pain, but even now, he can't avoid me. He needs something to serve him, a thing that only the Order can give. The answer is partially revealed in his violent yet desperately driven eyes. He wants power.

"I have been promised a nation through the Order," he admits.

I laugh, and he doesn't seem to like that.

"You can't just have a nation." I shake my head.

He looks away for a moment, "I was given an arranged marriage to the human Arch King's daughter."

"Titus, you could never be a king, you follow like a good soldier. I've seen you bend over backwards following Fyfe's orders, I've seen you lead your men on behalf of the king."

"I do not need to prove myself to you." Titus' eyes narrow. "You may have royal faerie blood in you but you will always be a grunt following orders."

"I am not the same woman you thought you knew in Jorthus." I sneer.

A sudden realization creeps over me. The one thing I should have asked Titus. How did he get so far into Daeyed without anyone noticing?

"Did you kill them?" I ask, stepping backwards.

Titus looks away. "The Order is everywhere, but it took years to gather support in Daeyed—"

"Did you kill them?" I snarl through my teeth.

"Those faerie bastards? They killed nearly all of us!" Titus narrows his eyes. "Aurelia, three of us made it out."

I cross my arms. "And you nearly killed me, we were trapped, and both Tionne and Rowyna died!"

He shrugs slightly. "People die in war. We needed to get you out, and a nice explosive distraction for them was the plan. You should've stayed on the grass for us to collect."

I shake my head.

"There has been enough death," I say. "Leave now, make your way back to your Order—if you can—and tell them Aurelia is siding with the fae."

Titus frowns.

"You've changed," he says, patting his satchel and pulling out his canteen for a sip of water. "I can't force you, perhaps we can part ways as friends? Or perhaps you'd want to see Cicero first?

He holds out a hand for me to shake.

"You have Cicero?"

"So fond of him." Titus nods. "We found him lying in a ditch after we attacked your group."

Jupa and Tian were so quiet behind me, I turn and see them bound, two faerie warriors holding blades to their throats.

I feel dizzy. "I'll see Cicero then decide from there."

"You can say hello to Cicero when we get back to camp," Titus smirks and pulls me along.

There is something hard in his eyes.

* * *

There was a small cavern beneath a grove after hours of walking. I may be dizzy but I don't put up a fight. If Titus is working with the Order, the fae could have something to do with this. Fae supporters of the Order more than likely helped Titus and his men travel through Daeyed, though not without risk.

I shake my head, my thoughts flowing like cold honey. The only thing that remains clear is that I need to find Azlyon.

Titus whistles a tune I did not recognize. Then another whistles back before we proceed further inwards. The cave itself looks as though it were made of molten gold. Smoke slithers on the roof, fleeing through the entrance.

I smell some sort of meat cooking. Around the fire sit eight others, roasting what appears to be a rabbit. Each of them looks glum and focused.

"I thought you said three," I mumble, out of breath and trying to make sense of my surroundings.

"Three made it out, but we had more hidden back in case something happened." Titus laughs.

"Aurelia?" The sound of a familiar voice feels like a blanket over my skin.

I see Cicero standing there. For a moment, I forget everything in the world, all that mattered was that the prince of lies figured out how to find me. My stomach drops and my heart quickens.

"She didn't want to come on her own?" a woman asks, standing up and looking at my sour face.

"Let's just say that she will need convincing," Titus says. "This is why you are still here, Cicero, and not back in Jorthus."

I walk over to my mentor, fumbling each step of the way, before throwing my arms around him.

"I thought you were dead." I bury my face in his shoulder. Even though the cat told me otherwise, I needed to see him with my own eyes to believe he was alive.

I reach for him. *Did Kynus make it out?*

He did, though he was frantic because we couldn't find you.

I sigh in relief.

"Not quite yet." He presses a hand to my neck, answering my verbal question.

Shall we end this charade or perhaps listen for information?

The latter, I respond, pulling back.

"Someone missed their master," Titus said with a frown.

"I barely saw him," I breathe. "If Cicero is with you, so am I."

Titus looks at us together. The Cicero we both knew was very formal in presentation, though this side of him is Azlyon. Cicero would never remain this close to me.

"Still, in this place, you treat Cicero as family." Titus crosses his arms.

"I trust Cicero with my life," I say. "If he deemed your cause worthy, then so shall I."

"Can we speak in front of her?" the woman asks.

Titus licks his lips. "No, not until she has an audience with the kings."

"She can't even think for herself." The woman narrows her eyes at me.

"And were these the only humans found with her?" a male faerie asks, looking back at knocked out Jupa and Tian.

"We lost Tionne, and the spy I sent for Jorthus died," Titus says.

"Do you not care that she died?" I ask Titus.

He blinks as if not understanding me. "I knew she would die the moment Fyfe told me to send her. As for Tionne, well I assumed he could handle himself."

I feel Cicero's hands on my shoulder, pulling me back.

I am sorry for your loss, Aurelia.

Tionne deserved death, and Rowyna was just a human. I try to sound cold.

"And how will you tell Queen Selene?" I ask.

Titus smirks, impressed with how much I've learned. "You will tell her since you know how he died."

"Do you want to know how he died?" I step closer to him.

"I don't care how, Aurelia," Titus yawns. "What I am more interested in is how deep those creatures got in your head."

"As if I would tell you what I've had to endure here," I growl.

"Aurelia," Cicero warns.

"I won't talk to you, but I will talk to the Order's leaders," I lie.

Titus must realize just how much I loathe him. Whether I am telling the truth or not, he sees just how much I prefer one master to another.

Titus narrows his eyes and steps closer to me whispering, "I always knew you loved your precious Cicero. The way you followed him, did as you were told, and watched only him in a room filled with people—including Jorthus royalty. Aurelia, you forget you would be dead if not for me. I trained you to be strong to survive in the capital. Yet you only looked at me with scorn."

I feel Cicero step to my side, being very careful of Titus' anger.

"Now is not the time to fight," Cicero says carefully.

"Aurelia, you need to answer some of my questions, to prove your loyalty to us," Titus says as he tries to calm himself.

"I will," I say. "However, there are things meant for the leaders of Rhion."

"There was a faerie present with you, that was not among those who came to Jorthus, is this faerie important?" Titus asks.

"Which one? Didn't Cicero brief you?"

"He did but he mentioned you were closer to them than he." Titus blinks. "The important one that rode beside the proud prince."

What should I say? I ask.

It is up to you.

"A Seelie lord," I answer. "He is meant to accompany Prince Kynus to the castle."

"What is his name?" The woman asks.

"Lord Gidlain, though it may not be his true name," I turn to the woman. "Fae rarely tell their real names to mortals."

The half-fae man smiles. "My mother is from Daeyed, she never gave her true full name to anyone. Not even me."

I want to talk to this man, I want to ask him how he grew up in such a place as Flokael, to see how he learned to be the best of both.

Titus sighs. "This country is cursed, the amount of fae that tried to kill us… I don't doubt their protection of themselves. But I don't understand just how names are so precious to them."

I see Cicero slowly walk away from me to the others sitting down by the fire. He is growing annoyed about where this conversation is heading.

"I doubt we could truly understand, for we are not fae," Cicero responds. Cicero the liar. Azlyon the deceiver, blessed by his goddess.

"Tell me," I say. "What does the Order want from me?"

"We don't know in great detail," the woman says. "We are just soldiers meant to take you back."

Titus looks at her, silencing her. "Your role is important, Arch King Whistryn and his consort want you at their side…in a sense."

I nod.

I step closer to the fire watching Cicero meet my eyes.

They are useless. I doubt they will have any more information, Azlyon says.

I nod slightly.

Do not move, Aurelia, no matter how tempted. His voice was quiet in my mind.

Azlyon, in one fluid motion, rips the hearts out of the two closest to him, blood spattering everywhere. The cave is silent for a split second as their minds try to rationalize the sight.

Before Titus can physically react, Azlyon dips and dodges an assault from the half-faerie. His fists hit the ground, causing stone spikes to impale all of the other soldiers. Their blood soaks my face and chest but I keep my feet planted.

There are drowning screams as their lungs fill with blood. The impaled human bodies harden and turn into a fair marble as they slowly become stone. Those with faerie blood simply spat out blood as they died. They will rot while the others preserve in time.

Then Azlyon sheds his disguise. Their faces are paralyzed in fear as if the presence of a high faerie could stop their hearts.

Titus is the only one who remains unscathed. His eyes are wide and his teeth clenching, yet he decides to charge Azlyon with his iron forged longsword anyway. There was a moment when I thought the blade would hit the prince.

"Who are you?" Titus growls. "You sure as hell are not Cicero!"

Azlyon twists away from the sword, grabbing it at the blade. His skin sizzles when it makes contact with the cold metal. Still, he manages to snag it away from Titus as though he were a child playing with a long branch.

A cool wind whistles through the cave, turning the copper flames into a pale violet. The bloodied moans of the dying faerie soldiers stop and Azlyon grins, looking utterly monstrous.

A metal clatter echoes against the cave walls. I thought he was immune to iron damage.

The sword glitters on the ground, reflecting the firelight while Azlyon's hands are at Titus' throat. He could use magik to kill him but he chose to watch the life leave the general's eyes while he squirms to escape.

"Titus, I am not Cicero," he says. "Cicero is a creation of mine. You should be honoured to know the truth before your life passes from Arcadia."

"I've done n-nothing to yo—" Titus is barely able to speak, his face turning purple as Azlyon's hands press deeper into the human's throat.

"Oh, but you did." Azlyon licks his lips as a final weak breath leaves Titus' chest.

When the body hits the floor, Azlyon bends down and whispers something into Titus' ear.

I could finally exhale.

I could've stopped Azlyon but I made no effort to move from where I stood. I've seen him act the part of a prince, friend, and human, but never a warrior.

"All bloody." Azlyon stands and tucks a bloodied strand behind my ear.

I meet slowly his eyes. "You told me to stay still."

He smiles again, crimson all over him.

"What happened to your hands?" I ask him.

He looks down for a moment. "That is quite the story, but I need you to pick up the sword and bring it with us."

"I thought you were immune to iron," I say, picking it up.

"I am."

I look at the blade. "Then what—"

"I will tell you someday. For now, your friends need tending to." Azlyon runs one hand along the other.

"They aren't my friends," I say, looking at Tian and Jupa, who still wear gags at the mouth of the cave, shouting muffled words.

"Aurelia, I know they mean something to you," Azlyon says. "I am not the one you need to worry about knowing that information."

I nod, looking at his hands once more before rushing over to the humans. Tian is wide-eyed and Jupa is frozen. I feel heartbeats through the air when I get close enough to cut their binds and remove their gags.

"Keep that monster back!" Tian falls backwards, keeping his eyes on Azlyon.

Jupa simply slides his eyes to meet mine and asks in a low, shaking voice, "Are we saved?"

I nod. "He won't hurt you, he saved us."

I need to calm them down. They need to see that Azlyon is not the villain he appeared to be minutes ago.

"Relia, do not trust him, do not trust them. Do what you need to do then get out," Tian utters.

I lean closer, whispering into Jupa's ear, "When I tell you to disappear, you will go see the kings in Flokael. You will leave Daeyed and me underneath whatever peril looms."

Jupa frowns. "Why can't you come?"

"Hush, now is not the time to worry about me." I press a finger to his lips.

Jupa sighs but helps Tian stand up. Their heart rates slow, I can feel it but I have no idea how.

"I trust the prisoners won't run," Azlyon walks over, now wearing gloves from a dead faerie. They are still soaking in blood, "or they may share a similar punishment."

I glare at Azlyon. This is not helping me convince them he is on my side. Perhaps they are right, Azlyon is dangerous, but I hope out of respect for me, he wouldn't try anything.

Chapter 27: Daelin Isle

Court of Daeyed

We stop at a nearby creek to wash off. The water is cool against my skin, yet comforting like wrapping up in a silk blanket. Underneath the water, my skin is no longer gold, but a pale bluish-grey, much like a true creature of the water.

"Strange," I say to myself. What exactly did the font do to me?

I clean my clothes after my skin is clean of blood, smoke, and dirt. The fabric lets go of grime in one or two swipes. I could almost smile. Back in Jorthus, it would take me hours to clean my gear to Cicero's standards. If only I used magic then.

There is a crunch and I turn sharply to see my familiar, thick fur fluffed in the breeze. I am completely naked, but half covered by the boulder I lean against.

"Why does Azlyon's familiar do whatever he says," I ask, "and you don't?"

He looks at me carefully with a slight smirk. "They've built trust over the years."

I grasp a soft and partly deteriorated stone to scrub my tunic. It is quite strange to see my skin changing colours as the water submerges my hands, but my mind is far too spent to even question it any longer.

"Are you going to leave me alone?" I ask.

The cat merely peers at me with a smile. "Maybe one day. Aurelia, tell me, what are thinking?"

I shake my head. "That the Order created me. The only part I don't understand is why my mother chose to die like that."

The cat licks his paw. "She was being tracked and going to die regardless."

I shake my head and change the subject. "How am I going to save Tian and Jupa? They need to live."

"One of them may die after the ritual." He looks me in the eye.

I pick up my trousers when I step out of the water. They are still damp but I can't walk around naked.

"I still am unsure if I trust you, cat," I say.

"I would tell you to trust your instincts but they've led you into trouble several times now." He stands up. "Behave like the princes, know what is proper, and when to act like the fae."

I watch him walk away into the brush. I'm not sure which side he is on but he does have a point.

I wring my tunic between my fingers, letting the water drip at the ends before I braid my hair down my back. A pale blue water pixie begins to tie in some flowers.

I dig out a Leviathan scale from my trousers and give it to the tiny creature as payment.

"He waits for you in the deep, when you come into understanding, when an unlikely alliance follows a cataclysmic change, you will be heard, and you will listen, when another shatters your mind and betrays your family," the pixie replies, its tiny buzzing voice reminds me of a hundred bees flying.

"What?" I ask.

"I deliver a message and mark your hair in river weed and flora," it says again before flying off.

Once I dress, I meet the others back at our makeshift camp.

"You aren't that bad," Jupa says as Azlyon passes him a red apple.

"I've had practice dealing with humans, something the others have not."

Tian still looks unsettled. "What if killing us meant you could, I don't know, rid this world of humans? Would you?"

"In a heartbeat. Just because I am treating you with kindness does not mean I won't murder you if it suited me." Azlyon pauses. "Ah, Aurelia, come to join us finally."

I shrug as he tosses me another red apple. "I have more to clean than the three of you. Is this apple safe to eat?"

Azlyon nods. "Nothing special about it other than giving you very basic sustenance."

"Aurelia," Tian says. "Would you kill us if it meant getting the life you've always wanted?"

I laugh. "I don't know what I want but I suppose I may. I know you both would try to kill us if it meant safety from the fae your entire lives."

Azlyon walks over to me and gently touches my hair, smiling slightly. "It is very becoming."

I shrug, "I may as well start becoming the faerie this world wants me to be."

"Don't lose sight of who you are though," he says more quietly, his hand gently falling down my back.

I hold my breath as though the world were about to burst at any given moment. I knew the exact amount of space his hand covers my spine, each pressure point he touches causing waves of instability, and all I can do is remain silent and let the quiet helping anchor me to the world.

"Your highness, you forget that I could break your hand right now." I smile at him. "I am not a fragile woman."

"Oh, I am aware." He removes his hand. "If you were that would be a shame."

I laugh.

"I'm not sure if they are trying to seduce or kill one another," Jupa whispers to Tian.

I freeze. I heard it as though they spoke loud enough for the world to hear.

"Both." Azlyon looks me in the eye while speaking. He knows I heard them, and he seems all the more curious about it.

Have you been keeping something from me, little river?

I bite my lips.

I saw death and he was not kind, is all I say back to him.

Azlyon knows better than to press on.

"How long until we reach Daelin Castle?" I ask.

"We are close to the Geanaul ferry that will take us to Daelin Isle," he replies.

The rest of the walk is easy and quiet. I walk next to the Prince and the humans follow. They know better than to run, for that would be a death sentence. The mountains once again grew jagged on each side of us. Azlyon mentions that each mountain that lined the road was named after royalty from the courts.

On the northern side, I hear screeching, growling, cackles and hooves beating against the ground. There is a high concentration of Unseelie faeries here and this time. When Azlyon says to stay on the road, I listen.

A faint echo of a whistle fills the valley, like a soft song longing for folk to hear.

"He will eat you whole if you follow the whistle," Azlyon says. "Stay focused ahead."

I nod, making sure Jupa and Tian are listening.

They pause, looking like the melody is scooping the brains from their skull. Azlyon ends up having to press mud into each of their ears.

"Who is it?" I ask.

"A fallen god called Pan. When he fell and lost the majority of his magik, he was left only with his flute and his whistle to lure food to him. He is now a simple faerie with a grudge against those who caused this to happen," Azlyon explains. "Humans fall in love with his sound more than the fae, which is why without stuffed ears, they will stop at nothing to find Pan."

By the time we meet the ferry, there are plenty of sentries standing post. They shackle up the humans and offer us silk robes lined with white fur, each symbolic of the different courts. Mine is blue and patterned with the waves and Azlyon's a deep forest green with gold branches.

A familiar face appears in a crimson cloak. "You're late."

"Kynus!" I nearly trip over the fabric.

He catches me and whispers, "I'm pleased to see that you've made it out. You must remember that you are royalty among the fae, they won't respect you unless you win over their favour."

I nod.

"Choose your interactions wisely, for the world will be watching you," he chimes.

I nod as he places a rune stone necklace over my collarbone. We are being shown off to the entirety of Daelin isle.

The ferryman is an old hooded gnome. He has no eyes and his mouth is sewn shut but I feel his stare on me the entire time. I try not to look but I can't help it at times.

The payment has already been discussed and paid in full before I even step on the pale longboat. Kynus, Azlyon and I stand at the centre, and two sentries are posted on each side of us while the gnome stands at the helm. Tian and Jupa would be arriving in a small rowboat after us.

The sun glimmers above us and the water sparkles in thousands of blue and green shades. The gnome is using magik to pull the boat through the water.

"Will we see the sea wyrm?" I ask.

The gnome's face shoots towards me in an instant.

"The wyrm should be long dead," a sentry says.

I nod, not believing a word of it. They just haven't seen him.

"You lack faith, the old ones will come, they will right the wrong, blessed be The Morrígan," I say in response.

They all nod and continue their watch.

The ride along the intricate waters is a calm hour-long journey. The silence fills the boat with unspoken words and questions. The faeries are unsure of me.

Azlyon's familiar is waiting along with three other horse-like creatures. They are different from the others I've seen. They are brown, but their legs are made entirely of small branches.

The familiar changes its shape when I look back. It is more like the others but its eyes are ghost-like as if they can't change no matter what shape it takes.

"Aurelia, you will ride my familiar," Azlyon says simply. "These others will not take kindly to a half-blood on their backs, no matter your status."

I nod.

A sidhe wearing pale grey robes walks over with a dozen knights. "The return of not one but two of the old blood is a cause of rejoice," he beams as the knights take their place surrounding us. "Many have gathered to see the return of your highnesses."

"This will be the final return before everything changes," Azlyon says without looking at the high faerie. "Let the walk begin."

The walk? I ask.

When royalty returns, we will be paraded down the cold path. It is tradition, he responds.

I climb the familiar and we start down a path hidden by rocky ravines and flowing willow trees. When the path ends at the stone wall of a cliff, we simply pass through it as though it is nothing more than an illusion.

That is when I see it. The capital of Daeyed.

Daelin castle is a place where the soaking bones of earth erupt in a towering mess of crystal and trees. With every glance, there is something new and extraordinary. From carved statues to living faerie guards patrolling and hiding.

There is a pale mist hovering over the bottom as waterfalls cascade down the grey mountains that encircle it. The road changes from dirt into glittering azul stones. The reflection from each stone looks different. I see myself as a child, as a warrior, and as a pure-blooded fae. With each blink, there is something else that leaves my mind even more confused.

Bordering the road are enormous dark oaks that are bigger than some of the buildings in Farlenfell. Worn with every generation and battle, they grow sombrely in this mountain valley. The pulse of energy is great here and in tune with nature itself, a song of wonder and a song of new beginnings.

Small pixies sit cross-legged on the branches waiting for our arrival, while several tawny elves sing soothing haunting melodies of return. I feel as though my muscles are soaked in honey water and my feet are as light as the clouds themselves.

As we pass, each faerie presses its body to the ground in respect.

My heart thumps as I look at the families of faeries. They are creatures who watch hope pass by them dressed up in lies and careful deception.

Vikorus would laugh and spit in my face, I cannot do what he asked of me. The one chance I had to impress him was gone, it left with Rowyna's death. If I acted differently then, we all would have died. If she didn't do what she did, any chance to save this world would be gone. I only blame myself. If Tionne didn't let go, we wouldn't have made it out. I couldn't do anything when I felt his grasp leave mine. I should have felt pleased or avenged, yet all I felt was the loss of another parent at that moment.

I look over at the centaurs, who stand beside the fawns, and in between them, I see an all too familiar cat. Grehyl. He looks at me curiously but also with a silent understanding. A cat who is all too familiar with the shadows of life.

I nod to the creature, knowing that somehow, we will rely on one another for quite some time. At this very moment, we both know I hold a degree of power over the princes and Arcadia and the meddling gods. Though bound by a promise, there are still things I can accomplish before this one power is relinquished.

The air around me begins to sparkle in morstone all around us. Butterflies and dragonflies flutter by us. I could have sworn I saw a silver dragonfly as large as a human next to the pools of water just behind the trees. It seems like every creature on this island came to see the return of the Seelie prince to Daeyed's capital.

When we reach the steps of the castle, two faeries are holding a human by the neck with a rope. He has muddy long matted hair, a loincloth to cover his waist, and skin so bruised and bloody it is difficult to see what he looked like.

I slide off the horse-like creature and stand in between the two princes.

I was instructed to fold my hands in front of my body like they did before I came here.

"We bless this day, may the gods rejoice at the arrival of our salvation." They kiss the ground before us.

"Why is there a dirty human in our path?" Kynus pulls one of the faeries' chins up with his boot.

"A gift for the arrival of the marine heir," one of the fae males says, "stole him away from his bed and showered him with the respect he gave her."

The second faerie pulls the man up by the hair. His bones are showing; there is little muscle and no body fat.

"I don't know this man," I say.

"Oh, we did our job well then, thank you, your highness." The faerie smiles.

The human rolls his eyes up and immediately I see him for who he is. I did not recognize him at first, in such a mangy, beggar-like state he was left in. Another memory of a face now sunken in hollow dips. The body can change but the eyes tell the truth no matter who you are, faerie or human.

"Beau," I say. The first man I loved and the one who broke my heart as a girl.

"May I suggest a new name? We have been calling him Claye since his capture," the faerie says.

Azlyon lifts his hand and Beau shoots back hard into the castle wall. I hear bones popping and cracking.

I step in front of the Seelie prince and slowly walk over to Beau, hearing every step on the stone. The wind shifts around us, hair lifting off the nape of my neck as I touch his face. His eyes have sunk so deep inside his skull I almost pitied him.

"Claye," I say simply. A name that strips his title and his legacy away from him. There were five common servant names among the humans who served the fae and Claye was among them. "Do you know who I am?"

This man wanted to use me once. He pretended to love me in my youth and he broke my trust in love.

The human looks at me with heavy-lidded eyes and nods. "A-Aure..."

"Hush now," I say, holding his face with my right palm. "Do you remember how you danced the night away with those girls? Do you remember how you wronged me?"

Beau lifts his head slightly in a nod.

"You love to dance? I loved watching you dance." I smile. "Beau, you are going to dance until I tell you to stop."

I let go only to touch his nose with the tip of my index finger. Magik swirls around me like a strong wind.

I watch him get up and begin to dance all by himself. He is performing the only tribal dance he knows, meaning fast steps and quick turns.

He can barely stand but my control over his mind remains firm. I give him the sensation of burning slowly.

"If you promise to dance until I say stop dancing, I will make the burning stop."

Beau grunts, "I p-promise."

I turn to the faeries closing in on the castle grounds, the curious ones who want to peer closer at the faerie meant to represent a court long lost. They want to know if I am like them or the humans who raised me.

"This gift to me will in turn be a wondrous gift to the court," I say before raising my voice for them to hear. "This human wronged me, in turn, he will dance for all of you until his feet bleed. Do not touch or alter this performance, for it will be the human's grand finale."

I hear their murmurs and whispers before a chorus of grins and animalistic cheering. I could feel the hoofs of the goat and horse fae rumble against the soil and stone, the fluttering laughter of elves, and the slight wind increase as the air fae fly higher and higher to see Beau dance.

"From now until his death, he will have no name, simply the human. He is not even worthy of our servant's names," I declare.

Warty trolls wearing fine silk open the doors of the palace. If they could tame a troll, if they could educate them enough to wear such fine garments, then they are truly remarkable.

I slow as I pass Beau. "I hope she was worth turning against me."

Without a second glance, I walk through the doors and shut him away from my mind. He will dance himself to death, unable to stop as his feet grow bloody and broken.

Chapter 28: A Visit

Daelin Castle, Court of Daeyed

The palace is made of crystal and stone. Carvings on the walls tell stories through images and glyphs. I can see up to glass-like minerals shining in the colours of the sun and ocean from above.

In front of me is the grand staircase leading to four stone thrones. Orbs float above each throne—black, violet, green, and red. No doubt they represent each court, unified under one roof.

Ice crystals and sparks of light float all around us.

I thought you were against torture? Azlyon asks after a while.

"That was then," I respond out loud after a few moments.

"They finally have arrived," a voice cuts the air after me.

I look to my left to see Septimius in fine silks embroidered with dragonhide scales. Vikorus is nowhere in sight.

"Good day," I say, "Prince Septimius."

He walks over with a simper. "My dear Aurelia, you couldn't follow a simple task! Though your actions outside, well, they were ever so delicious. Tell me my darling sea faerie, did you enjoy Daeyed?"

I tilt my head as the prince pulls my hand to his lips. "Enjoy is such a fickle word. Though I can say I wasn't bored in the slightest."

"Of that," he drops my hand, "I have no doubt. And how did the princes behave?"

I smile. "As best one can expect from the Bright and Seelie Courts."

Septimius lets out a slippery chuckle. "Ah, Prince Azlyon and Prince

Kynus, you both must be exhausted, I could show Aurelia to her room."

"I can do that, it is in the East tower, is it not?" Azlyon asks.

"It is, but you both deserve a period of rest." Septimius takes my hand.

It is Kynus who cuts in. "It is a very kind offer, and we thank you."

Septimius only smiles broader before turning to me. "My dear, what trouble you appear to have been. I would enjoy a walk with her, oh so many stories can be told along the way."

"I assume we will have a celebratory feast?" Azlyon asks.

Septimius nods. "I believe the dining hall has been prepared for a feast an hour before midnight. It should give you time to rest and change into clean garments."

Kynus and Azlyon watch as I take Septimius' arm before walking up the stairs at his side. I remember so many things from my delusion and of our last time together. Septimius, while holding the same rank as Vikorus, will always be lesser through Vikorus' influence.

"Where is Prince Vikorus?" I ask. "I need to apologize to him."

Septimius' eyes wander the halls. "He watched you through the human girl's eyes at the end when her life was forever silenced. Do not lie to him but do not beg for forgiveness. Vikorus is meditating to the Goddess of Death, for he communes with her every second eve."

I look at Septimius. "I suppose, it is getting close to the solstice."

The wyvern prince yawns. "It has nothing to do with the solstice and everything to do with Acantha."

"Who is that?"

"His anam and love," he says quietly.

It all makes sense now. Vikorus wants The Morrígan to bring back his love. Perhaps he has an additional contract with the goddess of fate and death to bring her back. I see no other reason why he would commune with her so often.

"She may be our fate but she only delivers souls to Mag Mell, wouldn't The Morrígan need to consult with Lord Donn?" I say.

"My dear, you have been learning well and just. Lord Donn is fair when conducting the dead, though he has been stripped of all titles other than

Mag Mell's overseer." Septimius touches my hand with his free one. "He once allied himself with the Tuatha Dé Danann, for they were the golden gods to his darkness. Their power eventually overtook him and now he obeys The Morrígan."

I nod, remembering all too well his face and words.

"We all love, just as we all fall in the end," Septimius says, and in his words, there is a warning not to press Vikorus on the matter.

I decide to change the topic to safer waters. "It is interesting that you chose those two words as separate, love and anam."

"Sweet Aurelia, has Kynus been feeding you the sugary side?" He chuckles. "An anam is simply half of your soul in another body, It is something you cannot ignore yet it also represents a burden. To have an anam in your life as your lover is both chaotic and hypnotizing. Most prefer to keep their anam at arm's length, knowing others can use them whenever a terrorizing situation occurs. Most importantly the majority of fae never reveal the identities of their anams. The ones who do usually are lovers and have an easier time protecting one another."

"If the wrong person knew, they could use one against the other," I say simply.

Septimius nods. "Oh, they would go mad trying to keep them away from an oppressor. The gods enjoy tricking us just as we trick mortals. The cost of having someone so close is a fascinating torment."

I feel a slight lump in my throat.

"How was he, when Acantha died?" I ask.

"Why so curious?" Septimius looks at the paintings we pass. "Her death was a relief. She was in what you now call the Dead Lands, captured and tortured with cold iron and treated like a slave. I have never seen him so desperate, he would've butchered any fae or faeling if it meant bringing her back. You see, she was also with child when she died. The wicked man who took her sent her head to Daelin castle. Imagine you are a scribe and your writing hand is being cut off, yet you always find yourself reaching for a quill but you never are able to grasp it again. Imagine forever suffocating through words buried in memories. Feeling so empty that nothing can ever replace who you were once. When she died he took his first breath again, she wasn't suffering anymore but it also took his goodness away."

I never even once thought he was capable of compassion, but perhaps it is just lost deep inside his soul, each moment fading further away from conscious thought.

"Have you been in love before?" I ask Septimius.

He smiles. "That is an interesting question. Yet you must ask yourself who could ever love a faerie like me genuinely? The love you appear to believe in must be presented by both involved, otherwise, it is just a pathetic one-sided admirable obsession."

"Oh my," I say, "that is quite the mouthful of advice from someone who appears to be refused."

"Refused? I'll have you know there are so many who would enjoy me as a lover. I am possibly the last skaelean in existence, an infertile prince, and let's not forget the relations I have to the sidhe. All qualities that many females wish to taste before they settle down."

I know he's jesting but part of his words are venomous. He can't have an heir, he is different, and though he has connections, he will always be the messenger.

"Tell me, what exactly happened since last we spoke?" Septimius half-smiles.

I swallow. "I nearly died, went to a revel, then was forcefully escorted to Order of Rhion soldiers, and finally I came here."

"Details, darling human." He licks his lips.

"Perhaps I may tell you another time, right now I am tired and wish to rest," I simply say.

Septimius only chuckles. "I look forward to our next conversation then."

"You don't care that the Order made it past the border?" I ask.

"No," he says.

"Why?"

We stop in front of a large golden door.

"We had this room prepared for you, it is tailored for one of the Cold Court," Septimius says.

A branch crawls out of the wall and pulls the door open. I stare in awe. While there are still vines along the crystal and stone, it is more elegant than back at the fortress.

The room is large, the floor a cold, pale blue marble, that glitters and swirls around my feet as though I were walking on water. There is a large window that appears to be a door to a balcony. The bed is lavish, blue and green silk blankets and the wall behind is covered in coral.

"It looks so…"

"Normal to me," Septimius says, then points to an archway beside the lounging puffy bench, "through there is your wardrobe and bathing chambers, as well as a decent desk to work on whatever you work on."

"It is amazing," I shake my head. "What is the symbol on the roof?"

"The sigil of the Cold Court," he says. "A wave with the moon at its centre, since most of your court was active at night."

I nod then walk down the hall archway. At the end is a large pool to bathe, and a desk was peaking to the left. I don't see the wardrobe, only a large tapestry with the leviathan and other asrai fae. I see the members of the royal court, and most importantly, my mother

"Where is the wardrobe?" I ask but when I turn back, Septimius is already gone, the door shut behind him.

The first thing I do is have a hot bath. The water feels nice, the steam clearing my lungs. This sunken pool could fit several people.

Once I am done, I wander back to the main room where I see something new laying on the bench. A pale, thin dress. Upon putting it on, it looks like I was wearing a tight sheet over my body; it is so light, I feel nearly naked in it.

If this is the only clothing here, Septimius is going to pay.

I go back to where I left my existing clothes and they are gone.

"Of course they are."

It is annoying but at least the dress goes past my knees. Maybe it is just something to sleep in. Regardless, I need to figure out where the rest of the clothes are kept.

I step into the hall to see a small sprite sitting on the edge of the painting.

"Who are you?" I ask.

"Your door guard," it squeaks.

"Someone stole my clothes."

"No one did, it was the brownies cleaning, they will return them," it replies.

I sigh. "Are they always around?"

"Yes, but the castle brownies are spellbound to clean before sunset or they will burn alive if in the room," it says. "The Princes' rooms are the same."

"Where are the clothes."

"I am not permitted inside your highness," it says.

I shake my head. "Can you take me to Prince Azlyon?"

The small thing only looks down the hall. "All royal chambers are in the East wing, though his are down the spiral and before the tower of Seelie."

"Tower of Seelie?" I ask. "Which way do I walk?"

It points. "That way, and you'll know because the banners will turn emerald, just as they are navy here."

I nod and begin to walk. I must look quite foolish wandering barefoot on the cool stone floor.

Tapestries are hung elegantly on the walls, on them, scenes of dragons, creatures, and royal feasts sewn in vibrant silks. But there is one that catches my eye—the most beautiful woman I've ever seen.

Her hair was the colour of woven sunlight, and her eyes were bright cornflowers. At her back were thin sparkling dragonfly wings that fell like a cape. On her head was a golden crown that rose in a tangle of antlers. Her skin even appeared to glow. At her side was a man, one with a slender but muscular build, who had antlers growing from the top of his head. Power radiated off him, though he was just an embroidered image on a tapestry.

I decide to walk on, leaving the tapestry to greet another face.

I need to speak to Azlyon about another matter as well. We need to decide what anam means to us and how we will proceed. It is only going to be a matter of time before word spreads about this. Once Vikorus and Septimius know the truth, it will be much harder for him to genuinely maintain order and it will be dangerous for me to be around the two of them.

The banners change from blue to red and eventually to green. I'm not sure just how big this place is but it certainly puts the king's residence in Jorthus to shame.

But there is a problem. There is more than one door after I walk down a spiral staircase to a slightly lower part of the castle. Several at least. Behind each door could mean a number of things.

Azlyon, which door are you behind? I ask.

There isn't a response.

I look up at the floating lights.

Looking for the prince? A different voice echoes in my mind. It is a fading, almost feminine tone, yet there is something animalistic about it.

I turn around several times. There is no one near me.

"Who is there?" I call clenching my teeth.

Aurelia, I have waited for so long to finally have you here. Though something intrigues me. If you bow right now, I will make an oath to you. So long as you don't raise a hand to me, I will keep Azlyon safe, I will keep your mother's brother safe, it says simply.

"Lady Morrígan." I take a breath, feeling my legs shake.

It is one of my names, but child, you must remember who I am and why you should fall to your knees and bow, the voice was sharp.

I drop, gasping, and press my face to the floor. The light around me dims, and I swear her voice chuckles through the corridor.

"Are you here?" I say weakly, not daring to look up.

I am everywhere. A pause. *You will complete the ritual without hesitation, you will stand at Azlyon's side throughout our reign over this land, and eventually, when I leave, you will worship me as the chieftain of the gods.*

I feel a cold hand on my neck and gasp.

"L-Lady Morrigan, I will help so long as it does not interfere with other contracts I've made," I say.

It will not, for only a god's contact would interfere. Now child, enjoy your last few days with Azlyon for he won't be the same when I descend. Then the hand is gone and the hall is brightly lit again.

I pull myself off the ground and see light coming from the furthest door on my right. I look up to another sprite peering down at me.

"Who was behind me?" I ask.

It simply stares at me. "You were blessed with a visit. I could not see anything."

"I need to see him," I say with urgency.

"The prince must approve, or all the others would be rummaging through his things," it says.

I shake my head. "He is my anam."

Its eyes widen. "You may attempt to step inside, if what you say is true, there won't be an issue crossing the threshold."

I pause before entering and look up, "You must swear to never speak or communicate this to anyone or anything. I will end your life if you don't agree."

The creature tilts its head. "I am bound to serve the Seelie prince, I wouldn't speak of it anyway."

"Swear it faerie!" I state through my teeth.

It bows. "I swear to do so unless my prince tells me otherwise."

That is the best I will get.

I walk into the room as easily as stepping through any old door. An archway of light greets me in the hallway. Books pile on the floor, wooden trunks containing things from centuries past scatter along the wall.

It turns out the archway of light is a large study, one where more cabinets of books and parchment line the walls. Vines, flowers, and gemstones dissipate along the walls and roof. In the centre is a grand pale tree growing into the roof, hollowed out for the desk that was carefully placed inside. The morstone glows in smaller bundles throughout the tall circular room.

Azlyon sits at his desk quietly. It must have been years since he's been in his study at Daelin castle. The solstice is approaching and I have to make my decision by then. Even though I know what I have to do, it doesn't make it any easier. Seven days after that, I will help bring magik back. Still, here I look, at the man I have come to love, one who has shown me a grand adventure and helped me grow into my own skin.

"Aurelia," Azlyon says, shutting his book.

I walk over shyly, I almost forgot about the thin silks hugging every inch of my body. They are the only thing keeping me from his eyes. My chambers are supposed to be my private den of tranquillity but confuse me more than I dare imagine. I wonder if the brownies knew I would make this garment mistake.

"You do know that you are wearing an underdress, there is supposed to be something on top." He pushes the book to the corner of his desk and stands up.

I blush. "I couldn't find anything else!"

"There is a silver bell, we all have one, ring it and your sworn lady's maid will come and help you dress. Though if you prefer to dress yourself, the clothes are in the wardrobe hidden behind the tapestry. The brownies will clean after you so long as you do not insult them," Azlyon muses, then sizes me up.

"I have a lady's maid?" I ask.

"Of course, though you will have to swear her to your service before she can enter your chambers." He smiles.

I shake my head and laugh for a moment.

"Who is the woman with the golden hair and wings I saw on a tapestry?" I decide to ask. She looked familiar but also distant.

"My mother, Titania. The image is of her before Oberon clipped her wings to stay with him forever," Azlyon says. "He couldn't bear a world without her in it. It is strange what we will do to the ones we love."

He steps closer, touching my arms with his hands. I tilt my head upwards to look him in the eye.

Titania may have been Oberon's wife, but she still had a mind of her own. I can't help but feel sorry that she was forever bound to him like that.

"If someone saw you enter my chambers like that, well, they'd think all the wildest things and the court would whisper of us," he says, touching the fabric of my underdress.

It is different between Azlyon and I. His family and world are long gone, and I came from something else entirely. If he wanted to chain me to the throne, he would have already. In a way, he saved me from Jorthus that day.

"Let them think whatever they wish," I say, lacing my hands around his neck. "I love the prince of lies enough to withstand whatever storm they push our way."

He raises his brows and smiles. "You came to love me?"

I half-smile. "Why do you think I remained around this long?"

He rolls his sparkling silver eyes. "I did expect to have to hunt you down a few times, though I did wonder why you didn't."

"We made an arrangement, it would be bad to go back on my end." My heart flutters, my stomach tickles. I have half a mind to curse this exact feeling, yet at the moment or whenever he is near, my mind slowly grows chaotic.

This must have been hard on Azlyon. He is no doubt used to faerie lovers, and they were so much different from I. Especially the faerie who may have been the love of his life.

"I know I'm not nearly as beautiful or hollow-boned as Laeraan, and have little manners," I look away for a moment, "more than anything, I am not anyone your father and mother would have approved of, I'm not even a sidhe like her."

I remember how his brother was sealed away for choosing a human woman. I remember how Azlyon and the other fae reacted.

Loving humankind is a disgusting crime amongst them.

"My family is dead, along with the Seelie Court. We have lived long enough for our culture to distort and change rapidly." Azlyon guides my gaze back to him. "It took me a very long while to see humans as anything but lesser. My father was a very clever faerie, he knew they were more than he led us to believe. Yet to remain apart, he needed us to think of them as dull creatures. My time at the Skuflan great library, walking the streets of Aeolus and the other human capitals showed me there is so much more than I was taught. My darling Aurelia, you are more than I could dream of. The best of each world and I truly believe all fae and mortals can learn from your example."

I smile slightly. "Yet they all are going to die."

He knew I meant the humans. "I am going to send the children through the last portal to Gaia. The half-bloods will stay here of course, but they must swear loyalty to us."

I sigh. All of us will die if everyone stays. This is the lesser of two evils and I am a little surprised he even compromised with me.

"What changed your mind, Azlyon?"

"You," his voice is dulcet, tucking a stray hair behind my ear, "Àlainn,"

I tilt my head. "What?"

"It's a name I need you to remember should the darkest time come," Azlyon whispers.

I smile. "A friend of yours?"

"A name I can never forget," he kisses the tip of my nose, "and a name you cannot breathe until the time is right."

"I promise," I say.

"Now, Aurelia," his eyes flicker at the door, "how shall we sneak you back?"

I pause, my heart beating quicker. No doubt he can feel it.

"I know we have so little time left," I say, pressing my head against his chest. "I don't want to be alone tonight."

His arms wrap around mine as he pulls me closer. The crook of his neck smells of fallen leaves and fresh apples, the smell of summer's ending and the beginning of a new season, one where the earth must shed its skin before the new can thrive.

"We do have to make a midnight appearance in court, for dinner." Azlyon presses his lips in my hair.

"We still have a few hours." I smile into him, tugging at the hem of his shirt. "Perhaps we could find something to pass the time?"

He leans back to meet my eyes. His are pools of silver and mine copper.

"Do you know what you are asking?" Azlyon asks. "I am not human."

"I am also not human, at least entirely," I whisper.

I pull him through the doors separating his chamber and his study, right to his plush satin bed embroidered with the tree of life, framed by branches it. A thin gold canopy falls down the sides. It is a bed for a faerie, for a prince.

"Aurelia," he breathes.

I reach for the wine on a shelf. The light reflects off his pale skin just as his eyes appear to glow at an angle.

He looks at me curiously as I pour a glass and bring it to my lips.

"A drink for you?"

"I don't want that."

I tilt my head. I am about to take a swig when his hand stops me.

"I would rather taste you," he explains with a wicked grin.

My cheeks redden. "I doubt I taste as good as this wine."

"I doubt the wine will taste as good as you. Though I must ask one more time, little river, is now the right moment?" He pulls at the tie on the slip. "We don't have to do this now."

I only nod, dropping the goblet.

As the burgundy wine spatters on our legs, my hands reach for his face.

"Once I start, there is no stopping." Azlyon loosens the strings further, revealing part of my breasts, which were normally taped close to my body.

"I don't plan on stopping." I rip the rest.

He grins like a man in love. He has seen me naked before, just not in any context that mattered. I wasn't dying or injured. Right now, at this very moment, I feel as though he is seeing me for the first time. There is no charade, no roles to play. Just me. Just us.

I push him down grinning just as wide as I lift his shirt over his head, thankful he dressed casually this evening.

My fingernails slowly caress his chest, I could see the shivers on his skin as each intricate touch sent waves of sensation in the form of goosebumps. He is muscular but his bones feel hollow at the touch, unlike my own or any human I've met.

I kiss his jaw, his throat, and over his heart. His breath is warm against my hair. His hand reaches to my back and slowly traces circles until I lift my head and meet his eyes.

"Little river, you are far more gentle than I imagined."

"Azlyon." His name is like sugar on my lips. The sound of each syllable is music to my ears. "I am just getting started."

I smile as he sits up, pulling me into his arms, his hands trailing every inch of my body. The sensations make my body ache for more. His hands tease and play.

My hands dig into his hair and his back when he begins. I feel the warm blood fall down his back like little fountains. He only groans and pulls me closer when we truly became one and the same.

The world spills into colour. All I can focus on is the prince inside me, the creature I love, and the only one I would fight to the ends of the world for.

* * *

I open my eyes to see Azlyon sleeping at my side. My body aches and my legs are numb. If I could sink into this bed with Azlyon forever, I would. I doubt anything would ever compare to the night we shared. He smells of the sea and I smell of summer apples. His skin is pale and marked up, no doubt my skin would mirror his if he hadn't held back.

I smile widely, wondering if I could even get up for our dinner meeting in an hour. Right now, the world feels perfect in the arms of one another. Yet there all good things must come to an end, and both of us need to look presentable.

I begin pulling myself away when a hand grabs my wrist, halting my movement.

"Where are you going?" Azlyon asks.

I smile as his strange eyes look up at me. "We have to get ready."

Azlyon sighs. "Let us show up with sleepy eyes and not a care in the world. Come and lay with me for a little while longer, while I still am myself."

I lay back down, my face a short distance away from his. "Azlyon, you will overcome her. I will be at your side and together, we can do what needs to be done."

He looks sadly at the canopy above. "That would be a lovely dream. To rebuild the Seelie as myself and watch it grow and thrive, with you. Aurelia, I made the agreement with her knowing that I won't be coming back."

I take a short breath. "Have faith that we will overcome this. Right now the future is undetermined."

He smiles. "Whatever happens, you need to know it is for the better of

Arcadia, but not for me. Though I would willingly give everything for the fae, for the land, and our gods."

I lightly caress his skin, no longer smiling. He is the villain, the lover, the leader, the just, and he is willing to go to such lengths for his people. I only wish he could speak as though he has hope, instead of submitting entirely to a fate that may not yet pass.

"Are the gods all-knowing?" I ask suddenly, still tracing the lines of his chest.

"They gave up much of their power when they created us," Azlyon says. "I think they can never be certain of the future if it involves them."

The goddess is no longer aware of the fates of those in this world. It must have been why she intervened when the princes decided to take action.

"Azlyon, there is something I never told you," I say.

He looks at me with sleep in his eyes. "If you feel like you need to tell me something because you feel guilty for not telling me, I don't wish to hear it. You are allowed to have secrets."

I shake my head. "It's not that. I met Lord Donn, and The Morrígan watched as we fought and—"

"Donn is my—her puppet," Azlyon said. "Any form of freedom he thinks he has is an illusion. Whether he knows it or not, he is under the control of our goddess."

I look away, catching the slip. Her claws are sinking deeper into him and I can't do anything about it.

There is a shift in the bed as his arm pulls me close to his warm body. I feel his breath on the nape of my neck, but there is also an uncertainty between us like a barrier that keeps me from seeing the real him again.

Chapter 29: The Ritual

Daelin Castle, Court of Daeyed

The next few days have everyone on edge. The solstice involves winter faeries crawling out of their burrows and tree homes. Snow, holly, oak, and fresh spices decorate the main hall. Vikorus doesn't speak a word to me even though we share the same table. All of us wear pale shades of white and blue adorned with never-thawing ice crystals. This is when the Unseelie are at their most powerful, though not all are elemental faeries. The shortest day of the year gifts the Dark court strength with a lack of light. Kynus told me this was the time of year when Vikorus and Septimius are stronger than him and Azlyon.

Septimius whispers to me that Vikorus would prefer the humans to be the first to die once The Morrígan reigns. I believe he thinks I will break the silence between us and ask him where the humans are, but I won't give Vikorus any more reason to doubt my intentions.

Azlyon doesn't forget to formally ask me to aid the princes in the ritual. It fulfills my end of our agreement. While I feel hesitation, I know I have little choice. It is the only way to help Arcadia heal, yet I have to remember my bargain with the god of healing.

We stood on a balcony overlooking the night sky and harbour in the distance. We heard music and saw fires of every colour as the fae below revel in the starlight. It was there where I told him I would complete what was asked of me. It was there where he kissed me once on the forehead before walking away.

Since we spoke on that balcony, I remained in my quarters except for nightly feasts leading up to the Last Stand's remembrance day. When it comes, I wake with a lump in my throat and a sinking feeling about what I have to do.

"Grehyl," I say, placing my feet on the cool floor as a cat brushes up against me before leaping onto the windowsill.

"You need to go to the dungeons and let your humans run free. Once the ritual has been completed, the princes won't show mercy," Grehyl says.

"I think my uncle will," I say.

"Your uncle will not have a choice." The cat looks me in the eye.

I shake my head and walk past him to the wardrobe, where only a single black silk gown and robe hang. Black is The Morrígan's colour.

"She cannot set foot here," Grehyl says, "but her consciousness will be combined with his. They will become one."

I don't say anything. Since the night we lay together, Azlyon has been distant. I tried to get him to speak but it was Kynus who always intercepted me with things to do.

I slip into the dress, press black powder on my eyelids, and crown my head in silver. There is a wooden runic bracelet I was asked to wear but it is too itchy, so I slip it into the drawer and pull the sleeves of the cape down. I know they are just symbolic, but I also don't want to offend anyone.

"Aurelia," Grehyl sits atop the vanity, "you need to be focused now more than ever."

"I am," I lie.

"No, you are not." Grehyl's eyes narrow. "You must forget everything you feel for him because he will be no more. The earlier you accept that, the easier it will be to let him go."

I shake my head. "I can save him when the time is right."

Grehyl hops down to my feet. "Aurelia, this plan of the princes is layered with dangers to not only the humans, but to all of Arcadia. She wants to control that The Dagda won't let her have. She may say she will leave but she can lie, and she does so often. The only way to save him is to kill him when the time is right."

I bite my lip. "He is the only one in my life who knew me and still looked past the hideousness of my appearance. He is the only one who truly cares for me."

Grehyl sighs. "Aurelia, that may have been true at one point but there are still people who love you for you. Lucia raised you and cared for you, your mother died for you, and despite what your uncle says, he does care about you more than anyone since Lythe. Azlyon is playing a game with a goddess, he chose his fate and still travelled towards it, all while whispering honeyed words and talking of beauty. He may care for you but he will not trade Arcadia for you."

"He can't trade it, it will die!" I growl.

Grehyl simply steps away. "He could have let another prince take this burden on. She gave him a choice not too long ago when he was in Jorthus."

Grehyl can't possibly know that. He just wants me to relinquish trust in Azlyon. What Grehyl doesn't understand was that I simply have no choice but to.

I slip into wood-soled shoes and step through the halls with a knight down to a chamber deep within the castle. Though appearing dim at first, upon further glance, the chamber is clear and precise. There is a faint glowing pool at its centre, an abundance of morstone, candles, and runes. Along the walls are ten portraits carved deep into the stone. The gods.

A sylph steps out of the shadows next to me with a bowl and a knife. I open my palm to her and she passes me the knife. I carve a jagged symbol into my hand clench my teeth from the pain. This symbol was that of The Morrígan, one displayed all around the castle. Kynus mentioned that while the lady of fate and death was our salvation, she cannot undo our bind. We will be using her rune whenever we draw blood for good faith and bring her closer to this world.

Vikorus arrives next, wearing a black robe and eyes lined in kohl. His hair is braided with black oak leaves.

The sylph flies over to him and takes his blood.

"This is it," I say.

"It appears so." He doesn't look at me. "It is only once the ceremony is over that I will believe you have our intentions in mind, even though you did fail me."

I say nothing.

"I am not mad, you put on quite a show and seeing you broken was almost better than what could have happened," he says after a moment.

Kynus walks in with hair in braids at the sides, wearing black as well. His eyes are sharp and focused as he stands across from Vikorus on the other side of the pool before giving blood.

"Aurelia, you will have to read from the parchment Azlyon is bringing," Kynus says, "in order to release the magik, it has to be you."

I nod, feeling my legs shake a little.

Septimius walks in and follows our suit. He looks at each of us with a slight smile, as though he were excited and nervous at the same time. He is one of the youngest of the four, born after the original binding.

Azlyon walks in last, wearing black silks and a cape of crow feathers, reminding me of Cicero, taking his place between Vikorus and Septimius.

Azlyon hands the Sylph a fading parchment before cutting his palm and mixing all of our blood.

"Blood of the Seelie, Unseelie, Dark, Bright, and Cold bound together for the fibres of the land to replenish in glamour and magik," he says, pouring it into the pool.

The Sylph passes me the parchment. It is written in the common tongue and by Azlyon's hand. He must have been preparing this for such a long time.

I take a breath and begin to recite, "From the beginning water is at the fundamental of all the courts, of the land before the courts. It was there during darkness and in light, it is within all creatures of Arcadia and Gaia."

I pause feeling their eyes on me.

"To bind demanded a sacrifice beyond what has been seen during an age of destruction and blood," I say, "to unleash required a different kind of sacrifice, a sacrifice of being, a sacrifice of stability, and a sacrifice that is blessed by the gods. Our sacrifice is Az...Azlyon, son of Oberon and Titania of the old blood. Prince Azlyon offers himself in exchange for the renewal of magic, and through the use of one of the blessed gods. Fate has answered him, for she has the ability to prevent the sacrificial decay of the courts in exchange for dominion of faerie until it is cleansed of iron blood."

I turn to Vikorus. "Will you and the Unseelie obey and kneel before your saviour in the name of all gods just and whole?"

"I will." Vikorus falls to the knees.

"Will you and the Seelie obey and kneel before your saviour in the name of all gods just and whole?" My eyes meet Azlyon's, and he looks at me as though he were saying goodbye and greeting me as a new being.

"I will," Azlyon says on his knees.

I feel his eyes on me as I ask the same of Septimius and Kynus.

The sylph passes me a decanter of the same black liquid surrounding stones and flowers. I begin to pour it into the pool as I walk along its rim.

"Tosaigh arís, by earth, by blood, by water," I say, remembering to go counterclockwise. "Tosaigh arís, by earth, by blood, by water! Tosaigh arís, by earth, by blood, by water!"

"Tosaigh arís, by earth, by blood, by water," the princes repeat three times.

The room starts to shake as all the candles go out.

"Tosaigh arís!" I say again.

"Arcadia tosaigh arís! By earth... By blood... By water!" I scream as the wind around us picks up, whipping our robes and hair around.

"Through the blood of my human sire, I offer iron poisoning by humans to cease, they will no longer poison the land, and their decimation will be swift," I make out the words.

My head whips up to Azlyon, who is smiling at me. He knew my blood would aid them in two ways: Representing the Cold Court and ending the iron decay in human blood. He knew and he never told me, he never told me.

"Through us, we will slumber for three days while magik returns to each fibre of each blade of grass across Arcadia," I say, falling to my knees unable to stop reading. "Tosaigh arís, through us, the vessels of the new world returned old."

I hear the air whisper all around us as the princes begin to fall into slumber.

All except Azlyon, who stands and walks over to me, his eyes are wild with power and brilliance of light.

"Sleep, Aurelia, you will wake soon." He touches my cheeks as my eyes shut.

* * *

I am alone in the darkness, or so I think.

Across from me is a faerie woman with cloudy eyes. Her raven hair floats around her as though we are underwater. She is naked except for a talisman that hangs down to her navel. At her side is an earthly-looking man, stout yet strong, several heads taller than her. His rugged beard fades from a warm brown to silver.

The woman kisses him on the cheek before fading into the darkness. Though he looks much older than her, they appear to be lovers.

"Do you understand that this is the only chance to bring life back to Arcadia?" His voice is fatherly yet ancient.

I nod.

"After this, there will be no more chances to right what has been wronged." The man steps closer to me, looking like a giant. Behind him is a dark cauldron that appears to glow in a faint buttery light.

"I will try," I say.

He shakes his head. "You will do more than try, you must return her to me before a true mess has been made."

I look at him. "Return that woman?"

"She does not belong in Arcadia anymore," he says. "She will serve a purpose to you all but you must return her to me or face tragedy."

I blink. "The Morrígan."

The man tilts his head. "The Morrígan is my past, present, and future. With the return of what you call magik, you mustn't take any missteps, for it will be your end."

I nod and finally realize who I am speaking to. The Dagda, chieftain of the gods. He loves all creations, including humans, while his consort did not enjoy those so weak unless they fought bravely. She values power while he cherishes wisdom and balance.

"I am not going to obligate you to do so, I am not like my kin, but I am asking you to do what you need to when the time is right," he says.

I look at him and feel sleepy once again.

* * *

When I open my eyes next, I am sitting at a stone table in a room completely lit up by the sun above. I see the other princes sitting there, sleepy and dizzy. We are all wearing plain silver diadems.

"Good evening." Azlyon leans against the back of the head chair. "It is nice to finally breathe wondrous air once again."

The princes all look at him.

"I thank all of you for your contributions over the years, your sacrifices, and your successes. I will honour what you did in full. However, from this point forward, you are all stripped of your current titles," Azlyon says. "You will still be regarded as royalty through new titles as high generals, though now only be one reigning."

Vikorus stands up immediately. "That wasn't part of our contract! I am supposed to rule the Unseelie!"

Azlyon twirls his finger forcing Vikorus back down. Only this time, his head was pressing against the table. His eyes are facing me as his adjacent.

I can only stare.

"Does anyone else wish to raise their voice against me?" Azlyon looks around, his eyes resting on me.

What are you going to do? I carefully decide to ask.

He only tilts his head. *Do not speak unless spoken to. You do not hold power over the fae any longer.*

He turns his attention to the others. "Let us begin."

I watch him speak but his lips are different. I look into his eyes but don't see the person I knew. I can't be sure if the goddess has taken hold yet, but I hope she has, because if this is truly him then I trusted a monster.

"I have already sent a few fae into the human lands to gather intel before I declare war against them," he pauses, "It is taking longer for magik to return to the Dead Lands, yet that hardly matters. Each of you will command warriors against the humans in different regions when the timing is opportune."

"And what would happen to us should we refuse you?" Kynus asks.

"A valid question, but I have ensured your loyalty. Look at your wrists, the binding runes for the ceremony served more than just to appease the gods, they ensure you will do what is told of you or face pain so severe you'll wish you were dead. They activated the ororoot, which will not harm you unless you betray me."

I turn my head to face Kynus.

He was not expecting this. Azlyon plans for everything, as she instructs him.

"You don't trust us, my king?" It is Septimius who speaks.

I chose not to wear the bracelet. The itchiness must have been part of the spell. I feel my heartbeat rise in relief but I can't tell or show Azlyon any of this. I can't tell anyone.

Azlyon leans closer, hovering over the table. "I cannot allow any mistakes to happen."

I lie through my teeth, "Azlyon, we would follow you until the end without such measures."

Azlyon looks at me with a smile. "I think it is time you all understand that Aurelia and I have become close. I have not told you my reasonings behind why I put her before all of you in the past. It is simply because she is my anam. Don't look frightened, my dear, after all, lying is quite filthy. Would I have preferred someone easier to control? Yes, but I suppose I cannot be too greedy."

I feel my body turn statuesque as all the former princes turn to face me.

"Lost for words, love?" Azlyon's voice darkens, "Do not fret, you will stand at my side while these fae work for us. I have many plans for you."

I clench my jaw.

"Will she be our queen?" Vikorus asks.

Azlyon turns. "Once things settle down, I will discuss an arrangement with Aurelia, though none of that is your concern. Vikorus, please know that your only worry should be following my direct orders. For now, I will conclude this meeting. You may leave, High Generals."

I begin to get up and follow Kynus, but for a moment, I hesitate. I need to leave this castle and warn someone. It will be a massacre if I don't give the humans a fighting chance.

"Yes, Aurelia?" Azlyon tilts his head at me.

"Am I speaking to the Goddess or King Azlyon?" I question, looking at him.

"We are the same," He blinks.

"Who am I to you?" I ask carefully.

He laughs. "You are my anam, you are my tool, you are my pawn, and you are my cherished."

"A contradiction."

"Let me be clear then, you are mine. You will do what I tell you to do," he says.

"He is gone," I say, taking a step backwards.

"He is in here, deep down. The faerie you love. I would have ended your beautiful life if you were not my anam, for even gods must be wary against the first magik." His voice is barely more than a whisper. "You are only a half breed, not something the gods intended, simply an outgrowth of what we made. It would have been tolerable if you were pure of blood."

I shake my head. "Why are you telling me this?"

"To keep you in line. I have the power to keep this body and do with it what I will," he says. "That being said, if you do as you are told, you will have a wonderful life."

Outside of the room, the princes wait for me in complete helplessness.

"So this is what our goddess does to him," Vikorus says. "They are together inside, yet he carefully chooses not to resist her. He would not have told us about you both without her influence."

I meet Vikorus' eye, still feeling a bit shaken. "I do not trust him."

"You must though," Septimius says. "No matter what he does, it will be for the better of Arcadia and the fae."

I nod carefully. "I believe he will do that, but he is unpredictable."

"This is the Azlyon that I first met," Kynus sighs, "but not who he is now. He has given up himself for us, the least we could do is lay our lives at his feet and have him use us as his weapons to succeed in the great plan."

"He is her and she is him," Septimius says. "We are at the mercy of the gods."

"Be that the case, we must follow but always remain skeptical," Vikorus snaps.

They all nod. I try to pretend, but I am still so shaken. I am in a new game, one I have no idea how to play. I am not a leader in the way kings and queens are, I am only good at following orders. Once, I felt I could trust in my superiors, I follow without question... Until now. I am on my own if I want to save both Arcadia's soul and the fate of many who will die.

I walk away from them, trusting my intuition. I need to get Jupa and Tian out of here. Now is the time for them to run and hide. They need to go where the princes won't find them, and the only place is the Dead Lands.

No, perhaps they can warn Flokael and the Order. I don't want them all to be slaughtered and I have no idea what Azlyon and The Morrígan are planning. Whatever Azlyon said he would do for me can no longer be trusted. He can lie, and she may have different plans.

I have to be on both sides, but that may be impossible.

"Aurelia," Vikorus says, now at my side, "you need to remove the humans."

I blink.

Vikorus continues, "They are meant to be the first to bleed, and while I do not particularly care about human life, I know you do. I am certain Azlyon will be quite angry that his spectacle will disappear, and maybe he will push that anger in a different direction."

"Why would I betray him?" I ask.

"I am no fool, I didn't see your bracelet," he says, "and you may be able to help keep him from taking what is rightfully mine away."

I sigh. "Vikorus, you haven't proven that I can trust you."

Vikorus says nothing at first. "I trust our goddess' intentions but this wasn't how I thought it would be. We have had enough spectacles. The sooner we take our world back the easier it will be for us to claim our courts."

I nod. "I want what is best for him, and the land."

Vikorus shuts his eyes. "Your humans won't survive our world, but you can give them a final fight, which is a better way to die than for the amusement of court officials."

I wonder why Vikorus is telling me this, why he thinks coming to me is even a good idea.

"Where are they?"

Vikorus touches his chin. "They are inside the green cells underneath the castle."

"Thank you, Vikorus, and I will try to help you the best I can."

Chapter 30: Let There Be Blood

Daelin Castle, Court of Daeyed

I find my familiar lounging on my bed when I return. He says nothing but continues to watch me.

"I need your help." I change into my boots and strap a silver dagger at my waist under the tunic I quickly pull over my head.

"Does it involve something that I told you to do earlier that you must now rush into doing?" Grehyl asks plainly.

I look out the window, pressing bread and cheese into a leather satchel I found in the wardrobe. "You were right, I should have listened to you and heeded your advice. I need to get them out of here."

Grehyl stretches. "Let's head down then."

"Just like that? I don't have to beg you?" I ask, following the cat.

"I know in the future you will listen to my words," Grehyl simply says. "There is more at stake than my pride and I am here at your will."

I smile for a moment. "You are possibly the most curious faerie I have met."

"I am not a true faerie, I am a Child of Magik, as are most familiars," he responds as we turn another corner and down a few sets of stairs.

Warriors are lining the dungeon. A thick green moss covers the walls and pale flowers hang from the ceiling on vines.

A knight stands in front of the cell. He doesn't budge or move aside for me, and his eyes are bright and careful.

"I am to bring the prisoners to the king," I say.

"King Azlyon said he would be the one to come and retrieve them," the knight says.

I lean closer. "Do you know who I am?"

"I do."

"Would you risk angering King Azlyon by refusing me?" I say simply with a sharp smile.

The knight pales a bit. "You are the future Queen. Please go in, but the feline will stay."

"My familiar will come inside in case something should happen to me," I curtly reply.

He nods after a moment.

I smile and touch the knight's shoulder as he unlocks the door.

"For your sake, I wouldn't speak of this to King Azlyon, for he won't be as kind when he knows that you delayed me," I whisper.

Tian and Jupa are leaning against the wall, chained by thick vines. They are tired and weak.

"Please, stand tall and come with me," I say after Grehyl deals with the vine.

They get up and slowly regain their footing.

"Is this where we die?" Jupa ask.

I shake my head. "Follow me."

"Aurelia, maybe you should just leave us," Jupa says. "We just need an end to this pain we've been living in."

"I am saving your lives and setting you free. Follow me and do not say a word."

They both hold onto one another as they trail behind me.

I keep my head held high and my feet firm against the ground.

Grehyl pauses as we reach the stairs. "We are going a different way."

He makes a sharp turn and we follow, turning sideways between a crack in the wall. I can already feel a breeze bounce off the stone and moss.

After turning and squeezing our bodies around stone and root, we emerge at a forest behind the castle. The air is full of life and vibrance. I breathe in a world of unknown raw magik.

I pull Tian and Jupa to me, my arms wrapping them as they exhale.

"You both must go to Flokael and find the Order of Rhion. Warn them that a goddess sides with the fae to eliminate mankind. Tell them magik has returned to the land, if they don't already know," I inform them as I pull away.

Tian looks me in the eye, grabbing my arm. "You have to come with us!"

I shake my head. "You are in danger when I am around. Besides, I need to be close to Azlyon before he ruins everything."

"We won't go without you," Jupa says.

"I command you to leave and follow my orders," I say. "Once you complete what I command you to do, our bargain will be fulfilled. Only then will his sins converge over a stone eye."

They step back in unison, having no other choice. Our contract was bound in magik.

"Stay alive, my queen," Tian says, bowing.

"I am no queen." I take a breath. "Do not worry about me, I can take care of myself, just go and don't look back."

They are bruised and dirty but they still follow my orders.

"Grehyl, keep them safe and make sure they get there," I tell my familiar.

"Are you certain you won't need me here?" the cat asks.

I shake my head. "It is important they get to the Order safely. They won't survive the journey through Daeyed."

He nods and follows the men as they begin to cross the stream with the satchel of food I hooked onto Tian. I am not sure what Azlyon will do to me for this, but it will be worth it to give them this head start.

* * *

I make it to the main floor before nearly colliding into a few knights and Kynus. They are all wearing pale blues and greens, but their expressions are stoic and shadowed. There is a hint of pity in my uncle's eyes.

"What is the matter?" I ask.

"You are to be escorted with a knight, wherever you step," Kynus says. "It is for your protection and guidance."

To watch me you mean, I cast my voice to his mind.

There is a nod so slight it could have been mistaken as an adjustment. Azlyon does not trust us, and with good reason. I already betrayed his rule by letting my friends escape, by allowing them to warn the countries to the East.

"What is my knight called?" I ask.

A tall sidhe with inky black hair, amber eyes, and a sharp chin steps forward. "I am called Taelon, I am of the Seelie and Wild."

"Wild?" I ask.

"The courtless fae who once roamed the forests between the courts. The borders were wider than cities, to cross them was a feat in itself," Kynus says.

I nod. "Taelon must be at my side?"

Kynus shakes his head. "He will be behind you, for at your side would insult his majesty."

"King Azlyon must not be disappointed," I say to Kynus. "Where are the other Generals?"

"Each is occupied with their new duties, soon you will be called upon for yours," Kynus says.

I sigh and walk away, hearing every step the knight takes behind me.

"A knight surely has better things to do than watch one like me," I say to him.

"Those born without restrictions of court life are troublemakers, no matter the amount of fae blood in them," he says, voice like velvet and honey, "I know how to watch a demifaerie."

"When will I be alone?" I ask. "I grow tired of creatures around me all the time."

"When you sleep and dress, though your door will be protected by more than just a sprite, my future queen," he says sharply.

"My strong king is so thoughtful, I must thank him," I speak through my teeth. "He is always keeping me safe."

The faerie smirks at me. "Oh, how wonderful it must be to lie."

"Remember your place," I say as I turn away clenching my teeth.

"I will when I know what yours is," he says, "and where you hold your allegiance."

I stop. The faerie behind is so graceful I don't even hear his breath.

"What is that supposed to mean? Where do you hold your allegiance, Wild faerie?" I snap, not even giving him the satisfaction of facing him.

"I serve the Seelie King. You know, all Wild fae have these eyes. We can see through the intentions of fae and mortals, but half-breeds are trickier. My father killed my Wild mother before I could descend into a true creature of the wood. I serve the one who will bring balance, one who will end this mess that created other creatures such as you. You may be of royal blood but your human blood makes you disgusting to most faeries. The King will not side with you against me, for he chose me because I will not hold my tongue until you fully submit to the new world."

I am lost for words.

"If there is anything else, future queen, please let me know." I feel his smirk on my back.

"You say the Wild fae are creatures of the wood, yet you seem to only cater to your Seelie father's world. Tell me why you have markings on your hands that are not on any other knight or Seelie?" I challenge.

"Wouldn't you adore the knowledge that I hold?"

"I could command you," I say.

"And I have every right to refuse you." His voice is darker now.

"Excuse me?" I scoff turning to face him.

"Only the Seelie King holds that kind power over me, not the one who warms his bed."

I raise my hand to hit him but he grabs it faster than my decision to act.

"Now, go about your day. I will do my duty, it is best if you do yours." Taelon smirks.

"And should the Seelie King tell you to do as I say?" I pull my arm back.

"Do not ask questions in which you know the answer," he says.

I need to pack, though I will have to travel light. Taelon stands outside of the room and informs me he won't leave. I believe him, but there has to be another way out.

There is a stream below my window, but from this height, it will be certain death to jump. Walking through the front doors or finding a hidden passage will be difficult, but it might be the only alternative.

I make sure my gear was in shape, pack the bread and fruit that lay on my nightstand, and braid my hair. I hid the bag inside a pillow and gently set it back. Finding a plausible escape route was essential before I run.

Am I the only one with a Wild faerie knight? I call out.

It is the only way I can ensure that you walk the path of the fae. Did you think I wouldn't notice that your wrist is bare? Is Azlyon's only answer.

I wonder just who this Taelon was. A Wild faerie with a unique skill set no doubt, but there is something different about him.

I walk over to the window looking down at the water below. Following it could lead me to the ocean but then what? I will surely be devoured by the creatures that lurk below the glassy water. It won't matter if I am my mother's child.

* * *

I meet with Azlyon later in the main hall. He wears the feathers of crows and ravens, their skulls pinned at his shoulders. His eyes are more vacant than before. They reflect the dying, the weak, and the future. The Morrígan may not be able to set foot here in her true shape, but I still feel the goddess thicken the air as though this were all a lucid dream.

"Aurelia, you are not fighting today, perhaps you would like to change into something more…fitting for court?" His voice calls me over with a smile. I wonder why he chose to have our meeting so open.

"I feel far more comfortable wearing gear," I respond hesitantly.

"Your role is to be an ambassador of the fae, I intend to keep my word to you and let the children leave."

I swallow before I take it; his hands are cold.

"I wasn't expecting you to," I admit.

"My word is binding, though my promise was vague," he says, softer this time as he leads me to a chamber behind the thrones.

We pause at the closed door. "The children will be saved if you can see it happen. Already, the false human kings and lords have noticed a change in Arcadia. They have called a summit at Skuflan. You will go with Taelon but first, my dear, you must be wondering where we are going now."

"King Azlyon, how I can do all this myself?" I say.

He smiles. "Fail or succeed, it matters little to me. The humans will be gone one way or another. But the return of magic brought back something I did not expect. You see, the arches opened, and travel to anywhere in Arcadia no longer takes days or months, simply a matter of moments."

"I could travel wherever I want with ease?"

"Those with the blood of the Elder Sidhe can, those without require the permission from those with Elder Sidhe blood." He pauses, reaching for the handle. "We can discuss more later, but for now, I must show you something."

He pulls the door open and a bright light blinds me for a moment, then I see nothing but red. Blood, limbs, and faces were torn off. Heads decorating the walls and floor.

The smell of death and salt fills my lungs and I try not to gag.

"A small voice mentioned you visited the prisoners today. Then they mysteriously vanished." Azlyon pulls my chin between his fingers and points it at the room. "There is an interesting Arch just outside the village of Lorlan, and once I found out my prisoners were gone, well, I had to repay what would have been their spilled blood...tenfold. I can be a patient creature, I can be generous, but those who sneak and go against me will face a different side of me. These faces, Aurelia, do you recognize them?"

They are the heads of people I recognize, some mounted and some rolling on the ground. I see Rika Goulden the head fisherman's wife, and Jora Tredan, a boy my age who I once admired. More faces of more people I knew—more men, women, and children lay lifeless.

I clench my teeth, holding my tears.

"The children," I hear my voice falter.

"My dear, it looks like you were too late to save those human children. I rather hope you are early at the next village, for their sake." Azlyon crouches next to me.

"How could you?" Is all I can say.

Azlyon sighs. "As I explained before, it is better to be on my generous side, Aurelia. At least now I know you will behave, for I left one alive, the woman who raised you. I will let her remain so if you simply follow instruction."

I see fingers on the ground. Tiny fingers that could belong to a small newborn. What have I done?

My body shakes and his touch is like poison. "Just kill me and be done with it."

He whispers in my ear, "I love you so very much, Aurelia. Why would I harm you? When this is all over and Arcadia is won, we can finally have time to ourselves."

I don't look at him, my eyes still on those tiny fingers.

Azlyon stands, pulling me up with him. He nods at the door; it opens and creatures run inside. They are disgusting and leathery of skin, small and more goblin-like than sidhe.

"Clean up this mess, patient and kind folk," Azlyon says as we walk out.

I hear bones snapping and flesh being torn apart as the creatures devour the flesh of the dead. I've had blood on my hands, but this? All because I saved two men. Were their lives worth an entire village?

I see the other princes in the hall as we walk closer towards them. All of them look as though nothing happened. Septimius won't meet my eyes, Kynus looks firmly ahead, and Vikorus hides his disdain well, but I feel it in the air.

"General Septimius, you may leave for Flokael," Azlyon tells the dark faerie. "Kynus, go now to Lomel and Trilan."

The two princes walk out the doors of the palace.

Azlyon turns to Vikorus, looking him up and down "Jorthus will be yours to conquer, as discussed, and you will obey."

Vikorus bows once and leaves curtly.

"What of Skuflan and the Dead Lands?" I ask when I no longer see the Unseelie prince.

"Both are being dealt with, simply worry about your task." Azlyon smiles, stroking the hair at the base of my neck.

Taelon emerges from the shadows, his eyes sharp and alert. There is a deep silence in his stance of understanding and amusement.

The fae are strange in their customs and humour. Slaying and desecration were humourous for them, but I have a different opinion.

"Go with him, sweet halfling, and save the children," Azlyon whispers in my ear. "I hope you do succeed before we claim justice for all our kin who died without such a mercy."

He holds my arm still, as he looks on ahead. "Remember what may happen should you walk on the wrong path."

He lets go in an instant as my feet widen the space between us. My skin still crawls and my heart is still so heavy. Would the goddess do this? Or is this Azlyon? Despite all he has told me, I still know little of who he truly is. He is the gatekeeper of my perception of him and no one dare speak about anything that could alter what he has told me.

Taelon bows when I arrive next to him. He leads me into a hall I have never seen before. The air around us is thick like cream. Stone and moss cover the walls. I cannot read the fading runes but whispers around me speak of walking the world through ancient doorways for the worthy fae.

"The Green King has allowed us to travel through the arch of summer-bright," Taelon informs me.

I say nothing.

"What the King did is no different from what you have done, especially to that human boy upon arrival." Taelon stops in front of an archway of red root.

"I never asked you for your opinion," I grit through my teeth.

"The quicker you accept your truth, the sooner you can be a true ruler," he retorts.

"Why do you care?"

"I do not personally care about you, but when you become a true ruler, my contract to King Azlyon is complete and I can return to my own life," he says.

"No one has meaningful allegiance to anyone," I say to myself.

"We do, but we do not care for those from different courts. You are of the Cold and I the Seelie," he says as the branches begin to glow.

I try to ignore him as I step through the arch.

There is a cool wind and blackness that drapes over the cavern. I start to walk but as my feet leave the ground, they go over the edge of a cliff.

Chapter 31: Skuflan

Great Library Citadel, Skuflan

I am walking on air that feels solid below me. Perhaps it was a test for those that wish to cross. These pathways are as old as Arcadia itself and anything was possible.

As we reach the other side, we step through a second arch. Through it, I see a bright room. Books, desks and plants fill the space beyond while old stonework marks the time passing.

There are few people in dark robes reading and another man standing in front of us. He is bald, with thick reading spectacles, holding a piece of parchment.

"Good evening, Lady of Daeyed," he says with an accent I've never heard before. "I am Ygram, overseer of the library. Follow me."

We walk a short distance, to a room Ygram calls "The Hall of Kings". He speaks little of the library and the room we are about to walk into. This was once where the Bright Court held war meetings but is now a place for general gatherings.

"We do not condone violence here, it is a place of peace and research," Ygram says before leaving us at the door.

I do not get the chance to respond before the doors open and I step inside with Taelon behind me.

Looking around, I see stunning details and rare items. The stonework is exquisite, with every intricate detail reminding me of Daeyed. The Fae craftsmanship is so apparent that the human kings would more than likely feel uncomfortable. Books line the newer, but still old shelves, and paintings decorate the walls. While there were also candles and lanterns lit, a massive skylight brightens the room.

Skuflan's rooms are intriguing and tempting but I have to remember that I am here for another purpose. This place is the only way the leaders of Arcadia could hold such a meeting, for this was the only safe ground for all kingdoms to meet.

My eyes flick over to a familiar face. A man under stress filling with absolute anger. King Fyfe of Jorthus. After such a long journey, we finally come face to face again. He has lost weight, his hair is greyer, and his eyes alarmingly alert. I could only smile at the poor king's state.

"Aurelia of Daeyed, daughter of Princess Lythe of the Cold Court," Taelon announces loudly, causing everyone to turn, "and the ambassador of Daeyed."

Another faerie turns his head sharply to me. His milky hair and bright eyes reflect every drop of light in the room. This was Lythe's mate, Arch King Whistryn of Flokael. He smiles warmly at me, as though we've been parted for generations. As though we are family.

"Good evening." Whistryn looks at me like he did in the false memory, like a father to his daughter.

Next to him is a woman with blonde curls, shining blue eyes, and laugh lines. This is no doubt Fyfe's former wife, Ambyr. The glow of her is playful and kind, I wonder how she lived with Fyfe for so long.

Fyfe does not look at her, but his wife Selene does. She embodies joy, for she hasn't seen her sister in quite some time.

"Why is the half-breed here?" Fyfe says.

Taelon walks forward at the king, smiling sharply. "Bold words, coming from a lowly human, perhaps I will slice your tongue out for saying such a thing to Cold royalty."

The leaders of Lomel and Trilan are silent as they watch the spectacle. I felt a wave of anxiety when Taelon spoke.

"King Azlyon?" the King of Lomel spits. "How come he has never been mentioned before! This so-called king of the fae."

Word travels fast.

I smile, mustering my courage, and take my seat at the round table while Taelon takes his behind me. "He has not been around the fae for quite some time and wore many faces, the latest would be Cicero of Jorthus."

"You housed this madman, Fyfe?" The Queen of Trilan scoffs at my former king.

Lorkus walks in and my heart stops. I did not pay attention to his announcement if he even had one. Prince Lorkus, fair-haired like his mother but the same build as our sire, Tionne. He has always tested and irritated me throughout the years but it is difficult to look at him the same way with what I know now.

"That is why they wanted him." Lorkus sits next to his father.

Whistryn sighs.

"Since we are all here now, please tell us what the Faerie King wants," the King of Lomel presses on, looking directly at me. "We noticed a change in our land."

"He desires nothing from you, for you have taken so much already," I say, realizing that there was no way the two humans made it to the Order, even with arches.

"Then why attend this summit?" Fyfe snaps.

"Because I have been given reign over what he is willing to offer," I say, ignoring his tone. "All of you will die, that much is given. He wants blood for the sins of your ancestors, and he wants to heal Arcadia from iron poisoning. But he is willing to spare the children—he is willing to send them back to Gaia—the world humans came from. He is willing to accept the demifae into his new world, so long as they swear allegiance to him."

There is silence for a moment, then the caramel-skinned Queen speaks. "We are to die then. Does your king understand that we will unite and go to war against him? Faerie or not, four nations against one, it is self-explanatory, is it not?"

But they don't have the goddess of war and fate on their side.

So I simply smile. "There is a reason why they have waited this long. For they have been planning mankind's downfall since the Great War. King

Azlyon fought in it, he saw as nature was sickened because of it. He is not mad, nor is he foolish."

"I knew Azlyon, son of Oberon," Whistryn says. "The man I remember was cold of heart but loyal beyond duty. He was trained under his strongest kin, Anul and Enal. Surely you've all heard of them through stories. I have not met them, for even I am not that old."

"We don't care for that information in Jorthus," Fyfe snaps. "Faeries are abominations."

Whistryn shakes his head. "We are the gatekeepers of magik, contracts, and nature. We came before humankind. At least try to understand us before you meet with me, King."

I try to hide my smile.

"I have travelled across Daeyed, I have been under the mounds, I have revelled, visited ancient citadels, met with fae of all sorts, and I have visited Lord Donn as well as seen the Font of Lystál," I proclaim. "I watched as Rowyna was eaten alive, I bore witness to my human father's death."

Selene looks away, holding her breath. I almost forgot about their relationship. I can feel her hurt and I will have to speak privately to her later.

"You visited Lord Donn? And lived?" Whistryn can't help but smile with pride. "That is very impressive."

Even the other Arch King of Flokael smiles.

"Yes, yes, yes, let us all drop everything to praise this traitor instead of discussing the situation at hand." Fyfe shakes his head.

"As I was saying before," I ignore Fyfe, "these experiences nearly killed me, faerie magik and glamour are deadly. If you think you can stop King Azlyon and his generals, you are mistaken."

"Magik has come back to Arcadia," Whistryn says. "Since mortals cannot wield it, you will rely on Flokael to deal with the brunt of everything. If you sit back and let us deal with the fae, this war is lost once we fall."

"Are you saying we are to be slaughtered willingly then?" the second Arch King of Flokael says.

"No, but our children, they cannot fight," Whistryn presses. "We can give them a chance at survival no matter the outcome."

"So we appease this girl and her king?" the King of Lomel chimes in.

"Aurelia, please let us discuss this in private," Whistryn speaks with intention.

I look at them. "One of you will wait with me, should things turn differently."

They all look amongst one another, thinking themselves too high to wait. But it is Selene who stands and walks over to me. I need to speak to her about Tionne, it is the least I could do.

Fyfe says nothing, for once, but Lorkus' eyes are on us. He has been rather silent this summit. It is quite sad, I was hoping to show him up for once.

Taelon follows us like he and I are attached by a string.

We sit on stone benches in a larger hall painted with murals and lined with books. The air around us is light and calming. It truly is a unique place.

"I am sorry about Tionne," I say.

She looks at me, eyes glazing over with tears that refuse to fall. She tried to remain strong in the presence of others, for she could not cry for her lover when her husband, the king, was beside her.

"You have changed, Aurelia," she says.

I nod.

"How did he die?"

"We were trapped. We had to jump over a cliff to another side. He was tricked by the dark one who lived there and fell. I tried to pull him up but my strength was failing. H-he told me to let go. He told me he has a letter for Lorkus and I," I say the last part carefully.

Her eyes widen a bit before her head leans on my shoulder. I have no idea how to respond, this is the Queen of Jorthus.

"You know then," her voice is little more than a whisper.

"I do, but it was not he who told me that your son is my brother," I say.

She shakes her head and smiles slightly. "You cannot tell anyone, for my son needs to ascend after Fyfe."

"Is Lorkus part of the Order?" I ask.

She shakes her head. "I hope he will be or all of this was for nothing."

"Tionne loved the both of you," I say. "Regardless of anything, Tionne would have done anything for you."

She nods. "He would watch over you, when you were a child he would watch you with Lucia from a distance. When you were in the capital, he would make sure you had fresh herbs for your poisons and elixirs."

"I always wondered why there was always stock. Cicero would tell me once they were out I would have to get more…but I never had to." I laugh.

There is a moment of silence.

"Does Lorkus know the truth about his father?" I decide to ask.

"He does now." A male voice sounds out from the archway.

We both turn to see the prince of Jorthus watching us with narrow eyes.

"Taelon, why did you not say anything," I say quietly so only the faerie can hear.

He simply smiles back in response.

"Son," Selene stands up.

He raises his hand silencing her. "I always felt something familiar with you, Aurelia, but to know that we share the same father was not something I would have expected. Much less to know I am just a…bastard."

"Lorkus," I say, "you are the prince regardless of what has been said. You need to become king."

"All this time, that man who I've spoken with on many an occasion, he knew," Lorkus says, shaking his head. "My mother knew. Aurelia, I now understand what it is like to live with betrayal from family."

"Lorkus," I say simply, "Tionne is dead, your mother would be if she said a word to anyone."

I stand up and walk over to him. Behind his glassy eyes is a child, a boy who simply does not understand. One who is afraid to understand.

"As if I care," he says. "I am a pawn, aren't I?"

Selene tries to reach for her son but he dismisses her. "You are much more than that."

"Lorkus, look at me," I say, "I was bred a pawn as well. I was born the bridge between humans and faeries. I was born to ultimately help the Order of Rhion, just as you were. If you jeopardize anything now, you may be killed or stripped of title and thrown out, Queen Selene will fall to Fyfe's blade, the Arch King Whistryn will declare war on Fyfe because his consort is your mother's sister. With everyone against one another, it will make it that much easier for Azlyon to slaughter you all."

Taelon steps forward. "What are you doing?"

I look at him. "Giving them a fighting chance so they are not slaughtered like sheep."

"Azlyon will not be happy," Taelon says in the faerie tongue.

"If the Azlyon that is my friend is still there, he will understand. He will still win but helping them prepare themselves will make a better song than a short slaughter," I respond in the same language before switching to the common tongue, remembering to think simpler. "We've waited long enough, I am heading back inside."

"When did you learn to speak like them?" Lorkus looks bewildered.

"I didn't learn," I say. "I've always known, just like any with fae blood."

We walk back in and both of the Jorthus royalty sat down back in their seats. I stand behind mine with a clear mind.

"Flokael will send all human children to Gaia," the Arch Kings speak in unison.

I nod and turn to Lomel's ruler.

"I will not send my subjects away," is all he says.

"Neither will I," says Fyfe.

"We will," Trilan's Queen says, "and when we win, we will claim them back."

I nod. This is more than I expected. Fyfe's answer does not surprise me, this just means I have more work. I need to go to towns and evacuate the children.

"King Azlyon will honour those who send their children away," I say.

"Of course I will," a silky voice came from behind.

I turn my head and see the king tossing a crystal sphere up and down behind us. He shouldn't be here.

Whistryn stands and meets Azlyon's eye. "I hoped to never see you again."

"Whistryn, it truly has been a long time," Azlyon laughs. "You look ever so foolish as a—what do you call it? Arch King?"

Whistryn's face is frozen in a statuesque state. "Why are you here?"

"Do you have any real power?" Azlyon asks darkly. "You also forget that you are still Seelie, you are mine."

I feel darkness surrounding us.

Whistryn remains firm. "Aurelia will not stay with you forever, Azlyon. Mark me, she will abandon you and join her family in Flokael."

He needs to stop talking.

"Her family is with me, her family is with General Kynus." Azlyon examines the sphere. "You are just a lost pet, never good enough for Lythe's family, and you will never be good enough for Aurelia."

He raises his arm as if to command the room. Instead, in the blink of an eye, he throws the crystal at the King of Lomel and takes his head clean off. Blood splatters everywhere and everyone leaps out of their chairs, ready for battle.

"Jorthus declares war on Daeyed!" Fyfe growls.

"As does Trilan!"

"Lomel will make you pay!" the now widowed queen howls through her tears.

"Flokael will see Daeyed fall," Whistryn carefully declares, shielding Ambyr.

Blood is everywhere. It stains the fabric. It stains the skin.

Azlyon looks at Queen Selene and grins.

She has no chance to respond as something unseen rips her body apart. Blood and flesh splatter everywhere as Fyfe cries out for her. Lorkus freezes, staring at a chunk of flesh that lands in front of him. What was once his mother is now no more than a bit of meat.

Ambyr screams and falls to her knees.

"Azlyon, stop, not like this, not now," I say to him my heart pounds.

He blinks and looks at me. "Aurelia..."

Then a bolt of fire shoots at him and he simply slides out of its path, pulling me back with him. The flicker of who he was is gone. There is only the goddess and I. My path was clear, she needs to be stopped and I would have to gain an upper hand to do so.

"Let there be war, the final war," Azlyon tells them as we walk out of the room hand in hand. Taelon follows behind us as we step through the arch and disappear.

To be continued

Pronunciations

Faeries

Aurelia: Are-elle-ia
Azlyon: Ahz-lie-on
Septimius: Sept-eh-mus
Kynus: Kine-us
Vikorus: Veek-or-us
Sithen Dochtúir: Seeth-en Dok-ter

Countries

Jorthus: Jore-thus
Flokael: Flow-kale
Lomel: Lom-elle
Trilan: Tree-lawn
Daeyed: Die-edd
Skuflan: Sku-flane

Acknowledgments

This book would not have been possible without the help of my friends and family.

I want to thank Leonardo Nunesmaia. From cold nights at coffee shops to long conversations across the world, he was the very first person I shared my words with. His insight into the Crown Of Lies world through multiple drafts helped me create what it is today. To my friends Daniela Vasquez Davila and Devon Lockhart who always encouraged me to write when procrastinating and having faith that I could one day publish. I want to thank some of my family members, especially my mother and my sister, Kaitlyn Nicholson, who encouraged my passion for writing from a young age. Other family and friends I want to thank are Nicholas Miklic and my grandparents.

I want to thank professors from my undergraduate studies Sally Haney, Sean Holeman, and Patti Edgar for helping me improve my writing skills. And to my former coworkers who dealt with me daydreaming of magic and monsters: Navpreet Garcha, Cynthia Raymer, Simran Dhaliwal, Saeed Rahman, Han Nguyen, Bernadette MacGillivray, Chad Russell, Rob Montgomery, Andrea Smith, and Cory Colluney.

This book would not have been possible without the help from my editor, Isabella Betita, and cover artist Kelly Ritchie.

And finally, I would like to thank those that took the time to give this book a chance. Readers, I thank you most and I hope something about this story brought joy to your life, be it a smile or more. We all are heroes in our own journey.

Explore the world at www.alexandranicholsonauthor.com

Exclusive content password: CrownOfLies2022

About the Author

Alexandra Nicholson was born in Calgary, Canada, and graduated from Mount Royal University with a Bachelor's Degree in Communications, majoring in Journalism. From the time she could pick up a pencil she knew writing was her dream. She has published many articles, videos, and photographs. When she is not working she enjoys going to the mountains, hiking, and spending time with friends and family.

You can connect with me on:

- https://www.alexandranicholsonauthor.com
- https://twitter.com/alexandran001
- https://www.facebook.com/CrownofLies
- https://www.instagram.com/a.nicholson.author

Manufactured by Amazon.ca
Acheson, AB

12271961R00189